Carol Birch was born in 1951 in Manchester and went to Keele University. She has lived in London, south-west Ireland and now Lancaster. Her first novel, *Life in the Palace*, won the 1988 David Higham Award for Best First Novel of the Year. In 1991 she won the prestigious Geoffrey Faber Memorial Prize with *The Fog Line*. *Little Sister, Come Back, Paddy Riley* and *Turn Again Home* are also published by Virago.

'Always understated, yet crammed with incidents of the highest drama, the novel's best moments come when the intense feeling that underlies it breaks out into densely weighted fragments of speech. It is at least as good as anything on this year's Booker shortlist' D. J. Taylor, *Guardian*

'With it's imaginative density and elegance of style, *The Naming of Eliza Quinn* is a polished and engrossing novel about the power of the past' Patricia Craig, *Independent*

'Immaculately researched' Emma Lee-Potter, *Daily Express*

'Muscular prose and precise vision . . . characters are drawn expertly and readers will appreciate Beatrice's independence and intelligence' *Financial Times*

'A spellbinding display of fiction' *Glasgow Herald*

Also by Carol Birch

Life in the Palace
The Fog Line
The Unmaking
Songs of the West
Little Sister
Come Back, Paddy Riley
Turn Again Home

The Naming of
Eliza Quinn

CAROL BIRCH

Virago

VIRAGO

First published in Great Britain in 2005 by Virago Press
This paperback edition published in 2006 by Virago Press

Copyright © Carol Birch 2005

Extracts from *Poem* (in the stump of the old tree . . .) by Hugh Sykes Davies
reprinted by permission of the estate of Hugh Sykes Davies.

A CIP catalogue record for this book is available
from the British Library.

ISBN-13: 978-1-84408-146-2
ISBN-10: 1-84408-146-X

Typeset in Bembo by M Rules
Printed and bound in Great Britain by
Clays Ltd, St Ives plc

Virago Press
An imprint of
Little, Brown Book Group
Brettenham House
Lancaster Place
London WC2E 7EN

A member of the Hachette Livre Group of Companies

www.virago.co.uk

For Diana Scarth

ACKNOWLEDGEMENTS

I am grateful to the Author's Foundation for a bursary, which assisted in the writing of this book.

Thanks to Martin Butler, Emily Atherton, Nina and Dave Bleasdale, Charles Root, Donal Mac Neamhabhnaigh, Somhairle, Mic Cheetham and Lennie Goodings.

The following books were invaluable:

Letters from Ireland during the Famine of 1847 by Alexander Somerville
Famine Echoes by Cathal Poirteir
The Great Irish Potato Famine by James S. Donnelly Jr
The End of Hidden Ireland: Rebellion, Famine and Emigration by Robert James Scally
Black '47 and Beyond: the Great Irish Famine in History, Economy and Memory by Cormac O'Grada

PART ONE

1969 – early summer

1

'. . . but do not put your hand down to see . . .'

Last night I saw a light high up on the mountain. It was as if a door was open in the rock, letting out light from within; and there was a shadow in front, like a man smoking, gently rocking to and fro as you might if you were just standing there in the cool of the night, looking out over the sea and having a last pipe before going to bed.

My front door is like a stable door; I had the top half open and I was leaning out to get some more of the summer night air, when I saw it on the hillside. I pulled in the shutter and locked and bolted, and then I didn't think about it any more. Here, as soon as the dark comes down, I draw the curtains, taking care to leave not a crack anywhere for an eye to peep in.

Everything around here is named. Darby's House is what my house is called. Who's Darby? That was the first thing I asked. Oh, he was before my time, that's what they say, these stocky Irish farmers I encounter in the lane. I've been here three weeks. I like to sit and feel my silent presence in the room, with the miles of darkness pressing in, and the sea singing very far below; it sounds distant at the moment, though I know that when I step out of my front door in daylight it will hit me in the face, and for a second I'll reel with vertigo. Though really, to fall into the sea you'd have to walk about half a mile down a rocky path then clamber over three or four grass ridges.

My house sits solitary in a stony hollow in a hillside high above the Atlantic Ocean. It has no electricity and I draw my water up from a hole in the ground surrounded by a tumbled stone wall. Three nights ago when I looked out, I saw the tip of a lit cigarette. Someone was standing down at the end of my track in the pitch black. There was no moon that night. I saw the light move up, brilliant as someone took a drag, then move back down again. But that was nothing, just old Pierce O'Donnell from down below. Nothing at all to what happened this morning, that thing I found, my hand upon the sudden something.

I was standing beside the old hollow tree out back, looking into the dank earthy hole that went down like a tunnel inside, like Alice's rabbit-hole; it made me remember a poem my Granma Lizzie used to scare me with when I was a child, a poem about the stump of an old dead tree. '*But do not put your hand down to see*' runs the refrain –

> *but do not put your hand down to see, because*
>
> *in the stumps of old trees, where the hearts have rotted out, there are holes the length of a man's arm, and dank pools at the bottom where the rain gathers and old leaves turn to lace, and the beak of a dead bird gapes like a trap. But do not put your hand down to see, because*

– and there it was, this hole for me to put my hand down to see, in fascination; so I did and what I found there was a dead baby.

She was just bones. I knew she was a she straight away, I don't know how. I had to walk all the way down to the village to telephone, it took me half an hour and I didn't see another soul on the way. I didn't know who to call, so I dialled the police. The switchboard lady said there was no one there. I mean, *no one* there. Can you imagine calling the cops in New York and finding no one there. She said she'd transfer me, and I stood and waited in the booth in the village street, listening to all the clicks and hums on the line, watching the way the tall grasses on the wall outside were quivering very finely, as if they could sense something, as if they were straining and listening with everything stretched. A feeling of weeping was coming up inside me thinking of the shock of the bones, but I swallowed it down into my chest. I didn't let it get to my eyes.

A voice came on the line. 'I found some bones,' I said. 'I think it's a child.'

There was a long pause, then, 'You say you found some bones,' the man repeated, as if he were writing it down very slowly, as if I'd reported a lost purse.

'Bones,' I said emphatically. 'Little bones. A child.' A shudder seized me, a blast of cold. 'In a tree at the back of my house.'

I heard him sighing in a weary kind of way. 'Your name?' he asked.

I told him my name was Beatrice Conrad, and he said at once: 'Darby's House.'

Everyone knows everything about me. I don't know him but he knows me.

'Must be rough living up there, I'd say?' he remarked pleasantly.

I had a wanderlust in my thirty-seventh year. It was the tail-end of the sixties and I'd had to get out of New York. I had a nice apartment on the Upper West Side, but it was full of people I hardly even knew. I had money and I was an easy mark.

Granma Lizzie's the reason I'm here. The day I learned

5

she'd left me a ruin in Ireland I tasted the taste of the strawberry sodas she used to buy me, and the past came flooding
back in a Proustian leap. I knew her well as a child. I stayed
with her a lot at her house in Nyack, I was her unabashed
favourite, and it was me she left the house to, not my brother.
It's not worth much but none of us even knew she had it. She
never spoke of it, and though she loved her country, she
never wanted to go back. Soon as I saw the address written
down on the deed, I knew I would come here. I fell in love
with it on paper: Darby's House, Kildarragh, Lissadoon,
Boolavoe, County Kerry, Ireland. There was a map with my
boundaries marked in red. Ireland, whose praises had been
sung in my ears since the day I was born, arose in my mind.
I used to be a total sucker for all the old shamrock bullshit
when I was a kid, the St Patrick's Day Parade and all that. My
mother used to take me and my brother every year. I'd been
to Hawaii with my parents, and Mexico a couple of times,
but never Ireland, though I'd always meant to. And now I had
a house there, a ruin.

There I was thinking of change, and Ireland just kind of
jumped up and grabbed me. It came at a funny time. I was
working in Stack's Music Store, bored; I'd been thinking of
going away for a while. I'd turned thirty-seven in the spring
and I'd barely spent a day alone in my life. It's like I was
something getting used up, a bar of soap infinitesimally
shrinking day by day.

I wrote to my mother's cousin Dec in Lissadoon, with
whom, out of a sense of duty, I'd been exchanging
Christmas cards religiously since she died. I asked him what
kind of a state the house was in, and he wrote back immediately. It had been used for cows for the past twenty or so
years, but was reasonably sound. Said it had a tin roof that
leaked a bit, the doors and windows were boarded up. There
was a spring. The spring did it. Something happened when

I heard about the spring. The sound of clear water rising out of the ground joined the taste of strawberry soda, and that sealed it. All I can say is it was a kind of hunger, but it wasn't a hunger for anything I had or had once had. I didn't miss any of my old beaux. I was independent, doing OK. I'd never had to work at anything I didn't want to do. I didn't know what it was I wanted. But it was simple really. For the first time in my life I was just hungry for quiet. And I was curious too. I'd heard so much about this place from both my mother and my grandmother, yet they'd never taken me there. For all their misty-eyed longing, neither one had ever wanted to return.

I thought I'd go over and camp in the house for the summer, see about fixing it up, maybe use it now and then and perhaps rent it out. I arranged it all with Dec, sent money over for someone to go in there and clean it out before my arrival, give me a window or two, put the doors back in. I had an idea of Ireland, all green and soft and lovely. You can't imagine though till you see for real these houses in the old abandoned villages: ruined, their ownership lost in time, whole families gone overseas. Kildarragh's all but gone, whatever it was. My house is standing, and old Pierce O'Donnell's, but between us lie the remains of a dozen or so dwellings, all tumbled long since. The grass grows over their fallen stones. When I first saw Darby's House I fell in love, it was just so beautiful. A low grey cottage, a door and two windows like a picture a child might draw. The roof shone. The hollow in which it nestled on the side of the mountain was purple with foxgloves. There was a stone wall out front, and the ghosts of old potato ridges running up the hill behind, left over from before the great famine.

There was a rainbow that day. It seemed to come down in the little patch of earth at the back of the house. But then as

I walked further up the track I thought it was on the other side of the mountain, by Lissadoon, the pretty village of pink, green and blue houses I'd come through that morning.

In the stumps of old trees with rotten hearts, where the rain gathers and the laced leaves and the dead bird like a trap, there are holes the length of a man's arm, and in every crevice of the rotten wood grow weasel's eyes like molluscs, their lids open and shut with the tide. But do not put your hand down to see, because

The bones were making me shudder through the wall.

I couldn't stay there in the house waiting for them to come and take her away. She was coming through the walls at me. I went out and stood on the track looking down towards the sea over those lost famine lands, those lost crowded dwellings, smoking a cigarette. The track meanders up from the low road that rounds the cliff, looks in at my gate then snakes its way higher and higher through house-high rocks and running streams. There are hares and wild goats up there. The mountain too is named. They call it Quilty's Door. I'm living on Quilty's doorstep. A black car comes beetling along the lower road and turns up my track, the stocky strut of old Pierce O'Donnell following after. No show without Punch, as my mother used to say. The car grinds to a dusty halt and stands sighing and creaking and clicking, cocked at a weird angle on the uneven track. Father Lynch and the garda and the doctor and Matthew Kelly from the village store slowly and solemnly emerge.

'It's this way,' I call, leading them round the back and up the hill a way, head bent, hands shoved up my sleeves.

I'd laid her skull and a couple of bones on the grass by the old tree The rest of her was still down there with the weasel's eyes. In my mind, I see them give a synchronised slow reptilian blink, and a shot of fear goes through me. I'll never put my hand down to see again. How am I going to stay here tonight all on my own? How can I not? I have builders coming to look over the place Tuesday. I have this gilded silence I've been nurturing. I'm one with the big sea. What's fear anyway? Only fear.

Her skull, the eye sockets black and huge, and two tiny bones lie at our feet.

'Hrrm,' says the garda, a sweet uncertain young boy with a mop of chestnut hair, 'these look like human remains to me all right.'

'These are very old bones,' says Father Lynch, who smiles habitually, whose eyes revert to humour in repose, 'very, very old indeed. Wouldn't you say, Matty?'

'Jesus, Father, how would I know?' says boxer-faced Kelly, shaking his head. He has taken off his brimmed hat and it dangles by the knees of his baggy black suit.

'The older the better,' says the doctor, a gingery-bearded man with the look of a seaman. I don't know why he's here. He can't do a whole lot for her now, can he?

Father Lynch is unsmiling. Strange to see him serious, his mouth a straight line. 'Well, boys,' he says, and hoiks up his sleeve and steps forward.

'No no, I'll do it, Father,' the sweet young policeman protests, but the priest waves him aside with his free arm, the other plunging down and reaching, feeling about amongst the weasel's eyes and laced leaves. 'Stand there, Barry, I'll pass them out to you.' His face is plump and firm.

There's something so moving about the way they bring her out, piece by piece, very gently, the priest's big soft hands coaxing her from the sticky bowels of the tree, handling her like porcelain, handing her on to the waiting boy, who lays each little pale stick of her side by side in the grass. They're so careful. Other men from the village and round about turn up.

9

One of them is my uncle, Dec Vesey, a rotund old man with a red face and cropped grey hair. They know all about me, all of them, or think they do, and I know nothing about any of them apart from Uncle Dec, who isn't really my uncle but my mother's cousin; and all I know about him is ancient stuff my mother used to tell me, about what a fine strapping hunk of a boy he'd been. I can't relate that to this stout shambling farmer, nodding to me from the little crowd that's gathered on the hillside around the fragile haul of bones.

I step over to him while they're wrapping them in sacking.

'Hello, Beatrice,' he says gruffly.

'Hello, Dec.'

'Strange business.'

I've asked him before but try again. 'Dec, do you know much about this house? Who lived here?'

He shakes his head. 'No one's lived in that house for years.'

'But someone lived here at some time.'

'Oh, sure.' He shrugs affably, smiles, rubbing the back of his neck. 'Will you be all right here on your own now, Beatrice?' he asks kindly. 'You know where we are.'

'Oh, I'm OK,' I say very firmly, smiling to prove it.

People are moving away. The bones are in the car. No one seems to know what will happen to them now.

'You will let me know,' I ask the young garda, 'you will let me know if you find out anything about them?'

'I will indeed.' He's in the car, leaning out. 'Don't you go getting upset about this, Miss Conrad,' he says. 'Those are very old bones. God knows how long they'd been in there. Long before your people, I'm sure. It's just some old story, nothing for you to worry about.'

'I'm OK,' I say, 'Thanks.'

'Come down for your tea, Beatrice,' Dec says shyly, 'Rosemary might know something about this old place. She has more of a memory for that sort of thing.'

10

I watch them go, and when I am alone I do cry at last, sitting on the high stool in the bare downstairs room where a manger still adorns one wall. Dec and his boys have made good use of the money I sent over, to bring in a stove, a table, a couple of chairs, the essentials. They have white-washed the walls and cleaned out the chimney and fixed me a fire in the grate with a bellows and fire-irons. The high stool must have come from a bar. Sometimes I sit on it and am just the right height then to look out of the small slit window that faces the sea, like an arrow vent in a castle wall; at sundown it frames a painting of vivid hue, a blood-red globe sinking slowly into the horizon, the rim of which is indigo under a luminous sky daubed and streaked with peach and pink and viridian. Tonight the picture is blurred and smeared by my tears. I feel so sorry for her all alone in the tree, all those years, her bones unburied for so long. I am actually trembling a little. I feel as if all the people who ever lived in this house are somewhere absorbed into the walls, all in there looking out at me. This won't do. I can't be chased away, not when I was getting used to the peace, to not being wanted for something all the time. The solitary condition is a good thing, I have decided; I was coming round to it, getting it licked; there's a way I found, a way to let the silence slip all over me like a new silk dress, some-thing to savour. It was scary, of course, but all the best things are. You just sit still and let it happen, and it comes good in the end. I feel like a lone explorer at the North Pole. Waiting for the Northern Lights, which will make everything clear. So I'm just fine here on my own with all the ghosts of the lost village till the end of summer. After all, they're invisible. I don't want this thing to chase me away. I have old Pierce O'Donnell a mile or two down the track, Kelly and the nice people in the village store, all the people in the lanes who stop and talk, and the countless

Veseys, my mother's people, who always say to me, 'You're Johanna's girl.'

But at night, no one comes calling.

As I walk over the high track with my back to the sea, going for tea with Dec and Rosemary in the evening, there's a rain that's so fine it's like a faint sensation of pins and needles all over my face. It's more of a climb than a walk. Sometimes I stop, breathless, and look back down and feel the dizzying drop. It's hot, and the rain is refreshing. I sit down on a rock and consider my situation; I cannot shake this sense of un-reality. My friends are very far away beyond that great water. Already the letters from home come strangely into my hands, and all those people, all the jangle of life, the rumble of the New York streets – all a dream. It seems to me now that I was fated to come all this way to that particular moment when I put my hand down to see, and touched someone who had not been touched for – how long? Fifty years? A hundred? How can that not be momentous?

When I get to cousin Dec's farmhouse, a strong square building set back from a winding lane of high dripping fuch-sia hedges that runs between Lissadoon and Boolavoe, I feel myself to be such an alien that at first I can hardly talk. I hardly know Dec and Rosemary, I've only met them once or twice since I arrived just a week ago, and so far they've been very good to me. The room is bright and many-patterned, the busy wallpaper on the walls, the tablecloth, the curtains, the pictures hanging from the picture rails, of wildly crashing turquoise seas and blue horses, and the soulful eyes of Jesus sadly watching in pride of place from above the cast-iron fireplace, a classical riot of columns and chalices and trailing laurels. A million small ornaments adorning every surface, and everything immaculately clean and very bright. Rosemary, a child-sized crone with a magnificent head of

12

white and grey ringlets, bustles forward and kisses me heartily, then plonks me down on a fat red couch. 'Oh the child,' she says, 'look at her! Now sit you down and make yourself comfy. Will you have tea?' Her legs are little sticks in dark brown lisle stockings, her shiny black brogues as ugly and heavy as can be.

They speak so quietly, Dec and Rosemary, such rippling little snufflings of sound, I can scarcely hear them, and whenever I open my mouth I am too loud. And they're small. And me, well I'm a sizeable piece of a lass as my mother used to say, God knows where you get it from, Beatrice. My mother wasn't tall, and Granma Lizzie was tiny. I stand six foot, near as damn it, in stockinged feet. My face is large and peculiar, my mouth too big, my eyes too small. My hair would not shame an Amazon, black and plentiful, my lovers have always enjoyed filling their hands with it. But I don't hunker over, I never hunker over, I stand up straight and tall. The air is thick with good smells of savoury food, and the turf fire, smoking gently in spite of the warmth of the evening, gives out a sweet aroma, a taste that settles in the back of the throat.

Rosemary seems slightly offended when I follow her into the kitchen and offer a hand making dinner, so I return to my chair beside the riotous fireplace. Cousin Dec, baby-faced and smiling, sits opposite me with his hands on his knees as she comes and goes. *He was eleven*, I hear my mother say, *and I was eight*. We had a house in Mineola. I'd come home from school and my mother would talk, her voice throaty because she chain-smoked. I see her standing by the window with a cigarette, looking out towards the turnpike. She was a hard woman, but Ireland she was sentimental about; a bone of a woman, tall, too thin and jerky, with shanks like a cat and all these memories of before she came to America, how Granma Lizzie took her to stay with her cousins in Lissadoon when she was a little girl living in England. 'Oh that boy!' she croaks. 'A golden Adonis! And I was only eight years old.' Strange she never went back. Maybe she was afraid it would disappoint her. And look at him now sitting there with his feet in brown tartan slippers on the fender, thick yellow fingers cupping a cigarette with a curious delicacy. His red face is double-chinned, his gut hangs over his belt. His eyebrows are terribly heavy and whiter than the tufty hair on his scalp.

'Do you remember my mother, Uncle Dec?' I ask.

'Oh now, Beatrice,' he replies, clearing his throat and leaning forward, 'I do, of course, remember little Johanna, but you know it must be more than sixty years ago. I remember her getting out of the cart with her mammy. My father went for them to Kenmare. Of course that was a very big journey to make in those days.'

I have to smile. She remembered individual cats and dogs and cows on the farm, buttermilk licked from a spoon, and the big boy Dec who hung upside down from trees and could row a boat on the sea.

'She remembered you,' I say. 'She had such a crush on you, Uncle Dec. She never forgot it.'

He smiles a shy inturned smile. 'I'm sure I don't know why,' he whispers, reaching for the tea Rosemary has placed beside him. 'She was with her mammy most of the time.' He looks sideways into the fire, stirring his tea with a tiny silver spoon, then shakes his head as if at a great marvel. 'Your grandmother – now *she* was a fine-looking woman. A very fine-looking woman indeed.'

'Granma Lizzie was a beauty,' I say. 'She was a beauty into old age.'

She had good bones. I never saw a picture of her when she was young, but you could tell she must have been something. She was some great age, ninety-two, ninety-four I think, something like that when she died last year; all bent over and a mass of wrinkles and liver spots, but she still had big eyes and thick white hair, and she'd kept her Irish accent till the end, very soft and sweet, with the sibilant t's.

Rosemary comes in with a dish of steaming floury potatoes. 'Sit up now,' she says, and we do. Pork chops with cabbage and potatoes, the gravy thick and red and salty. The first half of the meal we while away with small talk, then I weasel the conversation back to my house and who lived there in the past.

'It was your Uncle Pats had it,' says Rosemary to Dec. 'Pats had it,' she repeats, and turns her steady gaze on me. Her face is seamed and scored, there are white hairs growing out of her chin and her mouth is weathered and grown thin. There is something both fierce and calm in her face, and she speaks slowly, precisely. 'But this was a very **long** time ago, oh, fifty years or more; then his Martin had it; and after that, it fell empty, and then there were strangers living up there for a while.'

'I wonder how long ago it happened,' I say, 'when the child was put in the tree . . .' trying to make connections.

'Terrible thing.' She shakes her head. Dec, shaking his, agrees. 'Not in our time anyway.' She lays down her knife and fork and sits back, folding her arms across her cardigan. 'I'm sure it was not in our time.'

Dec drops me off at the foot of the track, turning the car and waiting to see me safely in with the lamp lit, honking the horn in a friendly way as he drives off, headlights sweeping the hillside. The sound of the engine hums fainter and fainter as I bolt the door and let the place settle around me. Rain whispers on the corrugated roof. I take my lamp and go straight upstairs and light the candle beside the rickety iron bed with the ticking mattress Dec's sons hauled up for me by tractor and trailer. The candle burns bravely in a saucer standing on a large flat stone about two inches thick and as wide

15

as a dinner plate. I found this stone under a thorny bush by the gate in the garden, and was taken by its perfect oval and the thin seam of something delicately green running straight across the middle like a ruled diameter. Then I found there was a whole beach of them if you struggled south from here along a meandering spine of rock that peaks suddenly on an unforgiving windy plateau. It's like the Grand Canyon or seeing the rings of Saturn through a telescope, one of those things that reduces you to nothing. God knows how they got it from there if that's where it came from, I think, letting down my hair. It falls heavily. There are caves there too, lonely caves far above the sea, and somewhere beyond, I know, an old famine grave. I'll take another walk over there tomorrow.

The room is pleasant by candlelight and dim lamplight. I get undressed and crawl naked into my sleeping bag, extinguish the lamp, put my arms behind my head and take stock of the day. The mountainside, running with rain, sings.

Something is different outside. She's gone from where she's been so long, and surely the mountain misses her. In stories, the disturbance of bones is often the prelude to a haunting. My mind's eye sees the light on the rock. But I'm not afraid, or if I am, I'm enjoying it. I have always loved a challenge. I find myself smiling, while the hairs on my nape prick up beneath the heavy weight of hair. I shouldn't be here now. I should have gone into town and checked into the hotel. I'd have been in bed, reading a book. There'd have been the sound of other people in other rooms, people downstairs in the bar. Instead I'm here all alone with the dark outside too big – oh God, *far* too big! – and that tree at my back, the tree where I put my hand down to see. The feeling grows that the finding of the bones in some way ties me to this child, for I have touched her, and she lived once and ran about and played and prattled, and some fateful line

16

drew me to stand just there just then, to think of a certain poem and not heed its advice.

That's the trouble with me. I always put my hand down to see.

I fall asleep while the rain patters on the roof.

'God, it's awful clever how they know these things, isn't it?'

I am in the post office in Lissadoon talking to some distant relation of mine. Kate and I have been reading in the local paper that the bones may date back to the famine, because it was not a baby after all, but a child of three or four, which means she must have been very badly undernourished. In any case, her bones are now so old that no matter what happened, even murder, it was all too long ago, and they are to be given a decent Christian burial in Boolavoe churchyard.

'God, the poor wee soul,' Kate says. 'Wait, Beatrice, there's something I want to tell you.'

She buys a bag of Taytos for her little girl, a stout sage in a green coat, then takes me firmly by the arm as we leave. Her basket bangs between us. Arm in arm down the dead centre of the main street of Lissadoon we walk, the three of us graded by size, like steps, openly watched by three long-haired boys of about eighteen who loiter with cigarettes by the water fountain. Kate comes up to my shoulder.

'Are you OK up there?' she asks cheerfully. For a moment I think she's referring to my height. 'I'd hate it. All the empty houses.'

'I love it,' I say. 'The carpenter and builders have been, you know.'

Lissadoon is supernaturally quaint; reminds me of a little old town in a Wild West movie, except for the Coca-Cola sign hanging outside Burke's Butchers. A donkey stands patiently, rhythmically twitching one ear, between the shafts of a yellow cart.

'So you're staying put?'

'For the summer.'

'Brave girl.'

We stop by her car, parked next to a yellow wall where an alleyway leaks out into the street. The back window of the muddy car is rolled down and a coop of chickens croons on the back seat. My sort-of cousin adjusts a polka dot headscarf round her shiny brown bangs. 'Listen, Beatrice,' she says, 'I just thought of this. Why don't you go see old Tiernan in Boolavoe? He's a local history man, does little books about round about here, you know. If you're after the gen on your old place he's worth a look.'

'That's terrific, Kate,' I say, 'I'll do that.'

She lets go of my arm and shakes out her car keys. 'Bill Tiernan,' she says, 'on the back road. You ask anyone in Boolavoe. Want a lift?'

I'm about to accept when it crosses my mind that it's Thursday and the minibus from the shop will be leaving for Boolavoe in about half an hour.

'Thanks, Kate,' I say, 'but I think I'll hang around and wait for the bus.'

A dog with a black lion's mane lies panting outside Murphy's Bar across the road, with its Sweet Afton signs, and the signs for Cork Dry Gin and 7-Up; inside it's brown and dim, cosy with a crackling fire, empty apart from two old men in caps, one at either end of the bar like bookends, a fuggy blue mist between them from their pipes.

'Now, Beatrice Conrad, what can I get you?'

It still shocks me how everyone knows my name.

Mrs Murphy, I suppose, a tall dark spiky woman with a gentle air, gets up from the fire and steps briskly behind the bar. I get a Guinness, chat the obligatory chat, then go sit under the frosted window to read the letter I picked up at the post office. Betty writes everyone's still living in my apart-

18

ment. The heat is atrocious. She has to meet Benedetti at Penn Station at four, they're going up to his dad's place at Ocean Grove for the weekend. Imagine stifling to death in Ocean Grove. Still, it'll be nice to get out of the city, she says. The club had a great weekend, she says twenty-eight turned up. Everyone's asking about me. They had a party afterwards back at someone's place and she can't remember how she got home.

The names of the people she mentions echo in my skull. Real life, far away, not just the measure of an ocean but light years of space, stars and galaxies and black holes.

The old man on the right of the bar addresses something unintelligible to me in a high singsong voice, and Mrs Murphy laughs. 'Now, Pats!' she says softly, 'don't be scaring the poor girl!'

I look at the old man and see for the first time how very ancient he is. His white, stark, prickled jaw reminds me of a cactus.

'I'm sorry,' I say, 'I didn't catch that.'

''Twasn't worth catching,' smiles Mrs Murphy.

The silent old man on the left chuckles into his stout.

'I said, did ye hear the ghostie yet?' barks Pats, hale and hearty, sucking vigorously at his pipe.

'Oh, please,' I say, 'don't tell me about the ghostie,' and a second later, 'Yes, please, tell me about the ghostie,' thinking of Rosemary Vesey saying to Dec: your Uncle Pats had it. There could be a million Pats around here. There are many ancient men. This one's eyes are pale blue and wet, full of a kind of mad humour.

'It's just a little voice,' he says, and his own is high and reedy and cracked.

'Now, Pats!' says Mrs Murphy sharply.

'What does it say?' I ask. 'What kind of a voice is it?

'It says: '*Is feidir liom thu a chloisteail. Teigh a chodladh.*'

There is a silence while we ponder this, broken only by the peaceful ticking of the clock and the crackle of the fire.

'And that means?' I ask.

A grin, absolutely toothless. '*I can hear you. You go to sleep.*'

I'm cold.

'And this was after a couple or five of these, I'll betcha,' says Mrs Murphy lightly, grinning and tapping the side of the old man's pint glass.

He pulls a strange face, an ancient baby grimace. 'Not at all, Maureen,' he says, sitting up straight-backed, turning to look at me. His eyes have an intense, dancing quality. 'I was just up out of my bed in the morning, first light, blowing up the fire, it was winter it was, and this little voice said as clear as day: '*Is feidir liom thu a chloisteail. Teigh a chodladh.*'

Mrs Murphy winks at me.

He lived there. He's Uncle Pats. He's Granma Lizzie's actual brother. I don't believe it.

'You don't want to take a blind bit of notice of anything he says,' she tells me, smoothing her skirt down as she walks back to her nook by the fire, 'he's an old eejit.'

I stand. 'Uncle Pats,' I say, 'I'm very pleased to meet you.' I shake his small, cold hand.

There's a bus to catch, and nothing more to be had from him that day.

Of course Bill Tiernan has heard about the bones. He is a dignified, handsome old man with a massive moustache like a white scrubbing brush wedged in under his nose. His hands are huge and rough and gesture constantly when he talks. And God, can he talk. Fortunately he's a raconteur, a teller of tales proliferating out of tales; unfortunately, he's the slowest person on the planet in speech and movement, a smiling, chuckling rambler of sidetracks that have nothing at all to do with the matter in hand – such as how to make perfect porridge, or the naming in sequence of every shop on the main street of Boolavoe, along with the names of all the people who'd had the shops before them. He tells me the history of a dozen families, none of them anything to do with me, charts the road to desolation of many a forgotten village, and finally, when I am mesmerised by the tight-stretched leather mask of his face and the persistent sonorous tolling of a bell from the Christian Brothers' schoolyard next door, he imparts to me that Kildarragh once consisted of fifteen dwellings, possibly more, most of them down on the more even ground closer to sea level. Looking at it now you'd never be able to count the houses. From the top of the hill it looks as if they've all been kicked around by a giant careless foot. My house, Darby's House, is away from and just out of sight of the others, higher, its plot of land running steeply up the side of the mountain.

Bill Tiernan consults his filing system, a bizarre arrangement consisting of about ten cardboard boxes with the tops cut off, all lined up around two of the walls of his plain square living room. Behind him, the window looks out over a row of bicycles tethered like ponies all along a wall. I envy him his slowness. Time must be different for him, I think. He acts as if he has aeons of it still before him. I never feel like that, I feel time running like sand through an hourglass. At last he shows me a document, a copy of a will. My house, he informs me, was left on her death in 1917 by Margaret Vesey of Lissadoon, widow of James Vesey of Lissadoon, in the joint ownership of her two youngest children, Mr Michael Vesey of Manchester, England, and Mrs Eliza Jakey of the Bronx, New York.

Such a lot of Veseys.

'Eliza Jakey was my grandmother,' I say, and think of Granma Lizzie. 'Her maiden name was Vesey.'

Two days later I got a letter in a shaky hand: *Dear Miss Conrad, I have been checking my files again and discovered that the Vesey family first took over the lease of your house in Kildarragh in 1848. Before then it was in the hands of a Darby Quinn. The only Quinn I know of in these parts is Luke Quinn at the saw mill. Trusting this is of interest to you. I have the relevant documents if you are interested in seeing them. Yours Sincerely, William J. Tiernan.*

So I am going to see this Luke Quinn at the saw mill.

I ask directions at the garage in Boolavoe and the man there says sure thing, my love, you just keep on the Lissadoon road till it goes over the bridge where all the trees start, then go left instead of straight on home. 'You after timber?'

'I'm looking for Luke Quinn.'

'Luke,' the man says, and smiles. 'He'll be there or up at the house, you'll see.'

I turn to go.

'You'll know him,' he calls after me, 'Your man's got funny eyes.'

2

I hear the saw mill first, a harsh silver voice coming through the trees, then I smell it, sharp and sappy. The woods hang out great vertical mats of rhododendron, past their best but still gorgeous, great purple blooms all crumpled and faded like hungover showgirls after a heavy night. Just off the road the whole area gets wild and tangled, impenetrable, like the forest around Sleeping Beauty's castle. Everywhere, the shiny green swords of earlier bluebells are growing limp. The saw mill appears, a massive shed in a huge clearing, open at either end, surrounded on all sides by stacks and piles and towers of wood, cut, uncut, higgledy-piggledy. The ground underfoot is shaggy, like the bark of a red-wood.

Two men, rough friendly types, sit smoking on a great log in front of an orange truck. I have to shout to be heard.

'Luke's up at the house,' one of the men shouts back, and points me the way further along the road. 'Can't miss it,' he yells, 'it's the only house you'll come to.'

The lane winds steeply upwards, high-sided, cascading with yellow and blood-red flowers, little bleeding hearts everywhere. At the side of the road there's a wide metal gate that clangs as I open it, setting a dog barking somewhere inside. A stone path leads through a rampant jungle of nettles and foxgloves and high-necked raggedy pink flowers to the solid grey house, high and beetle-browed, its front door standing open to a damp-smelling porch with a filthy door-mat and shelves full of clutter. High overhead, the forest hangs long arms that wave infinitesimally. The sound of the mill is less alarming here.

I rap on the inner door.

The dog's barking grows louder and someone appears behind the cloudy glass, cursing at the dog and pushing it back, then the door opens and an unearthly boy in a powder-blue sweater looks out, saying nothing.

'Hello,' I say, startled, 'I'm looking for Luke Quinn.'

His eyes are too far apart in his head. The irises are a subtle dove-grey and the pupils are strange, elongated. They are rather beautiful but scare me in an immediate physical way so that I feel a pulse begin to throb in my throat. Of course you never show it when a face makes your heart jump.

'I'm Luke Quinn,' he says, staring.

The dog, a Jack Russell, yaps round his feet and he kicks out automatically.

'Geddown!' he snarls, flickering his goat eyes. His face looks six years old but he's nearly up to my shoulder, or he would be if he wasn't all hunched up. Something changes in his face when he curls his cupid's bow lip at the dog, a wrinkling of the sides of his nose, a flash of baboon-like savagery, fascinatingly ugly and gone in a second.

'Beatrice Conrad.' I hold out my hand. He looks down at it, as if no one ever shook him by the hand before, hesitates for an awkward moment then takes it. We shake. 'I'm staying up at Kildarragh, near Lissadoon. I don't know if you heard about the bones that were found?'

'The bones,' he says, coughing. He takes his hand back and looks at it intently for a second as if it just appeared on the end of his arm. A little jolt of déjà vu kicks in from somewhere and ticks alongside.

'It was in the newspaper.'

'Hm,' he says, folding his arms again, sticking both hands under his armpits and staring. All seen before. His eyes produce

24

a feeling akin to panic so I have to keep looking away. Come now, I scold myself like Alice, don't forget your manners.

'Well,' I press on, 'I found out that a man by the name of Darby Quinn used to own my house a long time ago, and I wondered if there might be a connection with your family? I'm trying to find out about the house, you see.'

'Why?' he asks.

What a funny thing to ask.

'Luke,' comes a deep voice from inside the house, breaking the déjà vu, which has been oddly exhilarating, although I'm relieved it's gone, 'Who are you talking to?'

'It's a woman, Ma!' he calls.

She comes on two canes and pushes him aside with one of them. 'What do you want?' she says rudely, greying hair severely scraped back from a faded face.

'I'm researching the history of my house,' I say, 'and there's a Quinn connection. There was a man named Darby Quinn living there till 1848. I just wondered.'

'Well, I don't know,' she says anxiously, 'I've never heard of that.'

The boy fidgets manically behind her, looking down and grinning wildly to himself.

'Could we talk for a few minutes?' I ask as nicely as I can.

She draws in a long breath through her large hooked nose, licks her lips and sighs before saying unwillingly, 'Come on in then.'

The boy makes tea while she and I sit down by the range. The dog mooches up wanting to be petted. Mrs Quinn, a thin stick of a woman with baggy brown skin, stashes her canes, seizes the dog and holds it before her on her lap like a shield.

'What a lovely house this is!' I say.

It is, or could be if it wasn't for the decor. The pictures on the pink floral wallpaper are of holy scenes and gruesome sad clowns with wistful tear-filled eyes. The drapes are startlingly op art, full of strident brown and yellow squares and circles. Everything's dusty. Trees crowd the windows, looking in. Turning my head I can see through an open door: Luke Quinn fiddling about with cups and saucers in a dingy kitchen, fingers effete, shoulders round and frail under the powder-blue sweater a size too small. I look around. 'What a lot of books you've got!' The wall going upstairs is entirely covered with a hotch-potch of home-made shelves crammed with books.

Her bony fingers drum on the dog's head. 'My late husband's,' she says. She has a man's voice.

Luke Quinn drops a spoon in the kitchen.

'And you are . . .?'

'Oh, I'm sorry, I haven't introduced myself. My name's Beatrice Conrad. And you are Mrs Quinn?'

'I am.'

'My grandmother left me a house in Kildarragh,' I say, 'and I'm staying there for the summer. It needs a lot of work.'

'Sure, you're mad,' she says.

I laugh. 'Probably.'

She doesn't laugh. She looks as if she never laughs.

Luke emerges from the kitchen with a tray, his strange eyes cast down, elbows held stiffly out to the sides. He could be anything between twenty and thirty, I've no idea. He sets the tray down on the range next to his mother and retreats to perch on a stool by the window and looks at me with open, childlike rudeness. Both of them stare, waiting for me to speak.

'Well,' I say, 'I found some old bones in a tree at the back of my house.'

'I heard about that,' she says, pouring the tea.

'I'm just interested in the history of the place. Bill Tiernan on the back road told me it was owned by someone called

Darby Quinn till 1847, as I mentioned earlier. You don't think it could have been your husband's family, do you?'

'I never heard of any Quinns up at Kildarragh,' she says, handing me a cup and saucer. She doesn't look interested.

'Oh, well!' I sip my tea. 'It might have been different Quinns.'

She sits forward. 'Biscuits, Luke,' she says.

All this time I've been aware of him from the corner of my eye, watching me.

'They think the bones are from then,' I say, kind of performing. 'It was the famine time, wasn't it?'

She twitches her mouth. 'Would have been.'

'It's just my curiosity,' I say, shrugging and wondering suddenly why I am here. I laugh at myself silently. 'Sorry, I guess I had some idea that it would all just fall into place like in a book, and I'd come here and you'd have some marvellous old family story to tell that would solve the mystery of who's the poor baby in the tree.'

'Biscuits, Luke.'

Luke jerks to his feet and goes into the kitchen, returns with a caddy he hands to his ma like a good boy.

'On a plate,' she says.

'Oh that's OK.' I smile at him.

'On a plate,' she insists.

Poor boy, off he droops.

'The Quinns are mostly round Eskean or around here,' she says, sucking her tea, 'I never heard of any up at Kildarragh.'

'Oh, well. It was worth a try.' I sip. 'Sorry if I've been a nuisance. This is nice tea, Luke. Thank you.'

He smiles shyly, bringing biscuits on a small flowered plate. 'Judith would know,' he says, glancing quickly at his mother before retreating once more to his perch by the window and pulling a cigarette pack from a pocket.

'What?' She turns her head, irritated.

'Judith would know.'

'Judith's senile,' Ma says.

'She's not senile, Ma.' He puts a cigarette in his mouth then takes it out, jumps up awkwardly and jerks across the room, remembering his manners. 'Would you like one?' he asks me.

'Who's Judith?' I accept.

'My auntie,' he says, back on the stool, lighting his own cigarette but forgetting about mine.

'She's not your auntie,' Ma says.

'My dad's auntie,' he says.

'She's senile.'

'You would say that,' he replies gently, turning his beautiful misshapen eyes full on me. 'She's in the Cloverhill Home,' he says. 'You'll have seen their minivan. And she isn't senile, Ma,' he turns to her, 'no more of that.' But he keeps his voice soft.

'Your father's aunt,' I say. 'Is she also a Quinn?'

'Was,' Ma answers for him. 'She married a Rochford.'

'Do you think she'd talk to me?' I still address him. 'Would she mind, do you think?'

'You won't get sense out of Judith,' Ma replies quickly, slamming her cup down in the saucer, 'she's in her dotage.'

He makes a move as if to speak but subsides immediately, thinking better of it.

'I'd love to talk to Judith,' I say. 'It's amazing what old people can remember.'

She looks scornful.

'Ma,' Luke says, crossing one leg over the other and twisting his arms together in a painfully awkward knot, 'What was Aunt Judith's daddy called?'

'How would I know?' Ma turns her malicious old face towards him. 'Give her that William Tiernan thing if it's history she's after. Maybe that'll do her.'

28

He blushes at her lack of manners, unwinding himself; going to the stairs, reaches up to the top shelf for a book.

'Bill Tiernan's the man who gave me all the information,' I say, but no one replies and the silence is awkward. It's time to go.

'Well, thank you so much for tea,' I say, getting up, 'I hope I haven't been too much trouble.'

She feeds a sugary biscuit to the dog, ignoring me.

'Here.' Luke hands me a thin, very battered book and steps back quickly. 'Local history.'

Boolavoe and Beyond by William Tiernan. The line drawing on the cover is of Lissadoon Bay, with the Skelligs in the far distance.

'Thanks so much. Mind if I keep it a little while?'

He looks at Ma.

'She can have it as far as I'm concerned,' she says without looking round, 'I never look in it anyway.'

I like behaving extra nice and sunny to rude people, it drives them mad. 'Thank you so much,' I say graciously, 'I'll let you know if I find out anything.' And I smile at Luke, who grins and looks away. He walks after me into the porch. 'If you're in town next fair day and I chance on you,' he says under his breath, 'I could take you to see my Aunt Judith if you like.'

The wood round the window frames is rotting. Slug trails glisten on the threshold. I open the door on the sound of the mill.

'I'll keep an eye open for you,' I say. When I look round, he's gone.

Boolavoe on Fair Day. Weavergate, the main street, is blocked with sheep. I stroll among their soft brown eyes to the big square on the southern edge of town, packed with stalls and teeming with people: inscrutable farmers, women

29

in headscarves, scruffy little kids in rubber boots. Country music plays around the stalls. There are cattle with wild, rolling eyes and dripping pink noses, muddy sheepdogs trotting through dirty puddles rutted with cart tracks. My eyes are peeled for the funny eyes. He's been on my mind: that boyman, a faun of the woods, a Puck, living in the tangled forest with the Old Hag of Beare. As well as him, I'm looking out for Uncle Pats, who heard the ghostly voice. I meet a lot of other Veseys but not him, and finally some other old one tells me Pats has been having trouble with his chest and has gone off to stay with his daughter in Limerick. No one seems to know when he'll be back, and I guess at his age it could well be never.

Old Pierce O'Donnell is going into Finn's Bar on the corner of the square, so I figure I might as well follow him in; and of course who's sitting there but Luke Quinn himself, leaning on the bar and looking straight ahead through a fuggy cloud, obviously drunk. Finn's is packed, the air boils with smoke, thick beams of light stream in through the clear panes like heaven piercing the cloak of hell. A fog lies over the gold-leafed windows and mirrors. Layer upon layer, the voices go hubble-bubble, hubble-bubble as I squeeze up to the bar and order a Guinness. Luke sees me but pretends not to, covering one side of his face with a hand.

'Luke!' I call loudly.

The poor creature blanches.

I move around to his side of the bar and edge up beside him.

'Hello, Luke.'

He nods.

'So, did you mean it?' I say. 'About taking me to see Aunt Judith?'

He speaks but his voice is too quiet for the babble. I lean in. His collar's frayed but he's clean, smells of aftershave.

'Yes,' he says, too loud.

'Is she expecting me?'

He shakes his head. 'You could tell her,' he says, 'but she wouldn't remember.'

'The other day,' I ask him, 'did I offend your mother in some way?'

That makes him smirk. 'Oh, no. She's always like that.'

'Well, she was good enough to give me Bill Tiernan's book. I've been reading it but there's nothing at all in it about Kildarragh. Interesting though.' I drink. 'Your father had a lot of books,' I say. 'Have you read all those books?'

'Some.' Luke's face is flushed. He's not making eye contact at all, reminds me of a big hunting dog that belonged to a friend of mine. This dog would sit at the other end of the couch and take sly little glances at me, but whenever I looked at him he'd turn his head away, bashful. A terror in the field but shy as a maiden in the house.

'How old are you, Luke?'

His eyes dart quickly towards me then away. The colour, like you dipped your brush in violet and just touched it to the white, the merest tinge, then grey again. 'Twenty-five,' he says.

'Ah, a man then,' I say. I am twelve years older than him.

He's finished his drink and is folding his hands neurotically up into his armpits.

'So is it just you and your ma up at the house?' I ask. 'Just the two of you?'

'It is now.'

I think: Psycho, and in the space between draining my glass and setting it down on the bar, understand his unease. The whole place is watching us, including old Pierce O'Donnell who's taken up a position by my left elbow; and I am the only woman in here, larger than life with my hair all over the place. I feel it growing, coiling out from my head

31

into the mists of the bar, climbing up the walls like a creeper. I am embarrassing him horribly.

'Shall we go, Luke?' I say quietly. 'Shall we go and see Aunt Judith?'

He looks at me, his weird wide eyes from the gloom. 'OK.' He stands and pushes through the crowd to the door. Everyone has a nod or a word for him, and for me as I follow after, towering over him. I wish I was in a big city, anonymous. We walk along through the sheep pens, past the bars and shops. The raw beast smell is in the air. He lopes along in a high-collared grey jacket and corduroy trousers, a consistent three feet away from me, out of town, up the lane.

Poor awkward creature. I suppose he never thought I'd go in there; I suppose he was hiding, thinking he was safe.

'It's not far,' he says.

We walk along without speaking, striding out at a good pace. After ten minutes we come to a sign in the beech foliage: Cloverhill Retirement Home, tall gates standing open, a curving drive leading up through bushes.

'What was it like finding the bones?' he asks suddenly.

The house where the old folk live is large and red and square, surrounded by a big lawn on three sides, with trees and a few benches in the shade. A long glass extension has been made into a conservatory, and the old folk can be seen scattered all around it in various stages of catatonia.

'I've thought about that. And I can't find a simple answer for how it made me feel. I just put my hand down and there was this little skull. I can't get it out of my mind that she was a real child once.'

There is a long pause.

'That must have been a shock for you,' Luke says.

'You can't imagine.'

The Cloverhill Retirement Home is part hospital. We pass

32

the reception room and walk straight through the hall. Everyone knows Luke, all the attendants and all the old people who are capable of noticing anything at all. A nurse leads us past open wards full of old women in ancient beds of pale institution-green bars, speckled dark where the paint's flaked off. Boxes of Kleenex spit out their contents. Bottles of Lucozade make rings on narrow bedside cabinets. Beyond this is a corridor with squeaky linoleum, then a very large rusty twilit interior with long curtained windows at one end and a wide-screen TV at the centre front. Ancient men and women sit immovably in small groups of easy chairs, and a woozy somnolence weighs down the air.

'Now, Judith,' the nurse is saying loudly, 'there's someone to see you, darlin'.'

We have stopped before a harpie, a death's-head. Her great age inspires dread and awe. Her tiny size beggars belief. Her legs stick straight out in front of her like a child's.

'My good boy,' she says fondly, putting up her monkey paws to Luke. The crisp intelligence in her voice shocks me. I'd been getting ready for gaga. Ashamed, I wait to be introduced.

'Howya, Aunt Judith.' Luke stoops to kiss the thick, cracked leather of her cheek. She smiles alarmingly, showing a full set of horsey yellow teeth.

'This is Beatrice, Aunt Judith,' he says. 'Aunt Judith, Beatrice is over from America on a visit and I've brought her to see you.'

'How are the girls?' she asks me, seizing my hand and holding onto it.

'It's not Briege,' he tells her, 'It's Beatrice, not Briege.'

'How are the girls?' she repeats, still taking me for whoever Briege is.

We sit one on either side of her. 'They're absolutely fine,' I assure her.

'And the little one?'

'Fine, too.'

'My husband was a schoolteacher, you know,' she says, 'and a very good one.'

'Was he?'

'You've grown your hair.'

'That's right. How did I have it before?'

'Up on top,' she says, wiggling her finger about over her head, then turns to Luke and says crisply, 'How's your ma? Batty as ever?' She smiles and her lip folds like a leaf.

He gives a little snort, biting his nails.

'Do I know you?' she asks me.

'I'm Beatrice. I wondered if you could tell me anything about my house at Kildarragh.'

'She pretends to be ill, you know,' she says. 'Mind you, I'm glad poor Luke has my husband's books to look at. We brought him up as a reader, you know.'

'Luke?'

'Of course not.'

'She's talking about my dad,' Luke says.

Her lids of mottled lilac droop and flicker.

Luke takes out his cigarettes. 'She's falling asleep,' he says.

But she opens her eyes and looks right at me. 'My brother Tom, you know,' she says, 'now he never read a book in his life. He drowned, you know. Went over the cliff at Kildarragh.'

'At Kildarragh?'

'Was it at Kildarragh?' Luke asks, 'I never knew that.'

'Now he was a lovely boy.'

'My grandfather,' Luke tells me.

'Girls all right?' she asks me.

'Fine.'

'Oh, that's good. And the little one?'

'The little one's fine too.'

'Aunt Judith,' Luke says, 'Beatrice is staying up at Kildarragh.'

'Who's Beatrice?'

'This is Beatrice.'

'My grandmother came from here,' I tell her. 'Lizzie Vesey. Vesey was her maiden name.'

Something happens in her face. She is looking at me but she is looking in at herself. wheels turning, cranking.

'We don't like the Veseys,' she frowns.

'I'm Johanna's girl,' I say. That always seems to place me, but I am unprepared for the remarkable effect it has on her. She wriggles, thrusts her turtle neck forward, peering at me as if she would lean toward me in her chair, though being so frail she cannot.

'Little Johanna,' she says in a tone of wonder and sadness, 'little Johanna.' Then: 'Is she happy?'

'Did you know her?' I say, amazed.

'Know who, dear?'

'My mother.'

She frowns. 'Well, I don't know, dear,' she says, 'what was your mother's name?'

'Johanna. And my granma was Lizzie Vesey.'

She sucks her teeth noisily. 'She's one of ours,' she murmurs.

'Aunt Judith,' Luke says. 'Did you know something odd was found over in Kildarragh? In a tree at Beatrice's house. Aunt Judith, do you know if any Quinns ever lived at Kildarragh?'

She looks perplexed.

'You don't have to tell her about the bones,' I whisper, but she picks up the word, God knows, her ears are sharper than her wits.

'What bones?'

It seems wrong to talk about death to someone so close to it, but Luke puts it straight: 'There's been some bones found,

Aunt Judith,' he says, 'in a tree near Beatrice's house. The bones of a little girl, they think it is.'

'I knew your granma,' Judith says. 'Lizzy Vesey. Oh yes, she was a Vesey, you see. We didn't have anything to do with those ones.'

'Why not?' asks Luke.

Her head tips over and she starts to snore softly. We sit for several minutes.

'I guess that's it for today,' I say, but she revives and looks at Luke. 'They used to play in that tree,' she says.

'Who did?'

'My daddy did.'

Her eyes droop.

'My tree,' I whisper, a kick of excitement inside. Her father played in my bone tree. Her brother Tom drowned in Kildarragh.

'Is she happy?' she snaps suddenly, opening her eyes.

'She's very happy,' Luke assures her.

'Aunt Judith,' I say, 'Johanna did OK. She went to live in America with her mother and father and sisters. She got married and had a nice place to live and a lot of friends, and she had me and my brother.' I could add that Johanna died nine years ago in Manhatten State Hospital from secondary pneumonia after a very bad bout of influenza, but I don't. I feel oddly displaced, here in this overheated room full of people as gnarled and withered as ancient trees, people grown back to babyhood, people with proud necks stuck high out of their crocheted shells, reeking softly of curdling bodies. No one knows me at all, I could be anyone, I could be this Briege she takes me for. I could be anyone I wanted.

'He gave her the one chair,' she says. 'Our Tom. A lovely boy. He made it. He was good like that, that's where *you* get it from.' She places her trembling leaf of a hand on Luke's knee.

'Aunt Judith,' I say gently, 'how do you know my mother and my grandmother?'

'Are you a Vesey?' she asks me, putting up her tiny paws to get a grip on the yellow ribbons threaded round the neckline of the odd garment she is wearing, something like an overgrown baby shawl, 'We Quinns never had nothing to do with those ones.'

3

Luke is peculiarly persistent and persistently shy.

He appears early one evening on a rock above my house, and thereafter every night. He sits on the rock until I take notice of him and wave; then, surprisingly nimble-footed and graceful on the mountainside, down he comes through the old potato ridges and sits by my fireside, where he blushes furiously and chews his nails. Poor baby. Tying himself in knots. He hardly speaks, but listens to me ramble; in a way it's like talking to myself. I try to make sense of whatever it is that's emerging, coming through static, appearing like the pattern on wallpaper persisting through several coats of paint, like the marks of the famine coming through the landscape.

He came this evening while I was lounging in the deck-chair in the yard I'm making out back, trying to write a letter home. I'd written two or three sentences in half an hour. The idea was to clear my head by getting something down on paper but all I ended up doing was gazing at the horizon, chewing the pen and drifting. This place induces a whole host of sensations, peculiar and disconcerting, that I used to but no longer have. Three or four times in the past two weeks I've been nudged by déjà vu. I used to get stuff like that when I was a child and in my teens, but I can't even remember the last time it happened. I thought they'd gone with youth. Why've they come back? Because this is like another youth in a way, everything quite new?

Luke sits in front of my bone tree. His thin neck sticks out from his too-big collar; his Adam's apple lurches up and down when he swallows.

'Of course, to some extent,' I say, 'all this stuff about my mother and grandmother has taken my mind off that poor child in the tree. I suppose I feel that story's so far back I could never reach it now. But there's a link between the Veseys and the Quinns. And this house is the link.'

Something about the Veseys in the scrambled brain of that ancient woman, something she holds against poor old Granma Lizzie; and that I *can* reach, I think, given time.

Luke coughs asthmatically. 'Aunt Judith gets things wrong,' he says.

'It must have been sixty years ago when she used to know my mother and Granma Lizzie, because the one time in her life my mother was here was when she was eight years old and she was smitten with Dec. Now, let's see. How old is your Aunt Judith?'

'Old,' he shrugs.

'Just trying to get my bearings,' I say. I look around. I went to town and brought packets of seeds: nasturtiums and lovage, which I've sown close to the cottage. I don't know what'll grow this high up and so close to the sea. In the ditch round the side I found a big iron cauldron with a handle and three short legs, wonderful old thing, and now it sits by the door, planted up with some periwinkles Rosemary gave me. Maybe it was Pats' old cooking pot. Maybe it hung on a chain over the fire. Maybe it's older than that, maybe the Quinns boiled their potatoes in it before the famine.

'What do you think of my garden?' I ask him.

'It's very nice,' Luke says politely, 'what are you going to do with the tree?'

'Cover it with flowers,' I say. 'What else?'

He smiles, twisting his fingers together and lapsing into silence.

'So, what do you think? Are you making sense of it? Judith's ramblings?'

'Only that her father came from Kildarragh.'

'He played in my tree. Her brother Tom drowned somewhere near here. Your grandfather.'

He gets up and walks over to the tree, stands with his long hand resting on its bark, looking up at the mountain's rising levels. His forehead is extremely pale and thin-skinned, blue-veined. I don't know why he keeps coming up here. If he was older I'd think he was after me, but I don't think it's that. Maybe it's the place pulling him up here, the place where his – what? – great-grandfather played in the tree? I need to write it down. Let's see: Luke's father was brought up by the childless Aunt Judith and her schoolteacher husband after his own father drowned, so . . .

'We should make you a family tree.' I say to Luke, and he laughs as if I've made a very funny joke.

'I found all kinds of things while I was digging the ground.' I rise and head inside. 'Come and see.'

On the window sill I've placed a rusty spoon, a long green glass earring, some old accounts carefully written in a neat sloping hand, and a small bottle clogged full of what looks like human hair.

'I feel like an archaeologist with one of those little brushes they use,' I say, 'delicately exposing some buried artefact.'

He picks up the bottle. 'This is a pishogue,' he says.

'A what?'

'A spell.'

'A spell? How fantastic. How does it work?'

'I wouldn't know. I don't believe in all that.'

'Me neither. Still, it's a rare thing, isn't it?' I walk over and stand next to him and he sways disconcertingly towards me then jerks back in a peculiar way.

'What should I do with it?' I say.

40

'Leave it where it was.'

I am at work on two excavations: one for a lost, possibly even murdered child, through layers and layers of silted time and memory; the other excavation, completely separate and all in my mind, down into Luke Quinn. I'm getting used to him. What's odd about his eyes is not the colour or the indigo rims, nor the strange wide placing in his head; what's odd is their mutability, and the speed with which they change. Sometimes they're blank marble, sometimes beast intense.

We go outside and look down the sloping track to where the old ruins of Kildarragh slumber above the sea.

'Imagine all the people moving around down there,' he says, quite unprompted, 'all the people who ever lived here.'

A bird skims over the Atlantic Ocean.

We lapse into silence and I take the cigarette he offers.

When he's gone, just before dark, I bury the pishogue where I found it, then go inside, light the tilly lamp and sit down by the fire to finish my letter. Still, I keep drifting. I think of New York, all the poets and posers and phoneys. *Say hello to everyone for me,* I write, then get a sudden flash of Granma Lizzie in those last years when she was living with my aunt, tiny, with hunched shoulders and big wide watery eyes, straight white hair, lively, aged face. She kept cats and her smoker's voice was gravelly, deep and from the chest, but quiet. She was a cotton throstle-spinner in Salford when she gave birth to my mother. A cotton throstle spinner – I love the sound of that. She never talked about Ireland, though I knew she'd grown up there. My mother was always putting her down, hiding her away whenever any of her la-di-da friends were going to be around.

The people are nice to me here because they know me, I write, *I am Johanna's girl, of the Veseys.* There's a Vesey Street in New

York, in the Financial District. That's nice, they'd like that, my new Vesey kin. They like to hear of the ones that made good over there. So when they ask about my mother I tell them yes, Johanna did well, and she did too. She was a clever girl, she married my dad and had a beautiful house and made a garden that was her pride and joy, probably the greatest achievement of her life. People were paying to see that garden by 1958. All that I tell them, but I leave out any bad bits because they don't want any of that, they want the eight-year-old she was when she last appeared in these parts, hanging onto the hand of her handsome mammy.

4

'Which one are you?' Aunt Judith asks, frowning.

In the few weeks I've known her, the texture of her face has yellowed and thickened everywhere except the sharp bridge of her nose, where the skin is so thin it seems the bone must break through at any moment.

'I'm Beatrice.'

She's not placing me. I've come alone today.

'Johanna's girl,' I say.

'You're too big.'

I laugh. 'I know.'

'I remember Lizzie Vesey,' she says. 'I saw her that time with the little girl. And God forgive me for what I said to her, for the poor child was upset and jumped up and put her arms around her mammy's neck.'

'What was she upset about, Aunt Judith?'

'I always blamed her, you know,' she says, 'because she got him drinking. He was a lovely boy, Tom, a lovely sweet creature and he wouldn't have hurt a fly, but he was downright stupid about *her*. And she was up and off without a word to him after all she put him through, and it was after that that he went wrong.'

I sweat in the heat of the hushed conservatory.

'She never dared show her face till he was dead,' she says.

'Who, Aunt Judith?'

'Which one are you? Briege?'

Then—

'Bold as brass she says to me – this is my little girl, Judith. This is my Johanna. And I look down and see this child she's got with her, and the child's got just our Tom's face – just his face – and, and I says to her, I says –'

And Aunt Judith says very coldly and distinctly, looking into my eyes:

'You killed him, you whore. You killed my brother sure as if you stuck the knife in his heart, you brazen bitch.'

'Well, she bursts into tears. And little Johanna bursts into tears too, and she stands up on her tiptoes and gives her mother a big big hug. And that was wrong of me – very wrong – for it upset the child.'

And if that's true—

Straight from there I went to the saw mill.

Luke's working in the big shed with the men but he comes out when he sees me.

'You're my cousin,' I say.

He looks worried. 'What?'

'You're my cousin. Well, sort of. Second cousin, half cousin, something like that.'

'I don't understand what you mean.'

Aunt Judith believes my granma, Lizzie Vesey, and her brother Tom Quinn were sweet on each other, and that my mother was their lovechild. I tell him but he says nothing. I write him a family tree on the back of an envelope.

'Aren't you pleased?' I say, 'don't you want to welcome me into the family?'

He laughs uncertainly, scratches his head in a buffoonish way and laughs again. 'That's really funny,' he says.

'Shall I tell your ma?'

'Sooner you than me.' He starts backing away. 'I have to go back to work.'

'Won't she like it?'

'She likes things to stay the same,' he says, 'she doesn't like things to change.'

'Will I see you later? Want to talk about all this?'

'Maybe.' He hovers. 'Maybe.'

'Aren't you impressed at all, Luke? Not at all?'

He just grins, inneffable.

On Weavergate, Uncle Dec pulls up alongside me at the kerb and offers me a lift. I start babbling away about my findings: Tom Quinn and Granma Lizzie, and what does he think? Thank God for Dec and good sense. 'I have absolutely no idea,' he says like a rock, 'it's all long before my time. I recall seeing your granma that one time when I was only a boy. She was a beautiful woman.' He drives stolidly. 'Tom Quinn – I have no idea – no idea at all.'

I ask him to drop me in Lissadoon. I'll walk from here, I need to think. The churchyard calls me. Wandering among the graves, I find a whole host of Veseys but no Quinns. The older stones are all weathered and lichened, their letters here and there fading to tantalising ripplings on the stones. The stately building with its clocktower and cross looms like a sphynx above me. A railed path runs back up the hill to the front of the church. I walk slowly, my head spinning with Veseys. They are a liability, these Veseys, this long trail winding behind me. They're too much to take. I get mixed up with all the greats and great-greats and great-great-greats. They could all go lie still if they hadn't left me their cabin with the child in the tree. I never asked for that. I should just go back home and forget all about them.

I'd thought Luke Quinn would come and talk to me. Surely he's curious. First I thought I must have missed him. Surely he must have wanted to know?

A day or two go by, and I tidy the place, change the flowers, bring down the seamed stone from upstairs and place

45

it on the window sill, and on top of it a small glass jar containing two yellow flag irises. What a weight that stone is. Everything's clean and fresh. I've brought in driftwood from the shore, polished smooth and white by the tides. The turves are neatly stacked by the fire, an Indian cloth with a swirling purple and green design is thrown over the table. I sit quietly, taking stock, reading Bill Tiernan's book, waiting for Luke Quinn to come, but he doesn't. I think about getting some of my friends over here maybe. I imagine us sitting outside with a bottle of red wine, lighting cigarettes and joints to keep the midges away.

The builders come in September. I'll be home by then. The floor needs fixing, the roof mending, new doors, new windows. A pump to bring the water into the house. A flush toilet, septic tank. Electricity's more of a problem but not impossible. What do I *do* with this house now it's mine?

I go over the options again: sell it, rent it, live in it, leave it to the rain.

Live in it. Stay. Collect shells. The sand on the strand is shells, a million tons of mother-of-pearl. There's worse things to do with your life.

Leave it to the rain. To the mist and the wind and the bright sun and salt air, all the soft days and starry nights. Let it sink into the lap of the mountain. Quilty's Door.

The first visitor I do get, on the third day, is Pats Vesey. I'm in the front garden trimming the grass between the stones on the path when I look up and see a tall thin old man in a flat cap and baggy grey clothes approaching from below at a remarkable pace, the sea at his back. Before he reaches the gate I recognise him. He's taller than I'd imagined. In Murphy's Bar I'd never have credited him with being able to move so fast. I stand up and go to meet him.

'Beatrice Conrad,' he says, a spiky man coming through the gate, 'put the kettle on.'

'So you're back from Limerick?' I say. 'How are you?'

'Fair.'

'Back for good?'

He laughs. 'Who knows?' His toothless mouth is an absolute cavern. 'I hear you've been looking for me.' His voice a cracked reed.

'That's right. I want to pick your brain, Uncle Pats.'

He seems incurious about his old house. Once inside, he only glances about once, quickly. His eyes are gummy and shrunken, but somewhere in their narrow slits a slightly crazy humour dances.

'Tea, Uncle Pats? What can I offer you? I have some cake. Would you like some cake?'

I keep, for just such occasions as this, Battenberg cake and Dundee cake from the shop in Lissadoon. I feel deeply honoured to have old Pats sitting by my fireside in my one good chair, ('he gave her the one good chair,' I remember Aunt Judith saying) filling up his pipe while I slice the cake nicely and let the tea brew. His back is very straight.

'What do you think of your old place?' I say.

He waves a hand. 'Ah, she's sound enough still.'

'I've got the builders coming in in September. It's a lovely old house and it's so beautiful up here. I don't know what to do. What do you think I should do with it, Uncle Pats? I don't want to sell it. I couldn't live here all the time but I'd like to be able to keep coming back. Do you think I'd find a tenant for a place like this?'

'Not these days.'

'You don't think so?'

He grins, looks sideways. 'Who'd want to live in this lonely old hole?'

'You did.'

He lights his pipe with a reedy sucking. 'That's right, but I wouldn't live here now.'

47

'Granma Lizzie was your sister,' I say. 'What was she like when she was young?'

He smiles. How old is this man? He has a long gnarled jaw, peppered white with stubble. Older than Judith, older than Granma Lizzie; I can't get my mind back to where he started. Look at him, puffing away there on that black tobacco, no wonder he has a bad chest. The air all around us reeks with its strength. I can taste it in my chest, black tobacco, turf, sea-weed, tea made with spring water.

'Lovely,' he says, 'she was lovely.'

After a while, he lays down the pipe and dips his slice of Battenberg in his tea. 'That stone,' he says, pointing to the window sill, 'Did you find that down by the gate?'

'Yes. Under a bush.'

'Our old dog lay under that.'

'Really?'

'Died of old age,' he says. 'Nice dog.'

'What was he called?'

He thinks, his face cracking up into that odd grimace I remember from before. Baby to baby he's gone, full circle. The effort of remembering is too much.

'It doesn't matter, Uncle Pats.'

'Oh Jesus, what was that dog called? What was that dog called?'

'The Quinns used to live here, didn't they?' I say, and he chews his tongue in an avid, slightly obscene way.

'Long before my time,' he says.

'I've been talking to an old lady in the Cloverhill Home. She says she used to know Granma Lizzie.'

He doesn't respond to this.

'That old dog,' he says, 'it'll drive me mad now.'

'It'll come to you,' I say, 'in the middle of the night. That's what happens. Did you know Tom Quinn?'

An ancient person puts so much energy into the act of

48

thinking. It becomes a heroic deed, a retrieval.

'Tom Quinn,' he says eventually. 'I remember Tom Quinn.'

'What was he like?'

Pursed lips and puckered brow. 'Decent enough,' he says.

'Did he know my grandmother?'

I have to tread carefully. After all, it's his sister I'm talking about.

'Ah, I suppose. Everyone knew everyone else. Did your granma not tell you?'

I shake my head.

'She didn't talk about us?'

I make a vague, negative gesture. 'This old lady in the Cloverhill Home,' I say, 'She says Tom Quinn was her brother. She says he died falling over a cliff.'

He thinks again, consciously, for two whole minutes, then says: 'He brought it up from the stone strand.'

'He did what?'

'He brought that stone up here from the stone strand.'

'Where the caves are?'

'Near there.'

'Tom Quinn brought that stone up here?'

Pats puts down his mug and reaches for his pipe. He nods, relighting, stands up. I wish he'd stay and talk a little more.

'Are you walking back, Uncle Pats? Will you get there before dark?'

'No trouble, Beatrice,' he says with his gaping smile, 'I've walked that road many-a night.'

I go down the track with him as far as the lane. The sun's turning red, going down west, towards America.

'Will I see you in Murphy's bar?' I ask him.

'Sometimes I'm there' he says.

'I've heard no ghostly voices,' I say.

'*Is feidir liom thu a chloisteail.*' He smiles, '*Teigh a chodladh.*'

'Do you think my house is haunted?'

'If it's a ghostie,' he says, as we part, 'it's only a very little ghostie.'

Why does this reassurance prick the hairs at my nape?

'How do you think those bones got in the tree, Uncle Pats?' I ask.

'Before my time anyway,' he says equably.

A few steps on, he turns back. 'Captain,' he says. 'The dog was called Captain.'

More and more I feel a part of this place. I'm alone up here so much, and now it no longer seems a condition to be feared or endured. There are times when I am sitting like this at my door watching a silver downpour and the sea shining, and I feel utterly happy. This is a very full solitude. When the skies teem and all you can hear is the rushing of water, there could be a million small voices hidden under that white noise, and it seems the place is alive, throbbing with Veseys and Quinns. The Quinns were here before the Veseys. Where are they now? Bill Tiernan's book hasn't told me much; it scarcely mentions small places like Kildarragh. The land around here, it says, was owned by a Lord Tarlton, who died a very old man in Dublin, of gout of the stomach, which sounds horrible.

Some places, it says, suffered far worse than others during the famine years. My famine images are all of Africa and India, thin brown people, ragged, naked, in a land where nothing grows and no rain falls, where flies have won the day. Strange to think it was here in this place, its leavings beneath my feet. The abandoned potato ridges ripple here and there all over Quilty's Door; one lies, a patch of corrugated green, at the side of my cottage. My little corpse girl knew hunger. Was she a Quinn or was she a Vesey? Was she neither, just a dumped dead child, forever to be nameless? If Judith is right I have the blood of both Veseys and Quinns in me, and so did my mother. What if I'm related to the tree child – what if she's in the family? Does it make a difference if there's a line of blood between her and me? I think of imaginary invisible bloodlines, spreading out behind me like a peacock's tail, every eye a story.

The rain that drummed on the roof for the past half hour has stilled to a gentle fall that shimmers in the bright air. Outlines are clear and sharp. The mountain whispers. Luke Quinn is walking slowly up the track. He comes and sits with me at the door and neither of us says a word, though we smile in greeting, a peculiar piercing smile that passes between us like the clashing of teeth. He's wearing a high-collared grey jacket and a pair of jeans.

'You haven't called by for ages,' I say. 'Did she keep you from coming?'.

He keeps smiling, looking nervously at me. 'She can't stop me from doing anything if I want to do it,' he says.

'Well, you're a funny person,' I say, 'first you're up here all the time, then I go and see your mother and she shouts at me, then I see neither hide nor hair of you for days on end.'

'Her nerves are bad,' he says, 'Sometimes she can't be left.'

'She said *your* nerves were bad.'

'Well, she would,' he says. 'She thinks everyone's nerves are bad. It's really her own.'

He's an odd-looking boy. He takes out his cigarettes and offers one.

Cigarettes are flirty things. 'OK.' May as well go along with this. I accept his light, trying to catch his eye. Then the rain comes down steadily again, turning the sky above the rocks a beautiful sodden blue-grey; and it turns a little cold, but not unpleasantly so. I have a bottle of red wine I was keeping for something like this. I consider getting it out, but the silence between us grows so pure it seems a shame to break it. After ten minutes or so, he moves his head and locks eyes with me. His face has taken on a fixed, goblinish appearance, glazed, and he doesn't blink. I have known him

51

all this time as shy, and now he does this, turns scary on a pin. I don't blink. We stare each other out for so long the world makes a change around us, infinitesimal.

'At night you close your curtains very tight,' he says.

It was him. The cigarette glowing in the dark down at the end of the garden.

'Tonight,' he says, 'leave your curtain a little bit open.'

He stands and walks quickly away, through the gate, down the track, out of sight. I sit on for a while, watching the way the light dances in tiny spots in the air before my eyes. I sit and sit and the mountain chuckles and croons, rushy water all around me, a silvery cadence in my ears. Being here is a dream. I fell asleep in my apartment and dreamed I was here. It's two hours till dark.

I fill up every container with water from the rain barrel and get a bathload on the stove for later, lock all the doors and windows, pull the drapes, leaving the smallest chink, just enough for an eye. Then I go upstairs and light all the candles. Those cigarettes in the dark, sometimes they were at two, three a.m. He knows how to hang around. I open a bottle of red wine and make some strong black coffee, then pull out the tin tub and position it carefully, making believe it's Cleopatra's barge, before the open fire. When the bath's ready I take off all my clothes and bathe by fire and candlelight.

Things were different there, then, on that isolated hillside. I didn't know how I'd got into this. I didn't care. Every night for the next five nights I left the smallest little gap in the curtain. I didn't know if he was there outside. It didn't matter. He didn't come by in the days at all. I found myself thinking about him. Has he ever been touched? Ever been kissed? On the sixth night I left the curtain closed and took a break.

It was so quiet I could hear the mountainside yawn, then tap tap tap at the door.

The lamp flickers. I rise and flit to the door silently, put my ear there and listen.

Luke says, 'Beatrice, it's me.'

My fingers slide back the bolt. Everything's bright, the moon very nearly full. He grins, awkward as ever.

'Come on in, Luke,' I say. 'I'll make you some coffee.'

I let him in.

And, of course, he turned out to be the wolf. He fell upon me clumsily, frightened by himself, and I took him straight to bed. His hair was very tangled, as if he'd been hanging around on the mountain for hours. We had a fierce, sweet night of it and somehow fell asleep in the end, towards morning.

We'd drowsed no more than an hour when he sat up abruptly, as if called. His ghostly eyes were open but he was fast asleep.

He said: 'There are three children playing on the tree.'

PART TWO

1900 –
about seventy years ago

5

The Vesey house, solid and square, stood a little back from the main Boolavoe – Lissadoon road. Lizzie was out in the yard with her mending when she saw a cart coming along the road driven by a man who was not one of her brothers. She didn't get up from the stool but did several things almost unconsciously: bit her lips all over, licked them, tilted back her head, straightened her back and flexed her shoulders; so that when the old green cart drew to a creaking halt just beyond the gate she was ready. She was seventeen and bold. A lean young man dressed in old clothes, a blackened clay pipe in his mouth, sat up front with a dog. A bony brown horse snorted between the shafts. On the back of the cart were a couple of baskets, three or four buckets and a large barrel with a tap.

'Would you be wanting any water?' the man called over the wall.

'Don't you see the pump there?' she said, nodding towards the dairy.

'I'll tell you what.' He got down from the cart and leaned over the gate. He had long brown hair, a straight mouth and a fine-boned jaw. 'I've got some beautiful apples. All the way from America.'

'You'd have to see my brother,' she replied.

'Well, where's your brother?'

'He's beyond,' she said, and suddenly smiled at him. She had big teeth and full lips, and her neck and shoulders were graceful. Smiling was something she practised in front of the mirror. He didn't smile back. She indicated with her thumb, somewhere that way, past the outlying cluster of thatched sheds.

'I can deliver apples,' he said, 'any time you want. I go this way regular to Tadhg O'Donnell's.'

Lizzie got up and came to the gate, still with the mending in her hands. A thick grey stocking hung down. 'Does Norah buy apples from you?'

'Yes, she does,' he said, his elbow over the gate, 'and plenty more. I can get things for you. What do you want?'

'Nothing. You'd have to see my brother.'

'Tell you what I have got,' he said, 'a good pup.' He turned, went round the cart and returned with a basket in his arms. He was handsome in a spiky boyish kind of way, she thought. She leaned over the gate. A very young brown pup was asleep in some straw at the bottom of the basket.

'That's a runt,' she said.

'Don't you be hasty.'

'I know a runt when I see one,' she said, 'poor scrap.' She reached and lifted it out to look at its belly. 'Boy,' she said. It mewed pathetically. Its breath smelt of onions. 'We have two dogs as it is,' she said. 'What happened to his ma?'

'In the sea,' he said.

'Drowned?'

'All but this one. This one fell out the bottom of the bag. He's got the luck with him.'

'Has he, now?' She was watching the hawker to see what effect she was having on him. There was always an effect, always had been.

'He's grand.' The hawker said everything in the same serious way. 'He can lap. Feed himself. Look.' He stowed his basket on the cart, came into the yard without being invited and took the pup from Lizzie, setting it down next to a metal bowl in the dogs' corner. Its legs squashed out sideways.

58

'He's got very short legs,' Lizzie said.

'He's just tired.'

'No,' she said, 'no dogs, no apples, no water. Not today thank you. I'd have to ask my father and I'm not waking him. You might see one of my brothers if you're going over the top. They might want something you could get, I don't know.'

A slight smile hovered on his face but only for a second. He scooped up the dog. 'I wouldn't get the cart over the top,' he said.

'Come to think of it, you wouldn't. You're better by road.'

'Tadhg was in a very bad way last time I was here.'

'Still is,' she said.

The man ran his finger under the frayed neck of his wilted flannel shirt. 'That's a good dog, I guarantee,' he said. 'I won't take any money for him, he's yours. I'd have him myself, only this one I have here would kill him if he got out of the basket.'

Lizzie looked at the black and white dog sitting quite still and calm on the cart, gazing down the road as if deep in thought. 'That one doesn't look fierce,' she said.

'Oh, no, he doesn't look it, does he, but he's got a nasty nature on him, that dog. He can't live alongside of another creature.'

'I don't believe a word of it,' she said. 'Now take the poor desperate creature away with you.'

She followed him to the gate.

'Wait,' she said, 'Can you get me some ducks?'

'You want ducks?'

'I've had a hankering to keep a few ducks.'

'I can get you ducks.'

'I'd rather geese,' she said, 'but my father won't have them about the place.'

'Geese are fierce creatures,' he said.

'I have a hankering for geese.'

'I can get you geese,' he said, 'I can get you geese, I can get you ducks, I can get you whatever you want.'

'Get me ducks,' she said. 'Two. White ones.'

He grinned. 'Done.' He began climbing back onto the cart with the pup held in one fist but then turned back. 'I couldn't just trouble you for a bit of bread, could I?' he said, 'I'm famished.'

She sighed and went into the house, stood blinking for a moment in the gloom.

'God bless you,' he said when she returned with a hunk of soda cake, ate it down in two great bites and wiped his mouth with the back of his hand. She watched him get up on the cart. He put his hand in his pocket and brought out a small wooden whistle. 'I got this for the baby,' he said, 'Tadhg's grandbaby.'

'The baby can't play that!' She laughed.

Two clay pipes followed. 'For the little girls,' he said, 'for blowing bubbles.' He stashed his presents away again and fixed a navy blue cap on his head. 'What have they named the wee man?' he asked.

'Pierce.'

'Well,' he said, '*there's* a name for the gentry,' and grinned. He gave the reins a shake. 'I'll have you your white ducks on the next Fair Day,' he said, 'I'll be in the square.' The horse moved wearily forward. 'Or shall I bring them up to you?'

'Bring them up.'

Only after the sound of the cart had faded away did she realise the pup was still in the yard, nosing around in the turf mould on its stumpy legs, wagging its bit of tail. She sighed, looking at the stocking dangling from one hand. This was one mild day come suddenly from nowhere, early in the year. Tomorrow in all likelihood it would be cold again. The cats were sleeping on the roof of the dairy, the hens scratching contentedly. There was still a lot to do before the family started drifting home and she didn't feel like doing any of it. The pup, realising all at once that it had been set down free in a paradise of smells, tottered rapturously this way and that on the stones before squatting to pee, then darting wildly at a thin black hen that was scratching about near the puddle under the pump. The hen was a fierce old harridan that was having none. She flew forward, screeching. The stupid pup yelped and the cock flew up onto the turf pile.

'Ssh! Don't you go waking him up!' Lizzie grabbed the pup and shook it in front of her face. Her father, who was very bad with his head and stomach, had gone to bed at two o'clock this afternoon after a dreadful night of groanings and wanderings. 'Not a sound or I'll skin you,' she said, dumping the thing down and letting it stumble round after her as she brought in an armload of sods for the hearth, topped up the kettle and hung it back over the fire. She closed the bottom half of the door against the hens, but left the top open for the steam. A pudding in a cloth bubbled in a pan on one side of the chimney. On the other, a foul scum had risen to the top of the ancient vat in which her father's handkerchiefs had been steeping in simmering water for the best part of a couple of hours and now needed slopping out and rinsing. Leave it, she thought, and played with the dog instead, rolling it over and over on the rug till it was frantic, then sitting down on the floor in front of the fire and letting it suck her fingers; only when it continued to whine and fret did she realise it might be hungry. She put it outside to finish the old stirabout in the dogs' bowls. It was an ugly, undistinguished creature with a smug face, but at least it could feed itself. Enough, she thought, leave it outside; but it whined and she let it in so as not to waken her father, and in keeping it calm and quiet, fell sleepy and passed into an idle state, just sitting

61

and thinking about the way that tinker had fooled her. The cheek of it, she thought. And look at me with the holes in my apron. I'd like him to see me swanked up going into town, buckle shoes, lace collar. Bet he's not seen anything like me in a long time. Fellow like him knows he's no chance. He was much nicer looking than bold Robert Emmet though, her mother's hero, whose portrait hung above the table. Robert Emmet was grandly dressed with sword and epaulettes, but she liked the face on this tinker much more.

Her oldest brother Henry came in, reeking of sweat, threw a spade down in one corner, grabbed a bucket from the stack by the fire and went out again, acknowledging her with a silent nod. It was time to get up, drain hankies, peel potatoes, make tea. When she put it down under the cane chair, the pup yawned, showed fine white needle teeth and fell asleep immediately. Lizzie got the potatoes and turnips on low, checked the pudding, took down the tea caddy and enamel mugs from the corner shelf and spooned tea into the teapot. By the time she heard the cart draw up and the voices of her mother and Hanna, the whole kitchen was steamy. She looked out and saw the white donkey in the yard, front legs black to the knees, tearing with its teeth at the shrubs that grew along the dairy wall. Henry was unhitching the cart. Her mother swept towards the door, Hanna following with the market bag.

'Shilling a yard!' her mother exclaimed. 'Look at this, Lizzie,' throwing back her hood and unfurling a length of blue cotton over the table.

Hanna unbuttoned her jacket. 'What is *that*?' she cried, spying the dog at once.

Her mother had taken off her cloak and hung it on the door, and was already tying on her pinny, a great voluminous thing that went over all and made her look stouter than ever. 'Not another dog!' she moaned.

'That's the ugliest dog I've ever seen,' said Hanna.

'A hawker left him.' Lizzie held the cloth against herself.

'Where's your father?'

'Still sleeping.'

'What's it doing in the house?' Hanna asked.

'It made too much noise in the yard. I didn't want it to wake Daddy.'

Her mother came and took the blue cloth from her. 'Later,' she said. 'Now, where in the world is Mike? Lizzie, go and call. Hanna, go and see after your father.' Margaret Vesey rolled up her sleeves and starting taking down the plates from the dresser, sighing and muttering to herself. 'Lizzie, you could have seen to your father's handkerchiefs at least, couldn't you? What have you been **doing** all day? Take that creature outside, you know your father won't have a dog in the house. Off with you! Out you go!'

'Youse are all heartless,' Lizzie said as the pup was chased scuttling out the door. Following, she scooped him up in one hand, opened a gate between the pigsty and the dairy and strode up the mound to stand and call as loudly as she could for Mike from the top. She could hear the dogs barking, and the sound of a bell very far away.

Lizzie was the youngest and last. Ever since she could remember, she'd been given to understand that she was the most beautiful and remarkable person in the world. Oh, what a lovely baby! they'd said. Then: oh, what a lovely little girl! Now, it was looks they gave her more than words. I'm going to keep the pup, she thought, and I'll get my ducks too. She always got what she wanted. Why can't I have my geese anyway? I will, one day. Everything comes in the end.

The dogs' waving white tails came in sight in the valley, then Mike's white shirt. She waved to Mike and he raised a hand.

Her father was up when she got back in the house, standing at the foot of the stairs tying his paisley handkerchief round his neck, and she walked straight up to him and held the dog up right in his face. 'Daddy,' she said, 'can I keep him?'

'Let the poor man catch his breath!' her mother said, turning from the pot she was draining. 'Now, Jamie, don't let the little'un softsoap you.'

'*Please*, Daddy.'

Her father's serious bloodshot eyes softened. 'No, Lorelei,' he said, 'absolutely not.'

'I hope you didn't pay good money for that, Lizzie,' her mother said.

'I didn't pay a farthing. The hawker man just left him. He was selling apples and I said I didn't want any and I gave him a drink and when he'd gone he'd left the dog. What was I supposed to do?'

'No, Lorelei,' her father said gently, 'no dog,' putting his hands on her shoulders. He smiled fondly. The fact that he was a big man and she very small made her feel more than ever like a child. A horseshoe-shaped scar puckered his left cheek, just under his eye, from where a cat had bitten him when he was three or so. Since the beginning, it was a story: your daddy was bitten by a cat. Ripped his cheek out when he was a tot.

'Well, what am I supposed to do with him, Daddy?' she shouted, 'drown him?'

'Lorelei, you remember who it is you're talking to!' He pushed her away and she threw herself down onto a chair and sulked, still holding the pup.

'Put the poor thing out, Lizzie,' her mother said, 'you know he's going to have to get used to it.'

She pushed the tears out over the rims of her eyes.

'No, no,' her father said more kindly, 'let the littl'un carry it round with her for the night if it makes her happy. In the morning she can take it over to Kildarragh. Pats's Lady's on her way out, maybe he'll want to train this one up.'

'*That* one?' snorted Hanna.

It was the best she was going to get. Lizzie raised her eyes but didn't smile. She sat up straight and stared coldly at them all. The dogs were barking in the yard. Mike came in.

'Lizzie's been codded by a tinker,' Hanna told him, 'he's left her with a runt.' She was beating the potatoes, grinning, her thin brown face crooked in the firelight.

Mike grinned, strolled over and poked at the dog. 'Ugly thing,' he said pleasantly.

Lizzie ignored him.

'What's up with her?' he asked.

'Lizzie, get up,' her mother said, 'stop acting the princess.' Her mother went to the fire, pulled out the kettle on its chain and poured boiling water onto the tea. 'Run and see if Henry's coming for his supper.'

Lizzie got up with a loud sigh and sauntered out, swaying her hips, the dog cradled ostentatiously in the crook of her neck. Her oldest brother was in the shed, in the dying light, surrounded by tools and the plough on its side.

'Ma says do you want your tea,' she called from the door.

There was a long pause, then his quiet voice from the gloom: 'Bring me a lamp, honey, I have to finish this off. Tell her to leave it on the side.' He was a gaunt scarecrow under a ceiling of hanging shadows, strings of onions, dried fish, bundles of rolled beef. Lizzie went back to the kitchen and wouldn't do anything but slouch against the wall playing with the dog, despite all entreaties to put it outside; while Mike scrubbed up and her mother and Hanna dished up the food. The ridiculous bundle ran up her shoulder, like a tic. Her father limped over and stood looking at her. An old man now, silver-haired, stout and tall. His thumbs were hooked in the lapels of his waistcoat, from which a button hung loose. 'Now now, Miss,' he said, 'none of this.'

'Tell her to stop sulking, Daddy,' Hanna said.

'Now now, Miss,' her father repeated, 'sit up to the table and eat. All's settled.'

'What was on you to take a whelp like that, Lizzie?' Mike said, appearing in the doorway as she crossed the floor, 'He must have been a talker, this tinker.'

'He wasn't a tinker.'

'He was a robber,' her mother said, 'asking money for that. It won't last the week.'

'I didn't pay money!'

Mike sat to eat.

'He was a bit of a charmer then, this tinker?'

'Mike!'

His mother clouted his head and turned to Hanna. 'Take your brother's on a tray. Poor Henry working away! For pity's sake, Lizzie, change your face!'

But Lizzie kept it up till the lamps were lit and everything cleared away and washed up, and all the work of the place over. She wasn't even sure why. It wasn't the pup. She'd never thought she could keep it in the first place. It was just a feeling, as if they were all of them laughing at her in a way she hated; as if everything she did and said were no more than the mewlings of a pup. Well, if that was it, if they laughed at everything she said, well, she just wouldn't say anything any more, so there. But she got so sleepy again; sitting there with the pup asleep in her lap because her father said she could; and the blanket she was making spilling in folds to the floor. And everything peaceful again, the fire-light flickering up in the rafters on the hooks and on the horseshoe her father had hung there, and the lamplight reflected in the steel hook poised in her mother's hand. A strip of lace hung down. Hanna and Mike were at the table, talking in stifled bursts of laughter; they were close in age. Her father was smoking his pipe and gazing into the flames, frowning.

Sometimes at these moments a terrible sadness would come over her, a kind of mourning for the moment as it passed. Such things as her mother's pleated black cloak hanging on the door would fill her with a terrible sweet rush of love. Tears would prick her eyes and her nose would start to run. It was happening now.

'Now come on, Lizzie,' her mother said, 'be a good girl now.'

'Oh, she's grand now.' Her father smiled at her. His teeth were missing at the side. 'She's a good girl now, aren't you, girlie?'

But the tears rolled out.

'Girl, what is the matter with you?' he asked. 'You know there's nothing to cry about, Lorelei. What a silly girl you are.'

'I know,' she said, sniffing.

I don't want you all to die, she was thinking. She didn't know where the thought came from and it frightened her: as if the thought itself might strike them down. They smiled at her kindly. A bobbin was under her mother's arm. A mug of tea was handed to her.

It's just the little'un bawling again, they were thinking. She's always been like this. Cries easily.

'Come on, Lizzie.' Hanna got up and shifted her chair. 'Let's comb your hair, it's all over the place.' Hanna's brisk fingers took out the pins and set to with the tortoiseshell comb. Let down, Lizzie's straight fair-brown hair was startling. Hanna parted it neatly in the middle. Mike came and sat on the floor by Lizzie's chair, chafing her bare feet tenderly.

'There now,' Hanna said, and she combed and combed,

lightly and smoothly and rhythmically till Lizzie stopped
crying.

Every night the two girls argued about the window. Lizzie
always wanted it open for the fresh air; Hanna liked it shut.
They shared their bedroom with a few sacks of meal that had
nowhere else to go. Lizzie hated the smell of them, subtle as
it was; she said it was like dirty babies. But that night Hanna
didn't care about the window. Lizzie had kept the dog in the
room with them because it howled, and Hanna said the dog
stank. She said she'd rather freeze to death than have to smell
that dog.

After the candle had been blown out and darkness fell
sudden as a scythe, Lizzie was glad of the faint scent of hedge
coming in, and the soft onion breath of the dog faintly upon
her face. It lay fat and warm across the pillow, snoring gently.
Drifting, she tried to guess the age of the tinker. How could
she know? Twenty-four? Twenty-three? Young enough. She
couldn't quite remember his face. She heard the jingling of
her parents' iron bed as her father tossed and turned. Terrible
nights he was having. Hanna turned over. Lizzie made her
hawker walk into the yard all over again. This time she took
him into the house and let him sit at the table. The kettle was
boiling. 'A cup,' he said, 'no more,' but when she rose to get
it for him, he reached out and took hold of her hand and
stood staring down at it as if he had no idea how it had come
to be there.

She heard her father's heavy footsteps descend the stairs,
heard his muted groan in the kitchen, saw the ghostly candlelight appear in the crack of the door, and realised she was
awake. He was poking about amongst the canisters on the
high shelf by the chimney breast. Maybe he was making himself a cup of tea.

Next day she walked over the mountain to Kildarragh with the dog in a basket. A snappy wind was blowing, clouds flying. Far out to sea there were fishing boats with red and brown sails. At the top she let the pup out of the basket and chased about with it for a while, across the rath where, according to the old people, the fairies lived; where the white bog cotton grew tall, down the slope that dipped steeply to where the cliffs went on for miles and miles, pink with thrift, white with birds. There were caves here, safely high and dry above the sea line and easily reached, where she had liked to hide when she was younger, to sit and look out towards the Skelligs and be soothed by the hollow booming of the sea and know that no one could find her. A little further and you could look down on the stone strand where seals sometimes rested. But there were none today.

Kildarragh from above was a scattering of grey houses, mostly ruined, one or two inhabited further down the track towards the sea. After that there was nothing till you got to where the track ran into the crossroads a mile or more beyond the townland, where Tadhg O'Donnell's long low shebeen with hens roosting in the thatch nestled in a crook of land above a small shingle beach. A little away and above from the main cluster was Darby's House, where her brother Pats lived with his new wife Minnie. God alone knew why Pats wanted to make something of that place is what Lizzie's father said, grumbling over his pipe of an evening. There was no good land up there. But Pats had whitewashed the cabin and thatched it neatly, and though the ground was steep and stony, there was room for twelve rows of potatoes on a wide sloping patch beside the house. A white goat was tethered to an old twisted tree at the back. Minnie came out and stood with folded arms, headscarf flapping, watching as Lizzie came down.

'Well, look at you,' she said, 'don't you look nice.'

'I've brought you a dog, Minnie,' Lizzie said, as the mutt galloped clumsily forward. 'I got him from a hawker but they won't let me keep him. Daddy said you needed a dog.'

Minnie picked up the dog. 'The dote,' she said gravely, 'we'll have him.' She was a firm, handsome, steady woman who almost never smiled. 'Patsy!' she called, 'come see what your little sister's dumped on us!'

'He was going to be drowned,' Lizzie told Minnie.

'Come along in, Lizzie.'

It was dim inside. There was a clunking noise and Pats came stumbling down the ladder from the loft. 'Is it Lizzie?' he cried. 'Well, this is nice!'

The hearth was ashy, the floor a mess. Tadhg O'Donnell's ginger-haired grand-daughters, in identical gingham dresses, sat on the settle blowing soap bubbles through short clay pipes.

'Here, girls,' Minnie said, 'now you can run outside for a bit and play with the puppy.'

'Jesus, is that ours?' Pats sat down by the fire, picking up the tongs and rearranging a few sods of turf to make the fire draw. 'Tea, Lizzie? That's a pathetic creature you've brought us.'

'Shoo!' Minnie clapped her hands, 'shoo! Take him to Lady, girls, he'll be grand. Old Lady, she'll sort that one out.'

'The Young Pretender.' Pats grinned, striking a match against the chimney breast.

'What way is Tadhg?' Lizzie asked.

'A bad way.' Pats lit a cigarette, picked up the shovel and stood.

'The priest is down below,' said Minnie, scooping a dipperful of milk from the churn.

'He can't piss,' Pats added, lowering his voice so the little girls beyond the half-open door wouldn't hear.

Lizzie's eyes fell on the clay pipes discarded on the settle, a few dribbles of soapy water leaking from them.

'I'd sooner go quick than linger,' Minnie said.

'I was sweet-talked into that runt,' Lizzie said.

'By a hawker?'

'Well, no, he tried to, only I wasn't such a fool. "Take it with you," I said, but he left it in the yard and I only saw it after he was away. Did he not come here?'

'Tom Quinn was here,' Minnie said.

'Tom Quinn?'

'He's your hawker. Bit of a rascal.'

'Said he was going to see old Tadhg.'

'That's right. They used to go fishing together out of Dingle.'

Pats dribbled turf shreds over the fire. Minnie poured tea.

'He's going to get me some ducks.'

'She's mad,' said Pats to Minnie, 'the old man hates ducks.' He laughed, coughing out smoke. 'He'll wring their necks.'

Minnie handed Lizzie a mug. 'Tom Quinn was in my school,' she said. She pulled off her headscarf and scratched her curly head. 'He was a nice lad,' she said.

Lizzie left the pup living in the shed with Lady. She looked back once when she was halfway up the hill, and once more at the top. There was barking, and the high voices of Tadhg O'Donnell's grandchildren. The white goat had wound itself in on its rope and was feeding on the long lush grass from which the tree's trunk coiled, snake-like, throwing up its old tree arms in anguish. On top, the breeze blew ripples across the wide rath and her hair whipped about. Twenty minutes in the cave, she thought guiltily, and found herself running down the tracks above the sea, turning sideways once or twice, jumping here and there over the crumbly bits, till she reached the best cave, the one that was always dry and sheltered from the wind, well above the water line where no one else came. Its overhung, thrift-grown mouth was the size of a door, its floor a rock. The space it made was like a large cupboard, the back blocked up with rocks. She liked to sit here and do nothing at all but watch the sea. Sometimes a fishing boat far out would slowly cross her line of vision. So his name was Tom Quinn. So what if he was only a hawker? He had a nice face. He looked at her in the same way as Bob Jakey did, as if seeing her more deeply than everything else around her. Bob Jakey was a townie who'd slept in their barn for a week last summer, over from Salford with her sister's husband on a walking tour. Lizzie couldn't even remember her sister, she'd lived in England since before Lizzie was born. So, there were these two Manchester men in the barn, Bob Jakey a coach driver, and Cathy's husband a shipping something. The two men were strange and wealthy in their wing-collared shirts, full of loud laughter and an odd kind of energy. Bob Jakey was much too old, probably even older than Henry, but he'd taken a real fancy to Lizzie, and she was only sixteen at the time. Anyway, all she got was teased. Mike and Hanna went mad over it. She got used to Bob Jakey following her around like a dog, house to dairy, dairy to shed, shed to house, slick black hair carefully parted in the middle. His customary stance was hands behind his back, a smile on his kind, large-featured face.

He was nice, you could tell by his eyes, but he wasn't a patch on Tom Quinn.

Next Fair Day, late, she went into town with Henry. She wore button boots and a flounced blue skirt and one of her mother's lace collars, with a five-pointed yoke that set off the navy of her blouse. Henry left her down on the pavement at the top of Weavergate and headed off for the sawmill. The square was packed with carts with horses between the shafts, clusters of cattle hanging their heavy heads to the puddled ground. Around the edge of the square were the poultry sellers and their crates, pens for sheep, the occasional pig. If

Tom Quinn had ever been there he'd gone, so she walked down Weavergate where it was cleaner underfoot, and bought oranges from an old woman in a white cap. She needed castor oil for her father, soap, a new covered dish to replace the one Mike had knocked onto the stone floor of the dairy with his big clumsy elbow the other day. Weavergate was crowded, loud with the crying of wares. She kept her basket held out in front of her as a buffer against the press.

'Lizzie!'

It was Norah O'Donnell, Tadhg's daughter-in-law, with the baby screaming in a creel on her back and a huge basket pulling down one arm. God, she looked awful. Her fierce brown face was wrinkled and old, though she was only thirty-five. 'I'm worn out, Lizzie,' she said. 'Come on in here with me till I set this lot down,' seizing her arm and steering her into a place where a few people were sitting on benches. A woman ladled lemonade and ginger beer from two iron pots on a counter that was a plank over two barrels. 'Fetch me a ginger beer, darlin',' Norah said, dropping her basket and flopping down, 'while I sort this one out. Here, there's money, and you can get one for yourself too, darlin', I'm dead if I don't get a drink down me this minute. I was up all last night again.'

'With Tadhg?'

'*And* this one.'

Pierce was all worked up into a frenzy and purple in the face. Norah pushed him under her shawl to let him feed, stifling a yawn.

Lizzie fetched two ginger beers and sat to hear the news.

'He's had a Mass said in his room,' Norah reported.

'Ah,' said Lizzie.

The ginger beer was good. The door stood open and all Lizzie could do was keep her eyes on the street, looking out

73

for Tom Quinn and her ducks. Men with sticks passed the door, women in shawls, boys in caps, dapper gents in bowler hats. A sheep was tied to a drainpipe. A horse with its head in a nosebag deposited steaming droppings onto the cobbles. Norah leaned forward and put her long brown fingers on Lizzie's arm. 'Tadhg's ranting, Lizzie,' she said softly. 'He's talking to someone who isn't there.'

Lizzie looked at Norah with sympathy. How must it be in the shebeen, one dying, one just born?

'That's how it was with Granda,' Lizzie said. 'They do that.'

'Quite unsettling.' Norah placed the child on her shoulder. 'The way Tadhg's like a baby.'

'Granda was the same.'

'He says some strange things. He started crying this morning. Said, "Sal's screaming for her baby". I tell you, it makes my blood run cold sometimes.'

'Sal's screaming for her baby,' Lizzie repeated in a tone of wonder.

'He has some story no doubt. You'd never get it out of him in sense though.'

A cart laden with loaded sacks rumbled by on the cobbles. A man in a long black buttoned coat with a cape sat up front.

'Was there a man called Tom Quinn out to see Tadhg?' Lizzie asked.

'Tom Quinn's a rogue,' said Norah.

'Why? He was supposed to be getting me some ducks.'

'Oh well, I dare say he'll get you your ducks. He's had money out of Tadhg, I know that. He's a gambler.' She shifted the baby to the other arm. 'Tadhg likes him.'

'Have you seen him today?'

'Not today.'

'I should go,' Lizzie said vaguely. She rose, giving her

74

finger to the baby to hold. The grip of life, not like the cold weak hold of the dying old. She left Norah sitting on a while, talking to some woman she knew, and went out into the street.

How dare he do that, she thought, what is he? No one. First he gets the laugh on me with the dog, now he doesn't turn up with my ducks. She walked along as far as the station. A few post-cars were drawn up waiting for passengers. A man was selling papers and comics, so she bought a newspaper for her father. There was a haze on the hills over the trees and rooftops. The stalls had run out and there was nothing much beyond the station but cabins with dogs lying in front of the doors and a few women sitting on stools, so she turned and walked quickly back down Weavergate, the angry feeling swelling, went into a shop and looked at the plates and dishes. Her mother wanted something plain. The man behind the counter tried to sell her something with a cherry pattern.

'I don't want that!' she snapped.

These people would swindle the hair off your head. How could she be so stupid as get taken in by a tinker? If he wasn't a tinker he wasn't much more.

She bought a plain covered dish and walked back up the town, looking at all the stalls on the way. She kept meeting people she knew. Everyone was there but Tom Quinn. She filled up the market bag, treated herself to a slice of apple cake and ate it while watching the soldiers exercising their horses in the barracks yard, then it was time to meet Henry by the square. Already the lamps were being lit and it was getting chilly. The cart was there, loaded up, but no Henry. Lizzie sat up on the seat and hugged her shawl about her, shivering, breathing in the sweet reek of the horses. Perhaps they'd come too late. Perhaps he'd been here in the morning with her ducks and couldn't stay.

75

Maybe he'd thought she wasn't coming and sold them to someone else.

Then there was Henry walking towards her in his big coat with the collar raised.

'Did you not get what you wanted?' he asked.

'No.'

He smiled. 'Never mind. Ducks, was it? Daddy would never have let you keep them.'

'Yes, he would. Once I'd got them, he would.'

He shook his head. They rode sleepily home, hardly speaking. Henry's presence rocking beside her was solid, enduring. His hair was going grey already and it didn't seem he'd ever marry now. He'd be here for ever. Mike would go soon, she thought. His America money was steadily growing. And her? What would become of her? She was so sunk in thought she hardly saw a thing of the passing countryside in the gathering dark, till the slate roof of their house appeared suddenly, shining wet against the lowest shoulder of the mountain.

Her father stepped forward to hand her down from the cart.

'Why the long face, Lorelei?'

'She was after buying ducks, but there were no ducks to be had,' said Henry, jumping down.

'God in heaven! You don't want ducks *or* a goose. We had all this with the geese. Your hens are destroying the thatch as it is.'

'Don't you vex yourself.' Lofty, Lizzie swept into the house. 'I won't be getting any ducks.'

Her father followed, muttering, 'Dirty creatures!'

Her mother was putting the irons to heat. 'What are?'

'Geese. Dirty things.'

'Ah, well. What have you got there, Lizzie?' She laid the tongs in the ashes.

Lizzie showed her mother what she'd bought.

'What were you getting ducks with anyway?' Hanna asked, turning from hauling a piece of bacon from the pot oven.

'My egg money.'

She put the oranges in a bowl.

'*Your* egg money?' Hanna smirked.

'*My* egg money.'

'Enough!' said their father.

'I saw Norah O'Donnell.' Lizzie sat down and started rolling down her stockings and her father turned away. 'Tadhg's had a Mass said in his room. He's talking to people who aren't there.'

'Like Granda,' said Hanna.

Mike came in all scrubbed up from the pump.

'Take those potatoes out now, Lizzie,' her mother said.

'I'm only just in!'

'So you are. Now, take those potatoes out, there's the girl.'

Lizzie put on a clean pinny and did as she was told. I'm not feeling bad about *him*, she thought, and smiled at her mother and was pleasant to everyone; and after tea swept the floor, packed turf on the lids of the ovens and filled up all the lamps without being told. Then she sat down by the fire with her father and read to him a little from the daily paper she'd bought in Boolavoe that day; and the white cat came and sat on his lap and purred loudly along with the ticking of the clock. He didn't mind cats. He stroked this one on the side of its face with his rough old finger. Once she'd seen it put up its paw, claws sheathed, velvet-soft and loving, stroking the yellow-red cat-scar under his eye.

A rap came on the door and Mike opened. It was one of Henry's men after his wages. He came in and stood waiting. 'Tadhg O'Donnell is dead,' he said, making the sign of the cross, 'God rest him.'

★

Her parents weren't going to Tadhg O'Donnell's wake. They didn't go about so much these days since her father was so weak, and he didn't approve of wakes anyway, he said they were barbarous. Henry brought the big sidecar to the front of the house. Lizzie had done her hair with papers and fluffed it out. She'd tied a ribbon around her neck. She hadn't had a good dance in ages, and there would be a lot of boys there, maybe even Tom Quinn. Hanna came out and hauled herself up beside her, adjusting her hat, then came Mike, smelling of soap and raw under the chin from where she'd shaved him that afternoon.

'Ladies,' he said with mock gallantry, handing them up a blanket, 'for later when it's cold.'

'Up with you, Mike,' called Henry over his shoulder, and Mike got on the other side. The big mare danced a little, Lizzie clutched the rail, Henry clicked his tongue and they were off.

For upwards of fifty years, Tadhg O'Donnell had presided over the shebeen at the crossroads. Now he lay in his coffin in the parlour there, under a crucifix, candlelight flickering on the rosary between his fingers. His youngest son and daughter-in-law sat by to receive the guests. Lizzie looked down at the face of the old man who'd been such a friend of her grandfather's, a square, corpulent face, putty-grey, with massive grey whiskers that all but covered his cheeks. She kneeled and prayed, then stood and touched Jack's hand, then Norah's. 'I'm sorry for your trouble,' she whispered, 'I shall miss seeing him.'

Norah nodded and smiled. 'He's better now,' she said.

'He is indeed.'

Lizzie went through into the crowded smoky house. The table had been pushed against the wall. Tom Quinn was with a group of men taking snuff by the open door. Minnie, handsome with her dark hair piled up, called her over to sit by her on a bench against the wall. Marty Blake was there, the one her sister Hanna would probably take if she ever got down from her high horse.

'That's a very pretty frock, Lizzie,' Minnie said.

One of the little girls brought Lizzie some punch and she drank deeply.

'You'll never guess,' said Minnie, 'Pats has it that we're haunted.'

'Don't say that.' Lizzie crossed herself.

'No, he does, he says he heard a tiny voice.'

'What did it say?'

'Something in Irish.'

'Now don't go scaring me, Min.'

Minnie leaned forward, 'It said: '*Is feidir liom thu a chloisteail. Teigh a chodladh.*'

'*I can hear you,*' Lizzie said softly. '*Go to sleep.*'

An ancient with a big wooden rosary and a shawl thrown over her bonnet seized Lizzie by the shoulder. 'What way is your father, Lizzie?' she demanded.

'Only very middling, Alma.'

'God be with the good days,' the old woman said portentously, 'the old ones are fading away.'

The daughters were bringing things out of the pot ovens. There was a stew made of chicken and turnips, a soda cake too big to go on any of the plates, buttery cabbage and potatoes. Drink flowed. An old man named Scanlon remembered how well Tadhg O'Donnell had played hurley when he was only a slip of a lad.

'Didn't he play for the county?' Minnie asked.

'That he did, Ma'am. When he was only sixteen.'

'You should have seen him,' old Alma Sheehan said, 'and wasn't he the handsome boy? They were all after him, you know. There was hearts broke when he married Curly Callanan.'

Norah was taking things from the ovens still, setting them

out on the table. 'Eat up now, everyone,' she said, 'Come on now, there's plenty.'

After the food the fiddlers arrived, along with a boy of about twelve carrying a melodeon. They set up outside on the flat triangle of land above the shebeen, an upended barrel making a table for their drinks. People spilled outside. When the dancing began, Lizzie walked straight over to Tom Quinn, who was drinking whiskey and smoking a short clay pipe, and punched him on the arm. 'You rap, where were you with my ducks?' she said.

He grinned sheepishly. 'I swear there were none to be had. How is the great little dog?'

'Great little dog? The runt, you mean. They called him Captain. Grand name for a runt. He thrives. I gave him to my brother, him over there.'

He peered through the smoke.

'Do you still want the ducks?'

'My father won't let me have them.'

'I know who you are,' he said, 'you're Lizzie Vesey. Your brother Pats lives above.'

Norah went by with Pierce screaming on her shoulder. 'He's mad for his supper,' she said, smiling.

The people were clapping the rhythm, slow at first then faster and faster.

Hanna danced with Marty Blake, Henry with Minnie. The night drew on, fine with a full moon. A piper turned up. The old ones sat indoors and the children started running about playing games, pushing each other on the swing that hung from the elm tree. Tom Quinn had a thin, comfortable smile. 'Will you dance with me, Lizzie?' he said. It didn't matter. So much dancing, with everyone, with old men and women, children, brothers, sisters, sweet young men who'd drunk too much, sweet young men who didn't know where to put themselves. So she danced, simple-headed, with Tom

Quinn and anyone else who would. So much was drunk and still so much more that the glasses were never empty. Lizzie must have had more than she'd ever had before. The moon shone bright on the sea and all the land was lit up. She danced as she never had, as free as if this was some dream and anything at all could happen, things that never happened in real life, laughing uproariously, losing all her family in the crowds. She felt she'd gone into a place she'd never gone to before, and after that, everything happened outside the real, everyday world. Like the cave: that was outside the real. So was this place she came to after drinking so much at Tadhg O'Donnell's wake.

Early in the morning when things were quieter and the children had mostly gone asleep; when the old people, who could outlast any of the young, were still mumbling and yarning and ruminating by the fire, a whole bunch of them went up the mountain to the rath to scare themselves witless. Pats and Minnie were there, and Mike, and Tom Quinn. It was so light they could see each others' faces. The white of the bog cotton was sprinkled all over like fine snow. They ran about in the big circle and shouted and whooped, silly people, young and drunk, daring whatever lived there; moonshine. They came together at last, ten or twelve of them sitting in a huddle in the centre, giggling. Minnie said there was a whistling seal came and laid on the stone strand of a full moon and they should all keep quiet and listen. But there was nothing but the whooshing of the sea in its holes.

'Let's go down by the stair,' said Pats, 'past our house and through Kildarragh, 'tis quicker now.'

But no sooner had they set off than they all started telling stories about the fairies, and Tom Quinn stood still and hung back, turning his head and looking towards the cliffs.

'Tom!' called Minnie, 'come on now, they'll get you.'

He held up a hand as if to silence her.

'What?' asked Lizzie.

'I hear it,' he said.

'Oh, dear God,' Lizzie said, 'he hears something.'

'Ssh!'

The others were going on. Lizzie and Minnie lingered, arm in arm.

'Listen.'

Nothing.

'I'm going to look,' he said and set off towards the cliff that overlooked the stone strand.

'Ach, the man's mad,' said Minnie, setting off after Pats, who waited ahead. Lizzie giggled and ran after him.

'Lizzie!'

After waiting a minute or so and Lizzie not returning, Minnie walked on.

Lizzie caught him up on the other side of the rath, coming alongside reckless. 'I want to see a ghost!' she said. 'My head's spinning! Tom! My head's spinning!'

'You're very drunk,' he said, taking her arm to steady her.

They drew near to the edge, to a place from which they could see the moonlight gleaming on the rock striations under the caves.

'Did you really hear something?' she whispered.

'Whistling,' he said, 'very faint.' His arm went round her waist.

She slid her arm under his jacket. 'There's nothing to you,' she said, 'I can feel your ribs.'

'Feel them,' he said.

They kissed clumsily. Tom Quinn had a smooth chin, though his whiskers had encroached a long way onto his cheeks. She felt the kiss in her armpits and the soles of her feet.

82

'Lizzie!' came the voices, 'Lizzie!'

They stood apart.

The strand was bright. Three fat grey seals lay on the shingle.

'They'll have my hide,' he said.

She took his arm. 'I can do what I like.'

'Lizzie!'

She was very silly, that much she remembered afterwards. She laughed every time she fell down. He walked her back across the rath and half carried her down the mountainside to where Pats and Minnie waited below. Lizzie couldn't care about a thing, she had her arms round his boyish neck and was smiling madly. The feeling of his kiss was still in her armpits. She looked down. Something white was going round the tree at the back of Pats and Minnie's house. For a second her blood chilled, but then she realised it was the goat.

'What are you doing to the poor man, Lizzie?' called up Pats.

She laughed. She didn't care. 'I'm chasing him!' she shouted. 'I've chased him all around the rath.'

There was a wall to get over. Everything seemed funny to her, she couldn't stop laughing. Tom lifted her off her feet. 'You're only a wheeshy little thing,' he said, striding over the wall, whirling her round and depositing her on the other side. She staggered. For a moment she thought she was going to fall over, but then he righted her and she breathed very deeply till things stopped whirling.

'Are you all right?' His voice. 'Lizzie? Are you all right?'

The others were all there, around the ruins. The dogs were barking, old Lady and Captain. Pats had brought a bottle of whiskey from his house and it was being passed around as they ambled back along to Tadhg's.

Tom stopped suddenly and looked back at the ruins. 'Which of those is Darby's House?' he asked.

'Our Pats' house is,' Lizzie told him.

'Is it now? Back there?' He walked backwards.

Ahead they were singing sporadically, a ragged rolling sound, straggling back to Tadhg's. There were the lights. A mist, rolling up from the sea, gave them a slight haze. They walked separately now, smiling at each other with no need for words from either side of the track.

'There you are, Lizzylie,' Mike said, 'did you find the whistling seal?'

'We did,' she replied, 'three.'

'You know what I'd like? I'd like one of those big flat stones from the stone strand,' Lizzie said. 'For the dairy. To put on top of the cheese.'

They were sitting on the cliffs, looking out at the sea. Six or seven of them. Inland the fiddle's thin sweet whine. Tom peeled away and started running towards the shingle where the boats were shored.

'The man's a raging lunatic,' said Mike.

He didn't come back. Time passed and they went back inside where it was bright and warm. She kept looking for him whenever anyone came in the door. He'd said not a word, just off like that, was he mad? Another hour passed. The lamp was turned down and Alma Sheehan started berating the young ones for going up to the rath. She said they had no respect for the Gentry, that's what she called the fairies she truly believed lived there. 'Many a one's lived to regret that kind of disrespect.'

Alma's husband was there, old Matty, completely drunk.

'Matty,' she said, 'tell them about your lady.'

They pulled nearer to the fire.

'I used to be drilling with the Fenians up by the rath,' he said, 'this was after terrible times, after the hunger. And we looked across and a woman was walking from beyond the

84

rath towards us with a basket on her back. We knew at once she was not a woman of the townland. She was the most comeliest thing I ever saw, very tall and long in the face. When she came near, it was as if something made us stop, afterwards not a one of us could tell how it happened, only that we were waiting and she drew close and put down the basket from off her shoulders onto the earth and says, says she, "Let your eyes take a glimpse of that good food." I saw great fat strawberries and pancakes and figs and soda bread. And she had wine too, in a leather bottle; she said it came from the Indies. But she put the fear in all of us and there was some fell down in a faint and remembered nothing. So we all turned away, and Cathal Buckley who was our captain called us back to attention and she went on down in the direction of the cliffs over there where you can look down onto the stone strand.'

Then Pats told the story of the small voice as he was blowing up the warm sods in the morning – '*Is feidir liom thu a chloisteail. Teigh a chodladh*' – and Lizzie felt the hairs prick up on the nape of her neck because she knew that Pats was not the kind of man who would lie.

Pats called round next day. He said Tom Quinn had come back with a big stone for her after she'd gone. He'd taken a boat from the jetty below Tadhg's and rowed round to the stone shore. Later he'd hauled it all the way up to Darby's House and left it at the gate. Pats laughed. 'There's devotion,' he said, and Lizzie turned away and smiled.

'Ha!' she said, 'he did that?'

'He did. You want me to bring it down for you?'

She thought for a moment. 'Not really. Leave it where it is.'

Every day she expected him.

He left it a week and then turned up while she was in the

dairy beating the butter into rolls. She heard boots heavy on the stone steps and thought it was Henry but when she looked up it was him.

'Hello, Tom,' she said lightly, looking away and dipping the wooden bats in water.

He said he'd been in Mallow. Mallow was a grand place, he said, setting a heavy bundle down on the stone floor. There was a jug of buttermilk on the table, and she gave him a tumbler and told him to help himself. When he drank he threw back his head and gulped hungrily. Fascinated, she watched the movements of his pale throat.

'That was a wild thing you did,' she said, 'running off like that and taking Tadhg's boat.'

He set down the tumbler, half full.

'Were the seals still there?' she asked.

'The seals took no notice of me at all,' he said. 'They were like dogs. Three wild dogs. I was not too near them. I walked about for a while finding the right stone. Was it the right stone?'

'It was the very one,' she said, and laid down her bats to take a drink. The buttermilk was bitter cold and sharp to taste.

'See what I got in Mallow.' He stooped and opened the bundle. Out came long scarves made of gauzy material, yellow, green, orange. 'Which one for you?' he said.

'Oh, the green.'

'The green it is.'

He put it round her neck.

'I have to do the butter,' she said.

They kissed quickly.

'Where are your brothers?' he asked. 'Your mother and father?'

'Working. My mother's in the village. I don't know where Hanna is. Is she in the house? Did you see her?'

'No.'

They kissed again, more furtively.

'Will you come for a walk with me, Lizzie?' he said.

'Not now.' She laughed. 'How can I?'

The sound of boots in the yard. It was horrible and sudden and made her laugh recklessly. She put her wet lips very close to his ear and was going to whisper something, but no words came, so she stuck her tongue deep into his ear and licked. It tasted salty and dark and he squirmed in her arms, arching his neck and ducking his face into her throat, then pulled sharply away as footsteps clattered down into the dairy. Lizzie turned briskly and set about wrapping the butter in muslin, but she couldn't keep the outlandish smile off her face, even when she saw her father standing in the room with a face of thunder.

'Hello, Daddy,' she said.

Her father's eyes darted to Tom Quinn then back to her. 'Who's this?'

'His name's Tom Quinn, Daddy. He has things to sell.'

Her father was in one of his rare states of quiet anger. Once more he glanced at Tom Quinn, but his worst look was for her. 'What are you wearing?' he asked.

'Oh!' She pulled off the green scarf. 'I was just trying it on, Daddy. It's nice, isn't it? Here.' She handed it back to Tom. 'I don't have money for such things.'

Tom stuffed the scarves back in his bundle. 'So I'll be on my way,' he said, drawing the neck of the bundle tight and hauling it onto his shoulder. He moved towards the steps.

Her father was not a man for losing his temper. When he suddenly shrieked, 'You will leave my house!' in a voice unnaturally shrill, Lizzie jumped visibly and burst into tears. His reaction, so extreme and unexpected, as if a soft old dog had suddenly turned, terrified her. 'You will leave my house and never show your face here again!' he shrieked, trembling.

Tom Quinn had gone pale. 'Sir . . .' he said. Lizzie's father blocked his way to the door.

'You'd cheat the girl. It's bad blood. Everyone knows. Bad blood from way back! Get out or I'll kick you out!'

'Sir, I am not a cheater.'

'All your dirty tribe are cheaters! Away! I'll have the polis on you!'

'Sir, I am not a cheater.' He spoke steadily. She saw how young and callow he was, how very shabby.

'What's the matter, Daddy?' she cried, running to him and seizing him by the arms. He wouldn't look at her. The look in his eyes was something other than pure anger, a complicated look of profound hurt, of sheer embarrassment at the ferocity and nakedness of his emotion.

'So this is the wind-up of it!' he gasped, and stood aside.

'Daddy!'

Tom walked up the steps, shifting the bundle on his shoulder. Her father shook her away and followed after, coughing with rage and crying out: 'Filthy set! Beggars and cheaters! Bad cess to the whole lot of ye!' Then came Lizzie, crying in bewilderment. Her father aimed a kick at Tom but missed. Henry, coming round the side of the house and knowing nothing of what was going on but seeing that his father was chucking a tinker out, put down the bucket he was carrying and strode forward, squaring his shoulders. The dogs barked. Tom's dog barked, quivering, up on the cart. Hanna appeared at the door in a white pinafore.

Tom got out into the lane and climbed up onto the cart and shook the reins and was off in the direction of Boolavoe, his dog looking back fearless now they were on the move, hurling challenges.

'What's up?' Hanna came out.

Henry was laughing. 'Well, he'll not be back. What did he do, Da?'

Her father turned on Lizzie and roared. 'Bad, Lorelei! Bad! Bad bad bad!' and stormed away into the lower pasture with the dogs slinking at his heels.

'What was all that about?' asked Hanna.

'I don't know,' sobbed Lizzie, 'I was just in the dairy and he was showing me some scarves he had for sale. What have I done?'

That night at supper her father, chewing furiously, denounced the Quinns. 'They've not shown their faces round these parts in years,' he sneered, 'You'd think they'd know better, they was always a bad lot.'

No one spoke. Lizzie's mouth was sullen. Her mother sighed. Mike caught Lizzie's eye and raised a brow. She stared coldly back. He knew, of course, that she'd been up on the rath with Tom at Tadhg O'Donnell's wake. Tell him then, her look said, just see if I care.

'Vagabonds,' her father said. 'Scum. If my mother had not been so kind to them she'd have lived to see her grandchildren.'

'Jamie . . .' her mother said, covering her father's hand with her own.

'Why?' Lizzie put down her knife and looked at her father.

'Don't be bold,' said her mother, and her father leaned forward, stared gravely at Lizzie. 'Because, girl,' he said, 'your grandmother, Eliza Vesey, died of the fever that came with the famine. She caught it from walking up to Kildarragh, to Darby's House, every blessed day with food for the Quinn children. That's what a good woman my mother was, and she caught the fever off the Quinns.'

There was a long silence. All Lizzie knew was that her grandmother was a saint who'd died years and years before any of them were born, when her father was a child himself.

'It wasn't their fault though, was it?' she said.

'Why do you think you know everything, Miss?' he asked evenly.

'I don't.'

'I tell you the Quinns are bad in the blood. Do you think I don't know what I'm talking about?'

She said nothing.

He pushed back his plate. 'Kindness itself she was, and the Quinns run away with her character in return, putting it about that she spent time with the fairies. That's the kind of thing we're talking about. That's the kind of fools will put a bad name on a good woman.' He spoke quickly and gravely. 'They are nothing but badness and they've come to no good ever since those days and they never will, and if a daughter of mine ever thought to simper and smirk at the likes of one of them –' He turned his tumbler upside down, stood up so abruptly his chair fell over, and walked out.

For a moment no one spoke. Hanna righted the chair. Then her mother, seeing that Lizzie was stretching her face in a peculiar manner and sniffing, hissed, 'Pull yourself together, girl! See how you've vexed your father.'

'How was I to know all that?' retorted Lizzie.

'You should have known better than to bring a strange man into the dairy.'

'I didn't bring him in, he just walked in.'

'Even worse. Of course your father's annoyed. Someone like that an' all!'

'Like what? He was at Tadhg's wake. He knows Pats. He was at Minnie's school.'

'He's still a bogtrotter,' Hanna said.

Lizzie beat her fist on the table. Mike laughed, pounced sideways and tickled her. 'Lizzylie's got a sweetheart again!' he crowed. Lizzie screamed.

'Stop it, the pair of you!' Her mother got up. 'Mike, stop teasing her, Lizzie, clear the table, Hanna, pour some water.'

'Youse are all horrible,' Lizzie said.

Sometimes she could have killed Mike and Hanna. She was sick of being the baby, the little'un, the one they spoiled and teased. She couldn't ever have an admirer, she thought, not with Mike and Hanna. It was like the Bob Jakey thing all over again only much worse, because then she hadn't cared at all, and now she did. They teased her about Tom Quinn all night long, on and off, till she could have screamed. Crying made it worse. They tried to coddle her then, as if she was a baby who'd lost its rattle. A weight was on her. Her father's fury had seriously frightened her. Nothing seemed to account for it, but it made seeing Tom again an impossibility.

Hanna started again when they went to bed. It was the same old argument about the window. Lizzie said she felt sick with the smell of the meal sacks stacked against the wall, but Hanna flatly refused to open the window even an inch. 'I'll say one thing, Lizzie,' she said, thumping her pillow happily and nodding towards it, 'you wouldn't want for fresh air with the likes of him. You'd be under a hedge.'

Lizzie turned over and refused to speak. How stupid, she thought. Anger gritted her teeth. How can my father blame a man for things before he was born? It's not fair. It's not *fair*!

It was months before she saw him again. It was after the GAA sports that were held in the big field on the edge of Boolavoe, out past the sawmill. She and Minnie had been to the hurling and then to listen to the music in the square. It was getting late. On the stalls that had been set up all around the perimeter of the field, the traders were lighting candles and placing them in bottles. She was wearing her straw hat with the little blue feather and showing a good bit of leg above her buttoned boot, and they were counting out the pennies and farthings between them, seeing what was left, when she noticed the thin brown horse with its nosebag, and the solemn dog sitting up there waiting as patiently as ever on the cart.

'Look,' she said to Minnie, 'there's Tom Quinn's cart.'

'And there's himself,' said Minnie.

The cart was drawn up with some others by a fire of sticks on the edge of the green, where a fat woman with bare feet and a black cape was dishing up tins of stew for the traders.

'Where?'

He turned from talking to a man in a grey tweed suit and she saw his face, blank-eyed and thin-jawed, not seeing her.

'Tom!' she called.

'Lizzie, you be careful,' Minnie said. 'Your ma and everyone'll be along any second.'

'I'm doing no harm.' She walked over to speak to him. Minnie stood and waited.

'Hello, Tom.'

'Hello, Lizzie.'

'What are you selling?'

He smiled. 'Nothing,' he said.

'Nothing?'

'Nothing.'

Not a word came. They stood awkwardly.

'I'm sorry for my father,' she said.

'What's he say about me?'

'Tom,' she said, 'it's all ancient history. Whatever he's on about it's nothing to do with you.'

He looked sideways, always smiling, slightly shifty.

'Your people lived in our Pats's house,' she said.

'Only it was our house then.' He looked back at her. 'My grandfather built it.'

'Lizzie!' Minnie called.

'Really? Your grandfather did?'

'So I'm told.'

92

'Who tells you?'

'My father told me. He was born there. They lost it in the famine.'

'*My* father was on about the famine.'

'Lizzie!'

'There's Minnie,' she said. 'You went to school with Minnie.'

'True.'

'In Eskean.'

'In Eskean.'

'God, but you're a lovely girl,' Tom said, very fast and low and clumsy.

Minnie came up and took her firmly by the arm. 'Hello, Tom,' she said.

'Minnie.' He dipped his head.

'Here's your ma, Lizzie,' Minnie said softly, 'we must be going.'

There was Hanna's striped skirt and her mother's bonnet, coming along through the stragglers. Lizzie became aware at the same time of a tall heavy-laden woman who had been standing off to one side all this time watching them. Tom retreated into the shadows before the fire glow.

'What are you doing, Lizzie,' came her mother's harsh voice.

'Goodbye, Tom!' Lizzie said clearly.

'Bye,' he said, turning and walking quickly to his cart.

'Where have you two been?' Hanna cried, 'We're dead looking for you.'

'We watched the dancing,' said Minnie.

'Minnie, you should know better,' her mother scolded, 'letting her talk to that man when you know how upset her daddy was about it all before.'

'I was there all the time,' Minnie said, 'they were only saying hello.' She squeezed Lizzie's arm.

Henry and Mike were already up on the cart. Mike got down to help his mother up.

'It's not fair,' Lizzie said.

'Not another word! You know what your father said. No more!'

'Am I not even to be civil to people any more?' Lizzie hauled herself up lightly on the other side.

'Not to him.'

'Ah, come on, Lizzylie.' Hanna plumped down beside her. Mike tied the rope across. 'You don't want to waste your time on him. There's better fish in the sea.'

Like Marty Blake? she wanted to say but didn't.

They stood in line to get out of the field with all the other carts waiting along the hedge. Tom Quinn's cart was a little ahead and to one side. She could see stray strands of brown hair coming out from under his cap at the back. His dog's ears were pricked up. Lizzie felt an urge to do something ridiculous, pull down the rope and jump down, hit Hanna or something. A handsome young woman with a big creel on her back and a basket over one arm walked by and stopped a little further along the line.

'Is there any room up there for me, Tom?' she asked. She wore a tattered coat, a man's cap and boots, and her face was brown. Her right hand, clutching the ropes of the creel, was long and graceful and strong. It was the woman who'd watched as they talked.

'Room and to spare, Marie,' he said, and up she got and set down her load and settled beside him, taking out a pipe and lighting it. The carts began to sway forward. Ahead of them, the woman's tousled black hair, the tender back of Tom's boyish neck, swaying. Hanna settled a blanket over both their knees. 'There!' she said comfortingly. It was cold. Lizzie shivered and felt a sinking in the pit of her stomach. She was being ridiculous. Of course her mother and Hanna were right. How could she possibly contemplate a man who had friends like that? Look at that woman sitting up on the cart with him so familiar. And the rags he wears. No pride. Anyway, it always goes hard with those divided by money.

'I've told your father.' Her mother sounded upset but defiant.

'Told him what?'

'About you and Quinn.'

Lizzie was hanging up her cloak, her mother had just come in the back door and was bustling about the room. Hanna looked up from the fire.

'Mother!' Lizzie's hands flew up to her face. 'You haven't!'

'I had to!' her mother hissed. 'Better from me than from some other! Standing there for all to see!'

'Doing what? Doing what? Just talking!' Her father and Mike came in. 'What's this, what's this?' her father said in his deadly quiet voice.

'She has a grah for Tom Quinn,' said her mother bluntly.

'I have not!'

Henry came in. All of them, looking at her, waiting for the flood. She wouldn't cry though, not this time. 'I have done nothing wrong,' she said with what she hoped was dignity. Her father looked around at them all. For a terrible second she thought she was going to laugh. His eyes! As if there'd been murder and death, and all she'd done was say hello to Tom Quinn.

'Hanna,' he said fraily, 'you, my girl, tell me.'

Hanna glanced at Lizzie. 'I don't know, Da,' she said. 'She was just standing there talking to him and Minnie when we came up. He went off when he saw us.'

He shook his head from side to side slowly, moving across the room and feeling for the back of his chair as if he was blind or in pain or much older that he really was.

'What?' Lizzie laughed. 'What?'

'Lizzie!' said her mother.

'What have I done?'

Her father sat down and covered his eyes as if he'd just received a terrible blow.

She picked up a pot of blackberry jam that stood open on the table and hurled it against the wall, where it shattered in an explosion of flying jam and glass shards. Everyone leapt back. Her father jumped up. Her mother took one stride and struck her hard across the face.

'How dare you!' her mother cried.

Lizzie stood horrified, one hand on her burning cheek.

'You clean that mess up now!'

'I'm sorry.'

'Lorelei,' her father said gently, putting his arms out to her, 'come and sit on Daddy's knee.'

Then she really did start crying. 'No!' she shouted, 'No, it's not fair! I haven't done anything.'

He came towards her and she flinched. 'I'm sorry about the jam.'

'Lorelei,' he said, with eyes of mournful reproach, 'you know I never laid a finger on you.'

There was a moment of stillness. Hanna coughed.

'I'll clear the jam up,' Lizzie said.

That was when her father slammed the wall with his fist rather than hit her, knocking some of the whitewash off. He did that once, then sat down forcefully in his chair, breathing heavily down his nostrils. 'I'll do away with him myself,' he said, 'true as God's above me, I'll do away with him if she so much as looks at him again.'

They were all wrong, she told herself. What matters? She asked. That he's a nice boy or that he's got a rough edge or two? No one mentioned Tom at all after that night. It was all over, the scenes, the long faces, her father's discomfort

96

with the effort of strong emotion. Things were back to normal in every way but in her mind. Every night lying in bed she burned with the injustice of it all, that something good and innocent could be seized on and made shameful. He'd brought that rock all the way up from the stone strand. That must mean something. And he'd been so dignified when her father shouted at him, though he must have been shocked.

She should have let it go, she knew. She'd already faced the fact of impossibility before her mother betrayed her so atrociously by telling her father. And there was that big hard woman sitting up there on the wagon with him. What did that mean? Was she just a neighbour? A sister, even, or a cousin? I have to find out, she thought. So I can let it go. He can't come here so it's up to me. Because if he really wants to see me, I'll go against my father, I'll go against them all.

She would have written but she was sure he'd not be able to read it. So she cadged a ride into town one day with Jack and Norah O'Donnell, saying she needed wool, and when they'd set her down and arranged a time to meet, lost no time at all in setting off. She was carrying a basket of eggs. A rising wind rippled the grass growing between the slates on the rooftops across the way as she passed the barracks and the forge, walking very fast, then the sawmill loomed up. Two miles further on a plank bridge crossed the river to Eskean.

The village was one long terrace. Outlying cabins were dotted here and there.

'Which way to the Quinns?' she asked a boy with a stick who was driving a bullock down the road.

He jerked his thumb. 'Go to the crossroads,' he said, 'take the left fork and go on to where the wood's on your right then you'll see a stile and you go over and up the boreen and

97

it's on your left. It's got a lady scarecrow in a red frock.'

It was a tiny mud-walled cabin with scraggy thatch. The lady scarecrow did nothing to keep off a horde of crows that strutted here and there over the lazy beds at the back. The house opened straight onto the boreen and Tom was sitting on a creepie outside the door, having his eyes bathed by a barefoot girl of about fourteen in a filthy pinafore. When Lizzie appeared in front of the cabin, he could not see her because of the water streaming down his face. A dirty child pushed another in a wheelbarrow. Seeing her, the girl stepped back. 'Tom,' she said, 'there's a lady.'

Tom straightened up and shook the water from his eyes.

'Hello, Tom,' said Lizzie.

He stood, flustered, looking around at the squalor as if he'd never seen it before.

'What's this?' he said, 'why are you here, Lizzie?'

'I brought you some eggs,' she said, 'we had so many. How are you, Tom?'

He wiped his face with a dirty handkerchief. 'I'm well,' he said, 'and yourself?'

'Very well.' She smiled at the bony-faced girl, who did not smile back.

'This is my sister Judith,' he said.

Lizzie still smiled. 'What's that you're putting on his eyes?' she asked pleasantly.

'Some herbs I got,' said Judith. 'From McGrane.'

'Do you have sore eyes?' she asked him.

'Sometimes I do.'

She thrust the basket at him.

'Thank you,' he said stiffly. 'Have we something to put these in, Judith?'

'Of course we have.'

'Very kind, Lizzie,' he said, 'very kind. Will you come in and have some tea?'

98

'Don't put yourself to any trouble.'

'No trouble, no trouble at all. Is there hot water, Judith?'

'Of course there is.'

'Make a pot of tea, there's a good girl,' he said.

It was dark inside. A girl of ten or so turned from stirring a pot on the fire. The floor was scattered with crumbs and ash. A bashed old fiddle hung on a peg on the wall. Tom showed Lizzie to the one chair, while he sat down on a box, twining his long fingers and looking at her. The children came in.

'Do you play, Tom?' Lizzie asked, indicating the fiddle.

He shook his head. 'It was my father's,' he said.

Judith made tea. All of them stared openly at her as if she was a strange animal. She had not worn her best by any means but even so she felt like a queen in a hovel. She looked about at the dinginess. 'What a pretty cat,' she said. The animal sat on a window sill, blue-eyed with wild black hair. A little boy went and got it for her and placed it in her lap, but its fur stood on end and it scratched, leapt down and flew out of the door.

'It's wild,' said Tom.

A thin red line appeared across the back of Lizzie's hand.

'You're scratched,' he said, perplexed.

'Oh, it's nothing.' She licked the scratch, took out her hand-kerchief and dabbed at it briskly, smiling. Judith gave the pot a stir and poured out the tea, strong and dark and bracing.

'That's a lovely cup of tea, Judith,' Lizzie said sincerely.

Judith, sitting on the table swinging her legs, ignored her.

'Have we any soda cake?' he asked awkwardly.

'No.'

'She could have a saucer of stew,' said the child at the fire.

'No, no.' Lizzie sipped her tea. 'Nothing for me, thank you very much, I've had something not long ago. I'll just finish my tea.'

99

There was an awkward silence, then Tom said again, 'Thank you very much for the eggs. It's kind of you.'

'Not at all,' she said, and knew that she must go now, there was nothing more to be said here with all these Quinns sitting around watching her every move, and him there with his misty eyes and his bare toes braced against the dirt floor saying nothing. She took the empty egg basket from the bench and stood. 'Well, thank you for the tea,' she said politely, 'I really must be going now.'

Tom stood up so quickly his box fell over. He saw her to the door.

Hens pecked about on the stones outside. 'Bye so,' she said softly, and set off, straight-backed, smiling triumphantly. A little way down the boreen, she heard, as she'd known she would, his footsteps behind her. He came alongside. 'I'll walk you back to the bridge,' he said.

They walked in silence till they were leaving the wood behind, coming to the crossroads.

'I hope your hand is not too bad,' he said. 'The cat's a terror.'

'It's nothing,' she said.

'That was a long way for you to bring the eggs.'

'Yes.'

They walked on. A couple of women passing looked at them curiously. A sense of danger crept through her. When they reached the bridge she stopped and faced him.

'Well,' she said.

He grinned nervously. They were standing on the bridge looking down at the water flowing under. 'May I say, Lizzie,' he said, 'that you are a lovely girl, much too lovely for me. That you have walked all this way to see me –'

'Do you still want to go for a walk with me?' she asked.

He clasped his hands on the parapet and bowed his head

down till his forehead touched his knuckles. 'I don't think your father would like that,' he said.

'No.' She said it resignedly but with a faint edge of surprise.

They stood for a long time. The sound of the river running over stones combined with the rustling of leaves into a hypnotic, low-throated music. I must be going, she thought frantically, I must be going, but she said, 'I do what I like.'

He raised his head and looked at her. 'Want to go for a walk?' he said. 'Now?'

Then she was all briskness. 'Not now, no time,' she said, shifting her basket to the other arm, 'I have to go and buy some wool, I must have been away hours. Come up to the rath above Kildarragh if you want to see me. I'll go up Sunday after Mass on the way to see my brother. Where we saw the seals? It's safe enough up there. We can go for a little walk. Yes?' She smiled brightly.

'Yes.'

'Good.' And she walked off across the bridge without a backward look, rubbing at her scratched hand.

That whole summer was like a falling drop, flashing for one second. Every Sunday they'd meet on the cliff top; every week waited for Sunday. The path down the cliff was safe but took a sure foot, so they'd hold hands and go down slowly to the cave, crawl in and sit at the back where the booming of the ocean and the cackling of the sea birds was muted, out of the way of the wind. It was like being in a mouth.

Though he was her first, Lizzie was no innocent. She knew as soon as she told him to meet her on the rath that she would take him there. Inside, with the sea shining in the cave's mouth, framed by wild grasses, they were out of the world. This had been her solitude since she was twelve or so. She'd never found anyone else there, never taken anyone there. He was greatly honoured, but that first time she didn't think he appreciated it so she didn't allow him to touch her. She knew all about what went on. It wasn't wrong. You saw it all the time, the cattle and sheep and cats and dogs. She'd been exploring her own body furtively for years and had noted how much it had changed this past year. She was small but her breasts were bigger than Hanna's. She smiled at herself in the mirror a great deal these days, or simply looked, occasionally stunned by her own face. He was right, she was lovely. She was some wonderful thing, full of power. *She* would say when, and she'd only relent when she was sure he was fully aware of the extent of his luck. She was a prize.

The first four weeks she let him kiss her but no more. Each time that was only after an interval of decorous conversation which both of them knew as a prelude. They talked about everyday things. He went away a lot, he said, working here and there; he'd been in England two years ago. In September, he said, he thought he might be able to get a start with a road gang in north Wales.

She smiled mysteriously, trying to keep her feelings secret. In fact she had no idea what her feelings were, only that she was mad in the head with the whole thing. 'Will you come back?' she asked.

'Oh, yes,' he said, 'I always come back.'

This gave her a premonition of tears.

'Why do you have to go away? Why can't you just stay here like everybody else? My brothers don't go away all the time.'

'Money,' he said, smiling, 'I don't have the land.'

And there it lay between them.

For three months they played a game. She thought about getting a nice painted wagon like the gypsies and going on

102

the road for a while with him. She told him and it became another thing they did: lying side by side on his coat in the dim belly of the cave, talking about the wagon, where they'd go, what they would eat and drink, and how in the evenings they'd make camp somewhere tranquil and light a fire. Only, of course, you couldn't really come back from a thing like that. It was just another part of the bigger game, the one that went on changing all the time, because you could do anything in the cave. It was not in the world. You could play.

6

After Christmas

Silly things, Minnie said, when Lizzie tried to explain all this. She'd come over the top and started crying passing the rath. It was mid-October and Tom had been in Wales or Dublin, she wasn't sure which, six weeks. His cousin had sent word there was work on the road gang, and if not, then he was bound to get taken on at Jacob's biscuit factory over Christmas and he could be back in the New Year. She had not been prepared for his distress when he told her this. He'd buried his face in her lap and mumbled things she couldn't understand. She thought he was weeping, and stroked his head.

By the time she reached Darby's House she'd fallen over and skinned her hands on the stones.

'What happened?' asked Minnie, pouring water over her hands.

'I fell,' she sniffed. The icy water brought tears back to her eyes.

The dog Captain sat upon the path, scratching for fleas. Still a runt, bandier than ever.

'You fell.' Minnie's voice was flat. 'What's wrong with you? You're always ill.'

'I'm getting a weakness.'

Minnie looked closely into her face, her eyes solemn; and then Lizzie had told her everything in a great outpouring. She'd thought about talking to Hanna but simply couldn't; she'd even tried, but couldn't say a thing at all, at confession.

104

She hadn't known till she got here that this was why she'd come out today, because somehow someone had to be told.

'Are you pregnant, Lizzie?'

'No!'

'Are you sure?'

'I can't be,' she whispered. 'He was very careful.'

'Dear God,' said Minnie, 'you are.'

'I don't know, Min, I pray God I'm not. I don't know what to do.'

Minnie put her stiff arms around Lizzie's shoulders, but Lizzie was tearless now. 'Maybe it will be nothing,' she said. It was a clear day, the sea and sky bright blue, everything out-lined with a clear edge. She felt pure suddenly, untroubled. There was a baby or there was not. It would be or not. The sun would go down, the moon would come up. 'I feel,' she said, 'I feel −' but couldn't say what, and anyway Pats was coming up the track and she couldn't say anything to him. She looked around.

'Don't say anything, Min,' she said, and knew with absolute certainty in her soul in that moment that she was going away. The goat that was tethered, the old hollow tree, the big green-striped stone resting up against the wall of the house, the dog nosing its nether parts on the path − all of these things she would see no more. That time was near. It was a little death.

Minnie went with her to see Doctor Gildea at the dispensary in Boolavoe. Later, all she could remember of the room was that he had a blind on his window, with a lacy edge to it that could be pulled down by a little tassle; and she remembered the thin sympathetic smile with which he confirmed her worst fear, and the way both he and Minnie seemed to expect something more of her than what she showed, which was what she felt, which was nothing.

Still later, much later, she would remember how serene she had been when she stood with Minnie, and listened to Minnie tell her mother the truth; how her mother had not wept or shouted or scolded but simply sat down and said nothing for half an hour or so then gone to find her father; and how terrified she'd been. How he'd walked through the door with his killing eyes, come straight over to her and pulled her into a long and dreadful embrace, breathing heavily, and it had made her cry and want to break away though she didn't dare to.

Then all of them knew.

Not a word against her from any of them.

It was horrible. A kind of mourning fell on the family, and the household was sombre. Lizzie carried herself through it all, erect and calm, like someone very bravely bearing a terrible illness. The worst of it was her father's eyes, which she felt burning upon her sometimes as she sat in the evening with her sewing. Of course, she had to go away, that was understood. Before Christmas, before he came back. She didn't fight it. Everyone was being so kind and making a path for her. It all happened very fast. They wrote to her sister Cathy in Salford and it was arranged that she'd go there to have the child, and it would be given out that she was recently widowed. And then when she came back with the child it would be given out here that she had a husband over there.

It was too much to think about. Her father didn't speak much. Once, in the middle of a meal, he stopped eating and said darkly to no one and everyone: 'If it were not for the Quinns, I would not have lost my own mother.'

A silence followed.

Her mother told her he'd said he'd die before she'd marry Tom Quinn, not that she'd ever seriously expected to. Everyone knew Tom Quinn would never make money and

Lizzie Vesey would never go and live in a hovel. These things didn't happen and there'd be no happy ending. So now, when she thought about him and the things they'd done in the cave, she felt slightly sick and refused to see his face.

No sooner had the forms been filled in at the post office and the money found for the passage than a letter arrived from England addressed to Lizzie alone. Something about the firm script jogged something in her memory. Miss Lizzie Vesey was in larger letters than the address. It was from Bob Jakey, the English coach driver who'd stayed in their barn with Cathy's husband, the one who'd taken such a fancy to her. Bob Jakey wrote that he had discovered her situation from his very close friend, that he realised this might sound precipitate but would she accept his sincere offer of marriage. He had often thought of writing to her before but had not found the courage. He said that she must believe him to be absolutely serious about this, and that he would wait her reply. *PS: I will never cast it up at you and will raise the child as my own.*

Her trunk was sent on to Manchester.

The night before she left, though it was cold, she went out and walked about the yard and the sheds while the others were all inside. Familiar things held a kind of wonder, simple things shone: the bits of rock that hung from the pigsty roof, the puddle under the pump. She could smell her mother's cooking, listen to the soft crooning of her chickens settling down for the night. When she went in, her mother was chopping cauliflower and Hanna was slicing the pig's cheek. Everyone was coming for a farewell meal. They wouldn't let her cook or do anything at all.

It was a wonderful meal. Everyone came, and later, her father got down the whiskey for the men. Mike sat and stroked her feet and Hanna combed her hair, and Minnie had brought some little cakes she'd made. Her father said very little and hardly looked at her; her mother smiled bravely every time she caught her eye. Lizzie laughed and was very charming, and when they toasted her with wine, drank hers down in one quick gulp and laughed more, and said wildly, 'I can't believe it! I can't believe it!'

She couldn't remember Cathy's leaving. She couldn't even remember Cathy, even though she was going to be living with her and her husband and their five children. She couldn't imagine it, any of it, couldn't imagine Bob Jakey either. She hadn't said yes and she hadn't said no. She couldn't stop laughing, it ran away with her, trying to remember what he looked like and seeing only his hair with the dead straight parting in the middle, but no real face under it, only an impression of something good-natured but not particularly marvellous.

It was all so bright: the candlesticks, the bottles and canisters on the ledge above the chimney breast, the glasses and egg-cups on the top shelf of the dresser, the long-handled slane resting by the fire, the font at the foot of the stairs. And the pictures of poor Robert Emmet who was hanged, and Parnell and the Blessed Virgin Mary, all made strange with leaving.

Hanna gave her a beautiful rosary carved out of bog oak. Her mother threw her apron over her head and wept. 'Oh, Jamie!' she sobbed, 'Oh, Jamie!'

'Hush!' said her father, 'She'll be back.'

'I'll be back, Mammy.'

'Of course you will, of course you will.' Her mother blew her nose and wiped her eyes.

Her father did not come into Bantry with her. He didn't like to travel far, and Bantry was as far as he'd ever been. It was a gloomy grey morning three weeks before Christmas, a faint rumble of thunder grumbling over the distant ridge of mountains that ran down the Cork and Kerry border. He came as far as the gate, to the sidecar which Henry was driving, and reached up to where she was sitting with her mother and took her hand.

He smiled. The scar beneath his eye was white, tight-looking. 'Well, it's seldom we'll see you now, Lorelei,' he said softly, 'whatever way things work out. So you be a good girl in your life now, won't you, Lorelei,' and then the tears came spouting out of his eyes, shocking.

'I'm coming back, Daddy,' she said.

He wiped his face with one great swipe of his palm, stood back and raised his hand to wave solemnly as the cart swayed forward into the road. It was freezing. Henry had a sack over his shoulders. Lizzie wore two petticoats under her skirt, and the thick stockings her mother had knitted. But the rain kept off till Bantry, beginning in a soft silvery fall through the sun-motes falling through the dark clouds over the bay.

There was not much time before the post-car left, thank God. Now they were curiously formal.

'Well, Lizzie,' Henry said, hugging her swiftly, 'safe journey.'

'Bless you, Henry.'

'God bless.'

Her mother kissed her. 'Here,' she said, shoving a small bundle into her bag, 'for if you get hungry.'

She climbed on board in her tight black button boots and sat as elegantly as she could. Opposite her sat a small boy with a big white collar and a corpulent man in a thick tweed coat. A woman with a tightly-rolled umbrella and smart kid gloves got on. Then it was all rattling and movement and waving and smiling, and her mother and Henry were gone. Soon after, everything she'd ever known was gone too.

Only when she was standing at the rail watching the lights

of Cork City moving in the darkness as the ship sailed past Blackrock Castle and Spike Island, did she suddenly recall, clear in every detail, Tom Quinn's face; and then the whole unutterable vanished sweetness of the thing poured through her in a great torrent, along with the mournful lowing of cattle in the hold; and she cried at last, bitterly and drainingly, and finally, standing there on the deck. And after that she never cried for him again.

PART THREE

THE VESEYS
AND THE QUINNS
1845 – late summer

7

Now what is he about bringing that child home with his cheek damaged? He didn't have to go up there anyway, he could have sent a boy; he didn't have to take the child at all, and if he did he should have made sure he was safe and not running around with those rough little bodies. Said they were playing on the tree, the three of them. Blood pouring down his cheek, my poor baby. Brave lad.

'Jamie, what have they done to you!' I cried.

'S'alright Mamma,' he said, 'I didn't cry.' Though the tear streaks were like stripes on his dirty face.

'You mustn't play on that horrible tree!'

Phelim standing there like a lump. 'It's not that bad, Eliza,' he says.

Child with a hole in his face, scarred for life, and he says that.

'What would you know?' I say, dabbing away at the bite with a bit of cloth. The blood still flowing. There can be deep poison in a cat's bite. And a cat up there in that place.

'Twas only a kitten,' says Phelim.

Fool. I'd have killed it. One smash of the loy.

'Why weren't you watching him?'

He scratches his head like an imbecile. 'He was with the boys,' he says, 'they were all together. And I was only inside with Darby after tying the pig.'

'He's only four. You should have watched him.'

'It's not bad, is it?' He leans down with a frown, big dirty fingers stretching towards the child's face.

'Don't touch it! Your hand's filthy.'

The hand darts back as if stung.

'I'm sorry, Eliza.'

'It's not me you should be apologising to, it's him, he's marked for life.'

'No!'

'He is,' I say.

He is. The boy sits on my knees, dirty legs dangling. Mrs Vesey, they used to say, when I took him into town, what a beautiful baby. What a beautiful child, Eliza. Everyone said it. Everyone. Now look at his poor face.

'You must never, never play on that tree,' I say, 'It's a bad tree.'

'It wasn't the tree, Ma,' he says, 'It was the cat.'

'Then the cat will die.'

'He was with the children,' says Phelim again.

I left the boy with his granda the next evening and off I went. I had to wait but I don't mind. I sat absolutely still above and looked down like the eye of the Lord on Kildarragh and saw Darby Quinn walking between the lazy beds at the side of his cabin. There are seventeen houses in Kildarragh and not a shoe between them. Darby built his the highest, away from the rest and out of sight of them. He stands and surveys his patch as if it was great lands. He works for us and he works for others. Those Quinn boys had fixed up a plank of wood and were playing seesaw next to the old dead tree at the back, and the cat, a skinny black thing, was on the window sill. Both bigger than him, the Quinn boys, and they let my Jamie get hurt.

I can wait and wait. I can move and make no sound. I can get out of bed at night and go out of the house without waking a soul. I'm invisible. I hold a raven's feather between my fingers. I have some words in my mind from nowhere, saying, the circular web. That's all it says, the circular web, over and over again. It happens like that, words in my mind. I don't mind.

Darby Quinn walks around to the front of his cabin and his wife, that one Sal, comes out of the house with the babe toddling at her skirts and her belly pushing at its apron with the next one on its way. He used to be a traveller. He carried a loy and went about between here and Kenmare for work, digging, booleying, whatever presented, but he settled down with Sal. He comes behind her, even with the child there at her skirts, and puts both of his hands under her enormous breasts and squeezes them like fruit, and she sticks her arse into his stomach. Around her black hair she wears a red kerchief as bright as poppies.

Then it smites me in my soul that I hate Sal Quinn.

I wait.

When the light was fading, and they were all inside, and the little ones eating their stirabout, I came down; came so slow and silent, invisible. The cat was on the sill. I killed it with one touch, without a sound. Little puss, little puss, I whispered in the darling's ear. There was blood and slime from pussy's mouth and nose.

I crouch beneath the window. They're talking in Irish.

Phelim is a shy man who hardly knows himself because he's spent his whole life standing back, stilling his wants because of the tidiness of his soul. This man would have stayed in the womb if he could, it was all so easy in there. My heart went out to him as soon as I saw him, a childish youth when he first came to our house with my father. A bad fairy had touched him in the cradle so he'd grown with a bent nose, long, jagged teeth, pale freckled skin, hairy nostrils, huge ears and a large Adam's apple. And he's always had a silly smiling amiability that makes people think he's simple, but he's not simple at all, not Phelim.

115

I fell in love with him because of a dream I had when I was thirteen years old. In this dream I'm a small child in a downstairs room in a very old dark house, and there are grown-ups talking over my head as if I can't understand. An old woman like my grandmother, but not her, says, 'She's not to go, she'd only get upset.' But I sneak out anyway and go up a staircase that runs right up the middle of the house. I push open a door and there's a boy of about sixteen lying dying all alone on a narrow bed in the middle of a very large, very dark room. He seems to be in a lot of fear and pain. A long beam of pure white light shines out of his right eye, going straight up to the ceiling. He's my brother and I'm stricken with grief. That's it. Actually I never had a brother. But when I saw Phelim I recognised at once the silly pale awkward dying brother in the dream and that was that. I was nineteen then. I had the choice of the two of them, him or Tadhg. I chose him because he was soft. He wanted to please. Tadhg was a bit wild. He was in with those Ribbonmen running round making trouble for the landlords. I could have had better than Phelim as far as money went, and far, far better for the looks. But I do love him. I brought him six more acres, glass for his windows and a feather bed.

He never asks where I've been. He knows I go walking.

Jamie mo chree
Pussy's in the tree . . .

My little boy lies sleeping with his hands thrown above his head. His bloody cheek is staunched with cobweb.

'I'll take the pig to Lomas's tomorrow then,' says Phelim as we get into bed.

He's getting none of me tonight. Last night he was down at the shebeen. She goes there, Sal Quinn, with her husband. It's like her that she would. She's been everyone's fancy at one time or another, even Phelim's, but that was years ago, before me. There's a great deal of nonsense goes on when it comes to all that. She never had a chance with him, she was not his kind. They can sing their songs about it but there's never been a good match between high and low. And if Phelim's low to some, she's lower still. We are not living in the Middle Kingdom with the fairies, the place where stories happen. We live here on this ground. In the Middle Kingdom a king is not like a king here and a queen is not like a queen here, not like that fat queen over the sea. In the Middle Kingdom a king can fall in love with a beggarmaid and turn her into a queen. But not here. Anyway, let's hope the one in the belly's not as sickly as the last, the peery one. I delivered her. I delivered all her lot. She's a brood mare, and all the doors were open, but that was a poor weak thing she had, a little girl baby all pale and quiet like a stillborn but with a shocking smile on its face and its strange eyes wide open. And that's the creature she has to go and name after me, would you believe? Oh, you're so good, Eliza! You bring all my babies into the world. Still, a girl. I'd have liked a little girl, but after Jamie came the long bleed. It went on for thirty-six weeks, four days and six hours. I thought it would go on forever. I put an iron knife under my pillow for the strength. My mother used to say it was our power over men, that blood. My mother had only me and I have only Jamie. She died when I was twelve. Her belly swelled up very, very big and then she died. Then there was only me and father, and the land. We have twelve acres now. The Quinns have only two of conacre, and that's scattered everywhere. But they have those two big healthy boys, and the girl that's not right with my name, and now another. It isn't fair when those that can't look after them get them, and those with the means don't. But my boy's the best of them all, the best boy in all the worlds, the best of all those I ever held in my arms all slimy from the womb. And there's been a good few. How many? It's all the same, every babe's a blessing when it comes, every poor tiny scrap. Doesn't matter if it's a hovel or a glebe house. It's when I look at the mothers I worry. All these bonny babes born to become what I see walking around me every day, for human beings can be very ugly. Surely life's terrible to do that to us, to start us pure and twist us as we grow? Then again, sometimes I am so stroked with wonder at these times that I feel like a nun seeing Christ in the face.

This has been an awful rainy season. Phelim says the crop's been bad upcountry. There's maybe the taint, he says, and we're not yet through the meal months. Hey-ho. Last time we had a hunger was when my ma was alive; she and I used to go down on the strand for kelp. My ma could always get us something. We did fine. Well, the earlies are pitted and safe anyway, and there's plenty of oats, so we'll do.

I was shaving my father, he was all suds, when a girl came and called me up to Kildarragh to look at Scanlon's child that was ailing, and while I was up there I met with Sal Quinn in her red kerchief like a Queenstown whore. She's got the two boys with her, proper little spalpeens they'll make, and the queer girl wrapped in a blanket slung round her body. That child must be one now and it's still completely bald. I don't like it, it has no hair anywhere. I don't like its eyes because I don't know what it is about them. I wonder was she up there on the rath about the time she fell? Now that I'd like to know.

Sal looks wild, her eyes all a-stare. Have I seen Darby down the way? I have not.

'Oh,' she says, 'I need him here, he's got to come!'

'Why, whatever is it?'

'There's an awful crying,' she says then, and those poor

scared boys looking up at her with their dirty scrubby faces, 'I can't stay there,' she says, 'It's like a voice in the ground.'

She doesn't even think to ask after the little one.

'Come,' I said, 'I'll walk up with you, there's nothing frightens me.'

So we all trail up there and the sound, coming the louder as we approach the cabin, would curdle your blood in your veins.

'Holy Mother of God!' she whispers. 'It's a soul in torment.'

'It's the cat,' I say, and up I go to the old tree and throw down stones and sods till it stops.

'It's dead now,' I tell her.

'Down there?'

'Must have fallen in and got stuck. Never mind, it's out of its misery now.'

'Oh the poor thing!' she says, and then she remembers. 'How is Jamie's cheek?'

'Mending. He'll have a scar.'

'Oh, surely not!'

'Oh, surely.'

'Oh, poor little man, and he's such a brave boy.'

'He is so.'

Then Darby Quinn arrives on the scene. Well, he's a handsome enough man, fair, too squat for my liking, but a hard-built, strong man. 'What is it, allanna?' and he's straight to her and she's all soft and silly with him.

'The cat's dead,' I say. 'It fell in the tree.'

Those two boys are peering down there.

'You'll see nothing,' says I.

'How is the little boy, Eliza?' asks Darby kindly. He has a nice soft voice. Picks up his little girl and rubs his long soft hair against her pate.

'Mending.'

119

'She says he'll be scarred,' Sal tells him.

He looks closely into my eyes. 'I am very sorry for it, Eliza,' he says, 'I am very very sorry it happened here.'

I nod.

The baby holds out its arms to me.

'There, she's giving you a love,' says Sal, 'she does it with everyone.'

Look at their foolishly smiling faces. Darby is one of those soft-eyed souls, transparent. They see no flaw in that child. All of them, the boys as well, they bow down around her like the sheaves of corn in the dream in the story of Joseph and his brothers. It's always baby Eliza this and baby Eliza that, and look at what she's doing now, as if there'd never been a baby before. Well, she'll get her nose put out of joint when this new one comes along, won't she? I reach out and touch her hands. Same chubby hands as any child. Her eyes flash red for a second. Dark wine red.

It's funny how the boy knows the way I'm feeling. I've said nothing and I thought I showed nothing on my face but he came up and put his hand on my knee. 'What's the matter, Mamma,' he said.

'Oh nothing nothing, my sweet baby.'

I'm known as a woman of knowledge. I have always known that if you do this thing and that thing – certain actions which must be taken at the appropriate times – good will follow. I have a very strong will and nothing yet has defeated me. But I know too when a time comes that topples the old rules. When you do this at the right time and that at the right time, exactly as you have always done, and it's all been right before; but now it isn't. Like a cold stream in the blood, all those sure things are gone. Like a falling in the blood. That's how it was when my mother died.

How did he know I was feeling like that?

'Never mind, Mamma,' he says and puts his arms round my neck and hugs.

So we hug and kiss and rock and make everything good again.

It'll be hard. It's been hard before. We don't know what it is. It's not the taint and it's not curl. I've not seen it like this before. The look on Phelim's face when he came in from digging the potatoes told me. 'Come and see this,' he said. I know all the expressions of his face, and this was like nothing I'd ever seen. I didn't want to go and look. I don't know why, but it made me feel as if I was suddenly dreaming, a bad dream I wanted to wake up from. I didn't want to follow him, but I did. We went out to the pit. It was pouring down. The spade stuck out of the pit, and when Phelim shifted it, it raised a stink like a rotting sheep. The spade came out from the potatoes with a sucking noise, all covered in black muck. 'Oh, Jesus!' I covered my mouth and nose with my apron. God, it was like breathing poison.

'The whole bloody lot,' he said. 'Rotten. Rotten rotten rotten.' He threw down the spade.

We stepped back and took in fresh air and rain. My mouth had filled with spit. Our eyes watered.

'That is sheer rotten,' I said, 'Are you sure it's the lot?'

'As far down as I've gone with the spade. I couldn't go down more, I was nearly sick.'

Jamie came running.

'Jamie darling, don't go near!'

Summer was the lean time. Always so, summer lean, then the harvest. I looked at the slimy pit and was angry.

'But it was a good crop,' I said, 'they've turned in the pit. It must be how you put them in. What did you do?'

'What I always do,' he replied tetchily. 'What I've been doing for years. They're all gone, Eliza. Do you know what this means?'

121

'It means we'll get heartily sick of stirabout before we're through. Here, Phelim, go down to Bob Neary's and see if they've got the same. Sniff around. Come in, Jamie, you're getting soaked.'

I took him in and played trit-trot-trit with him on my knee. I remembered the last time. There were some died in the uplands, but we saw nothing of it. The beggars multiplied. There was a little cove where you could go for the mussels, and we waded in up to our thighs. I used to love wading there with my mother. She always knew what to do. She had a smile that never quite left her face, she even died with it on. I have a nervous feeling in my chest, a peculiar thing like the string on a fiddle vibrating very high. There must be within my inner soul a girding, a hardening, a rock wall of being that will not fall, let all the seas wash over it for a million years. I am iron.

He comes back and says it is not so at Kildarragh but it is so at Neary's and Gilhooley's and all along the strand beyond Lissadoon village. Jamie has fallen asleep sprawled across my lap. Phelim sits forlornly on the stool with his thin-fingered, gentle hands loosely clasping one another. 'It's going to be a bad winter, Queen Eliza,' he says.

He worries. Always has. Even when there isn't anything to worry about he can't be easy. I'll have to pull him through another bad winter. I'll pull us all through. I put my hand on his knee. 'We'll not go short,' I say, and smile.

My poor heron looks into the fire and his eyes are black. 'I know that, love,' he says, 'it's the debt I'm worried about. I told Lomas I'd bring the debt down come November.'

'Well, we can't do the impossible. Have sense.'

'Oh, I'll have sense,' he says, 'I'll have sense alright, but will he? Anyway, it's not Lomas that counts.'

Not Lomas, not even Cloverhill in his big house. Tarlton's the man. We are all in his pocket. Tarlton is a big lord, lives in Dublin, owns everything between here and Kildoran, which lies beyond Boolavoe. Owns us and owns Kildarragh, owns Lomas, owns even Cloverhill. Cloverhill's his middleman and Lomas is Cloverhill's agent. Everyone's got his master.

'There'll be folks put out,' Phelim says darkly.

It won't be us. The Quinns come into my mind, and all at Kildarragh. But their crop's not touched, he says.

Phelim and me have plenty, with the oats and the barley. As for the debt, it's older than the two of us, it'll wait a while more. Lomas can bring in Kildarragh's rents, we can't do the impossible. Theirs have rotted now like ours, and the late crop's got the mould under the leaves. It's all the talk and there's people crying. People do love to cry and wail. I was up there seeing Becky Scanlon again, and there was Alma Sheehan and Nan Fox both after me wanting to know what way things are with Lomas. Phelim's seen him, I told them, as far as I know there's no cause for alarm. Well, he has seen him, but they'd never tell you anything. Well, we can't do the impossible, can't keep carrying others too, not necessarily, not if Cloverhill gets nasty. I said as much to Phelim, and he says: 'We'll do what we can, Eliza. It won't come to that.' Well, of course. But you ought to see the prices in town. Doesn't take the hawksters long to take advantage of misfortune. I said to that woman in Moran's store, 'What's this?' I said. 'What d'you think people are made of? I paid the same last Thursday week here for a loaf and it was twice that size.' She just says, 'I know, 'tis terrible, it's what they're going for.' And as for those awful lumpers, God knows where they're getting them from, three times the cost and they turn to mush in the pot.

I get home and my da's up stomping around in the yard like an old turkey cock, stirring up the chickens. Pathetic whingeing old thing, takes more looking after than Jamie. Says his legs are bad but he's getting about, isn't he? When he wants to.

'Eliza,' he says, puffing and blowing as if the next breath's all too much, 'there's been a fellow looking for Phelim.'

'What's he want?'

'I donno. Says there's papers from the government. I told him he was working for Cloverhill today and surely he'd just come from that way. He must have seen him there. He's gone back looking for him.' He has a wheedling miserable way about his speech.

Papers from the government. What's all that?

'Get back inside, you old rep,' I say. 'What are you doing out?'

God, the man gets under my feet.

'Just getting a breath of fresh air, Eliza,' he says.

'Well, it's going to tip it down any minute,' I say, shooing him, 'go on in,' and I take Jamie's hand and we start off down the lane to see if we can see his daddy coming, but no sooner do we reach the cross than we hear the sound of a cart; then it's round the bend with a little brown pony trotting smartly, and sitting up there with two government men in their good warm coats and high hats, looking strange and grey in his old working clothes, is Phelim. The man driving pulls on the pony's mouth and they stop and Jamie wants lifting to stroke the creature's nose. One of them says to me, nice as can be, 'Would you climb up and ride with your husband now, madam, you'll be getting soaked.' And in fact it is starting to come down now, the clouds over west are like cow's udders desperate for milking.

'A ride in a cart, Jamie!' Phelim says, and jumps down to hand me in like a lady. There's nothing wrong here, I can tell by his manner and the way he smiles at me over Jamie's head. We're home in a trice, hedges and ditches flying by, and me

124

and Jamie snuggled up with my shawl wrapped round us. Jamie says nothing, but his face is a picture. They're nice men. The one who isn't driving has a jolly demeanour and pretends to steal Jamie's nose off his face. My father's all agog, hanging round the door. I could bet you ten shillings he's got the place in an awful state being up and alone all afternoon, and of course he has. The dust's like grey sand round the fire, and the table's covered in slops. I have to clean it up quick so they can spread out their important papers. They're not real government men, they're only from Boolavoe. The papers are instructions telling us what to do with our rotten potatoes, and they want Phelim to give them out in Kildarragh.

'They have a schoolteacher up there,' I say, 'he can read it out to them.'

When they've gone Phelim goes through the whole thing very slowly, stumbling over some of the words. It says you can cut out the bad bits and eat the good bits quick before they rot, as long as you boil them well.

'What good bits? Ours were rotten through and through. God knows what eating slime would do to you. What good bits? That's what I want to know.'

'Eliza,' he says, 'let me read.'

If they stink it's too late. You have to break them up then –

'– imagine the stench – break them up in my good pot?'

You'd be scared to use it again.

Break them up, he says, and get the starch and mix it up with flour and make bread. Couldn't you just retch at the idea? I wouldn't eat it.

We ate well that night. I killed a chicken yesterday and we had the broth with some of the meat and some bread. Next day, when Phelim went up to Kildarragh I went with him. I took some broth in a can for Becky and found her running about again, so all's well there for now. There was a bit of a gathering in the house of O'Carroll, the schoolmaster, a tiny beaky man with straw for hair. He has some very nice things. Over his fireplace hangs a white carved pipe, very long, made out of ivory. I was looking at it and he came over and told me it came from very far away, and named a place I'd never heard of. He was very civil. He has a clock on his shelf. Matty Sheehan and Darby Quinn were there, and old Nan Fox with Peader, her long streel of a husband. And Tadhg was there. When O'Carroll read out the bit about how vital it was to separate the good from the bad as soon as possible, Tadhg laughed loudly and said it reminded him of in the Scriptures where the Lord separates the wheat from the chaff and throws the chaff into everlasting fire, and we all know damn well who the chaff is, don't we?

Tadhg'll be fine, thank God, with his boat and the she-been and his bit of carpentry. I could've been there at the crossroads instead of Curly Callanan. Now his daddy's dead, he's the man. See me, mistress of the shebeen. Not that I'd have wanted that, not like some, larking and wasting time when there's work to be done. He and me would not have made a pair. They're all wild, those Ribbonmen. Guns and pikes and lurking about in the dark. Good luck to them, I say, but don't marry one. I look at Tadhg sometimes and wonder what my life would have been like if I'd had him. I imagine sleeping with him in our feather bed, waking up with his dark square face and the big side whiskers that grow on his face like bushes on the side of a rock. Didn't choose the handsome one, did I? I still think I got the better bargain.

Make sure it's all dry, O'Carroll's telling us. Don't pit them any more, they have to be ventilated.

'It's the wet,' Darby says. 'God willing, we have a drier season coming.'

Tadhg laughs again. 'And what'll we plant?' he says. Tadhg always laughs when there's nothing to laugh at.

Nan Fox snorts and picks at her peeling nail, the end all broken off and crooked. Man, woman and child, the cottiers all have a long spike of a thumbnail for peeling spuds; not that they'll be needing them now, not for a while anyway

We walk back over the top past Darby's house. Darby walks along with us as far as there, him and Tadhg. Now we're out of the general company, Tadhg's face is grim. Cloverhill and Lomas have it coming, he says. He says there's ships of grain sailing out of Cork Harbour and people going hungry.

'Whisht,' says Darby in a weary way, as if he's heard it all before.

Sal's at the front of her cabin, with the girl. She waves. She's showing now. Looks like another girl to me, I have a feel for these things. Two boys and two girls she'll have. Tadhg stops and says, 'Well now, my little lady!' to the child, who holds out both her arms to him and crows in a weird breathy little voice as he scoops her up in his arms and kisses her cheek. She croons delighted nonsense, and he carries her on into the house as if he lives there. Sal gives him a smile as he's going in the door. I feel ashamed for her, giving a man who isn't her husband a smile like that, but no one seems to notice. The brightness about Sal is the thing. Her eyes are dark and glittery, her big red lips shine, her teeth shine, her hair springs vital from her head. Mine doesn't. Mine is plain and straight and thin, and I have no red kerchief or a single ribbon about me. Yet still I have something. I can sit and sit and it grows and grows. And I know I really could have had either of them, Phelim or Tadhg, because there is something very strong in me that gets what it wants, even though I'm very, very small, and very, very thin with no breasts; even though my face is dark and narrow.

'I want to do right,' Phelim says as we pass by the rath.

Phelim is a weak man. We're going to want every penny we can get.

'You will,' I say, 'you always do.'

'I'll talk to Lomas tomorrow.'

Phelim is a good man and nothing wrong with that. But he's a soft man in a hard life. Rent day's coming up, and no word yet from Lomas about Cloverhill's decision. If he insists on the lot, he'll get it but we can't carry our labourers this year, the Quinns and the Foxes, the Sheehans and the Scanlons. They give us work, we pay their rents, that's how it's always been, but not this year surely. Of course it's hard but they'll not starve. There's plenty of meal. And Tadhg's still out there with his nets and his boat.

I haven't got Phelim to agree to this yet but he'll have to. What can we do? How many years we've seen them through with Lomas, even when there's not been the work. No good comes to them if we go down. And next year things will be better. Even they can see the reason in that.

8

I have always had another person inside my head. She even has a name. She's called Juliander and she comes from the Middle Kingdom, the place where things not real live. She has accompanied me throughout my life and been a great comfort, though she hasn't always had her name. First I used to play with her, then I realised that she was not outside but inside myself, that she was in fact me, though she had another name from me; it came to her about that time. But this is all a very long time ago.

She's like me but different. She's always the same age. She has a history, her own life and beginnings that I have discovered. No one knows her origins, she was left as a newborn outside the cabin of poor cottiers but they all died in one of the hungers. All of this happened somewhere up the coast from here. She left behind everything she'd ever known and walked the roads of Ireland till she came to Dublin City, where she had many adventures. She'd never worn a shoe till she came to Dublin City. Now she is rich beyond your dreams and her life is full of adventures. Everyone loves her. She knows everyone I have ever wanted to know and all of them admire her. Not only is she beautiful, but even though her life has always been one of tragedy, she's wise and brave and clever and full of love for all things. Nothing changes this. She is bereaved many times, suffers terrible sorrows, grieves deeply and never forgets, but grows still wiser and somehow more pure in spirit, though she is a woman of the flesh. Of her many lovers, none has survived. Her lovers are strange, dangerous, fiery men, lonely and intense; her love affairs are holy passions.

When I first met her she was a little girl playing with acorns. She became my best friend. Thereafter she came every night of my life, through all my growing years, and she still comes. She's small and light, like me; in fact she's exactly the same size as me, but with a finer bosom. Her hair is black as the raven's wing, her eyes the blue of deep twilight. She comes when all is over, at the moment when you turn over and know it's the final slide into sleep, she comes and plays out her life in my head, a little at a time. Her life, like mine, is a gradual thing. It changes.

Wherever in the world she goes, someone will love Juliander. There is something about her that demands it.

Lomas says Cloverhill's prepared to stand for half and we can make it up when things are better. I knew. We won't take anything from Kildarragh. We'll carry them.

It was a terrible winter. Terrible. Nothing worked. They said it was a fungus. They said it was the wet. I suppose it's like toadstools, they love the wet. First you heard of places not touched, then it was everywhere: up the mountains, down by the shore, everywhere. And all that about how to store them with the little turf roofs on for the ventilation, all that came to nothing. They still turned to mush.

Sal Quinn sent for me up to Kildarragh because she was feeling scared about the child she's carrying. I was taking her up milk. Her place was in an awful mess. They're a dirty couple, that's what it comes down to. The pink-eye's still a baldie. She'd spread her stirabout all over herself, and the mother was letting her totter about like that any old way. She's at the falling over stage, and the two little ruffians in their raggy breeches were there, Young Darby and Mal, following after her like faithful servants ready to catch her at a moment's notice, or pick her up off the filthy floor and set her upright again.

'Oh, she's the clever girl,' says Young Darby, 'she's the clever, clever girl.'

They see something in that child I don't. They see a darling thing. I think she's like a maggot. I remember a dream. There was a creature wrapped in swaddling clothes like the baby Jesus, and it had a white face like a seal pup but without the big eyes, because its eyes were closed and it was scarcely even aware. I think it was very ill. There were thin white whiskers all over it, but when I leaned over it to see if it was wanting anything, it didn't have nice fur like a seal pup. It had skin of a kind of horrid white creamy consistency that made me shudder. I decided I couldn't have the thing about the place any more because it was turning my stomach, even though it hadn't done anything wrong. So, quick and spry, as you would if you were cleaning away a maggoty lump of something found in the drain, over I goes to it with cloths on my hands, and picks it up firm. But then it opens it mouth and screams at me in dreadful distress, and the feel of it, even through the cloth, is so hideous it sends shudders all through me. I dropped it and it lay on the floor crying very piteously, a poor thing in pain, absolutely helpless, and I wanted to stamp it away as you would a grub, but instead I took it out and put it down at the end of our long field and just left it out there because I couldn't have it inside, it was making a terrible noise. And then I felt awful. It was a fearful cold windy rainy night, and I remember I was looking out of the window all the time down towards the thick hedge, thinking of the helpless thing suffering out there.

I gave Sal a potion. I'd say she'll not have a problem with the milk. Her bubs have swollen up like bladders and the blue veins stand out on them like roads. She's sitting on a stool by the fire, and she's not her normal self. She's a vain woman.

131

She has a penny looking-glass on the ridge above the chimney stack. She has high round cheeks and she never looks drawn. Now she's pale. There are dark rings under her eyes. Black hair straggles out from its pins. Her soft lower lip juts out and the light shines on it. I like to see her looking dull.

'Are you sure you can spare this, Eliza?' she says of the can of milk. 'This is awful good of you.'

I shrug. 'It's necessary.'

She gets up and stretches her back and groans. She's very big for her time, God spare us twins.

'Ach, what a world, Eliza,' she says, stifling a yawn, 'this one'll have to be dainty. A girl, I hope. Not a great big boy that could eat a whole horse, like these ones. God, I'd give anything for a good watery lumper! Melting in the pan.'

'It's a girl,' I say, 'set your mind at rest.' Though God knows it looks like an eater.

'Well,' she says, 'you've never been wrong before.'

Look at her. I don't know who she thinks she is, the Queen of Sheba maybe. There's none like her round this way; there was that Bridget one that rubbed soot on her eyebrows but she's gone now, married into Eskean. People talk about Sal, they've said things to me. Nan Fox said, she holds herself in high esteem, that one. That's what Nan Fox said to me. And they don't like it when someone sets themselves above, why would they? Phelim brought me a green ribbon once, it was given him by a lady who was staying at the House, for your wife, she said, because he took up eggs and beastings. Well, I've never worn it out. They'd think I was putting on airs. It's very pretty, hangs above the bedroom door.

'God willing,' she says, 'next year will be better. I have to have a lie-down.' She's a very lazy woman. Others have to keep going. 'Boys, take baby out and play. Keep an eye on her, give your poor mother a little time. I'm heavy, Eliza. It's lying like a stone.'

Going back over the track I look down and see the boys walking the baby down into Kildarragh, slowly, a hand each. All the little fields run in a muddle over the hill towards the sea.

I have said in my heart that I hate Sal Quinn because when I look at her I'm angered and grieved. She's never wanted for anything. It's not that I like hating her, I wish I didn't. And because I know I should not hate her, I must do good to her. It's a grim seam.

Christmas came and went and for fear of fever they were whitewashing the back lanes in Boolavoe. Sal Quinn got bigger and bigger all over till she was like a big seal cow lying on a rock. Her ankles swelled up terrible. I have graceful ankles. One of the things Phelim's always liked about me is my daintiness. He's a man of nice words. Once he said to me you move across the grass leaving no trace, as if there's no weight of you on the ground. Queen Eliza. He used to carry me when we first married, pick me up and carry me about like a child. My arms round his neck, my eyes close to his pimply neck. I liked to rest my head there and he would kiss my hair. Here's the strange thing. I know my face is wrong. I know it's too narrow and a little twisted but I can make it the only face in the world he wishes to see. I think it so. What he sees then when he looks at me, though he doesn't know it, is Juliander. Not her features but the tincture of her as it were. And no man can resist Juliander.

The weather goes on foul, rain, rain, endlessly splashing in the yard, making mud. The sky so low it sits below the tops of the mountains. The air swirls. Everything streams, the earth sings and gurgles through January into February. And on a dragging day as foul and dark and cold as any other, I put Jamie down for his afternoon sleep in our big feather bed with his granda, who's taken it over for the day and is lying

133

flat complaining of backache, and find myself quiet and restless and mad to be out of this damp-smelling house; so I put on shawl and cloak and boots and all and walk out as far as the end of the cow's grass, look down over the wall past the mound at the land, the small fields in a hotchpotch and our own bits and pieces of it scattered here and there, and see a man come running over the ups and downs from the long strand as if his life depended on it. Sometimes he stumbles. Then I see the dark green uniforms of two peelers running along about a half mile behind in pursuit. Well now, what's this? One of our good boys running from the law. The little man zigzags across the boggy land, towards me. It's Tadhg. My heart gives a lurch. The fool, didn't we always know this could happen? What's he done? They'll shoot him. I get down below the wall and watch. Poor Tadhg slithers and slides down into the big hollow leaving long scorch marks through the muddy earth, hares across it and comes pounding and scrambling up the rough gorsy hillside towards me. Now I hear his breath, scraping itself out of his chest like a knife. It hurts. I scuttle back down the length of the cow's grass and wait, quivering.

Here he comes, clearing the wall with a great leap and pounding on. He sees me. His eyes, never timid, are deadly scared, scalded and beat and miserable, like a child's. For that one second, his eyes like that meeting mine, it's as if he and I are naked together.

He sobs, can hardly speak. 'For God's sake, Eliza –' his knees give way and it's as if he's begging me to have him, '– help me, I'm dead.'

No time. I'm standing aside watching myself, exulting in some strange way. I think my eyes are cool.

I say nothing, grip his arm and haul him along after me as if he was Jamie, take him in the house and through to the room where the two of them are in our feather bed. Jamie's well away but my da's awake, sour-faced and flat on his bad back. His eyes show only mild annoyance when we burst in, as if we're an irritating draught coming in the window.

'Move over!' I command.

'Get in!' to Tadhg.

And they're lovely, all tucked in together the three of them, Jamie still sleeping rosily at the wall, Granda outraged in the middle, Tadhg squeezed in at the side heaving like a bellows with what I think is now a kind of laughter.

'Be still!' I hit him through the quilt and glare at my father. 'Ssh!' And in another second am outside going for water with a pail over my arm when the two peelers land like bullocks in my yard, red-faced and bristling with their bayonets and carbines. One carries a sword.

It's starting to spit rain.

'Is it the man you're after?' I whine. 'The one that was running?'

One's stout, his chest heaving. The other, a weed of a man, says in a high voice: 'You saw him?'

'Oh, I did,' I say, 'he went over the wall beyond as if it was the devil after him. What's he done?'

'Which way?'

'That way.' I point towards Lissadoon. 'What's he done?'

'Do you know him? His name?'

'Oh, sir, I never saw him before.'

The stout one with the moustache and wide arse heads for my door.

'Oh, sir!' I run. 'Please be quiet, sir, my baby's asleep and my father's not at all well!'

I trail him in while he stalks about my house. He throws back the curtain. There's my poor father with his watery old eyes staring. There's Jamie, sweetly sleeping with his red cheeks and surprised eyebrows, all hot and sweaty. There's no movement under the covers. The polis turns away and makes

135

up the ladder, but there's nothing up there, only a few stores and my father's old chaff bed. Then he's off after his friend. Puff, puff, puff with their load down the lane towards Lissadoon. I'm back inside.

'Not a word from a soul!' I say in a terrible deep voice.

And make them stay there. It's no hardship for the child, he knows nothing. What's he dreaming? Where's he gone? I wonder if a child goes back to where he came from when he sleeps? When he's there, does he understand everything? And when he wakes, it's gone like the morning mist that sits so low upon the land. There's nothing from the man all squashed and sweated up in his boots against my father's side. Perhaps he's fallen asleep too. Perhaps he's back in mammy's womb. Perhaps his killing breaths have finished him off. My father's piercing eyes stare like an aggravated baby. God, look at him. He's not a man, he's hideous. 'Eliza,' he says, as if he had any say in anything, 'what, for the love of God, are you doing?'

'Not a word till I say so!' I make a fist and show it him. You dare, you old fool. I pull the curtain across fiercely.

He'll not stir. Neither will any one of them, they'll stay so still and quiet as little mice knowing puss is there, till I come and set them free. Ha. The rain's pounding it down now. Oh, I do love this moment. By the back door looking out when the rain's just setting in good and proper and making the back wall drip and gleam and everything like a cascade of silver music, all smelling so fresh and new. Times like this I wish I was learned and could make a poem.

I'll leave them a while. Serves them right. Except for my little boy, who's done no wrong but he knows nothing of all this anyway. I sit by the door on the creepie and watch the rain and wait and wait and wait until I'm as sure they'll not come back as I am sure of anything; how much time that is I do not know; and then I stand, as if waking up from a lovely dream, go back inside and put back the curtain and say softly, 'Up now, Tadhg.'

Meek as a lamb he follows me. The door stands open.

'You'll not stay here,' I say.

He has tears in his eyes. 'God save you, Eliza,' he says, 'you're a grand woman,' and hugs me up off my feet in his turf and sweat embrace. His whiskers scratch my cheek. I struggle down. 'Go now,' I say, 'you can't stay here. What have you done?'

'We went for Lomas's oyster beds.'

'You didn't!'

'We did.'

'You and who else?'

He's still pale but he smiles. As if he'd tell me that. 'The keeper fired on us.'

'Why?'

'Why! Because of the oysters!'

'You must have done something.'

'We threw stones.'

'Ah!'

'Eliza,' he says, and pulls a pistol out from his clothes, 'take this for me, I daren't be abroad with it. Please, Eliza.'

'You fool!'

'Bury it for me, Eliza.'

'Take it away from here!'

'They won't come. You're Phelim's wife.'

'So?'

'Eliza,' and his voice cracks and falls, 'if I'm caught with that I'm dead.'

I've known Tadhg O'Donnell since I was five. 'No, you're not,' I say, 'you're transported.'

His eyes cloud over with misery. I look at him for a second then grab the gun and put it in my apron. 'Oh, go on, Tadhg O'Donnell,' I scold, 'out of my sight, you bad man!'

'Eliza!' he leans forward and grips my arms. His thumbs dig in. 'Eliza,' he says bitterly, 'they're going short in Kildarragh and Carraroe and Malahies and Scarran. When times call for it, you do what you can.'

'Would you rob *us* then?'

'Never!' he chops the air angrily, then he's off at a lick in the rain along the lane towards the gap.

That was stupid of them, I think. Lomas's oyster beds. If you were going to go for anyone, you should go for Cloverhill at least.

I'm not one to panic. I thought about burying the pistol. I kept it safe in my apron, it lay at my navel very heavy as if I was bearing it like a baby. I walked through to where my father still lay, grumbling and mumbling. Jamie was sitting up.

'Jamie, my love,' I say, sitting down on the bed, 'your Uncle Tadhg was here but you missed him. Now up and play. Granda's getting up too, he'll take you and show you where the snowdrops are beginning to push through at the side of the ditch. Won't you, Pa? Take him for a walk while I get these sheets washed.'

My father's had enough. 'You remember who you're talking to, girl,' he splutters, a vain attempt at the kind of authority he may once have had twenty years ago.

I pick up Jamie.

'Up, Daddy,' I say.

'I have a bad back!'

'A walk will do you good.'

'It's foul!'

'No, no!' and I run to the open door. 'It's stopping, see? Go and look for the rainbow.'

I go back and pull and push him from the bed, him groaning all the while.

'What nonsense is this with Tadhg O'Donnell?' he complains.

'Not a word, Pa. Not to anyone or I'll skin you. Not to Phelim, whatever you do. Do you understand, Pa? Do you? Do you understand?' I am staring into his eyes in that way that scares him. I bring my face to his, my eyes very close to his, till both of us are squinting, and I stare and stare and never give up. 'Do as I say. You saw nothing. Nothing happened. Unless you want that man shot by the peelers, and you carried him on your shoulders when he was a gossoon.'

'Eliza,' he says, 'you're an awful bold girl, you'll be in trouble yet.' He's pulling on his breeches over his long flannels.

'Maybe so, Da,' I say.

Finally I get him up and staggering out with his collar turned up and a tremendous air of injured dignity. Jamie runs ahead. Look at the state of these sheets, full of mud from that man's big boots, I say to myself. They'll need a good soak. Never mind. I work steadily, build up the fire, put the water to heat. Soon I know what I must do. The pistol lies hard against my belly. They transport you for bearing arms. I must get it off our land.

Nine at night going up to Sal Quinn's, called there by the eldest wee boy, I meet Tadhg going over the rath. He must have known I'd be coming, he's been waiting for me; he jumps down from the bank on the other side and runs across to me. 'Eliza,' he smiles, 'my saviour and my queen.'

He's a terrible man. He married Curly Callanan but he puts those eyes all over me still.

'I destroyed it,' I say, 'if that's what you want to know.'

He looks at me, his eyes bright and playful. 'Now how did a little scrap like you destroy a big gun like that?'

'It's at the bottom of the sea. I threw it over by the stone strand.'

He laughs. 'Tell me you're joking me, Eliza. Do you know how much a gun like that costs?'

'I do not,' I say.

He walks crabwise alongside me. 'Twenty eight shillings for a gun like that.'

'Fancy.'

'You know, you're wasted on Phelim,' he says. 'I have not thanked you. Is your father safe, you think? Will he talk?'

'He hardly sees a soul. He wouldn't talk.'

'Have you told your jackeen?'

'Don't call Phelim a jackeen.'

'But he is. Thinks he's a cut above the rest of us, doesn't he?'

'That's because of me.'

'Exactly.'

'I *am* a cut above,' I say. '*You* couldn't have me.' I say it, it comes out of my mouth. He looks startled, even scared, opens his lips as if to speak but falls dumb. We walk on, side by side, silent. On the descent, he turns now and then and offers me his hand like a gentleman, and I take it like a lady, all very nice. But we don't speak, and I sense he's gone shy. At the bottom, in sight of the Quinn house, he says suddenly, 'Don't tease me, Eliza, you didn't throw it in the sea, did you?'

'Yes.'

'No.'

'I did, Tadhg,' I lie, 'I really did throw it in the sea.'

He gives a great exasperated sigh and closes his eyes for a second. 'You shouldn't have done that.'

'Why? So you can kill a man and get hung?'

He breathes heavily down his nose. 'Oh, Eliza,' he croons softly, 'Oh, Eliza.'

The gun is in the tree. It's lying on top of the pussy cat. I came over when the night was quite black. I see well in the dark. I sing as I come, to lighten the way, a thin high song that no one can hear, a gnat-like sound in the low place just beneath speech. I came over in the pitch black when they were all asleep, and dropped the weary burden of my apron down the tree. Now no one'll find it, and if they did, it's not on my land. I don't like guns. Too hard and heavy. They're better kept away from hands like Tadhg's.

'Did you shoot at the keeper?' I ask him.

'No.' His lips press inwards and I believe him. 'I had the gun and I didn't even use it.'

I smile, seeing the tree from here, ugly misshapen thing scragging its long witchy fingers out across the green hillside. I wouldn't have it reaching at my house like that. I wouldn't live there. I like the idea that I know something no one else knows. It gives me a little power, though I'm not sure over what or whom.

'I don't care what you've done with the damn gun,' Tadhg says earnestly, 'I thank you from the bottom of my heart and I can't say more than that. I'll never forget what you've done for me.'

I won't let you, thinks me. There's a thin wisp of smoke from the chimney. 'Well,' I say, stopping, 'there'll be hard work here tonight. She's not a coper.'

'She's strong though.'

'Not with pain she's not.'

Sal screamed the place down when the girl was born. I remember clearly, Eliza Quinn was born with a caul. I still have it.

'Poor Sal!' he says.

You too, Tadhg O'Donnell. I'd like to meet a man who was unmoved by Sal. I remember even when we were little girls, five or six, her swanking it like a Dublin whore even then, hand on hip, rolling gait. And the lads, even then, with their google eyes.

141

'She'll weather it,' I say.

She will. She was made to bear babies, she was made to hate pain. She's a screamer.

'Birth,' I say, 'is a great leveller. Like death.'

Tadhg watches the cabin, grey and peaceful with its wisp of smoke, as if there were no mighty struggle within. 'I have more cause to have thought of death than most recently,' he says throatily.

I laugh. 'Listen to him! More cause than most! As if there weren't poor people much worse off than you starving.'

He was ashamed at once, his mouth dropping weakly. 'Forgive me, that was stupid,' he says.

'And there's been deaths they're saying. Where? Up in Clare?'

'So they say.'

I breathe in very deeply, girding up for the task ahead. 'It's exaggerated. There's always deaths this time of year. There'll be more, of course.'

'Well,' he says, 'no more talk of death tonight. Look after our lovely Sal, Eliza.'

Our lovely Sal, is it?

Here's Darby coming, tight-faced and haggard. 'Nan's with her,' he says, 'she's desperate for you, Eliza. It's been all day since a little before noon.' He has a chubby strong face by nature, but there are long bags hanging down under his doggy eyes. I'd guess he's not slept.

'Where are the children?' I ask.

'Below at Scanlons.' He rubs a square hand over his face and gives a great yawn. His fingernails are chewed to the quick. 'God bless you, Eliza,' he says, smiling wearily down at me, 'she'll be better now you're here.'

I'm a woman greatly blessed. If I had a penny for every time I've been blessed I'd be rich as the Queen of Sheba.

It's dark in the cabin, though the fire's burning and the

142

candles are lit. Sal lies on her side in her nightdress with one arm trailing down to the floor, her black hair free of its pins and hanging from the bed to the ground. Her knees are wide apart. Nan Fox is holding a hot turf wrapped in sack onto her belly low down.

'I'm such a scaredy, Eliza,' Sal gasps, starting to cry when she sees me, clutching the black and red shawl that covers the bed. 'You'd think I'd be getting used to it by now, wouldn't you?'

'You're grand, honey,' Nan says, 'you're faring just grand.'

'Let's take a look,' I say.

She smears her face with her hands and sniffs, hoiks up her nightie. Coming on nicely but the head's still a bit high. Water runs down her leg, her breasts are leaking too. She's a bag of water, a seal of the ocean. A pain takes her. 'Oh, Jesus!' Her knuckles are like hen's claws, fingertips biting down hard on Nan's long brown hand. 'There now, there now,' Nan says steadily, her gaunt old face stern. I count. A minute, more. Sal draws in a long breath as it fades, closes her eyes gratefully.

'It's a while yet,' I say. 'Put the kettle on, Nan. We'll have some tea.' Then around I go loosening the ropes of the creel, the knots that tie Sal's shawl on the door, the string that keeps the bundle of herbs above the fireplace. Nan's put a sheet and a clean flannel nightie to air in front of the fire. She's already got the rags steaming in hot water in the red ashes.

'Did you see Darby?' Sal asks.

'He's gone down with Tadhg.'

'Tadhg's been on at him to join up.'

'Darby with the Ribbonmen? Ha!'

'Oh, he has more sense,' she says.

I rub her back. The pains come and go. Scrawny Nan lights her pipe. We drink tea, the three of us, me and Nan on either side of her. When the pain comes, we rub her down, Nan at her back, me at her front, and she weeps and groans and whimpers and says she can't stand it. She cries on God. When the pain fades we wipe her face and tidy her hair and tell her she's a good girl. She wants to get up, but when she tries, her knees wobble and she has to bend down over the bed with her hands in fists on the old red and black shawl, panting like a horse. 'I can't stand it,' she says over and over again, 'I can't stand it,' in disbelief, endlessly, and I say, 'But you are standing it, Sal, you're standing it even as you say you can't stand it.' She hates me for that. I grip her hand and she grips mine as hard as she can and both our hands shake.

Three hours pass like this, till she crawls to the edge of the bed and calls for a bowl. Nan runs with one just in time. We clean her up and rub her down. Then she gets a bad one and starts screaming. This one goes on and on, and she screams all the way through it, jerking her head back as if she's in a fit. I hold her head. 'Enough now,' I say, 'you're fine now, not much longer,' which may or may not be true. There's a break. I grab the minute or two to look below. All's well. 'Oh, that's lovely now,' I say, 'that's coming along nicely, she'll be here in no time.'

'You, Eliza Vesey, you are amazing,' she says, smiling as best she can in the sudden lull. 'You have me convinced she's a girl. Have you ever been wrong?'

'Never. What name'll she go by?'

'Margarita,' she says proudly.

I snort mildly but smile too. Margarita indeed. Fancy. Hah, she'll only end up as Peg.

'Oh, Jesus!' She screams piercingly right down my ear.

Nan jumps up and grabs a hot cloth from the pot, stands wringing it out with her long hands held stupidly high. She looks like a hare. 'Ow!' she cries as it burns her hands, runs clumsily and lays it on Sal's stomach.

Sal screams and swears, pushes us both away with surprising strength, lurches from the bed and squats like a fat frog for a second or two before falling over onto her front.

'Come on, now, love,' I say, 'hold on to me.'

We have her, she's on her knees, sobbing.

I put my finger down and feel. 'Nearly there,' I tell her. We hold her hands and pray, all three of us in murmurous harmony. Suddenly she hauls herself upright and gives a great shriek. Nan gets behind her and holds her under the arms, and we start her pushing. This is the bit I like. This is when it's all up close, death and birth together like twins. I'm pushing it down with my hands. I'm pushing it out of Sal Quinn's body, and though I have said in my heart that I hate Sal Quinn, at this moment I feel like God dealing with her, and I almost love her in that passionless, indifferent way God must have for his creatures. Her belly is clay from which I'm moulding a new being.

'Now,' I say, 'lay her back very gently, Nan, and open that door,' and while Nan's at the door and the cold air creeps in, I give her a little shake to shake the baby down. A great gush of water comes, and a very strong pain that has her groaning like a soul in hell; I get between her legs and see the slimy head push against pot-bellied skin.

'Stop pushing.'

Nan's back. She holds her. It's going to tear.

'Don't push, love.' I put my hand there to steady it, the big wet head, black-haired, pressing up at me. 'Not so fast,' I whisper, 'not so fast.'

Beast. You'd tear your poor mother to bits.

'Now,' I say. 'Now. Easy.' Patting the head like a nervous animal. Steady now. And close my eyes and wait until I know it's good and time, then tell her softly in the ear, 'push.'

It comes. It takes a good few more pushes then out she sails, Margarita on a tidal gush, a bonny blue girl covered in cream. No caul on this one. Her eyes are wide open, shocked. Sal reaches down for the child between her legs, scoops it up into her arms and holds it fiercely against her breast. It cries once, sharply. 'Oh, a girl, a lovely little girl,' Nan croons, throwing a bit of warm blanket over the slippery thing, and Sal stares intently into its face. It won't suck, but after that first cry doesn't make a sound, only wants to look around with its wide open eyes. Alive and pulsing, the cord loops down from under the blanket into Sal. She starts to laugh weakly. 'Oh, I'm such a silly, such a silly,' she says. Nan puts her arms round mother and babe and laughs with her.

I build up the fire.

'More tea, Nan.'

Life goes on, whatever you think, life does go on. I have thought very often of the end. At every birth, I think of the end, and I think of Phelim. I think of all the things that have ended. My childhood. My mother. The doll that used to sleep in my oxter. Things are taken away, things are constantly taken away. I feel very lonely, sitting by the fire far away from the three of them, Nan and she and the babe, the Margarita, all cuddled up together there.

'It's coming,' she says.

No rush. Let it come.

'Yes, yes,' say I, 'coming, coming.'

'Eliza!' Nan calls, scared, 'Oh, Eliza, I don't know what to do!'

I feel very tired, not at all like getting up and going to that woman I don't like. I should be at home in bed, there's bad times coming. I feel them in my bones. I should be with my own. We're just poor stupid creatures, how are we to proceed? I've closed my eyes and am whispering a prayer: My God, my God, tell me what to do, when Nan says, 'Eliza, what shall I do?'

Cut the cord.

'Here it is,' I say. 'Here.'

'Now?'

'Time enough.'

Always, always, time enough. I think of them, far down there below in the darkness of tonight, Phelim and Jamie. Fifteen minutes later the afterbirth comes. I cut the cord with my birthing knife and drop it in a bucket.

'Go and tell Darby he's got another daughter,' I say.

Nan goes.

'She's not sucking,' says Sal.

I sit by her. 'Time enough.'

'Eliza,' she says softly, sitting up with the baby in her arms, thick lips smiling, 'will you come up here and see me sometimes? I don't feel very strong, Eliza.'

'You're stronger than you know,' I say.

'Not as strong as you.' Her eyes brim tears and look unnaturally large. 'Nowhere near as strong as you.'

'Look at you.' I reach for the pipe Nan's left. 'You're twice my size.'

'Will you?' she insists, 'Will you just keep an eye on me, Eliza? Just drop by once in a while?'

'Of course,' I say.

I take the baby and wash her then hand her back to ma, take a fist of salt for my pocket and pick up the bucket with its bloody smell, nearly colliding with Darby at the door, rushing in, bringing the cold air. She hurries the shawl around the babe.

Oh, look at this, he's down on his knees, she's his love. Throws his arms around her and weeps. Such a fuss for a fourth child.

Outside is a rare clear night about three in the morning, and a neighbour woman's coming up the road bringing something in a big pot that she struggles to carry. Behind her the high bright moon, nearly full, makes its path across the

147

calm sea. I slip round the back. The ground's hard but a place has already been prepared, into which I tip the big jellyfish with its knotted cord, the knots my own hands made. I sprinkle the salt and cover all, murmuring a prayer. I need to sit out here a while in the dark and cold, while the neighbours stir, bearing gifts. I yawn and rub my eyes. The see-saw the Quinn boys made is still there, next to the dead tree. I yawn hugely. I'd like to be lying next to Phelim, he asleep, deeply breathing and far gone in dreamland.

I'm chilled.

Tadhg's arrived. He's brought a sprig of thyme and he's smiling and a little staggery with drink. Because he's a special friend, he's allowed to lean over the mother and babe to place the scraggy herb gently in the baby's grip. Darby's turned into a pure fool. There's Nan, towering over the little neighbour woman, the two of them tidying up and making yet more tea. I'll wait a while in case she needs me, then I'll go down and sleep, and then I'll kill one of our precious chickens and bring her some meat, and the broth. I sit by the fire getting warm. Nan hands me a pipe.

Tadhg hadn't noticed when I came in. His eyes are all for Sal. Even like that, all of a sweat with her great udders sticking out, she takes his eyes.

148

9

1846

You heard terrible things, rumours to catch your breath, that a woman had set off to walk to her people in Westport, County Mayo, and had died with her children on the road and a cart ran over them in the dark. That a man in Dingle saw the devil pissing on a shrine.

Then I'd go out back and stand up on the mound, even on a foul day – so many foul days we seem to have now – and see the creamy hush of the waves far away and think inside myself that life is wonderful and God is kind. He's been good to *me* anyway. We have the grass of five cow's scattered here and there. We got eightpence the stone for our oats in town. Me and Jamie go down to the strand and we collect dulse and the big mussels, like I used to with my mother when I was no bigger than he is now. They do say we'll be fine if we can get a dry harvest, but for now the wet seeps in everywhere and the house stinks with it. The sky sits there wanting to burst.

My mother used to say to me, 'Do just what you want. Do it for me.' She had the most amazing eyes, bright piercing blue like a spring sky, and I always remember her smiling. I never knew what she meant because she never told me, even though I asked. She used to say funny things. But now I think I do know what she meant. She wasn't a good speaker; she was good with her hands and at doing things, but she couldn't talk well at all. I think she meant get what you want because life is very short; get what you want like she did, she always got what she wanted. She took a man like my father to do as he was told, and I took Phelim because he was butter in my hands. Him and me and Jamie, we'll sit here till it's all over and we'll do fine because I'm blessed – I've been blessed so many times by so many people – and I carry my protection around my neck in a small blue cloth bag next to my skin. My mother put it there when I was three. She sewed it up herself with tiny black stitches. I have no idea what's in it, for to open it would be to remove its efficacy. So we won't suffer, but there's some will suffer. God knows what Kildarragh will do. There's a miserable look up there, though there always is this time of year. I took them milk. The way word flies around, everyone's hearing things. Alma Sheehan came up to me and she says, 'I'd sooner die than go in the workhouse, Eliza.'

'What are you talking about the workhouse for?' I asked her, 'You're not going in the workhouse.'

'I couldn't stand it.'

Then it's Cliona Scanlon crying about the bellyache and Becky with the runs and thinking it's fever, which I soon put her right about. She's a sickly child but she's not got fever.

Lomas himself turned up on a terrible wet night. The sky had just burst like a bladder over the house when he came squelching through our yard, his horse tied at the gate. I peeped out of the shutters and told Phelim, who met him at the door. Lomas is a squat red-faced man with a wispy ginger beard. 'God save all here,' he says brusquely, whipping off his dripping hat and planting it down on the table to drip on to the floor. 'Is there room by the fire there, Phelim?'

Phelim indicates the chair and takes the stool for himself. 'Some tea would be nice, Eliza,' he says.

'Now let's not mince words.' Lomas shakes his head and sends raindrops spinning into the turves. 'Tarlton has three years of poor rates due, and there's not a chance in hell of him getting his rents. He has Cloverhill by the throat and Cloverhill tells *me* to bring them in. Now, Phelim, what would you do in my position?'

He sits forward, a hand on either knee, his stomach sitting on his thighs. Phelim frowns. Never a one to speak quickly, he puts his face in his hand, sighs and considers. After a time he says with slow deliberation, 'I don't know.'

Lomas laughs. 'Ah, Phelim,' he says, 'a man of firm decisiveness.'

Phelim smiles faintly. 'You can't get what isn't there,' he says.

'Quite.'

'You can tell Cloverhill we'll bear the fines for our labourers as we always do.'

I stop what I'm doing. He'll have us dead before he'll see sense. Sense is often unkind.

'As for the rest, I can't say.'

Lomas is clearly relieved. His dancing blue eyes smile up at me as I solemnly hand him his tea. 'Thank you, Eliza.' He takes a long slurp of it, hot as it is. 'Well, I'm very glad to hear that, Phelim. Very glad indeed.'

Then they sit and yarn there by the fire like two old fools, as if nothing were happening and the world not tightening its heart around them, steeling itself. The very sky is telling them. I leave them, slip through the curtain and sit by sleeping Jamie. Beneath the golden down there's a flush on his cheek, but when I put my hand on his forehead there's no heat. This is the healthy flush of a boy asleep. His dreams are serene as the rain beats on the shutters and the roof. Looking at him I cannot feel helpless, though I should. All I know is that as long as there is a will in my body no harm shall come to him, even if a million perish. What can I do? I'm not God, but I have a will. No one takes the food out of this boy's mouth while I'm alive, not Tarlton nor the Quinn brood nor

151

Jesus himself if he came crawling at the door. I'm charged with the keeping of one only.

I say as much to Phelim while Lomas is hauling himself like a bloated sack, dropping heavily onto his poor streaming horse's back.

'I'd not see anyone starve,' I say at his shoulder, 'but our own child comes first.'

'What do you want me to do, Eliza,' he says snappishly, 'we've had a year's labour out of them.'

'Shut the door, for God's sake, the rain's driving in.'

He all but slams it, walks ponderously to the fire and sits down in a rare state. 'What do you want me to do, Eliza?' he says again in a loud voice, peculiar for him, and turns his head from side to side as if there's something down his ears.

'Do?' I say gently, 'All I want is for you to be a good father and look after your child.'

He looks pained. 'I *am* a good father. Eliza, you're unfair. We are not so badly off. There's others far, far worse. We'll not starve, we can tighten our belts a bit and get through, even paying for our cottiers. It's what we've always done.' And then he looks so miserably into the fire, his pale grey eyes glistening with moisture, that I soften and sigh and put my hand on top of his head.

'All right, Phelim,' I say, 'all right, all right, we'll say no more.'

Christ, but this is a bloody awful summer. I've never seen anything like it, this weather going on and on. They're all getting sick and calling for me. That Doctor Carmody's been up there and sat a while yarning with O'Carroll in his house. O'Carroll told him some have had nothing but turnips since Christmas. That's not true. I know for a fact they've been bringing in cockles and mussels by the basketload, and now there's this Indian meal stuff coming in from America. And how wonderful that is. Bright yellow, spits up out of the pot and fills them up with nothing but gas. Phelim went down to the new depot in Boolavoe with John Scanlon and Matty Sheehan, and hauled back three sacks, up to Kildarragh. Everyone got the colics. I had a family down towards Carraroe ate it practically raw and near killed themselves, six of them all doubled up and retching, the ma and pa too sick to tend the little ones. Nothing much you can do for them, it just has to work its way through. It's the kind of stuff you can cook for hours and it'll never be done. You get all these little hard bits that just about break your teeth and scratch your throat going down. Some places there's been people bled to death from getting their insides pierced.

'You've got to soak it,' I tell poor old Nan, 'stands to reason.'

Nan's bad with diarrhoea, I'm feeding her a nice pow- dered tea, a spoonful now and then, but it's coming out both ends, she's bringing up blood, and her lips are turning creamy and making me feel sick. I look at her as little as possible. I haven't told her how worried I am. I like Nan. She never had any babies and I'm sorry for her for that. We've had no deaths near here. Don't be my first, Nan, I'm thinking. Carmody's been told but he's half dead himself running here and there and hasn't showed up, so I've stayed by her all night so Peader can get some sleep. He's been bringing his guts up all day too but he's just got on with it. Looks like a ghost but he's through the worst. And no one can look quite so like a ghost as long grey Peader, thin as a hound, even when he's well. I've heard people say the reason they couldn't have children was because they were both so tall and skinny but I've never given it any credence.

By morning there's no blood. The moans have stopped and she's fallen asleep. The air's foul. I go outside for a breath of air and look over and see Tadhg's boat tacking over the grey choppy sea and he a black hump at the oars. Nan and Peader's old dog comes over and sits beside me, scratching, his fur all wet and matted. Grey rain pours steadily down in thin rods. I wouldn't want Phelim out there. The weather could turn worse any moment. The fish are far from shore. I think of Tadhg and how he has always admired me and been so nice, how he had looked in that one scared moment when the peelers were after him with their guns, and how when I was picking along the shore with my mother, sometimes I'd see him bringing in the nets with his father and big brothers when he was just a little thing. He was different then. He was at ease. He's tight as a fiddle string now. Suddenly, a small revelation, I realise I love him. It doesn't make any difference, doesn't tear my heart or anything like that. I think: this is interesting. Then the feeling pushes itself out from me, like some invisible bubble blowing itself outwards all over the world, rolling over everything in its path. For one thrilling moment, I think it must be possible to love every creature in the world. Even Nan, draining her bile into the bowl. Tadhg's little boat rides the waves like a seal. Foolish, but then he is. Blackened his face with two or three others of them Ribbonmen and off to Cloverhill's and cut the tails off the cattle. I saw Cloverhill going through town a day or two after. All his guards round him bristling with pistols. I wouldn't like to be him in these days. He's a handsome man, with soft waving brown hair that bushes out around his ears, and he wears a very fine waistcoat. His mouth is large and red and curly. I could imagine kissing him.

Trudging up from below comes Sal Quinn with her baby tied on behind, 4 months old, a black-haired girl like her ma. She has little Eliza by the hand. Well, that one's had her nose put out of joint for sure. Look at her. Two years old and tottering along over the rocks drizzling like a miserable sky.

'You're abroad early,' I say.

She looks a wreck. 'It's her,' she says wearily, jerking her chin back over her shoulder at the gently snoring baby. That child looks sickly to me. Not like the pink-eye. 'She only sleeps when I walk about outside. Soon as I set foot over the threshold she'll be off again, howling the place down. How's Nan?'

'Still bad, but she'll mend.'

Sal yawns in her pretty way. 'And my little shadow here, of course, she never lets me out of sight for a minute.'

'Jealous.'

Slowly, Eliza Quinn turns her face up to me and what I see there sends a panic thrill up my spine. Her face is dirty, smeared with tears and snot, but she smiles at me in a sudden ingratiating way. She has an odd little face. She's not bald any more but what she's got is wispy and colourless, so you can see the shape of her head, a pale nut shaped like an elongated onion. It's a vegetable head. I would not be surprised to see a bug creep from its ear. Why has she got my name? The panic is not that she is so repulsive to me, but that her eyes themselves frighten me. What looks back is not human, nor is it animal. It's sly and dangerous and full of fun.

'She's been a good girl,' says her mother fondly, smiling down at her, 'and now she's a very very tired girl who should have stayed in her nice warm bed.'

In the Middle Kingdom, there is beauty beyond human beauty, and there is also, of course, wickedness and abomination. The thing I recognise looking out of the child's eyes is of this last kind. Juliander has her origins in the Middle Kingdom also, but she is noble and true and brave. It's not that she can't feel fear. She wouldn't be so brave if she didn't feel fear. She gets terribly scared, so scared that she cries and weeps and falls all the way down to the very darkest depths of the well. But she always gets up again. Finger's length by finger's length, she pulls herself back up to the light.

'Are you all right, Eliza?' Sal says, breaking in on me. 'You look a bit queer.'

'I've had no sleep,' I say, blinking. 'Neither have you. We're both in some half land.'

They go slowly on up the hill to their cabin. Eliza Quinn turns her head once as she walks, looking back at me over her left shoulder. She should not have my name. She can see Juliander. Creatures of the Middle Kingdom always recognise each other.

They were pitifully small, those green-tops we planted, the tiny poreens soft and watery, not fit to eat. I tried cooking them but they turned to black slime in the pot, so we set them in good hope and they've come through for us. This morning I walked between the ridges below our house. The potato's a handsome plant. Its flower is a white spiky star with a rude yellow tongue, and it clusters like bells in a belfry, many bells in many belfries rising up all along the ridges, pretty as anything. The flowers stand tall, the stalks are sturdy and green. There's a good few planted between here and Kildarragh. Not long now and there'll be a great lifting, and then, oh, won't we all be going mad for a lovely buttery potato with salt?

It's as if the long dry spell we had never happened. The downpour is dreadful, endless, and the seeping damp every-where, and those poor people out there on this new government scheme, they don't stop for any weather. I don't suppose they ever get dry. They're shoring up pure bog, and everything they clear in a day is flooded by morning. They're walking in from as far as Sneem and Cahirciveen for six in the morning to stand up to their waists in freezing water every day. There'll be all kinds of fever and grippe, you'll see.

It's harsh, but they're like that, these Whigs. Peel's gone. Peel wasn't so bad, at least he brought in the yellow meal. We cursed him for it too. Peel's bloody brimstone. At least they don't die from it any more. The millers learnt how to grind it, and the word came round on what to do with the damned stuff: which is simple: soak, soak, soak, boil, boil, boil, and don't take any chances. Whatever you do, don't say, oh, God, that'll surely do, let's just eat the stuff. Throw in some oatmeal if you've got it, makes it more digestible. Of course they haven't at Kildarragh, so naturally there's Phelim off up there with a big bag of the stuff hoisted on his back and his big heart pumping him along. God love him. I wouldn't have him out there on the Scheme in all this; thank God we're not reduced to that. They're all up there now, Peader Fox and Darby Quinn, John Scanlon, Matty Sheehan. They get six-pence a day to buy India buck. There's women there too, Nan's up with Peader, she gets fourpence a day. And children. They're making a road across Clunagarthy. Why they don't make one over to Kildarragh, I don't know, not many use the Clunagarthy track. Still, they're glad of the work, I suppose. Good luck to them, I should say, but they've left us in a pickle. We've got no one to lime the land. How can they expect Phelim to pay them a wage as well as clear them with Lomas and Cloverhill? Don't they know how good he's been? Of course it'll be a different story when the rents next fall due. I suppose they think we're made of money. I suppose they think we've had a fat winter and a full summer and don't drool sometimes at the thought of all we're missing. If they could see me walking between the ridges praying God and the Holy Mother and all the Saints to bless these potato plants and bring us in a decent harvest at last. There were so many potatoes before, they were dumping them in the ditches. They were using them as manure. And now look, these beds are so precious. Sometimes I have to stop and attend to this great weight in my chest. And yet sometimes, thinking of this foul year and how it's fared with so many, I know that the worst is past and I think of that good time of

year that's coming – the pulling down of autumn and the settling in of winter is cheering, when everything's in and the
meal months are behind us all again and we can breathe easy.
Then I'm so lightened with hope it's like a fountain bursting
up inside me, and I know again that the terror times are necessary in order for the fountain to renew.

Tonight there's a gap in the weather. We stand at the gate,
Jamie and me, looking down the lane at the growing dusk.
The earth is poised. Everything's damp and breathing, and a
dark figure wades through the fog that is creeping up from
the sea, lying low on the land. From the walk it's Phelim
coming up from Lissadoon.

'Daddy!' I say, and Jamie runs. Phelim lifts him and carries
him back on his arm, and smiles at me as he comes near. I
think that I am very lucky.

'Do you smell that strange smell?' says Phelim.

There is something in the air, now he mentions it, faint yet
distinct.

'It's in the fog,' he says.

'In the fog?'

'Well, it seemed to come on with it. The smell and the fog
at the same time. Didn't you notice?'

'I didn't notice anything till you said.'

We stand, the three of us in the foggy lane, sniffing the air.
Now I can't smell anything but dew and mist and sweating
plants.

'Maybe we're in for a storm,' he says, 'it's very still all of a
sudden.'

We can hear the murmuring of water in the hillside and in
the ditches, the dim far howl of the sea.

'I want a storm,' Jamie says, pulling his father's face round
towards him with rough affection.

'You may well get one, Jamie,' replies Phelim and we go in
and close the door and all the shutters against the fog.

158

All night it seeps in. In the morning the storms begin and rage for three days. It's nigh impossible to get out of the house, you open the door and the weather drives you back in and follows you. It's always trying to get in. If you do go out you can't see a thing. We're using up too much fuel, I know, but what is there to do but sit in by the fire and keep out of it? Poor Jamie, grizzling and griping away because he wants to go out and play, wants to be off with his da seeing to the beasts, but Phelim won't let him. You could die out there, it's winter in summer, on and on and on, howling and banging around your head till you could scream.

Till suddenly on the fourth day we wake to a quiet morning.

'Thank God for that,' says Phelim, getting up groggily and sitting on the side of the bed with his shoulders rounded. 'It's not raining.' He stands and stretches, yawning loudly before going into the room and blowing up the fire. I get up, dress quickly in the first morning chill and get started on the stirabout. Jamie's up but my father's still snoring vigorously. It's when Phelim throws open the door to the yard to let in what seems the first clear morning in an age that I know, with a hollow and terrible certainty in the pit of my stomach, that the catastrophe has struck. I have known it since the moment in the lane when I felt lucky and Phelim said, 'Do you smell that strange smell?'

What comes in is rotten in the nose and throat. Phelim turns back from the door and looks at me. Our eyes hold for a long time. I wonder what he sees in mine.

'Pooh!' says Jamie.

'I'll go and see,' Phelim says.

'Can I come now? The storm's gone.'

Phelim hesitates for a moment then takes his hand. 'Yes, you come,' he says gently, 'I think we'll find the potatoes have gone bad again, Jamie.'

'Oh no!' cries Jamie, holding his nose, but he has no idea what this means.

The three of us walk down together and stand in the field, just stand and gawp. Last night the stalks were upright and green, I walked among them in the rain. A dragon has come and breathed on them while we slept. They've fallen sideways and laid down their burned black heads, ridge upon ridge of them felled at one stroke. We don't speak. Phelim gets down on one knee and takes a handful of withered rot. The stench is wicked.

'Don't!' I say, and Jamie covers his nose and mouth.

Phelim heaves a great sigh. 'Oh Jesus,' he says, an appeal, not a curse.

A faint rainbow has its tail in the meadows beyond Lissadoon. The air shimmers over the sea. It's a soft warm morning and my father's up wanting his breakfast. I don't know what we're going to do. Maybe it's just ours. This can't be happening again. I got that child through the whole of the last year without a hungry day, and now what am I going to do? Oh, God! I'm not giving that child yellow meal, I'm not watching him cry with the wind. They'll have to reduce the cost of bread, they'll have to. We've still got oats. No, no, no, we'll get by, we will if we keep calm. There's a horrible wriggling of unease rearing its wormy head in my gut. Down, down. The rainbow in the warm meadows beyond Lissadoon has deepened. Distinct, I see the seven colours.

'You take Jamie in for his breakfast,' Phelim says quietly, 'I'll see to this.'

I could laugh. See to this?

'Go on.' He nods his head towards the house, its grey spiral of smoke climbing into the sky.

When I break the news to my father, his grey old face makes me sad. Poor soul, I think, he should have had a bit of peace in his dotage, not this again. He's seen it all before. He subsides by the hearth with his knotty old hands linked and his lower lip hanging stupidly. He'll endure. Funny that he survived all those hard years when my mother, who was so much stronger than him, did not. She had a thing in her stomach that swelled her up till she died. There's nothing you can do for a thing like that, she knew that and she told me. She was a very proud woman who always spoke straight to the mark, and she taught me to be brave. 'Eliza,' she said, 'I'm going to die and you're not to worry, you're to be a good girl and look after your father.'

'No,' I said, 'you're not really going to die.'

'Yes, I am,' she replied simply, with the smile I see always when I remember her, 'It's going to happen.'

She was always right.

I wonder what she would have done. We sit by the fire and wait, my father and I, while Jamie runs about in the yard kicking his ball, glad to be out and about in spite of the smell. The news comes in in darts from here and there, from Phelim coming and going, from Father Buckley who's making the rounds, from Tadhg who always knows everything, from Darby Quinn, pale-faced at my door and wanting help for Sal. The blight is total. Everywhere.

'She's very nervous, Eliza,' Darby Quinn says, pushing a thick-fingered hand through his springy fair hair.

'I should think she is,' I say unsympathetically, 'I should think we all are.'

'No, no, you don't understand,' he says patiently, 'I mean, she's ill. She keeps on crying all the time and it's upsetting the children. She says she can't stop.' As he speaks he grows agitated. 'I don't know what to do, Eliza. I don't know what to say to her. She won't get out of her bed in the morning.'

'Well, I can give her something for her nerves,' I say, 'but she'll have to wait till tomorrow.'

There's enough to do here. They think I can run to them whenever they want me.

'That's grand, Eliza.' Darby turns ponderously. 'I'll tell her you're coming. That'll cheer her up a treat.'

Tadhg brings me a fish. He's not on the Scheme, he's still got a business and his nets and goes out whenever he can, which has been precious little with this weather, but he got out first thing this morning before light, as soon as the weather cleared. He could smell it from out there in his boat. He knew, he says. He drifted in his boat, and he knew.

'People will die,' he says.

Like my mother. Simple.

I do not contradict him.

We cut down the stalks near the ground. You couldn't lift that mush. Here and there are one or two little poreens not worth saving, even smaller than the last lot. How could we ever have expected anything from them? Still, they put on a good show for us for a while, a very pretty show.

Kildarragh's in despair. I got up there late the next day with some milk and bitters for Sal Quinn. She has a pot of water over the fire simmering, waiting for Darby to come home with the meal. It'll be a good hour yet, then up they'll all come trudging from Clunagarthy with their sacks on their backs. God, they work them hard. Wait till they get over towards Corrabreac, it's covered in rocks.

'How are you, Sal?' I set down the can of milk.

She bursts into tears.

'I'm not good, Eliza,' she sniffs. She's lying on her bed against the wall, her children gathered about her, made solemn by the state of her. The baby's sucking fretfully.

I sit down.

'I've not enough milk,' she says.

'You will have. Drink this.'

'You're very good,' she says. 'I feel so scared, Eliza.'

'You're a strong woman. You'll do well enough.'

She drinks and makes a face.

'Nan's very good,' she says. 'She brings me some of her share every day, for the babies.'

'Nan loves babies,' I say, looking at my namesake who's squatting on the bed beside her mother's tousled head. 'You must calm down, Sal, you're upsetting them.'

'We thought we'd have the potatoes again,' she says.

'You have a husband who's working,' I say, 'and food in your belly. There's plenty worse off.'

'I know! But it's not enough. They're hungry every night and it's not enough for a man to work on and poor Darby's worn out.'

'There, that's going down nicely. You run out and play for a bit,' I order the boys, 'I'm talking to your mother. Go on, the rain's stopped. Go on,' and I shoo them unwilling out and close the door. The elf Eliza sits on her mother's pillow, watching me with her uncanny eyes. One hand rests on the shoulder of her baby sister. For the first time I notice how long her fingers are, long and pale. They look as if they could lift up their blind heads, wormlike.

'You know what scares me?' Sal asks with another gush of tears. 'You know what really, really scares me?'

'Tell me then.'

'The workhouse,' she says. 'I'd rather die than go in the workhouse.'

'What are you talking about the workhouse for?' I ask, amazed. 'Who said anything about the workhouse? You've got a husband in work.'

But she just cries.

'Some more,' I say, pouring from the can. 'This is doing you good.'

'Oh God, not the workhouse!' She throws back her head

163

on the pillow. 'Please God, not that! They'd separate me from the boys. If my boys were dying they'd keep them away from me. Children want their mothers. But all the little boys are taken away from their mothers. Oh, that's cruel! And the husband from the wife. Not even an eye to look at you in the way that it knows you.'

Her daughter croons, an odd small keening, leans over and tries to cradle her mother's head and the sucking baby both together.

'Sal!' She needs a slap and she'll get one in a minute if she carries on. 'Why are you upsetting the children with all this? Stop it at once and drink your milk.'

She blinks and sits up, pulls both her girls to her. 'You'd need someone with an eye that knows you, wouldn't you, if you was getting near the end?' she says. 'Don't you think?'

'You would,' I reply, 'but it won't come to that. Drink.'

I didn't go back over the top that night, I went along the low track along past Tadhg's shebeen and back along the road. It was as I was passing the lime kiln I noticed the queer light over the sea. It was dark. This dark summer is fading away into a dark winter. I'd love to see a blue sky again. The mizzle soaks me, and the queer light says another storm is coming in. Something has closed over the world like a tunnel raised above our heads. I have one of my moments where I must stop and stand. My blood thrills. This storm will be bigger than the last. It's coming in like blood in the sky. Below me I see men, women and children walking home along the shore with their measures of meal, heads down. They don't seem to see something rising over the sea, they just want to get home and get warm and eat. They've worked a twelve hour stretch. The men dig, the women pull box-barrows, the children load them. All in their own little worlds, they are, while the storm that is right for the times is coming in as sure as the blight settled from above. And they'll work through that too or they'll get no pay.

It comes with thunder and lightning and a heavy downpour in the middle of the night. It comes with a vicious, moaning voice that cries about the house. Many a time it strikes with a big crack over the great stones towards the coast. The ground shakes. The sea's up in fury. No one can sleep.

It goes on for days. No one can expect me to go slogging up to Kildarragh or down to Lissadoon in all this. They can leave me alone. We have enough fuel if we're careful, we have enough food. The weather has wrapped us up in our nest. My father stays in his bed. Phelim darts in and out when things need doing. I keep by the fire with Jamie, telling him stories and fashioning games and singing songs. I make up my own. 'Pussy's In The Tree' and 'Old Sow Got Caught In The Fence Last Spring'. He laughs. The fire's glow exaggerates the scar that will always mark his pretty face.

After a while, with the sky dark in the day as well as the night, with no one coming near, with the noise always howling and the wind pounding our house with angry fists; day after day, night after night of this, awake or asleep, I go into a strange state of calm. I become the eye of it all. It's a peaceful place to be and perfectly safe. At night the three of us huddle together in the big feather bed, Jamie warm in the middle. I throw an extra blanket on Father. He needs it more than we do.

The gales howl us into winter at last. It's never clear when summer ends. Some people are got down with the weather but not me. They call it a curse. All this palaver about the devil and God's wrath, it's all just a load of old dung. It's not God, it's stupidity and greed and politics, that's what Tadhg says. That's where ruin comes from, not the weather. That's what he said. But when the weather goes on and on and on, maybe even he wonders.

There was no way a man could go out on that sea, and the fish were all miles off anyway.

So he pawned his nets and sold his boat. He had to. He went on the Scheme. Now, there's a man growing bitter. Sold his boat! I can't believe he'd do that. But he's sold his boat and seethes and boils as he works on the road. He says the ganger's a bastard, he'll dock you half a day if you're a second late.

Phelim told me he'd been to see Lomas to say the people couldn't meet their rents this season, and Lomas had said that as far as he knew Mr Cloverhill didn't appear inclined to make any concessions come November. The cutting of his cattles' tails hadn't helped, Lomas said, though of course all that might change if anyone decided to come forward with information about any subversive activity they knew of in the district.

'So, what are we to do, Eliza?' Phelim asked but not as if he seriously expected an answer.

'We'll meet our commitments,' I said. 'What other people will do I don't know. That's for them to work out with Lomas, it's not our concern any more.'

He sighed.

'We can't pay for work we haven't had,' I pointed out. 'If they're working on the Scheme they can't work for us, it's as simple as that; and if they're not working for us we don't owe them anything. We'll pay our own way but no one else's. Face facts, things have changed.'

Another long sigh. 'I suppose you're right,' he said sadly.

I lay wide awake that night thinking hard for a good long spell. It was time for me to act. I didn't know at first what I would do, but I knew it would be something bold. The demons of the weather were still whistling outside. Let them. Sound, that's all it was. Sound.

I know how Phelim talks when he talks to Samuel Cloverhill, like a lackey. It's all your honour this and your honour that: yes, your honour, no, your honour, three bags full, your honour. That's the way everyone talks to Cloverhill.

Not me.

I march straight up the road from Boolavoe to his big gates, pull on the bell and stand there in the wind and the rain looking through the bars. After a while a surly old man with pointed ears and a threadbare black jacket and high collar comes trotting along the muddy path, stands a little distant and asks me what I want.

'Tell Mr Cloverhill that Phelim Vesey's wife requests a word or two with him if he would be so kind as to spare the time.'

He goes away and leaves me standing, getting soaked for ten minutes before coming back and unlocking the gate without a word, motioning for me to follow him. Phelim's done a lot of work for Cloverhill, so I'm admitted, up the rutted track through dripping shrubs and old beeches festooned with ivy, to the house; ugly, red and square in its circle of trees. It's very fine in its way, but I wouldn't want to live in it. I think it's gloomy. He takes me in a side door and puts me standing in a hall at the bottom of some stairs, listening to the soft ticking of a large clock somewhere, smelling dust and polish and a strange, almost mouldy atmosphere that evades the senses. The wood is very dark and the stair carpet has a pattern of green roses. You don't get green roses in real life. Juliander has lived in houses like this, well, very much finer than this one actually. I wonder what she would make of Samuel Cloverhill. For myself, I'm not sure. I've only seen him once or twice and I can't make my mind up. The picture of him in my head can go either way. The door to a room opposite is open and I go over and look in carefully. It's a lovely but stern room, full of books, and on the wall above the mantelpiece is a painting of a fine young lady I recognise as Samuel Cloverhill's daughter, only looking much prettier than the real thing, at least as I remember her. We don't see much of her in these parts nowadays, he sent her to school in Cobh in Cork City. Opposite her on the other wall is another picture, of a woman completely naked, lying down on a sofa with her legs wide open and her hand draped over her private parts.

I hear footsteps and move away, shocked.

A woman called Martha Colgan comes out of a room on my right and tells me to come this way. I know all about her, everyone does, she comes from Kildoran and she's a widow and his housekeeper; everyone says she sleeps with him but I can't see it myself, she's old enough to be his mother and she hasn't even worn particularly well. Very broad in the beam she is.

He receives me in a small study at the front of the house, where he sits scratching away at some papers at a small wooden table that has been polished up to a yellowish shine. The room smells of snuff and tobacco and he appears as a dark shape with the window behind him. I can't see his face.

'Do sit down, Mrs Vesey,' he says.

'I'll stand, sir, if you don't mind.'

I can't see his face to tell if he's surprised or not. He gets up too, and comes round the desk to stand facing me and say, 'Now, what can I do for you?' as if he were a shopkeeper.

I'll bet Martha Colgan's got her ear to the door.

I can see him now, no longer a silhouette. His mouth is sweet and soft but his nose is cruel. A serious man, disappointed. Trouble in his eyes. I am in no hurry. I would oblige him to look at me as closely as I am looking at him. Easier then to make him listen. 'Sir,' I say, 'I'm sure you're aware of the bad state of things.'

'Oh, indeed I am, Mrs Vesey.'

'I thought you should know, sir,' I went on, respectful, 'that the cottiers cannot pay any rent this season. None at all, sir, just in case there were any doubt. Not that they will not, they *can* not.'

He looks stern but says nothing.

'For myself and my husband,' I say, 'we will settle our own affairs but I want to inform you that we will be unable to carry any of the debt for Kildarragh as we have not been able to hire any help from there this year on account of they're all on the Scheme. It's been a very bad year, sir, and after last year, sir.'

He starts coughing, deep in his throat and phlegmy, sounding like a much older man. His eyes stay fixed on me all the time, still stern as they grow moist. When the coughing fit is over he wipes his mouth with the palm of his right hand and says, 'Mrs Vesey – Mrs Vesey – to the best of my knowledge there are two private charities operating in Boolavoe at this moment.'

'I wouldn't know about that, sir.'

He nods and looks away, thoughtfully gazing into a corner of the room. I know what he's thinking – he's thinking: they cut off the tails of my cattle and expect leniency. I think he's maybe quite a good man at heart, not like Lomas, who just wants life easy for himself. That man reminds me of a bladder. You should get out while you still can, I feel like telling Cloverhill. See if old Tarlton can get himself another fool to get shot. Suddenly he looks back at me sharply as if he knows what I'm thinking, and smiles faintly. 'You can't get blood out of a stone,' he says. 'I know the situation.'

'Mr Lomas has told my husband he thought there were to

be no concessions come November and it's what people are saying, and a lot of them are very worried. It's not that they wouldn't pay it if they had it, sir, it's that they can't because they haven't.'

'I am completely aware of the situation, Mrs Vesey, and I'm dealing with it.'

That seems to be that.

I smile at him. 'Thank you for listening to me, sir, and I'm sure you are.' It sounds insolent but not quite enough to anger him.

He blinks at me for a while very rapidly. The poor man's eyes are dark and hopeless. 'I'll speak to Mr Lomas,' he says, 'No one will be put out, Mrs Vesey. You can tell them that. No one who is honest has anything to fear.'

Lomas puts out that some rents are exempt till the first of May. So there you have it. We, though we're sick to death of turnips and cabbage and the scrapings of the oat barrel, *we* have to pay our share; and all that lot up there don't pay a penny. They have me to thank for that. They do because he was impressed, he must have been impressed that I'd just go marching up and say my piece like that. The one thing I can do is look a man in the eye. I've probably saved his life. Suppose I had not gone up there and impressed him with the truth, he'd have exacted his rents and there'd be weeping and wailing and gnashing of teeth, and one of Tadhg's Ribbonmen would go up and shoot him. I did a good thing, I saved a good man, two good men – him and Tadhg – because maybe it would be Tadhg himself to go and kill him and then get hung on a gallows. My mother saw a man hanged once when she was a very small child. She watched his face every moment of it, she told me. It went on for a very long time and his legs were kicking all the time. She says she knew the precise moment the life went out.

Well, I'll get no thanks and no one knows I spoke at all except Cloverhill himself.

At last the weather stops and silver shines in the puddles along the lane. I couldn't wait to get up and about and into town, so off we go, me and Jamie. Set free, Jamie's wild, running along the tops of the ditches. There's no rain, not even a drizzle, not even a fine mist you can feel but not see. It's clear and still, and the sea washes on the shore far away with its old gentle hushing sound. I've been cooped up so long and I have no money so I don't know why we're going, it's just for the sake of it. My father's crying out for a scoop of sugar to put on his stirabout. Well, we can get that at Neary's, then we can see if there's any stalls in the Square, and walk about the river bank for a bit and be home to get supper. It's still very cold though. The nip in the air whets knives on your cheeks, making them burn and flake. Your eyes water continually. But the sun's as bright as high summer, and the hedges are full of dark leaves and growths of bright bitter yellow fungi. The fact we're out makes us festive. The fact is we're getting through these terrible times, and Jamie's in high style, cocking it all along the ridges.

Coming out onto the high road down into Boolavoe, we meet with a tall old man like a grey wraith, hand in hand with a tiny hobbling old woman.

'The man's legs,' Jamie says, 'look at his legs, Ma.'

'Shh, I know. I know, Jamie, don't say anything. Don't stare, it's not polite.'

The man's naked legs are obscene white sticks covered in fat red boils. His head is much too big for his body. He strikes us dumb because he looks so strange, like a ghost, like whatever it is that wails in the wind. The old woman looks half daft but she doesn't scare me like the man; she's just a bent ugly old ball of rags, the kind you'd see anywhere.

'God save you,' says the ghost, wild-eyed.

'God save you,' I reply.

'Save you,' whispers the old woman.

'Is it far now to Boolavoe, ma'am?' the ghost asks. He has a fine strident voice and his thick grey hair is tangled and matted into a barbarous mane. His coat, all torn and filthy, is pinned tightly in three or four places for lack of buttons. Holes gape at the sides and under both arms, and it looks as if the hem's been hacked off hurriedly, so that it ends some three or so inches above his knobbly knees. Barefoot, he's striding out as best he can with his ridiculous thin shanks exposed so. I believe he has nothing underneath. Yes he has, an apron, a sack maybe, tied round his middle. But there's nothing up top. His sickly old flesh and the ribs that ripple under his skin, all's visible through the rents in the coat.

'Two more miles at most,' I reply. 'Have you come a long way?'

Sobered, Jamie walks holding my hand, peering round me at the spectral pair.

'From Portmagee, ma'am,' says the man.

'But that's miles away!'

'It's surprising what you can do,' he says, 'when you put yourself to it,' and smiles at me, a grinning skull with unnaturally brilliant blue eyes, fierce and intelligent. His wife turns her face away from me into his arm, like a shy child. She hums a soft high hum into the raggy sleeve, a sound like a little fly dying on a window sill. 'Not far now, Jess!' he says cheerfully. 'And is it true, ma'am, that they have a boiler in Boolavoe?'

'I believe so. Have you been out in all that weather?'

'We took shelter,' he says, 'we managed to stay out of the worst of it.'

Even so, they must have taken something of a battering. And us all snug in our house.

'It must be bad where you've come from?' I say.

His eyes sharpen. 'Bad? It's terrible. Terrible, ma'am!'

172

We shuffle on for a while. He says his name is Michael Byrne. His poor addled wife is called Susan. She never speaks, just totters along beside him with an idiotic smile on her face. He says they've not eaten since yesterday and hope to get soup at Boolavoe. There was fever on the way, he says, so they come away before it. If they can get to Cork they'll be fine, his wife has a cousin in Cork.

'No point in waiting to meet it,' he says, 'no point at all.'

I look at the boils on his legs, pustules with sore wet heads. I don't think that is the fever we've heard of. It doesn't have the fever smell. No, this is something else, perhaps he's being bitten by something, eaten away. There's poison in his blood. But it's not the fever, definitely not the fever. I would know a thing like that.

He says his son had looked after them, he'd been a labourer but there was no work and now he's gone and listed and they have no one. We've always had bad times. There's always been beggars and there always will be. We have accepted this destroying season that never ends because we know that there *is* an end if we just keep walking on through it, sensible, steady as she goes. But I've never seen anything like these two along any road I ever walked upon before. It takes my heart into a lower place and gives me a fear I had not imagined.

'Jamie,' I say, quiet in his ear, 'don't be afraid. These are people just like your mammy and daddy, only a bit older and they haven't got any money. They're souls like you and me. Don't ever you forget that when you see poor people, wherever you may be, always remember they are the children of God like you and me.'

'He looks like Peader Fox,' he whispers, 'only more so.'

'He's had a harder time than Peader.'

He has to understand these things. This is an awful time to have to rear a child up, poor scraps having to learn these terrible things for which there's no comfort.

173

'That's a fine lad you have there,' Michael Byrne says, rolling his unnatural eye Jamie's way.

'He *is* fine,' I say, 'the finest boy in the world.'

The crone turns her perished mushroom of a face to Jamie, smiling her fatal smile. Her eyes are slits, nothing of them visible. She frightens me now more than him. They are death, both of them. Death and the cold fear, walking down the same old road to Boolavoe. Begone! I would say if I could, away from me, but it's not possible to do so because they are too real, too apparent with their streaming noses continually wiped with genteel scraps of cloth kept handy for the purpose somewhere in their lousy rags. They are hungry souls on the road, the poor to whom the good Christian must always attend; and they are also death, smiling into my son's soft face.

We meet a woman with a wooden can on her head, coming back from town, who tells us there's no soup, only Indian meal stirabout in a big boiler in Fallon's Yard. As we walk on we keep passing them, more and more people on the road with cans on their heads taking home the meal. None are as ragged or hideous as my old pair, none so liable to cause thought of death. He reminds me, this tall bony old man, of a picture I saw on a wall once, it might have been in the schoolhouse, of Old Man Death with his scythe and his grinning skull peeking out from a loose black hood.

Things are hopping on the old woman's neck. We keep our distance. In town, they dither and dander, and in the end I take them to Fallon's Yard myself because it's easier than leaving them standing there. But my God, when we get there it's madness. It's so long since I've been into town, things have got worse, infinitely worse. I don't know where all these people are from, they must be coming in from all around, you don't see anything like this even on a Fair Day. At the back of Fallon's Yard there is a metal cauldron as wide across as our bedroom, and two big men stirring away with sticks; and there's Father Buckley and Father Dolan measuring out thin stirabout from a tap on the side of the pot, a pint into each can, and all the people lining up.

I'm not waiting with this lot. Jesus Christ, they're all bloody lousy, look at the wee black bugs thick on them, jumping round their filthy grey collars. I can't have Jamie in there. 'Stay here and don't move,' I tell him, and go in to where the old couple are standing uselessly at the back with everyone pushing in front of them.

'Here!' I say loudly, 'let these people through! They're old and they've walked all the way from Portmagee and they've had nothing since yesterday.'

'Have you a ticket?' a man asks. 'You have to have a ticket.'

'It's not for me, it's for them. Look at them, man, they're dropping. Come through, Mr Byrne, come through, Mrs Byrne dear,' and officiously I shoo them through the crowd towards Father Buckley.

Father Buckley knows me; he knew my mother and knows my father. 'These people are hungry, Father Buckley.' I say.

'A lot of people are hungry, Eliza,' he says, hard-faced.

'They're dropping, Father. Look at them. They've walked from Portmagee with nothing in their bellies since yesterday morning.'

'Have they tickets?'

'Where can we get tickets?' Michael Byrne asks.

'You have to go to Mr Lomas at Malahies,' Father Buckley replies. 'He's head of the committee. He'll give you a ticket.'

That's when I lose my temper.

'Oh, for God's sake, man,' I shout at him, 'they've just walked all the way from Portmagee and they're old and they're starving. Let them first eat and then get the ticket. Tell you what, you give them something to eat now while I go

175

and get the tickets for them. They'll not make it there and back unless they're fed in any case.'

Father Buckley looks vexed. 'Oh, come up,' he says impatiently in their direction, 'come up and get a tin can from Sean. But you'll have to get a ticket for the next time, you know, or I'm not supposed to serve you. And you, Eliza, you can't go for them, they have to see Mr Lomas in person. It's the rule.'

What a fate for human beings, I think, getting out of that place as Michael and Susan Byrne are having their pints doled out. What a thing to come to at their age. I swear, if it ever gets like that for me and Phelim and Jamie, I'll go and get that gun from the tree and I'll finish us all off. I swear it.

Ah, but that was only the beginning. Something turned in me that day in Boolavoe. Because I've known Boolavoe all my life and it was changed, full of creatures I could scarcely bear to think of as human beings because they were ugly and mad-looking, strangers to me. They were from other places, and with them came fear and starving and the end of everything as it had been. I passed back along Weavergate and into the Square, where a post-carriage was loading up for Limerick, and a couple of gentlemen onboard surveying the crowd with troubled eyes. The windows through which their anxious faces peered were mobbed.

'Think of the childer, sir!' a wild-faced woman cried, holding up her filthy baby, its loose-skinned legs dangling from a tatter of rags.

Where are they all coming from? We can't help them. We have nothing of our own.

10

Sal thought the room seemed very plain without her mother's old red and black shawl lying across the bed as it had done for years. She'd sold it in the town. So many nice things you could get there these days if you'd only had the money. People were selling everything they didn't absolutely need: caps and bonnets, stockings and blankets, gew-gaws that had stood for as long as anyone could remember on shelves and chimney pieces. As for the shawl, her mother had made it when Sal herself was only about eight and she could remember the making of it, her mother's big rough hands working away by firelight. She sold it in Boolavoe along with her mirror and a bunch of ribbons she'd had for best. She kept her red handkerchief though, folded and stowed away, but that would have to go too if things didn't improve next season. They said it was far worse up-country. Here life went on somehow. Darby brought home the meal.

And one day Tadhg, God bless him, brought a hare he'd killed up to the house, saying it'll make a meal for the children anyhow. He gave it to Darby on the path.

'Christ Almighty, man.' Darby's voice broke. He was a soft man, Darby, and these days often close to tears. 'This must be the last bloody hare on the mountain.'

'Not quite.' Tadhg smiled.

'What about you and Curly?'

'When we've mouths to feed,' Tadhg said, 'you'll be helping us out.'

Darby's eyes were big and swimming as he presented the

hare to Sal. Of course it should have been hung, but who could wait? It was meat. 'It'll do if we stew it a long time,' he said.

'I'll make a pudding with the blood.' Sal was already grabbing the sharp knife, reaching for a bucket, 'I'll make a pudding with the blood and –' She set the baby down on the floor to crawl.

'If I could get a couple of turnips –' he said.

'Go and tell John and Cliona –'

Margarita started whining. Sal slit the hare's belly and the innards slithered into the bucket. A rank smell rose up, making their tongues sting.

'I will, and the Sheehans.'

The Scanlons and Sheehans were their nearest neighbours. Between the three families there were nine children.

They came together in the Quinn house very late. The children were asleep except for Margarita, who was being passed around the circle of adults, picked up and set down onto her feet from time to time, to totter and gimble on her toes while they held her hands. There was a little tobacco, which they passed around in a pipe, its fug mingling with the smoke of the fire, and the steam from the hare that simmered gently over the turves in a thin stew with a bit of wild cabbage and nettle and a handful of meal. The hare was young and had bled profusely into the bucket when Sal opened it up. Now she was mixing a blood pudding with her hands. All of them were wet about the mouth but they'd all had a good feed of stirabout and could wait. The men talked half-heartedly about stealing turnips.

'You have to be careful,' said Matty, a tall, fair-faced man with curly hair, 'wasn't I nearly caught with my arse hanging out of a shed window one night over toward Kildoran.'

'You would,' Alma said, appealing to the room at large. 'He'll take one chance too many one of these days.'

'You were glad of the turnips,' he said, smiling.

'I wouldn't be glad of you getting transported,' she snapped, 'then again maybe I would.'

Everyone laughed.

John Scanlon said nothing but sat there solidly with his mouth smug, puffing on the pipe. Everyone knew he had a knack for stealing. Of the three men, Darby was the only one who had not stolen turnips. Sal wouldn't let him, not because she thought it was wrong – you could steal; God made a special dispensation for the poor at times like these, everybody knew that. What could you do? What other way could you live? – but because she didn't want him getting caught, and Darby was just the kind of man who *would* get caught. He wasn't a careful sort. Clumsy and genial, he'd always stumbled and bluffed his way through life, taking very little seriously and getting by on his humour and good nature.

'How long you reckon that'll be?' He nodded at the pot.

'Two hours to do right by it,' Sal said, yawning, 'but I can't see us holding off that long.'

The boys, Young Darby and Mal, aroused by the ineffably sweet smell of slowly cooking meat, crept up to the fire and were scolded for getting out of bed before time. Eliza came and leaned against her mother's legs, sucking her thumb and drooling, slumbering on and off. Darby watched his daughter's skimpy-haired head droop against her mother. Her thumb, festooned in saliva, slid from her slackening mouth.

He stood up. 'Hold off till I'm back,' he said. 'I'll get us a few turnips.'

'No, Darby,' Sal said sternly.

'No risks,' John Scanlon said mildly, too comfortable to move, 'not now.'

A peculiar smile crept over Darby's face.

Matty gave one of his deep scattershot laughs. 'Not you, Darby!'

Darby just went to the door, shrugging into his coat, taking a sack.

'Darby!' shouted Sal, and Eliza woke and started up with a little shriek.

'Give me two hours,' he said, and was gone.

'Oh, go with him, Matty,' cried Sal, jumping up.

'You will not indeed,' said Alma.

'He's such a big fool, he'll get caught!'

'He's a big boy, Sal,' Matty said, leaning back suddenly philosophical and poking at the pipe just passed to him by Cliona.

Sal ran to the door and stood shouting into the darkness, 'Darby, you come back here!' and Eliza ran after and peered round her legs.

But he was off.

He went to Mr Cloverhill's because he knew it, he and Phelim Vesey once having worked alongside each other there, digging ditches. No other reason. He knew Cloverhill had mantraps set around the place and had belled his cattle after their tails were cut, and he knew there was a guard on the shed where he kept the turnips, and a guard on the perimeter. Everyone knew these things, and that only a fool would go near Cloverhill because of them. Still Darby went there. He had actually thought about this many times and decided that if he ever did it, against her wishes, then he must do it daringly or not at all, and now that he'd decided, nothing in the world could have turned him around. He walked with a huge smile on his face, every now and again laughing to himself at his own boldness.

It took him half an hour's brisk walk across scrubby mountain and low-lying boggy fields made treacherous by the heavy rains, but it was land he had good knowledge of and he saw well in the dark. He approached the wall of the house slowly, under cover of darkness and light rain. The perimeter guard could not be everywhere at once. Dogs were worse. A dog charging you in the dark, snarling like a demon, was unpleasant. But Darby was a strong, stocky man and he carried a big stick, a long cudgel with which he felt his way ahead like a blind man, checking every inch of the ground before he stepped on it.

It was alarmingly easy. He scaled the wall, putting his faith in his coat which he doubled over on top of the shards of broken glass on top, and dropped down in the shade of trees and sombre rhododendrons.

He could be shot. They'd have guns. Luck of the draw, if you got a frisky guard or not. They could send him to jail or Van Diemen's Land. Still, he smiled and walked on, elated by the danger. Sal didn't think he could do this, but he knew he could. And when he came home there would be glory. The smile never left him.

He skirted a large mantrap, a wide patch of bramble into which his stick suddenly sank down with a sucking sound; moving on, slower and slower and ever more cautious, he reached the edge of the trees and saw the side of the house, with the stable off to the left, and the shed and the lean-to round the side, in which everyone knew the turnips were stored. He edged round towards it, keeping under cover. The rain fell more insistently now, pitter-patter in the leaves. Darby shivered. He had a clear view of the side of the lean-to with its narrow window high up. In front he could see a boy of about sixteen, his gun on his back, slouched in the deep doorway, keeping out of the mizzle, looking as if he'd rather be anywhere else in the world than shivering there. The yawn that stretched his already long face and practically wrung out his body was so palpable it brought tears to Darby's own eyes. It was followed by a deep sighing exhalation that settled inexorably into a long shallow snore, followed by three or four others. Propped up by the corner of the doorway, he was sleeping on his feet.

Darby stood for five more minutes before creeping past the sleeping boy, round to the side where the narrow window was. It was a stretch. You'd need Peader Fox for the height. He looked around. Nothing. Then he saw the arms of a barrow sticking out from round the back of the shed. It was an old rotten thing, slippery with rain, but he carried it round and deposited it under the window with its arms pressing into the sloppy earth and its one wheel facing the sky. He was completely calm now he was underway, sure what to do. He had to be careful not to catch the wheel with his foot as he stood up on the barrow's underside. The wood squelched and the whole thing tilted, but he was able to grab the sill and balance there till everything had stopped rocking. The few inches made all the difference. His hair dripped into his eyes.

Standing on tiptoe on top of the barrow, clutching with his toes, sticking his arm as far as it would go through the window and feeling around, he resisted an incredible urge to laugh out loud. He couldn't feel a damned thing. He'd have to knock the boy on the head.

'What are you doing?' a man's voice asked.

Darby froze. Everything went through his head, a gunshot and terrible pain, a prison boat leaving Cork Harbour, Matty Sheehan hanging out of a window in Kildoran, laughter in Kildarragh. There was a sound of snuffling and hawking and general pulling together, then a boy's high voice said, 'Was I asleep, Mr Cloverhill?'

'Of course you were asleep, Ted, you know damn well you were asleep.'

Slowly and silently, Darby breathed out.

'Sorry, Mr Cloverhill, I swear I was only out for a second.'

There was a shifting of feet.

'This is a bloody awful night again,' Cloverhill said.

'You shouldn't be out in it, sir.'

Darby's arm, held at an awkward angle through the slit of the window, was beginning to ache.

'And let you sleep? Have you seen Martin?'

'Not this while.'

'Damn.' More stamping and shuffling. 'Go up to the house and ask Martha to make you a drink.'

'That's kind of you, sir, oh, yes, yes, I'll do that . . .'

'Go on, Ted, for God's sake. If you see Martin send him down here.'

After the heavy footsteps of Ted had squelched away into silence, there was a long pause full of the dripping of leaves, then Cloverhill said, 'Come out of that,' stepping round the side of the shed, 'I have my pistol on you. Who are you?'

'Darby Quinn,' said Darby, unthinking, pulling out his arm and looking into the muzzle of the gun. He dropped the cudgel.

'What the hell are you doing?'

'It's to make the pot go further for the children, sir,' he replied, hangdog, dropping his eyes. No point saying anything else.

Cloverhill sighed. He was silent for an uncomfortable time, studying Darby moodily.

'I'm very sorry, sir.' Eyes down, head down, a dog.

'Oh, for God's sake,' Cloverhill snapped, 'don't you know you could be shot? I know who you are. You were on the drains.'

'Yes, sir.'

'What have you got there?'

'It's a bag, sir. For the turnips.'

'Do you *want* to be shot?'

'No, sir.'

Cloverhill snorted and was taken with a fit of coughing that made the gun quiver in his hand. He hawked and spat. 'I

183

told Mrs Vesey when she came to see me,' he said, vexed, 'no one would be put out at Kildarragh and in the townships beyond. I said it, and I've kept to my word. There is a relief committee. There are two private charities. There is a board of works. What are you doing here?'

'Yes, sir.'

'For God's sake, man!'

There was a trembling in Darby's hands and eyes.

'Are you armed?' demanded Cloverhill.

'Oh no. No, I'm not armed, sir, truly I'm not, sir, I swear I'm not. Sir, I have four children.'

'What about that?' He motioned with the gun at the cudgel Darby had thrown down on the ground.

'My stick, sir. For feeling my way. I was 'feard of traps.'

'Damn you!' Cloverhill holstered his gun furiously and pulled out a bunch of keys. 'Come here!' He turned and strode back to the front of the shed and set about opening the door. Darby followed. 'Quick,' said Cloverhill, 'take a few quick and go, and if I catch you here again I'll shoot you for sure. Do you understand?'

Darby gawped at him.

'Quick!'

Darby ventured into the dark of the shed. He was trembling severely now and couldn't see a thing, but he groped and groped and got a dozen or so turnips in the bag before a cold sweat broke over him.

'Quick! Quick!' Cloverhill was at the door. When Darby emerged he slammed it shut, locking it smartly. 'That way.' He pointed. 'Quickly. If you meet a guard, you're a dead man.' Then he turned on his heel and stamped away through the rain.

Darby fled as silently and swiftly as he could, but he'd left his stick behind and kept catching his feet and lurching into bushes, and most of the time had no idea where he was. Any

184

moment a shot would explode in his head. He'd fall headfirst into a mantrap. His breath sounded very loud in his ears, and the bag bounced about on his back and thumped him every time he stumbled. Finally he hit the wall and scrambled up and over, careless of the glass which slashed hard in one or two places and caused hot blood to trickle down inside his clothes as he fell on the other side. There was a moon. Once the house was back on his left he ran. The cuts on his knees and arms throbbed and his muscles ached but he was pushed on by a wild elation, and as he ran and marched by turns, up and up into higher ground, he laughed aloud to himself and even spoke in ragged bursts. 'Just take a few, he says, just take a few . . . well, well, fancy the man . . . ha! . . . I know who you are, he says . . . oh, Jesus, he can't go back on it now, can he, he can't go back on it now? . . . they'll never believe! . . . they'll never . . . Jesus! When I open up the bag . . .' and he saw them, their good familiar faces in the fire glow when he spilled out his haul, all radiant with appreciation for what he'd done.

Sal was cuddling Darby's old hat to her breast when he burst in, a big comical smile on his face. She threw it down and jumped up. 'How dare you!' she cried, taking three quick steps towards him, her neck thrust forward. 'How dare you frighten me like that! I thought you were dead.'

He stepped across the room and opened the neck of the bag, letting the turnips roll out onto the table. Sal screamed.

Matty Sheehan roared. 'You did it!'

Then they were all over him, slapping him on the back and telling him what a good man he was, and he started to laugh and laugh and laugh. 'I just did it,' he spluttered, 'I just put my arm in the window and kept feeling about and I took them one by one. The guard was standing round the front with his gun at the ready and he didn't know a thing about it!'

His coat was all torn from the glass on the wall, and when

Sal tugged it off him and saw the blood running down into his palms, she paled visibly and shuddered.

'It's my knees too,' he said proudly.

'God, Darby, and you're soaking wet.'

He was dried and fussed and petted, his wounds tenderly dabbed clean and dressed with cobwebs and strips of torn up sheet. Only the gash under his right knee was deep and troublesome and would leave a long scar.

'Jesus, Darby, I never thought you'd do it,' Matty said, chuckling and shaking his head.

'She's been a wreck,' Alma scolded, walking up and down and patting the baby's back, 'a complete wreck.'

Cliona scrubbed the turnips. 'Your father is a very brave man,' she told Young Darby and Mal.

'No, really,' Darby said, still plastered with a mad smile, 'it wasn't hard really. There's just this young lad having a nap in the doorway.' He hooted a fleeting relief-filled laugh. 'Honestly, it was so easy, all I had to do was stroll up and stick my arm in. Anyone could've done the same.'

'Ah, no, that's where you're wrong.' John Scanlon handed him a freshly filled pipe. 'You had to keep your head. You had to have the nerve. Not many would have done that. You did well, Darby.'

Darby shook his head, unable to believe his own bravery. His body was still trembling but in a good way now. Warmth seeped into his frozen bones and the aroma from the strong meat juices was almost unbearable. Young Becky chopped the turnips very small so they'd cook fast, and it was scarcely any time at all till everything was ready and the children of the three households were awakened for the feast and sitting blinking in the smoky glare.

Nine children got the lion's share. The adults had the broth thickened with meal, and plenty of turnips.

★

Later that night Sal began to cry. She couldn't tell why. Everyone had left and the children were fast asleep and she was lying in bed with the blanket pulled up over her head.

'What is it?' asked Darby, getting in and finally blowing out the candle.

She could only say she didn't know, it had been so awful thinking he was dead and now she couldn't stop the feeling.

He laughed. 'I was never in any danger,' he said.

'You were.' She blew her nose. 'Of course you were. They could take you away. They could hang you, Darby. What would I do then?'

He laughed again. 'What would *I* do?'

'Promise me,' she said, sitting up and looking down at him in the darkness, 'promise me you'll never ever do such a stupid thing again. Promise.'

But even when he swore on his own mother's soul that he would not, she didn't stop crying.

'What is it?' he sighed, desperate now for sleep. The wind was getting up again in fits and starts and tomorrow was another day of digging.

'I don't know,' she said miserably, 'I don't know, Darby, I really don't know. I feel so sad.'

He put his arms round her and drifted to sleep against her restlessness. 'I wish I hadn't sold my mother's old shawl,' she said, but he didn't hear. She started thinking about the red and black shawl again, how she'd sold it to a woman from Kildoran in the square. Her mother's hands were in every stitch of that shawl. She bought a loaf with the money. Six years since her mother died. I'm glad she's dead, Sal thought, she'd have hated these times. The sound of breathing filled the air around her and the wind blustered outside. The more and longer she cried into the dark, the more alert she became, till she felt as if she'd never been so wide awake and alive in her whole life. The crying settled into a rhythm, becoming luxurious, enjoyable. She drifted in and out of sleep, in and out of worry. Her stomach hurt.

A woman called Annie Porter had gone down with the fever on the other side of Lissadoon. They said it was terrible up-country. If it got here what could you do? Perhaps, Sal thought, drifting, she should stop going to town and keep the children in. Eliza Vesey might know of something, she'd been away with the fairies like her mother before. I'll go and get a charm, she thought, and something for Darby to carry with him when he goes out because he'll want to do that all over again now he's done it once and everyone making a great palaver over it. Hail the conquering hero indeed.

Margarita grizzled in her sleep in the crib next to the bed. Sal put out her hand. The only sleep her mother got that night was bad sleep. She was still awake when Darby dragged himself from the bed and started shivering his way into his breeches, grumbling and belching to himself in front of the smouldering fire.

Sal sat up. 'I think I'll go and see Eliza Vesey,' she said.

'You awake?'

'I've not slept.'

'Ah, go back to sleep, love.'

The rain swept the roof.

'I've not *slept*.'

'Too rough to go out.'

She flopped back down again. 'You have me worried sick,' she said pettishly.

They were whispering so as not to wake the baby.

'Me?'

'You? You? Hear the innocent. After last night. Darby, you have me worried sick.'

188

'Oh,' he said, smiling, 'did you not enjoy the feast then?'

'You know what I mean!' She was up again. 'I don't want to lose you, Darby.' This hissed in a vexed and scolding way.

He went and sat on the side of the bed, grinning. 'Poor Sal,' he said, 'you're stuck with me a while yet, I'm afraid.'

'I'm going to see Eliza Vesey,' she said, 'She's got a head on her shoulders. *She'll* give me something to keep you at home.'

Darby laughed. 'That old sourmug,' he said, '*she* doesn't know anything. She was up seeing Samuel Cloverhill, you know.'

'Who was?'

'Eliza Vesey.'

'Was she? How do you know?'

He stood up and went to mess about with the fire, squatting with his back to her.

'Darby? Who told you that?'

'Martha Colgan,' he said quickly.

'You saw Martha Colgan?'

'The housekeeper, you know.' He turned from the fire.

'I know who she is. When did you see her?'

'I met her on the road.'

'When?'

'Last night.'

'What? At that time of night? You were stealing their turnips and you stopped for a chat with the housekeeper?'

'Well – she didn't know anything about it, it was on the high road, nothing wrong with that.'

'Oh, Darby! Didn't she think it was funny you being out and about in all the wet at that time of night?'

'Oh,' he said, imperturbable, 'I said I'd been looking for work and was late coming home.'

'What was *she* doing?'

189

'She'd been to see someone who was sick,' he said, standing and looking about as if searching for something with his eyes. 'A relative, I suppose.'

Sal was quiet for a moment, looking distant and thoughtful, then she said, 'Well, I hope you didn't get too close to her then, Darby.'

'No, no, no, the colic was all it was, she said. No fever.' He was pleased with himself. This was easy.

She thought for a while. 'You never mentioned seeing Martha Colgan last night,' she frowned.

'Did I not?'

'No.'

'Oh, well now,' he shrugged, 'I met her on the way there, you see, and I thought it best just to chat as if everything was normal; so I just said I was back from looking for work, and, and she said, I think she said, she was off seeing someone sick. I think her niece it was, and then she said that Eliza Vesey had been up to see Mr Cloverhill.'

'What for?'

'She didn't say.'

'Didn't you ask her?'

'She didn't know. I don't suppose she stands there with her ear to the door.' He sat briefly on the side of the bed, peering down at the sleeping Margarita.

'Do you think she looks flushed?' Sal whispered.

'No, no,' he said, 'she looks fine.'

He looked in on the children.

'They'll sleep awhile,' he said, 'you go back to sleep, love.'

'I haven't *been* to sleep.' Sal flung herself down again, sticking out her lower lip.

But after he'd gone, she finally did drift off, briefly and deeply, waking only when the boys started yelling at one another outside. They'd been up and heated the stirabout and fed little Eliza, and there was a horrible mess all over the floor

190

where they'd eaten. Now they'd gone out and left the back door open and it was freezing cold in the house and her head was aching. It had stopped raining though, and the wind had died down. She blinked and scraped sleep from the corners of her eyes with her fingernails. Through the open door she could see Young Darby, Mal and little Eliza playing on the old tree.

She sat up and shouted, 'Close the door!' and the sound woke Margarita, who was sleeping late. The boys stopped and looked towards her, but Eliza went on walking round and round the tree in her shabby white dress. So young and dirty the boys were, poor big-eared vagabonds, muddy bare feet hard on the knuckles of the tree. Were they mad not to feel the cold?

'Come in here!' she called.

Young Darby jumped down, splashing into the mire below. The earth under the slope from which the tree writhed out was boggy, heaving beneath his heels, and he tavered and smiled, the spit of his dad but thinner in the face. Setting her feet on the floor, Sal felt the cold about her ankles. 'Come in and close the door, all of you! Now!' she fairly shrieked this time. Margarita, who'd been frowning perplexedly at the light for some time, set up a surprisingly deep, throbbing kind of a wail and had to be picked up and stuck on the breast with no more ado. She snuffled and squalled at the teat, red-faced and angry. Sal stared fiercely into her face, looking for signs of illness.

'Blow up the fire,' she told Young Darby, who skulked in the threshold with a silly grin like his father's, Mal in tow. 'Eliza! In now!'

That girl was getting naughty.

'Scrub yourselves up a bit,' she told them when they were in and the door closed. 'We're going to see Eliza Vesey.'

'Do we have to?'

191

'Can I stay here?'

'And nearly set fire to the place like last time? Away and scratch. Darby, you wash you sister's hands and face.'

There was nothing left in the pot but she didn't care, she couldn't have eaten much anyway, her stomach still felt uncomfortable from last night when she'd had too much. What a laugh. She washed her face and scrubbed her neck, then wrapped them all up severely and tied Margarita on with her shawl and set off with them up and over the top, telling them the walk would do them good. It wasn't too bad today, the worst of it had blown out in the night but little squalls still sprang up out of nowhere every now and then, racing visibly across the billowing hillside, which seemed alive like the skin of a horse. She was going to Eliza Vesey to get a charm if she could, or something at least to make her feel she was heading off the fever.

When she reached the Vesey house, the first thing she saw was Phelim clearing up around the dung-heap. His boy was with him, shovelling with a little spade.

'Hello, Phelim,' she called over the wall.

His head shot up and for a moment he looked confused.

'Oh, Sal,' he said, 'how are you keeping these days?'

'Never better.' She smiled very widely.

He gave a nervous laugh. She thought he was sweet, poor thing. He was looking grey and washed-out. He still liked her, she knew by the bashful sideways looks he kept sliding over her.

'Eliza at home?'

'She's inside, just go on in, Sal.'

But she lingered a moment or two. 'And how's the wee sweet boy?' she asked Jamie.

He looked away.

'He's grand,' said Phelim, 'say hello, Jamie one.'

Jamie mumbled.

192

'Not talking to me today, Jamie?' Sal put her hands on her knees and leaned down to smile in his face.

He looked at his shovel.

'Ach, he's a vagabond.' Phelim gave the side of his head a fond swipe.

The two big rough boys, Young Darby and Mal, ran off round the back. He wasn't to play with them. His mother called them hooligans. He and little Eliza stood looking at one another. The baby was awake and wide-eyed, quietly gazing over her mother's shoulder at Phelim.

'Look at her,' said Phelim, smiling, reaching out one long finger and stroking it swiftly down the baby's cheek, 'anyone can see where her mother gets her eyes.'

Sal laughed. 'You've got that the wrong way round, Phelim,' she said.

'No, I haven't.' His eyes threw her a quick humorous look and he laughed the nervous laugh again, which made her smile even more.

11

Look at her out there flirting with him. She doesn't even know she's doing it. She'd flirt with a donkey, that one. Not so round in the face any more, is she? Anyway, she can flash her eyes at him as often as she likes, he knows his place. That would have been a terrible match, that would. She's too good-looking for him, he's too nice and soft-bred for her.

Those boys are making a terrible din out the back there. That older one should be on the Scheme. Tuppence they're paying the children. But they've always spoiled theirs, the Quinns. Here she comes now. So what's she after this time? I meet her at the door.

'What do you want?' I fold my arms and lean on the door-post. I'm not pleased she's here, why should I pretend?

'Hello, Eliza,' she says, pleasantly enough.

'Oh, well, come in.'

It's cold. We're going very easy on the fuel. She sits at the table and her baby looks over her shoulder. The pink-eye sucks its thumb. In comes Jamie and stands gawping at it.

'Close the door, love,' I tell him.

'This woman, Annie Porter,' she says. 'Have you heard?'

'Course I've heard.'

'Is it the fever, do you think?'

'How would I know? I've not seen the woman.'

She looks at me closely, frowning. 'Are you all right, Eliza?'

I sigh. I'm not discussing this in front of Jamie. 'Run up to Granda, love,' I tell him. 'Away!'

But he doesn't want to go, gets as far as the ladder and stands there kicking his toes against the lowest rung.

'Take little Eliza with you, sweet boy,' says Sal, giving her child a push.

'Don' wanna,' growls the elf. Her voice is soft grey and furry like a catkin.

'Oh, Eliza!'

The child's thin white face crumples, then straightens out into a savage glare, directed at the floor. Her mother grabs and hugs her fiercely, her threadbare cloak falling open. 'What am I to do with you at all, my little funny one?' she cries. 'Go on and play now with Jamie and Granda. Go on!'

The child shrugs angrily.

'She never used to be like this,' Sal says wearily, looking at me with desolate dark eyes. 'I don't know, I can't seem to do right with her any more. They've got me run ragged, this lot.'

I can see it. She's got dirt in the corners of her eyes, and a big grey tidemark round her throat. 'Of course you can,' I say. 'This is how you do it.' And I put on my voice of authority: 'Eliza, do as your mother tells you.'

That's all I have to say for her to go, slouching sullenly across the floor to the ladder's foot. It's the same with dogs and horses. If you know you're the boss, they know it too. Sal Quinn's the weak one. And here's me, a brown small thing, got all the strength.

'It's the new one,' I say when she's gone, 'her nose is out of joint.'

'I suppose so.' She puts her hair back.

'You look tired.'

'Ha! I didn't get a wink last night. Not a wink.'

'She's not sleeping?' I nod at the baby, which has fallen asleep with its head on one side.

'Oh, she sleeps. It's me doesn't.'

'They're all cranky these days,' I say. 'What can I do for you?'

'I'm wanting something to keep away the fever, Eliza,' she says, 'if there is any such thing. This woman Annie Porter's at no distance.'

I sit down with her at the table, clasping my hands before me and giving a long sigh. What does she want from me? She starts to speak again but I hold up my hand for silence, and close my eyes. I need to think. She has a superstitious regard for my silence, she thinks I'm doing some magic, but I'm letting my sleepiness have its five minutes while I think what to do.

And what if there were fever at Kildarragh? What if it were at Boolavoe and Lissadoon and Kildoran and every little town-land between here and Kenmare? What do they want me to do? Am I God? Do I have the power of life and death? Can I think the world well, make the potatoes flourish again? Because I have the secret for myself, they all want it. Through the worst of times, my mother kept the fever away from us all, and she always found food. She had something very strong. What killed her was not a fever or a chill, it was some great malignancy inside, too powerful for any charm. Before she died she gave me the strong bag that lies always against my chest bone, the size of half my thumb and tightly sewn shut, never to be opened. I have no idea what's inside but it feels like powder and smells of must and faint spice, and because of this, all in this household are protected, even that old fool upstairs. But I have nothing like this to give anyone. I open my eyes.

Sal Quinn belittles me with her very presence. I am weakened, and that is a thing I cannot have and that is why I do not like her. This seems a great realisation. I also realise it's not her fault. She means me no harm, at least not more than she means to any. I hate her because she is as she is and I am as I am, and that is that. Such a hate is not proper and therefore I must, with all my might, do right by Sal Quinn.

I smile. 'What will I do, Sal,' I say, 'if the fever comes here? What will *I* do!'

She just looks at me.

'Do you think I have power over life and death?'

'No, Eliza,' she replies pertly, 'but I do think you're very clever.'

'Don't I have enough on my hands without having to nurse people through more sickness?' I say testily. 'Can I work miracles?'

'Only our Lord ever worked miracles on this earth, Eliza.' This is said in no pious way. She dares – she actually dares – to put her still cold hand on mine. If she knew how my innards cringed. I dislike to be touched, unless I specifically invite it, but I do not withdraw my hand even though it wants to curl up and creep away from her.

'Eat ramsons,' I say. 'Pierce an orange if you can get hold of one – ha! – put an onion under the bed, maybe it'll work, maybe not. I'm not God. I can't change the world.'

'I know that,' she says quietly, looking down.

I draw my hand away.

'I thought a pishogue,' she says, 'it's better than nothing.'

'I can give you a pishogue.' I stand, the fire needs blowing up. 'Come back tomorrow.'

I can give her any number of pishogues. But if the fever comes, it comes.

'You're an angel, Eliza,' she says warmly with her sudden big-toothed smile.

They'll all be after me. And then when a number have died, they'll stop.

'There's another thing,' she says, 'I'm a bit worried about Darby.'

I turn with the bellows in my hand, raising my eyebrows.

'I don't want him getting in any trouble. I don't know, I worry about him, not that he's a . . .' she trails off as if she thinks she might have said too much.

So what's he been up to? Come to that, when is it Tadhg

197

ends up on a gibbet? No, no, don't think that. Never, never, never, not Tadhg.

'I don't know,' she sighs, 'just some small thing, something to keep him safe or to stop him coming down with something, some . . .' she trails off again, looking sideways towards me at the fire. She has a sly look, or is it me imagining things? I'll pick her some centaury from up on the rath, steep it well. If she pours the water over him she'll feel better. I can't say it will protect him, not if he's determined to be a fool. I can't say anything will. But if he's a good boy it might just help him, I suppose.

'Come back tomorrow,' I say, pumping on the bellows and blowing up a cloud of dust. 'I'll have you something. Jamie! Come down now and bring little Eliza. Careful on the ladder, the pair of you.'

Like pale spiders, their thin grey legs, their curling toes coming down the ladder. Oh, my Jamie. Where have I been all this time? My blood runs cold. He is a thin young thing not getting enough, his belly gurgles all day. Those old knee breeches he has on, ragged, like a gypsy. What is happening to you, Eliza? Where are you while this unfolds? Come back. Come back from wherever you've gone. A year ago it wasn't like this.

'Well, then,' Sal Quinn says, standing at the foot of the ladder to greet the white-legged grub. She holds out her open, welcoming arms, and the girl jumps from the third rung straight into them. My teeth clench.

'I'd worry about that one if I were you, Sal.' It's out before I know I've said it, before I even know I've thought it. Her head swings round and she glares at me, a child on the front, a babe on the back.

'What do you mean?' she says in a low voice, covering the child's ears with her hands.

'Don't look at me like that,' I say, 'anyone can see she's

sickly. Oh, don't worry! I'm not talking about the fever, I'm talking about the look of her. When did you last see her laugh? There's a spark gone.'

Sal is studying her daughter's face anxiously. The child, like a cat washing itself, is fussing its hand about its ear. 'It was me told you she'd changed,' she says.

'Of course. You'd be the first to know. That's all I meant. She's been put out by the new one, that's all. Give her time. I'll give her a tonic.' I sigh. 'So that's my work cut out for me till tomorrow.'

Sal puts the child down and hoists the baby higher on her back. 'Well, if you're too busy, Eliza,' she says, a touch huffy.

'Not at all. But don't come before noon.'

I could have said more. I could have said what a scowling joyless creature the child's becoming.

'Keep her spirits up if you can,' I say. 'Don't you be standing for her moods.'

She walks out and stands in the yard, calling her boys to her like a hawker. She has another word or two for Phelim while she's leaving, another bright smile. Watching from the window I see him nod and grin, hear the murmured soft tones of him but not the words. Jamie comes up behind me. 'I didn't talk to her,' he says.

'What?'

'Granda tickled her. He called her a bonnie little gossun, but I didn't talk to her.'

Sal Quinn is walking away with a weary tread, the girl whingeing round her while she shifts Margarita to the front, to give her back a rest, I suppose. Young Darby takes his sister's hand but she shrugs him off. Mal tramps hunch-shouldered along the top of the ditch.

'I'm not talking to her any more,' he says, 'because you don't like her.'

Now, how does he know that? He picks things up, that boy.

'What do you think of her, Jamie?' I ask him, as if he were the same age as me.

'She's not nice.' He shrugs. 'She smells stinky.'

'Well, they're not as clean as us, love. Come on, let's get you all cleaned up nice, shall we?'

The water's only lukewarm but it'll do. I take a cloth and rub it all over his face and behind his ears, down his neck inside his collar; he complains it's running down inside. 'Never mind,' I say, 'never mind that,' and think that now I've started I may as well go the whole hog, and tell him to get his clothes off and we'll shake them out and air them a bit, he can put his nightie on for now and sit by the fire, it'll be up and roaring in a while. Jamie doesn't want to do this. He says it's too early for his nightie, so I tell him if he's a good boy and does what I say I'll wrap him up in my shawl and we'll have a little session, just the two of us by the fire, with singing and talking. That's when Phelim comes lumbering in from the yard bringing in the cold, and spoils everything.

'Gah, it's freezing,' he says, going to the fire and leaning over holding out his hands. 'What did Sal want?'

'The usual. Something for nothing.'

'Well, don't let her take advantage, love,' he says mildly, turning and smiling down at Jamie. 'There's worse off than them.'

'I know. She's scared of the fever.' I whisper this last not to upset the boy.

'Aye, well . . .' He lights his pipe.

'Well, the Quinns are no more likely to get it than anyone else. I don't know why she thinks she should be special, what if the whole lot of them come wanting stuff? I've told her, I can't do the impossible.'

'Of course you can't. She doesn't expect you to.'

'You'd be surprised what they expect.'

'Ah, she knows what's what, Sal does.'

'Are you in now or out?' I ask him.

'Out again in a minute after a warm and a smoke.' He stands smiling with his hands behind his back in front of the fire. 'Very cheerful, isn't she?' he says.

'Who?'

'Sal.'

'Is she? I thought she was looking rather miserable.'

'Did you?'

Very familiar, it seems to me, the way he talks of her.

'What do you mean by cheerful?' I ask.

'Cheerful. You know, cheerful. The way she is. Smiling and so on, you know.'

She was run ragged, fed up, tired. All smiles for him, of course, a man. She's one of those.

'Well, she didn't look cheerful to me. Go on, Jamie! We're airing Jamie's clothes.' I lower my voice, adding in a whisper, 'I'm checking for lice.'

Phelim knocks his pipe against the chimney breast.

'And we'll wash your hair, Jamie,' I call. 'Phelim, can you fill the big bucket?'

Yes, let's make the most of it. As I am rolling up my sleeves, I am unsure whether it's the fire or something in me that is making my face burn so; then I realise it's a variety of fury, something unaccountable for the present but which must have its way. It's so big it tightens my chest and blocks my ears and turns the world before my eyes red for a moment. Ah, but that's only the fire, burning and popping now, sizzling and darting on the small sticks I placed on top to entice the flames. Yes, let's make the most of it, my unaccountable hatred.

Phelim goes out for the water, humming happily to himself. Bucked him up a treat, she has.

201

'Jamie! Hurry!' I call up. Times when I've sat for ages gazing into the fire, chewing my lips and the skin inside my cheeks, hating Sal Quinn. A feeling like that doesn't listen to reason. Strangely, it is enjoyable, though it shakes my soul and sickens me. No, not enjoyable: necessary, as if suddenly the veil that is normally drawn between me and my true feelings is rent like the veil of the temple. Then I know that for most of the time I am lost, though safe enough, behind the veil. Now in my anger I am real. And an image comes strongly into my head, the picture of the woman on Samuel Cloverhill's wall, reclining open-legged on a couch, staring back at me. She makes me think of Juliander, who can do anything, even that. Even that. She can lie back slowly upon the couch, completely naked, and she can stare you out while she does it. Juliander lives on the other side of the veil from me but I can call her up. Come through to me, Juliander, I can say, I am too safe here without you.

A sudden clear day. The village is a single line under the mountain. Everything is blue and still, many blues, the mountainline vibrating, too bright to look at directly. It's such a lovely day I have to go for a walk, I must, I can't bear this house any longer. After all you have to take your chances.

Me and Jamie walk down to the strand. It's so strange. People are up and about, walking the lanes. We keep meeting others, and we always smile and nod and reassure one another, saying: this is the change coming, God bless and protect us all. Surely the bad weather can't last forever. Then we'll get the crop back and all those poor people up-country will stop dying. We've had our deaths here now of course. There's always deaths. In Lissadoon I meet Nan Fox just coming out of the shop with her ashplant and a wild grey look about her. More and more like a witch she looks. She's suffering on the Scheme, poor old Nan.

'Did you hear Annie Porter died?' she says. 'They've boarded the place up and the people are passing food in through the window.'

Nan's one of those who loves to be the first to tell you anything. She's enjoying this, I can tell, though her face shows no sign.

'So it *was* the fever,' I say.

It's here. We must all walk carefully. I look across to where Jamie's climbing about on the wall, making sure he can't hear.

'It's the others in the house I can't get out of my mind,' she says. 'Imagine. There's three in there.'

'Is she buried?'

'Oh yes. It's the typhus. They took her out straight away, they had to, they brought her out on a hurdle and buried her in the cemetery, but the others had to stay in. Please God it won't spread.'

'How many in there? Three?'

'One's only nine. Nine years old! Poor baby!' Barren Nan was always a weeper over children. She starts now, her watery grey eyes turning pink and small. I wouldn't have her with me at a birthing if there was a chance of a death. She'd be stupid. You can't be stupid at a time like that, it doesn't do. 'He's in there with the sister and the aunt. The sister's sick, they say.'

'It's hard on them.'

What can you say? It could be me, me and Jamie. Under my cloak, my palm is enclosing the little blue bag that rests upon my breast bone. It seems a small warm heart is beating within; my own heart, quite separate, beats a different rhythm beneath.

'They're putting the food in on a long shovel,' Nan says. 'Isn't it horrible?'

I shake my head. 'Horrible.'

She goes home towards Kildarragh, and we go on through

the village. I'm frightened. I have had fear many, many times. I know what to do. I open up my soul and let the fear have its way, as with the anger. It is another twitch of the veil. And this fear is very strong, rolling in like the ocean, the last wave, the one that finishes you. I'm coming, I'm coming, I'm coming, fear says. Standing where the village begins, I'm made a statue by fear.

'Horrible times,' I whisper.

Jamie is a child in horrible times.

I'll walk no further. The fear is in the village. I turn my back on it and make for home. If we sit tight at home we'll do well, if they don't all start coming to me, wanting this, wanting that, as if I can do anything when the great wave comes. Walking in. Hello, Eliza! Just marching into my house the way they do. I've got this awful runny eye, Eliza. I've got this big toe that throbs. This ache here. This itch there. This funny kind of feeling in my jaw.

The fear's in me all the way home. It's not for me, or even for Jamie alone, it's for everything I've ever known, Boolavoe and Lissadoon and Kildarragh and all the little townlands beyond. It's for all the faces I've ever seen. Still, there's nothing to be done. Aren't we only weak creatures after all, waiting like the spider for some hand to brush the web? Everyone dies. Some die worse than others. My mother had a very hard death, a lot of pain, and she was granted the time to know it. And she was a good woman. If that's what's waiting for you, there's no trick in the world will help.

Phelim's cleared a space at the side of the yard. 'That's where I'm going to put the dairy,' he says, turning his head as we come in at the gate. 'It'll be a lot of digging.'

'Annie Porter died,' I say, walk in the house and hang up my cloak.

12

Fever makes you lock the door. I never used to. First I started doing it because of all the theft there is nowadays – they'll come in and take your food out of the pot while it's cooking, and run away. It's not happened to us, but it's happened to plenty. I don't want to lock my door against hungry people. I've never done it in my life, and I've always given where it was needed. But what can you do?

Let them knock and I can decide whether or not they get into my house. You can't give to everyone; it's just not possible, there's too many now.

I don't go into Boolavoe any more. I was sickened the last time I went. I could never take Jamie there now, and he used to love coming into town with me.

'When can we go into town, Ma?' he says. 'You said we could.'

Seven next birthday, poor mite, and stuck here with my father all the time, and *he's* up and about and getting under my feet again all the time, wouldn't you just know it; they're dropping like flies and *he's* getting better. It's a mad world. How could I let Jamie see those children who don't do what children do, don't run or smile or play or even cry very much, who just stand there with their tin cans empty and their eyes dull as dust? All these people losing their cabins, running before sickness. There's middlemen less soft than Cloverhill putting them out by the dozen not thirty miles north of here. And in amongst them, standing around outside Fallon's Yard, I see faces from round here, faces I've known, ones who've dug alongside Phelim for Lomas, who've tipped their hats at me in the lane and sometimes come walking all day to see me and get a potion. And there they are queueing to get into Fallon's Yard with all the strangers, and when their eyes meet mine there is a terrible joining and a quick veiling, and then all goes blank because now everything is different.

The weather continues foul, even worse than last winter, I think, or at least it feels that way but maybe it's because this day and night battering has gone on for so long. It accompanies our work and our rest. We've grown quiet, beaten into submission. Life has diminished to a small round of necessary actions. I remember summer days. Hot days. But most I miss the spring and autumn, certain days that could be either. We've had no spring, summer, autumn. Only winter. It's as if winter has won and will never lift again. We are sometimes very cold, and this worries me more than hunger. We always have turnips and meal, but sometimes there's no more than a wisp to warm us because we have decided to ration, and we know it's wise. But it's hard. We'll cut turf next year. They say the Scheme's coming to an end so there'll be labour if they don't all die first. We had to sell our big eiderdown too, though that's a small thing compared to what other's are having to put up with. We can do without it. Last thing every night I throw Phelim's big coat over the other two coverlets, the big blue one and the lumpy quilty one we've still got. They're fine. It did look nice though, our big eiderdown. It had a pattern of purple flowers and came down from Phelim's parents who died of the pneumonia together under it. Fancy that, and now it's gone to strangers. Phelim took it into town and sold it to a hawker, and he brought home with him a newspaper that said they were thinking of finishing off the Scheme, that there's been people rioting over food in Cork, and that in

206

some areas the famine's completely out of control. I don't want to read about it. The word famine makes me think of the famine in Pharoah's time, in the Bible, where Joseph's brothers come and beg him for food. And he says go back and get my father, or something like that, doesn't he? He could save his own family but he couldn't save the whole of Israel, could he? No one could.

There've been fevers over towards Kildoran, the relapsing fever that comes and goes in waves. They've been eating such rubbish, you see. Worms. Crab apples. Mice. It's getting like that here too. Nan came to me crying because Peader slaughtered their old dog Mick that used to be always sitting panting by the door with the ticks all round its eyes. I had to laugh at that, after she'd gone, of course. Poor old Mick must have been tough as old leather. I'll bet they were picking him out of their teeth for days.

'Ma,' says Jamie, swinging listlessly on the doorframe, 'I want to go out.'

'Run out onto the mounds, Jamie. See if you can see a hare.'

But there are no hares.

We used to see a lot of hares, they used to box on the mound. When do you see a hare these days, or even a rabbit? Pretty things, they are. I wish they'd come back.

People pass by our house, coming back from town with bags of meal on their backs. This twilight, strangely, is quite beautiful, the wind has died down and there's just a gentle steady rain catching the last of the light. I'm out in the yard watching a family go by, a father and mother and four scrubby lads, all barefoot, each with a precious tin can. Their heads are bowed against the rain and they plod on at a steady pace, getting wet, enduring like horses pulling a plough, or sheep standing against a wall in the blast. They too are beautiful, their shadows through the rain becoming softer and more ghostly as they walk. I love a moment like that, when all is well though all is not.

When I turn there is another ghost, close to me in the yard, but I don't jump or scream. I have no fear of ghosts.

'Tadhg.' Tadhg walks past here regular on his way back from work to the shebeen. Curly's pregnant! What a time for it. She'll have to have more milk. We're grand for milk, we've been very careful, so I told him: Bring a can and I'll fill it up for you.

'Nan Fox is down with the fever,' he says.

'Nan!'

'She's down. Peader came to work on his own. Said she'd caught a bad cold and was feeling too weak to walk over. And then he gets home and finds her raving. Burning hot.'

'Oh, not poor old Nan again. Were you up there?'

'Just come from there.'

'Did you see her?'

'Jesus, Eliza, I wouldn't go in. I was in Darby's and they were full of it.'

'I'll have to go up.'

Then Tadhg does a very strange thing. 'Jesus, Eliza,' he says again, and takes me into his arms and hugs me very hard and slowly, 'You're such a little thing, you're nothing but bones. You've got yourself to think of, love, you have to take care of your sweet little self.' I feel like a child, held there against his broad chest, my ear flattened and his heartbeat thumping away in it like an army on a brisk march. He lifts me high off my feet and then puts me down.

'Oh, I'm all right, Tadhg,' I say, 'It can't touch me.'

He shakes his head. 'You're not invincible, Eliza.'

Neither of us mentions what has just happened. His bear's embrace has quickened me and I laugh. 'I am.'

He smiles. 'No, you're not.'

'Don't worry about me, Tadhg,' I say lightly, 'you worry about yourself.'

'I do.' He turns out of the gate and sighs deeply, looking down the lane. 'What a time to be bringing a mouth into the world. Know how many deaths now, Eliza?' He sighs. 'Six in Carraroe, eight or nine in Malahies, Barney Kelly's child in Scarran last night, and God knows how many in Kildoran and Boolavoe. What's happening, Eliza? What's happening?'

'There were a lot of deaths when I was little,' I say, 'my mother used to talk about it. We went round all the houses, she always took me with her, and not a thing touched us. Don't you worry about me, Tadhg.'

'But I do.'

I laugh and shrug. 'Worry then.'

Next morning I go up to Kildarragh for the first time in ages. It was bracing going over the top, over the old rath, with the sea all whipped up and the air a mist. I looked down on the Quinns' house. I'd call there first, get the lie of the land. Sal must have seen me coming because she's out waiting for me when I arrive, so eager to talk that she's bustling towards me up the track before I'm even over the stile.

'Have you heard anything from Cloverhill about the May rents?' she says.

Well, that's nice, isn't it? No time for a how nice to see you after all this time, Eliza. Nothing about poor Nan.

'Of course I haven't. Why would I?'

'Oh, I just thought you might have heard something.'

'Well, I haven't.'

She stands there frowning at me. 'Because Alma heard he was short of money and he might . . .'

'Of course he's short of money. Who isn't? So? He was short of money last year too.'

'She was talking to Martha Colgan's niece. He owes a lot apparently. His daughter's got to leave her school.'

I laugh. 'Oh, the hardship!'

Sal laughs too. 'I know, but . . .'

'What do you think, Sal? Think he's on the turn? He's not put anyone out yet.'

'I don't trust any of them!' she says, suddenly vicious.

'It doesn't really depend on Cloverhill anyway. It depends on Tarlton.' Which is, of course, true, though none of us ever think it.

'Nan's sick,' she says.

'I know. I'm going to see her.'

'Are you and Phelim sowing this year?'

'Darby after work, is he?'

I look at her hard in the eye but she hasn't got the grace to blush. That's it then. Soon as the Scheme ends they'll all come crawling back.

'He will be,' she says.

'We'll sow a few turnips,' I say, 'I don't know what help we'll be wanting, you'd have to ask Phelim.'

She nods, compressing her lips. We'll try the potatoes again too, even though Father Buckley's giving it out that no one should sow them any more. Anyway, Phelim wants to have another go with the poreens. We split them yesterday, but there's more eye than flesh about them. She offers me a cup of tea and I go in and stand looking around, speechless for a minute. It's disgusting. Look at the *state* of this place. The queer girl sits dribbling and drooly-eyed, wailing listlessly in the middle of the bare floor. The boys are just squatting with their dirty toes splayed in the dust, idle. That boy Mal never closes his mouth. Adenoids. The baby's asleep on a pile of rags.

'You need to clean this place up, Sal,' I say. 'What's it like? What's it like for Darby getting home from work?'

'He doesn't mind.' She sulks as she makes tea. 'Eliza, do shut up,' she says to her daughter, her whole face wincing.

They must have sold everything. Or pawned it. There's

nowhere to sit down but on the flat straw mattress, full of bugs probably. Oh, well. I sit. What I should do, what I *would* do if it were any other child, I would pick that whining girl up from the floor and walk about jollying her and shushing her up for her poor tired mother.

'What's the matter with her?' I ask.

'She's hungry,' Sal says.

The tea is weak but very hot and surprisingly refreshing. She sits there sullen-faced with her hair uncombed and hanging, just sits, saying nothing, doing nothing.

'So how are things with Nan?' I ask.

'Bad, it seems.'

'Any sign of a rash?'

'He didn't say. Peader told Matty she was rambling in her mind and sweating like a pig. I daren't go down there. I didn't want Darby to go to work today. He said Peader seemed fine yesterday, just the way he always is.'

'He probably is fine. It's the way of it. Some get it, some don't. The devil knows why.'

I can't take my eyes off the girl. There's nothing to her, no substance. Her mouth gapes, gummy like a crone; her milk teeth are falling out and nothing's coming to replace them. And that awful endless droning whine. I should take a good look at her but I can't.

'Oh, come on,' says Sal, reaching down and suddenly scooping her up into her lap. 'Come on, my little kitten.' The child moans into her mother's chest, and Sal croons, stroking down her wispy fair hair and rubbing her cheek. And there they rock together, crooning and moaning softly, till Margarita stirs on the floor and gives out a few sharp coughing little yelps, and Sal hands the girl over to Young Darby. 'Well, well, well,' she whispers, puckering her lips and seizing the baby under the oxters, 'you've had a lovely, lovely sleep, haven't you, my love?'

Little Eliza goes quiet, cramming her thumb in and slumping against Young Darby. I leave them to it. There's milk in my basket but that's for Nan. I put something in it to do her good if she can get it down. We'll see. Sal hardly glances up as I leave. The fine mist still shimmers in the air before my eyes, and the waves dance, and the bright white clouds run towards the sun. I shiver. I don't suppose it could be that the weather's on the turn, but something's different. Something in my nostrils and my bones. There's no one about. I stand still for a while at the turn of the bend, with the Quinn house above me and the cluster of dwellings below. There's no movement between the cabins, not a dog or a cat, and no creature stirring on the mountainside. The people are all inside, hiding from the spores of the air. I stride down, breathing deeply.

I knock and walk in. I can smell it at once. Poor Peader's sitting in the corner with his sharp pointed knees sticking straight up out of his britches and his great bony wrists up on either side of his face. He's been crying. 'Oh God in heaven, Eliza,' he says, 'thank God you're here.'

Here's the good wise woman come to set all to rights.

'Any rash?' I say.

Nan's a smelly heap on the mattress, twitching and mumbling in a fever sleep.

'I don't think so, Eliza.'

'What do you mean, you don't think so? There is or there isn't. Haven't you looked?'

'She won't eat anything!' he complains, 'She won't talk sense!'

Useless.

'Has she had a pee?'

'Not since . . . I don't know.'

I sit down beside her and say kindly, 'Now then, how goes it, my Nanny?'

212

She opens her eyes, blinking as if there's a very bright light, snorts and sniffles like an infant. Her lips, thin, white and wormy, champ and burble. There's blood on them. Gingerly I lift her upper lip as if she's a dog. It's the gums, they're rotten.

Peader's got up and is hovering behind me uncertainly.

'There's no rash,' I say. 'It's not the typhus anyway.'

'Oh thank you, thank you, thank you, thank you, Eliza!' he rants, as if it were anything to do with me.

'Are you managing for food?'

'Oh, we're coping, Eliza, coping you know. They're good people, they'll not let us starve.' He grins pathetically.

'She doesn't need to eat. Just keep giving her sips of this. I'll bring you some more in a couple of days. It's just thin whey milk with a few herbs in it.'

'God bless you, Eliza.'

'Oh, He does,' I say, and smile, and then he falls down beside me and blurts: 'they'll not have me back on the Scheme.'

'That's the way of it, Peader,' I say.

Nothing else I can do.

I leave, stand out in the cold and look at the sea. It may actually turn out a nice day. Still not a soul abroad. It's not the typhus, so she might pull through though I doubt it. If she were younger or stronger perhaps, but not Nan. I suppose it's a good thing she has no children. No orphans to worry about. Peader though, it'll go hard with him.

I go back via the shebeen but there's no life there either, and it's not a time for paying calls. I'll go back and wash myself all over and wash everything I have on.

13

The world's gone mad. They're putting things in to Peader through the window. Food. Water. I just walk in, I walk in wherever I want. There are others down with it now in Kildarragh but they've left me alone. They know I'll only tend our old cottiers, the Sheehans and the Scanlons and the Quinns and the Foxes. You have to draw the line somewhere. The Sheehans are a terrible family for diarrhoea. Too many greens. The Scanlons all seem to be fine, even young Becky, and as for the Quinns, I don't know why they don't put that boy of theirs on the Scheme while they still can, buy a bit of flour. Margarita's a healthy baby, I wonder if they're giving it all to her and letting the others go hungry. Sal wants to be careful. She wants to be careful of that girl. I'm thinking there is a thing up there I dare not name, in the house of the Quinns. Now more than ever I'm realising the truth, I've been lying and thinking about it, just lying and thinking about it all night long unable to drop off. Phelim keeps twitching in his sleep. She's come from out there, up high, the reeds and starry pools and rocks. But she doesn't scare me. I'm not scared of any of them, they don't scare me at all, and they never scared my ma. There's only one world and we have to share it with them, as long as you remember that, you'll not go wrong. And these things from out there come and look at us sometimes, and they have a certain look, a certain steadiness of gaze that cuts you to the bone just like the butcher's knife; and they have a certain smile. And that's one up there in Darby's house as sure as I can be.

But Nan though. Poor old Nan died hard, and was the first of ours to go at Kildarragh. There'd been three more down below towards the shebeen, people I did not know well, but Nan was the first of ours. We kept her going for three weeks, me and Peader between us. She did well for a while and got her senses back, but then she starts lapsing and being sick again. She'd been dead three days before I found out, and Peader was in there with her and no one would let him out and no one would go in. Last time I saw her she was sitting up. She'd had some milk with a sop of bread and she kept it down. I couldn't say there was any colour in her face but then there never was with Nan. She looked as if she was at death's door even when she was well. But she was sitting up and talking sense, and she even laughed. 'Eliza,' she said, 'it's a good job you're half gentry,' and she laughed. She meant because I couldn't catch the fever. By gentry she meant the other people that live in the Middle Kingdom. I didn't laugh with her because you shouldn't make light about things like that, but she meant no harm. She asked after Phelim and Jamie and my father.

I really wasn't worried about Nan, not to any great extent, I don't think I gave her much of a thought over the next day or so, and then we got some very bad winds that lifted the corner of the roof of the shed where we'd had the turnips, so that was a lot of trouble; and it was Sunday when Phelim came in and said he'd heard from Darby Quinn that she was dead but still in the house and no one doing anything about it because they were all scared.

'Peader can take her to Lissadoon,' I said.

'They won't let him out.'

'Who won't?'

'The ones nearest. They've built turf up over the door. They say the house smells of fever. They're still putting food through though.'

'The house smells of Nan,' I said. 'What do they expect? She can't stay there.'

I was for going straight up and sorting it out, but for the first time Phelim showed doubt. 'You're not your mother,' he says to me, but I don't think he was seriously worried. He knows me well enough by now. Still, we had an argument of sorts, I suppose. It was my da stuck up for me strangely enough.

'Give it up, Phelim,' he says, 'she knows what she's doing.'

Then Phelim says an unforgivable thing: 'Think of Jamie.'

As if I'm not thinking of him day and night!

'Do you think,' I said, 'that if there was even the slightest shadow of a threat to that boy I'd take the risk? Do you think I'd even step out of that door? They could be dying in their droves and I'd not lift a finger.'

He looked at me with his serious grey eyes searching, and I stared right back as firm as rock.

'I believe you,' he said faintly after a time.

'It's you that brings him home with his cheek ripped open,' I muttered as I went out to call Jamie to me. There he is on top of the mound, turning and looking back at me with his small surly face. He gets cross with me nowadays: I no longer take him to town, I leave him behind when I visit the townlands. Last time he thumped me in the back. But he's all right with his daddy, and this cannot be put off.

'That's not fair.' Phelim speaks at my ear. 'That was years ago. That wasn't my fault.'

I turn round and give him a kiss. 'That's enough now, Phelim. There's plenty of stirabout in the big pot. Don't let the old man grab it all.'

And I'm off to Kildarragh.

They're all in their houses and it's a lovely day at last, smoke curling up thinly here and there from the odd chimney. The silence chills me. I've thrown back my hood. How long is it since I've been able to throw back my hood and feel

216

the air? When I get to Nan's house I stand and look. Beyond is Flynn's and John Michael's and Bat Sheehan's, Matty's cousin. The door of Nan's house is all stuffed up with sods, and all the windows apart from one small one on the end. I stand there with my wet feet growing cold on the rocky ground, staring at Nan and Peader's barricaded house, and can't believe what's happening. I never saw anything like this in my life before. How long I stand and stare I do not know, but suddenly my temper's gone.

I run and knock on Flynn's door. The door opens and Mary Flynn's face peers fiercely through the gap.

'I want the Fox's cabin opening up now,' I say, imperious, 'tell Larry.'

I go on and call out the Sheehans and John Michael and Tim Felix and his crew, and they all come out shamefaced and stand at a safe distance, making excuses.

'It's all right for you, Mrs Vesey,' Bat Sheehan says, 'you don't have to live alongside; now that makes all the difference.'

'We all know it doesn't touch you, Eliza,' says Mary Flynn in an aggrieved voice, 'but there's children living here, you know.'

'I have a child,' I say.

'So you do,' says she, 'and he doesn't have to live next door to a fever house, does he?'

I shout at them. 'No one's asking you to go in or touch anything. You let that man out now to bury his wife and get himself to the fever hospital if that's what he has to do. You think it's healthy to leave corpses lying around?'

'It's not exactly something we like, Mrs Vesey,' says John Michael, a shy, ugly man with a shock of ginger hair.

'Here,' I say, 'who'll go down to Tadhg O'Donnell's and ask him to knock up a coffin as fast as he can and bring it up here?'

John Michael twists his lip. 'I'll go,' he says.

'Tell him it's not a work of art. It's a box big enough for Nan, and it's needed now.'

I don't think even then they would have made a move to pull down the wall of sods if I had not put them to shame and started doing it with my own hands. Then one by one the men set to.

'That's enough, Mrs Vesey,' Tim Felix says gently, touching my arm, 'this is no work for you. You go and have a sup of tea now while we clear this. But we'll not do any more than clear the door.'

'That's all you have to do.'

When the door's clear they all vanish. I feel as if I am at the mouth of the tomb of Lazarus, and have a sudden impulse to lean forward and call in a sonorous voice: 'Lazarus, come forth!' This I do, and I giggle as I go in. It is very dark inside and the smell from Nan is sickly sweet and evil though not as strong as I had feared. Nevertheless, it forces bile up through my gullet. I stand in the bit of light from the doorway. 'Peader!' I call softly, 'Peader!'

There's nothing, but then as my eyes are somewhat adjusting I hear a scuffling like the sound of mice and he looms towards me through the shadows. 'I'm not sick, Eliza,' he says in a high quivering voice, 'you mustn't be afraid, I'll not hurt you.'

'Out of this bad air,' I say, 'come on now,' and out we go.

He's very dizzy from the light and the fresh air. His eyes and mouth screw up like a baby's, and his knees give way till he sinks down on the ground with a faint moan, head in hands.

'Take your time now, Peader.' My hand on his shoulder, whispering. 'Take your time, there's all the time you want.'

Slowly he eases down till he's lying on his face against the earth. He's not hot, he's tranced.

'She took bad again, Eliza,' he says, eyes closed, fingers fiddling with the earth.

'Aye, she did.'

He coughs. They're all watching.

'We're going to get her buried now,' I tell him. 'Tadhg O'Donnell's bringing her a coffin.'

He starts to cry, a gentle steady rain. For ten minutes he lies like that, then falls silent. John Michael returns and stands a way off from us, calling out that Tadhg's started on the coffin and Curly's raising the roof saying she won't let him come up to Kildarragh any more. 'If there's anything more I could do, Mrs Vesey,' he says respectfully, then stops abruptly, struggling with some emotion.

'A wheelbarrow,' I tell him. 'You're very decent, John Michael.'

He nods sharply. 'I'll leave it about here,' he says, looking down at his feet.

'Get up, Peader,' I say, when he's gone, 'show them you're alive.'

After another moment or two Peader sits up and squats there in front of his door with his head held precariously erect. His eyes are red and squinty and he blinks frantically, as if they'll never again be clear, but I'd swear he's not catching. He's been sitting in that stench for three days and nothing's fixed on him. 'There, Peader,' I say, 'you're going to live a long time,' but he isn't capable of talk.

I sit on the hillside in front of Nan and Peader's old house and think how strange the world is; that I used to sit here a long time ago when I was a little girl with my mother, before all of this, and then, though there was always want and sickness – which is simply the way of life – there was never anything to touch this. And now she's gone and here am I. And there is dear Nan's body in there making the darkness in the cabin smell foul.

Peader will be an old man now Nan's gone. Sure as sure. If I were a poet or a shanachie or a maker of songs, I'd make a song or a tale that would make you bleed, knowing of Peader and Nan and all that they were. I have not got the words, so Nan will not be sung. I know only that Nan was Nan, not a bad woman, and Peader's an old man. That's all. It's not new.

Tadhg brings up the coffin, a terrible rough affair, after time elapses. How long? Who knows? Time itself stands back.

'Look,' I say. He won't come close, he's scared of Peader. 'When all this is over, you must not go back into your house till you've got some clean clothes left out ready and you've washed yourself thoroughly all over, then you take off the old clothes and burn them, and then you put the new ones on and go in. Do you understand?'

He gives the merest hint of a shrug.

'It's all right, Tadhg,' I promise him, 'it really is all right. Would I set you at risk, boy? Come now, would I? Would I?'

Smiling at him, I can put him at rest.

He's very serious of face, very scared. He's been drinking.

'Are you scared, Tadhg?' I ask him.

'I am, Eliza. This scares me more than anything.'

He smiles like someone who needs to vomit and is putting it off.

Peader and I put her in the coffin. It wasn't Nan, it was matter. Just matter that putrefied and smelt, though not as bad as it might have done. After all, this was not the height of summer. This was a dead creature left for longer than it should have been, and by now things were moving. Things lived in Nan. Her flesh bred new life. My God, my God, I prayed, oh, my blessed saviour, you too are in these wrigglers. As I writhe in spirit, so writhe they in her. As my spirit fails, so are you made strong. Uphold me, my Upholder.

We carried the coffin into the house. In the dark we felt for her, we placed her gently in the home-made box.

Tadhg had John Michael's wheelbarrow. We lifted the coffin on at an odd angle, and I couldn't help but think of poor Nan's thin bones getting bashed about in there, rattling and subsiding into one another like dropped beads.

I watched him wheel her away, with Peader.

14

Gawky, wide-eyed Peader became the Kildarragh corpse-shifter. It made sense. Nan was gone and he had no children. What else was there for him? He was a lovely man, Peader, and he came to his rightful place after Nan died and he was left to his occupation. Some of us there were who could not be touched, and I was one and so was he. And whenever we met after that, united over a burial, eye-locked over a corpse to be moved, something would occur. It was the strange love like a drink you've drunk, a deep potion, knowing no limits, so that I could love Phelim and Tadhg and Jamie and Peader all in their own ways that were theirs alone, and none could diminish another and there was no end. I never really knew Peader before Nan died. After, he was a long gentle thing that shifted corpses and lived all alone in a scraping in the side of the hill with a thatch cover. Everyone loved him. Everyone.

We're hard people, we've had to be.

We've all heard the stories; how our fathers and our mothers suffered. From that they grew, spawned in a bog of chance. Chance set us down here in these times, spawned of our chance-spawned parents. Walk through it, I tell myself. You are not God. Set down here, walk through it.

When the Scheme ended, there was work digging graves, but not enough. I don't know why the Scheme ended, it's not as if they even finished the road, it just stops in the middle of a field in the middle of nowhere. When I think about it, I don't know what any of it was all about, why some things happened at certain times and others didn't. I know there came a time when things didn't work any more, things we'd always had. Fear was always in my mouth like cobwebs, in my throat like coming illness. Nan started it. I knew things were seriously adrift when Tadhg returned and told me how they'd got her to Lissadoon and were redirected because the cemetery was full. They'd opened up a new place out on some headland called Briggan two miles further west, and that's where they wheeled her in John Michael's wheelbarrow, and tipped her in that old knocked-up coffin into a long trench for the outraged dead, caught surprised as they went about the endless palaver of living. There weren't enough coffins. Our Nan had one because of Tadhg, but they were tipping them in without, he said, from the townlands down the peninsular, all soft and soilable as they were, just throwing down the dirt on them however they lay. I wonder the souls didn't rise up crying out in anguish for their mothers and fathers. I wonder the mothers and fathers didn't throw off their immortal dreams and scream out the names of their children through eternity.

In bed I touched Phelim all night long. My hand was on him. I didn't sleep. He lay breathing steadily under my hand, and the night passed peacefully with me whispering my charms and prayers and saying in my mind: good man, you are safe, safe under my hand. When the morning came I fell asleep and dreamed of an eagle flying from the crest of Lissadoon Point out over the sea, a very beautiful bird both fierce and desirable, but then it was time to get up and start another day, and the endless bloody stirabout.

It's been mild and dry and I've been into town. They've turned the old bakery into a fever hospital and the Quakers have taken over a house on Weavergate and are dishing out soup. Cloverhill's daughter was giving out old clothes from a cart in the Square. A very plain girl, I thought, doesn't take after her da, but tall and graceful; I suppose it's the dancing and the deportment and all these things they learn at those fancy places. I feel sorry for her, she doesn't look easy in herself and I don't think she catches one half of what's being spoken to her, but I'll say this for her, she's got guts. I'm surprised her father lets her do it. I'm surprised he even let her come back here at all, but then I suppose she's a young lady now and does what she wants. She must know the Commissioner got the fever from talking to the people outside the poorhouse, and there was a clergyman and his wife at Kildoran both went down with it and died. And who should I see there standing in line for the clothes but Alma Sheehan and her three, and ragged little vagabonds indeed they do look. I didn't let on I'd seen her; she'd have been shamed. But I saw that she saw me, and she turned away.

Some of the men marched up to Cloverhill's house and made a protest against the May rents at his gates. Martha Colgan came down and said he wasn't there. 'He's in Dublin,' she told them, 'seeing Lord Tarlton.' Then as she turned to go back to the house she spoke over her shoulder: 'I don't know why you don't just let him alone, you lot. He's only trying to live the same as everyone else.'

Father Buckley was there, and O'Carroll the schoolmaster, who shouted out: 'That's true, Martha, but some live harder than others.'

Then Miss Belinda came down with her scarf wrapped round her head and opened the gates and came out. 'My father isn't here,' she said gravely, 'but you can say anything you have to say to me.'

But no one wanted to talk to Miss Belinda, and soon after, everyone drifted away.

'You have to admit,' Darby said later to his wife, 'Sam Cloverhill's daughter, she's no coward.'

'Why?' Sal asked. 'What harm's she going to come to with a big crowd of witnesses and O'Carroll there, and Father Buckley and all. What's going to happen to her?'

'Still. There's a few been shot.'

'Not young ladies, there's not.'

'True.'

'I'd go for Lomas myself,' Sal said, 'I hate the man.'

'Anyway, he's got to be back for the meeting, Tadhg says. There's going to be a hooley in the Square.'

'Well, you don't have to go. I don't want *you* in any trouble.'

'Why? Would you miss me if I was hanged?' He grinned.

'Oh stop it!' Sal was tipping the last of some whey into Margarita's mouth, around them the heavy triple breathing of Young Darby, Mal and little Eliza. 'No, she's not that brave. I'll tell you who's brave. Eliza Vesey's brave.'

It was Eliza Vesey who'd brought up the whey. A kind of awe was attaching to her after Nan's death. She was the only one who'd go into Peader's shelter. It was terrible the way Peader was living like a wild man in that hole in the ground and his good house there all shut up.

'She's turned out strange, Eliza Vesey,' Sal said. 'You have to admire her.'

Darby thought, leaning over to stroke the hair on the baby's head. 'I can't say I like the woman myself.'

Sal nodded. She knew what he meant. Eliza Vesey was hard to like. You felt it was terribly bad not to like her because she was so good, and yet. And yet. 'Sometimes I like her,' Sal said.

'Certainly she's a godsend.'

'You know, she was always sweet on Tadhg O'Donnell.'

Darby smiled. 'They don't suit.'

'I did a bad thing once,' Sal said suddenly, looking down into the ashy grate, 'really wicked.'

225

'What was that?'

She chewed the inside of her lip and shook her head.

'Ah, go on now, you have to tell me,' he said, and she turned her head slowly and gave a great sigh. 'It keeps coming back to me now she's being so kind to us. She must be a very kind woman, mustn't she? And fearless.'

Darby licked his dry lips and steepled his fingers.

'We was both at a dance once, me and her. A big dance on Cully's Field. Everyone was there, Phelim Vesey and Tadhg O'Donnell and all the boys from Lissadoon and Kildoran had come in and it was wild. Do you know what she was like then? She hadn't the courage she has now. She was an awkward stiff creature, and she used to stand there with a look on her as if she thought badly about everything. She was like a little old woman. And I went up to her and said, aren't you going to dance, Eliza? She looked at me and said, I *may* dance. I *may* dance.'

Sal put into her voice and tone everything she could of disdain.

'It was,' she spoke haltingly, 'as if – as if she was far too grand for foolery such as the rest of us might get up to. She could make you feel very small. I've just said she hadn't the courage then, but now I'm speaking I don't know: maybe she did have – she'd look at you and not blink, just look at you. When I say she had no courage I mean, it was so clear, I *think* it was, that she wasn't easy at all in herself about being with other people, with all the rest of us, and yet she was always there at everything going; whenever anything was on she was there, as if she just had to make herself go, even though it was all beneath her.'

'Go on,' said Darby, taking the baby from her. Thank God they were all asleep at last.

'Oh, I don't know,' she said, 'it wasn't really anything.'

'Go on.'

226

'We were all so young. We were fifteen or so. Well, I was, I don't know, we were all thereabouts. Very young. And there was a man from Killarney had come, I don't know who he was, he was one of the pipers, and he got up on a barrel and said there was to be a competition as to who, out of all the boys, could box the best; and who could sing best out of the girls. And the winners were to lead the dancing and get a prize. And then he called on the boys all to come up and give it their best, and of course Tadhg O'Donnell goes up there, with John Scanlon and Tim Felix and Dinny Buckley and a few more, and they do knockouts till there's only Tadhg left, wouldn't you know, victorious. And then the man says that there's to be another competition, for the girls, as to who could sing the best; and the winner was to dance with the winner from the boys, which of course was Tadhg. Well, four or five sang and none of them was too bad, and then I was amazed because there's Eliza Domican, as she was then, getting up and singing *The Green Linnet*. Eliza, who never joins in with anything at all. I wonder now I haven't ever told you this before, Darby.'

He laid down the baby between them on the bed.

'*The Green Linnet*!' she whispered wonderingly. 'You know what that's like, Darby. It's full of tricks. It goes everywhere. You need a damn good lilter now for that song.'

'Was she good?' Darby's eyes shone brightly in the very faint light from the candle stub.

'Blow out the candle, love,' she said.

He did.

'What about you?' he asked, 'What did you sing?'

'Me? I didn't sing. You know me, I have no voice at all for singing. And if I had I'd never have chosen something like *The Green Linnet*. I'd have chosen something easy.

'So was she good? Did she win?'

Sal was silent for a moment then pushed her hand to her mouth to stifle laughter.

227

'She was terrible. *Terrible*. It was the most – oh, it was the most! – it was agony. It went on for *ages* and *ages* and not one single note of it was right. She had an awful, weak, cracky voice, and she made that beautiful song sound as if it had no tune to it at all; just one long dirge she made of it, and it made you wince, it really did, it was like your ears were curling up and trying to close themselves. It hurt.'

'Oh God, poor Eliza!'

'I've never heard the like. I don't want to ever again.'

'Did she not realise?'

'Now, that was the funny thing. She did. You could see it in her face all the while she was singing. She knew exactly how awful it was but she didn't stop, she just went on and on with her face getting redder and redder; she was just burning up and dying of shame with every single note, but there it was. She sang it right the way through to the bitter end, and we all stood there with our mouths open listening as if she was as good as anyone. No one said a word. No jeering. No laughing. We were struck dumb, I think. And when she finished there was this little silence and then everyone clapped just like they had for all the others, and she got down and went and stood away from everyone the way she was before. You could never read Eliza's face. Have you noticed that? You can never read her.'

'Whatever made her do a thing like that, do you suppose?'

'God alone knows.'

'But that wasn't your fault, was it? What was this wicked thing you're supposed to have done?'

Sal sighed. 'Well, then, you see, when a couple more had sung their bits this man from Killarney said that because Tadhg was the winner of the boys he had to choose a winner from the girls. And Tadhg chooses Eliza. He gets up on the barrel and says, the winner is Eliza Domican, and the man calls her up and she still has that blank face of hers, and everyone calling: Well done! And she gets a bunch of lovely purple ribbons, and Tadhg gets a hurley stick, and then they both get down and they're supposed to lead the dancing like the man said. And that's when I did it.'

'What? What did you do, Sal?'

'I felt cross,' she said. 'He only chose her because he felt sorry for her making such a fool of herself like that, and no one said anything about it because they all felt sorry for her too, and you could see that she knew that. But no one was going to say anything at all. And what about all those other girls who sang so much better than she did and gave it their best? What about them? I don't know, she bothered me, she did, in those days. She was so bloody serious. And Tadhg had been pestering me for a dance all night long, he was very taken with me at that time, you know, and I'd been saying no just because, just for the fun of it because he wanted me to. She was so bloody serious and because of that everybody always took her so seriously as if she was something different and nothing applied to her that applied to common people, no one else would have got away with singing like that, but because it was her, somehow – anyway. I was standing next to her when she came down, and the dancing was about to begin. I remember it as clear as when it happened. We were standing by the punch tub and she gets in front of me, between me and Tadhg and her nose up in the air, and I, God forgive me, there was something of a hurley-burley all around at the time and I bent down and picked up the hem of her skirt at the back and tucked it into her waist. Oh, it was terrible, just on a whim, you know, it happened before I could stop myself, and I'm sure I was saying to myself as I did it, no, no, no, you mustn't do this, this is wrong, Sal, this is wrong, but I did it anyway. And next thing she's off in the dance with Tadhg, up and down as merry as can be – she was even smiling – and her showing her scrawny arse in calico drawers to the whole country for miles around, and her thin little legs stepping and kicking away and a big hole in her stockings at the back.' She covers her face but she's laughing. 'Oh, couldn't you just die? Couldn't you just die?'

'Well, it was bad, Sal,' Darby replies slowly, 'but you were very young.'

'That's neither here nor there. I've felt sick about it ever since. I felt sick about it then, but I did it. Aren't I bad?'

'No no no no no,' says Darby. 'How could my Sal be bad?'

'I am though, I am. It was very bad.'

'No.'

'What a spiteful thing to do to someone. Poor Eliza! And now she's so good to us.'

'Did she know?'

'Of course she did! Don't you think as soon as she finished that dance and she turned off the floor, they were queueing up to tell her. And she knew it was me too. Someone of them told her, I know. I know because of how she looked at me ever since, after that night. She's always known, and yet she's always been so good. And I feel so bad about it, Darby, I feel so bad!'

Darby put his arm across her shoulders. 'Hush now,' he said, 'it was all a very long time ago and you're older now and everything's forgiven. She's forgotten all about it.'

'No one forgets a thing like that, Darby,' Sal said, 'I know I wouldn't. Not in a million million years. Can you still love me? Oh, what a cruel thing to do!'

'I still love you.' She could feel the bulge of Darby's cheek smiling against her forehead. 'I'll always love you, Sal, you don't know what you are to me. You're not a bad woman. You're good! How could my Sal not be good?'

'I'm glad I told you that,' she said, 'glad.'

Margarita between them slept deeply, at peace.

'Ssh!' he said.

★

Then there was the riot in Boolavoe. How it fared with other places no one really knew, but for Boolavoe this was the big riot that people would pass down and tell to their grandchildren. Eliza Vesey was there, alone, which caused some comment.

They all gathered around the barracks where the meeting of the relief committee was being held, and all the big people were there, Cloverhill and Lomas and others. Tadhg was in the crowd along with all the wild boys, and many of the small farmers from round about, and the people of five townlands. Father Buckley stood on the steps and addressed the crowd while the meeting went on inside.

'We are not unreasonable in our requests,' he said. 'All we are asking is a simple commitment to life and health for the majority, something which cannot occur without yet another waiving of the rents. All we are asking is that facts be squarely faced. The poor have no decision to make. It is not that they wilfully withhold their rightful dues, it is a matter of no choice at all. If they desired with all their hearts and every nerve in their bodies to pay every single penny owing, if they vowed to sweat and toil to the last gasp of their bodies, it would make no odds. Blood cannot be got from a stone, and rents cannot be paid by those whose only concern is putting a sop of gruel in the mouth of the child who will not live the night without it. Tell me, my friends, what matters more to God? The life blood of Mammon bled from the poor to succour those in grand houses? Or a mouthful of thin stirabout to keep a child from death? Who is there here so inhumane that he would satisfy his landlord and deprive his dying child of comfort? Who? Who, my friends?'

A roar rose from the throats of the crowd. They became so restless that six gentlemen from the meeting came out and stood at the top of the steps, Cloverhill and Lomas among them. Cloverhill stood forward.

'The meeting is not yet concluded,' he announced in a strong voice that rang above the crowd with the conviction of authority. 'Your concerns are being addressed at this very moment. I can tell you that no decision has yet been made as to the collection of rents immediately pending. However –' and here he paused and let his gaze slowly rake the crowd, 'I can assure every one of you standing here this evening that our sole purpose here tonight is to find a way forward for us all – every one of us; man, woman and child, no matter what his station. Upon this I pledge my word.'

'That means nothing!' a voice cried from the crowd. Someone threw a clod of dirt and it hit Lomas on the left arm and left a dirty mark. That upset Cloverhill. You could see him flinch and the anger and fear flit across his face. After all, there could have been a gun. The crowd tensed and the six men turned stiffly and marched back inside, Lomas scowling and dusting earth off the sleeve of his jacket. And then the peelers turned up with their truncheons drawn at the ready and the dispersement began; but a few of the wilder lads, including Tadhg, turned over one of the gentlemen's carriages on the edge of the Square, and there was a fight on the steps of the cross. A few heads were bloodied.

Whether it was the hostility of the crowd that night or the prospect of his own eviction by Tarlton if he didn't get the rents in, something must have hardened in Cloverhill, because he put out at a meeting a few nights later that this issue of arrears could no longer be ignored. Last year the tenants should have paid half-rent but none had paid any. This year the May rents would be let go because of the continuing hardship, but come November all outstanding debts must be settled. And he called on all the farmers of the area to provide work wherever possible. People needed to get back into work, he said, that was the best way forward, and he himself would take the lead. A massive programme of planting must be implemented now that the weather was looking more favourable, and they must all pull together. But there must be no more non-payment of rents.

Well, Phelim is no saint. So much we've done, we can do no more. For their time they'll get a fair wage, but we can't pay their rent. Not this year, not next year. Not this year, Lord, anyway. Lord, this year, you pay the rent, you're able surely if anyone can, we're not. Hear me, Lord, we're just not. I have a child. Lord, Lord, Lord, didn't you ever have a child? You who know everything? Of course you had a child, every child that ever was born is yours, so you know, you know how it is for me and Jamie. You know.

I am afraid. Not of the fever, which nibbles and hounds away at the district, spreading like mould on bread. It's *want* I'm afraid of. Of course Cloverhill's a fool to talk of a big planting. What are they to plant? The funny thing is, those silly little poreens we cut up, me and Phelim, it looks as if they're going to yield; no sign yet of any blight there. But there's only enough for us, and as for those others who never planted because they'd got no seed from last year, what can *they* do? We can't feed them all. And now there's this new law, this quarter acre law. I don't know what that means. Everyone thinks it's bad. It was all the talk when I was up at Darby's house. I'm there again often these days, taking her whey. Tadhg and Darby, they're thick as thieves. I often see Tadhg there. And sometimes there's Matty Sheehan with his ridiculous grin and clever talk, or one of the Scanlons. Tadhg thinks it's lovely, the way I look after everyone. And so it is. They can say what they like, I'm a good woman, I've made sure of that. I know the things to do and I've done them, and maybe that will atone for the hatred in my heart.

They were saying you'd have to give up your land to get relief. You couldn't have more than a quarter of an acre or you wouldn't get anything. We've got twelve so we'd never qualify.

Tadhg was furious, I've never seen him like that. He had his mouth hard closed in a line and he was breathing heavily, in fact at one moment I was convinced he might burst into tears. 'There's a weapon to beat the poor man with,' he says bitterly. 'Starve or be landless. Whose land is it anyway? They'll have it all.'

'All but your last quarter acre,' Darby points out.

Darby has a single acre and most of it's mountain scrub. Now he's off the Scheme he takes in his ticket and gets meal in town. He won't be able to do that now.

'What will you do?' I ask him.

He gives a crooked mirthless smile. He's sitting on the mattress. They only have the one blanket now it seems, but that serves for the time because it's summer.

'What choice is there?' Tadhg spits. 'Starve or go in the poorhouse.'

'I'm not going in that poorhouse,' Sal says quickly, 'I'd rather die in my own house.'

The Scanlons and the Sheehans are in the same boat. So is just about everybody else in Kildarragh.

'They work you like a dog in the poorhouse,' Sal says, 'even the children.'

'They've all got the fever in there,' Matty Sheehan says.

'You'd not survive,' says Sal.

Matty sucks his big square teeth. 'They're not making me give up *my* wee patch, I'm telling you that.'

I don't know why they're bothering. They'll do what they have to do to stay alive because that's what you do. What good's an acre with nothing to plant on it? I think they're all mad. There's only the meal. They'll give up the land when the babies cry.

But not yet.

For now Darby Quinn goes out roaming. He goes past our house every day, he always gives us a wave but he doesn't usually stop, he's in too much of a hurry. He never begs from us. Why would he? He knows we do what we can anyway. He goes down to the main road and begs, and he gets what work he can. I suppose he steals too, I don't know, but I know he wouldn't steal from us. I shouldn't think he gets much. There's no pigs and sheep any more. There's scarcely a chicken between here and Kenmare. You can walk all day and not see so much as a rabbit. It's been change, change now, for so long, and never a change for the better it seems, though it must be coming, it must; nothing in this world ever lasted forever. Walk on. Every day another change. The last time I was up above, O'Carroll's house was all closed up. They said he'd gone away. Scared, I suppose. We went over and looked in the windows. He'd locked up so we couldn't get in, but there's nothing in there. All his nice things have gone, went ages ago, sold for food for Kildarragh. Why should the poor man stay and starve? So how will the children get their schooling? I said this to Phelim. And what about Jamie? Shouldn't he be out now playing with other young ones? Shouldn't I be taking him into Lissadoon? But there's no school there now either, because the mistress is sick; and no one dares send their children out to sit among others.

Phelim has fear too, I think, but it's hard to tell with him. He never lets on. His face is heavy with something though, some deep trouble he's trying not to show. When I tell him the things I've seen, he shakes his head and sometimes closes his eyes as if struck, and says, 'I don't know if I wanted to hear that, Queen Eliza.' But he never gets angry, like Tadhg, and he never shows despair. His shoulders hunch though. He stands sometimes, stick-like in the yard, leaning on his shovel and just gazing down the lane, but he's looking at nothing.

★

We have potatoes. Those silly little poreens we split so carefully and planted with so little hope and against Father Buckley's advice all came up a treat.

This is a muddle. How do these things happen? Poor Phelim's bewildered as to what to do. There's us and the very few who planted that have a yield, and no disease in sight so far and the weather fair; and if we're very, very careful and keep a few back for seed – and God knows that's going to be well nigh impossible the way things are – then we may, we just may – no, we will, we will, because we have to – we will get through.

God bless us. God's given this crop to us, then please God, we will be safe and I'll see Jamie grow up. Of course I will.

But there goes Phelim again, sitting with his long arms hanging from his knees and his eyes like all sorrow staring in the empty fire like he's daft, worrying about everybody else. I said we'll do what we can and we can't do more than that. First I feed my child. The rest is for God. We'll plant, my God, be it ever such a small patch, and we'll guard it day and night and we'll do what we can.

I made boxty. There are some scallions growing in the field and I mashed a few in. They talk about nectar and manna and food of the gods but there was never anything since time began to rival that boxty all mashed up with a few scallions and a splash of two-milk whey. My mouth fairly dripped as I smelt the white potato smell begin to rise from the pot with the steam, and by the time I had the bowl and was whipping it into cream there were tears of joy in my eyes. It had been so long. And their eyes, Phelim and Jamie and the old man, their eyes by the fire. We were very happy that night. It sounds funny but I think I can truthfully say that that was one of the happiest times of my life. Things have not always gone well with me. But that night even my father was not in a mood to complain, and when we had finally eaten there was a deep and sleepy silence between us all, and every-thing was good.

We have them stored and hid. Phelim goes up by night and scatters a few around Kildarragh where people will find them; he says it's fairer that way rather than having to choose who gets them. What would you do, he says, going up there and looking them all in their eyes and having to decide who got them? You couldn't do it, that's what he says. And he wants to pay their rents for them come November because we haven't done too bad with what he sold in Kenmare. That's where he had to go, all the way to Kenmare to sell them. He'd have got a price in Boolavoe but he wouldn't dare go there and have to face our own people and them all knowing what we'd got. So the way he sees it, it's no sin to sell a few potatoes for a good price in Kenmare and use what we get to pay the rents for our old labourers come November, the Sheehans and the Scanlons and the Foxes and the Quinns.

Or what's left of them, I say under my breath.

I'm easier in my mind now when I lie in bed. Now I know we'll manage. I've been very scared, perhaps I did not realise how much so at the time, but now I know that I've come through a kind of fear that rots the soul without you even knowing.

One night I wake in the dark and hear soft male voices and realise Phelim's side of the bed is empty. Half asleep I listen for a while until I'm sure of who it is, Phelim and Tadhg sit-ting up late and yarning pleasantly together for some reason. Unlike these two to sit so late and so companionably. Then Tadhg begins to sing, so I turn my head and draw back the curtain just enough to see the two of them in the light of a single candle, Tadhg singing softly and quietly because he doesn't wish to wake the household, a song about a girl little more than a child, a girl so beautiful that the small wild flowers open up as her bare feet pass by and the stars lean down from the heavens to sigh. He sings that she is his little dew-wet flower, whose song puts to shame the nightingale and thrush, more graceful in her movement than a fawn. A lovely singer, Tadhg, he brings tears into my eyes. Of course they're drunk.

Where he gets it from we'll never know but he still gets it even in these awful times, a strong sweet poteen that has you mellow as a summer moon.

They don't see me looking. A bottle passes back and forth between them.

'Oh, she was,' he says, 'the dew-wet flower.'

However he's to get home I do not know.

Phelim's bony hand shakes a little as he takes the shiny bottle, puts back his head and drinks.

'The most beautiful thing I ever saw,' says Tadhg, leaning back and looking at the ceiling, 'was Sal when she was only fifteen, washing her feet in a tub at her ma's back door.'

Phelim laughs softly. 'I used to walk by that way deliberate.'

'We all did.'

Mellow as a full summer moon, the two of them drinking, thinking soft thoughts of Sal Quinn. There is a feeling in me I cannot name, a toiling, moiling restlessness that never lets go, that lives constantly in the whole of me, body and soul. Because of Sal Quinn. What am I to do about it?

'Phelim Vesey,' I say from the bed, 'that's plenty you've had.'

They jump to, laughing.

'Come out and join us, Eliza,' Tadhg calls.

'I will not.'

'Ah, do!'

But I let fall the curtain and turn over on my side, and soon after hear Tadhg leave. I have no idea what time it is. Phelim sits on for a bit, silent, thinking God alone knows what thoughts, till he gets up and puts back the curtain and stands with the candle looking down at me. I'm stiff as a board. He sits, touches my shoulder. 'You're not angry, are you, love?' he asks softly.

'No. But it's time you came to bed.'

'It's not that late.' He puts the candle on the shelf. 'Wasn't that good of Tadhg to think of us? He's left us a half bottle.'

'Well, you'd better hide it well,' I say, 'if my da gets his hands on it, it'll last all of two minutes.'

He chuckles. 'Will you have a drop?'

'A sip.' I sit up and he hands me the bottle. The liquor burns its way down.

'It's a bit of fun in hard times,' he smiles, leaning towards me to rest his face against the front of my nightdress.

'You'll have a bad head in the morning,' I say, capping the bottle.

But he only laughs, and when he's in bed and the candle blown out, huddles up hot against me and wriggles like a child. 'Queen Eliza,' he murmurs, 'Queen, Queen Eliza,' and falls heavily asleep, snoring faintly. I can't sleep though. I can't even close my eyes. My body's as tight as a fiddle string in spite of the drink that warms my stomach. Why should he be asleep when I'm not? I push him. He rolls over and catches his breath. I hate him for smiling so stupidly in his cups over Sal Quinn. I wish she'd die. Why can't she take the fever? Why poor Nan and not her? Why is it misfortune never comes to the right ones? Not fair, not fair, not fair, I cry in the night, and after an hour and another hour and then another of night crawling over and around me, I give up and lie on my back with my eyes wide open, summoning Juliander.

She's alone by candlelight, plainly dressed in a blue skirt and black shawl. Her hair hangs long, combed out, and her eyes glow. She's thinking very deeply about life and its endless

239

turnings, contemplating the next step. The world's put distance between her and her lovers, but they are still there, strong presences within. Death has crept up close to the cottage in which she sits, death rubs itself all over the roof and every wall, obscenely amorous. A woman of supreme courage, she is acquainted with abominable fear. It has, she sometimes thinks, accompanied her every step of the way, she cannot even remember a time when it was not. And so it should be, so it must be, for there's nothing else that moves her on, keeps her walking through and through this madness the world has become. The strength of Juliander is that she transforms fear. It becomes the food of life, sustaining all. Beyond the glow of the candle, lighting her simple beauty, is a darkness full of death, and in it, the faces of the dead are clear. These are not times for play, they are times of testing. So what, in these times, does a woman like her do? She takes up her invisible staff and binds about her an impossible armour of humankindness, tempered in a fire she can no longer endure. What else is there now? She goes through the darkness to see what there is to see. And when she gets to the top of the hill, she looks down on the townland of Kildarragh so still and peaceful in the pale rising dusk of a new morning.

I have to keep returning to that miserable house in Kildarragh where the Quinns are starving. She keeps sending for me and it's driving me mad. If it's not one thing it's another. Poor little Eliza was coughing so bad last night. I'm a bit worried about Darby, do you think he looks a funny colour? And what about these lovely big lads, little broad men's faces, slit-eyed and callow, self-conscious. I suppose she loves them like I love Jamie. I suppose it's all the same, there's people all around loving each other like me and Jamie love each other. What a terrible weight that is, when so many are dying and we're all jumpy. I'll not let him pay their rent. There are soup kitchens, that's fair. The food's there if they want it. It's us or them. I've been sitting here gnawing my nails bloody all day. My da's up. He's off for a walk, he says he'll catch the good weather while he can. And Phelim, Jamie with him, is doing something necessary in the lower field down under the mound. They leave me to think here, looking out and biting on my raw hands and thinking what should I be doing? What should I be doing? I'm going to bash up some neeps tonight. I'll make them into little cakes with a few greens. I don't know, I daren't think what's happening above. There's far worse down below on those lower slopes. Our people aren't so bad, not amongst the worst. I keep thinking about Juliander and what she did last night. But then, she has no husband or child, she can do what she wants. She's outside of all that. She went through the night of cool breezes over the mountain by the light of a mellow full summer moon, she looked down on the sleeping townland. Then down, down, down, with small wild flowers springing at her feet, the small pink stars I make into a potion to protect; and the stars out, and the sea so many bright small silver-tipped black waves. It is easy to be drunk on the beauty of a night like this, whether or not you've had a drink of Tadhg O'Donnell's strong poteen. And being who she was she was suffused with joy, drifting down through those low cabins. There was a smile on her face. The night was indeed very lovely. She stood on a rock and looked out at the sea. Far away, somewhere down the coast, where the caves were and the long shingle where the seals come in, something strange called, a long, high, quivering call.

Then she walked down into the very depths, till she came to a cottage on the extreme edge of the settlement, under a high ridge that kept off the worst of the wind from the sea, with two or three faint ghosts of potato ridges rippling out the back and a bit of rope tethered to a tree, dangling forlorn.

The doors and windows were silted up with earth. With her cold hands she pulled it all down, scratched and scrabbled a way through, a small voiceless mole woman burrowing with strong claws. And when she gets in and the light's come though the door again and a window is clear, what does she find?

I didn't know the names of those people. They were not ours. The mother was dead in her bed, and a child lying beside her, a boy of about two. Who knows? He could have been older, he was starved small, a poor sweet monkey boy, still alive.

I'd seen them in town by Fallon's Yard, these monkey girls and boys and babies, but here? They grow hair. I heard about it and didn't believe it but it's true. They grow hair on their faces when they're starving. There was no fever smell, this was hunger alone. I'd heard of the hunger deaths, they were all the far side of Lissadoon, thirteen or fourteen I heard. But this was here, a walk away. A faint but foul smell rose from the mother. Her eyes were closed, her mouth was open, she looked as used and pointless as an old cloth screwed up and thrown out in the rubbish. There was no man. A girl of about thirteen lay across the floor, and a boy of ten or so on a sop of straw. They were horrible, not dead but no longer alive, dirty things with claws like mine, and sad flickering eyes. The place needed whitewash. I picked up the little one from his mother's side, and he lay across my arms with all his limbs dangling. He wouldn't stop crying. He couldn't keep up his head, and his eyes glittered black. He didn't weigh a thing. One arm came up at me, a rag on a pole, and I caught it in my hand and began to cry.

That was how Peader found me, crying with the little one in my arms.

'Nothing I have will do them any good,' I say.

242

'Of course not, Eliza,' he says, 'of course not.'

I am bewildered.

Peader says, 'you go, Eliza, these are beyond us.'

Nothing to be done but walk out into the air with the rag boy and watch the light go out in him as the dawn comes up fully, big and bright over the mountain. I sit for a while and study his face. The eyes of the dead are magnets, the shadow of the soul is there, a mere phantom. Peader comes out and touches my shoulder. 'I'll bring a hurdle,' he says. 'Leave it to me now, Eliza.'

I lay down the monkey boy.

Juliander sits with the dying night after night. There's nothing she can do but sit by their sides and hold their hands and watch them leave the world, and give them gentle words as they go: 'there now, my darling, soon better, soon all better now, soon, soon better.'

But here, as bright and loud as can be, are the Quinns. God, that woman is selfish. She thinks she's the only one in the world. Would you believe, she's wearing her red kerchief? It's like a slap in the face.

'You should have put that big lad there on the Scheme,' I tell her.

We're at her gate.

'He's only eleven,' she says, 'I wouldn't have had him killing himself like a man out there for tuppence and the ganger standing there doing nothing for four times as much.'

'He's a big lad and the times are not just bad, Sal,' I say, 'they're desperate. You should have let him go.'

'Well, that's what you think, Eliza,' she says. She's looking haggard.

'I would have gone,' says Young Darby.

'I know you would, my love,' she says, touching his head as he passes; then to me: 'Now you're here, would you mind

243

very much just taking a quick look at little Eliza? She's got that cough still and it keeps her awake.'

'It keeps us all awake,' Young Darby says.

I suppose one day there'll be rest for me.

I go in. The girl sits in the middle of the floor, whining and ugly.

'What colour's her pee?'

'Normal.'

I'm not touching her. I sit and wait and she coughs, a rough liquid grumbling pulled up from the chest. I sigh. 'It's no worse than before. Get her hot water to sip. Give it time. Where's Darby?'

'He'll be back today.'

Begging. I don't suppose it's anything much to him, he's done it before. Well, I think, I'm not waiting around here after a night like that, I need my own rest now. She gives me a funny look as I'm leaving, suspicious I think, though what it's for I don't know. Little enough any of them have to reproach me with. What do they want from me? To use me all up, every bit, till there's no more left of me? That's more or less what Phelim said when I got back. Of course he did have a bad head but I thought there's no need for that, taking it out on me.

'You can't just keep going off like this in the middle of the night,' he says. 'Not at a time like this. What about Jamie?'

'Jamie's safer here.'

He's listening to all this, the boy.

'So? What about you?'

'Oh, you needn't worry about me. If I was going to get anything I'd have had it by now.'

'It's not that, it's the wear and tear. Can't you see it? Look how tired you are.'

'I'll have a bit of a rest.'

'It's not fair on us, Eliza. On your own family. You don't

244

belong to everyone, you belong to us.' He threw down the rag he'd been wiping his neck with, just hurled it to the floor.

'Well, that's nice, isn't it?' I say. 'Shall I tell you what I've seen last night, Phelim? And to have to come home to this.'

'I don't want to know,' he says, and walks out.

I pull a face at Jamie. Like, isn't your da an old silly, making such a big fuss.

'Don't go there again, Ma,' he says.

'Oh, I'm all right, Jamie.'

'Dad says they're wearing you out.'

'Oh, yes? Who's wearing me out?'

'The Quinns.'

'I wasn't with the Quinns last night.'

But he's right, I suppose. She calls on me more than anyone, she does, and they haven't even got the sickness or anything. They've got off lightly. And there's a wearing out that's nothing to do with walking over the mountain in the middle of the night, there's the kind that comes from having a thing go round and round in your mind till it's like a tune on the brain, one you get to hate. I can't get it from me that my life would have been better if Sal Quinn had never been born. And there's that creature. I've been very good with putting her away at the back of my thoughts, but now as I lay on my bed in the morning with the curtain drawn against the light, she comes forward in my wandering half awake dreams. She's an abominable thing. She's walking along a mountain track near the sea, over by the caves. I never noticed before how bowed her legs have become. She's always in that dirty grey dress with her thumb in her mouth. She smiles a thin smile at me, and her face is all curving lines, the slits of her eyes and mouth, curls that go on curling up and up and up like grubs that clench at a touch. Her nose is a mere tweak of the clay. What is she? A cuckoo, a mooncalf. There's nothing

245

of the human in her, and what is there has its origins under the ground. She has the earth about her. Her substance is worm-holed, cracked and ancient, muddy at the core. Looking at her gives me an ill feeling.

Then I wake with a start and a dreadful headache. God save me from this feeling I have about the child. I won't go again, I'll do as Phelim says, and I'll stay home like before and let Juliander do her wandering alone. I toss in the bed and fall back soon into the netherlands of sleep, but just before I take the plunge over that final sharp edge into oblivion, a clear small voice says: Why else were you put here at this time if not to see it all? What other purpose?

And for all my fine resolutions, I was pulled in when the Quinns got sick, sucked back in as if by a sinking sand.

I was dreaming about them every night, and I was waking up, frightening myself with a curse aloud on my lips. Twice I woke Phelim. 'You were shouting,' he said, and stroked me with his hand. After all they were my nearest neighbours and they were all sick, all the children but the strange one in differing degrees. And who else was there to see to them? They don't call on each other any more, the Scanlons and Sheehans and Quinns. There's very little flitting between cabins now. Tadhg told us they were sick and I went up. Should I not have done that? Phelim cried last night. He says he's so heartsick and tired at the way things are going. He never shows it and now he's showing it, and I can't have him breaking. Not him. But there's something strange goes on when he's unmanned, a baby of a thing; there's something of a thrill that makes me strong. I sit him by the fire and cuddle his big stupid head and let him cry into my apron for a bit, then I sit on his knee and give him one of my big strong kisses that makes him well.

'Now when have I ever told you false?' I say. 'I'll not go

further than Darby's house, the worst of it's down below. It doesn't touch me and you know it.'

I touch my hand to my mother's charm, and tell him to stay in today with his sniffly nose and sad eyes, stay in and keep himself warm and put two potatoes to bake in the red ashes. When I come home the house will be full of the aroma. I take some soup in a bottle, a big lumper and a pint of milk. It's such a beautiful day, early autumn, a little cold and the scent of the seasons changing. I swear this mountain on such a day is the seat of the gods. There's nothing in all the stories and great tales, nothing anywhere in the world to compare with it for beauty. For a time I sit among the heather and gorse looking out over the bay and the distant blue line of Lissadoon village shimmering in the softness of the day. This is a lovely land. When we're all dead it still will be.

The Quinns are in a bad way. There's no fire because she's got no fuel. She's on her own, he's been on the road nearly a week and she's scared stiff he's dead. I told her not to be so stupid. Why him rather than another? Can you blame him staying away? I thought, but I didn't say it. Who'd want to wait around here to die? Look at you, Sal Quinn, just look at you, this hunger's a great leveller, you can say that for it. That brightness of the eye has gone, that was always one of her great things. I used to think she put something in her eyes to make them like that, it irked me because it was a secret I didn't have, and I have many secrets but not that one. But now look at you, Sal Quinn. And look at me. Serene and sure I go about my business in this reeking hovel with you traipsing, clumsy and big-shouldered after me with your frightened face all haggard and wild. You've cried into the soup, thin poor stuff, because of my kindness. 'If we had a morsel of turf,' you've said, 'we could soften the potatoes,' and I've promised I'll bring you some when I can, because

247

the last time you ate raw potato it gave you the most horrible pains and you were up all night.

All the food in the house before I came was a ladle of yellow meal with maggots in. You don't know what you'd do without me, do you?

Young Darby and Mal are raging hot and vomiting. Margarita's limp. She'll not last but I'll not tell her mother, she'll turn on me. They do that, as if it's your fault. The other one's quiet, just sits and watches the boys and sucks her thumb, the only thing about her that's clean. As for Sal – well, she's poorly herself and she's not coping.

'I'll not let him go again,' she says, picking at her knuckles.

'Right enough.'

'I need him here.'

'Of course you do.'

'He could get me some wood.'

'Phelim'll bring you some. He'll leave it over by the stile.'

'Oh, you are good, Eliza. You've been a true friend to us.'

I smile and send her for more water. These need cooling down. She takes little Eliza with her.

'Up, my fine lad.'

Mal's hair is drenched. He whimpers like a dog.

'Soon better now,' I say, holding his head and keeping back his hair. 'That's it, let it go, the more the better, good boy.'

A child can be miserable in a fuller way than a grown person. If he's well enough to cry, that's good. That baby's quiet as a mouse. Young Darby is a little still for my liking too, but when I go over and look at him, his eyelids flicker and he puts his hands up to me in a peculiar grasping way. How fine his hands are, long-fingered and with a gentleness in the way they touch the air. He gulps noisily and whispers, 'Where's Ma?' never opening his eyes.

248

'Ma's coming,' I say, 'she's just bringing you some lovely cold water.'

'Want Ma.' His voice a high wheeze.

'Ma's here.'

'Mammy's here, my big boy,' she says, sinking to her knees with a cold rag.

'He'll be fine, Sal, don't you worry.' I can say it as one who knows, reassuring her. And it's true, he will be fine and so will his brother, they're tough little tykes, but the baby's going to die. She breathes scarcely at all. She's hot but her hands are freezing cold, and there's no power at all left to hold the life in. Just nothing there. But when I pick her up and bring her close against my breast, I feel that she is suffering somewhere beneath the stillness, as if a mirror-calm pool concealed a boiling bed of mud.

I remember her birth a year and a half ago, when things were bad but not so bad; how her eyes were wide open from the first, and very bright. She had strength, all sparkle and shine like her mother, and her black hair glistening wet too.

She was wet now too, but dull.

'Margarita,' I whisper, blowing gently on her forehead, 'Margarita.'

Someone should be holding her all the time from now on. It's wrong for a baby to die unheld. She should have her mother. Even closed, you can see how large her eyes are, they bulge and stare behind the almost transparent eyelids, which are crazed, leaf-like, with thin lilac veins. The way I'm holding her, I can feel her heart running into mine, pouring in like a flood. The way it's going, there will be nothing left in her by the time death takes her, she'll be all in me, whatever she was. She hurts me, coming in.

'Sal,' I say, 'Sal.'

She turns from swabbing down Mal's scrawny chest. The child's ribs ripple like the sand on the beach.

'You should take her, Sal,' I say, and her face begins to collapse, but then in from the side runs the girl crying: 'Mamma, Mamma, Mamma!'

Sal shakes herself and seizes her elder daughter, lifts her high onto her shoulder and pats her back. 'It's all right, my baby, Mamma's here, Mamma's here,' and she swings her slowly from side to side.

That's when I feel Margarita go. She bleeds the rest of herself into me and, empty, dies with a slight shudder. Now, though I may put her down, I'll have to carry her forever. Dear me, it is getting crowded in here. Already we were Legion.

I count. They'd been forty-two in Kildarragh, I think. There was eleven gone now with Margarita. Peader would bring a box, very rough. There'd be no more wood after this; in fact, is there wood enough for Margarita? She's only very small. Forty-two take away eleven is –

'She's gone, Sal,' I say.

– thirty-one.

We can get that little bit of land. Some must live through this. That little bit of land would be ours. It would be easy. I could go see Cloverhill. Not that it's such a great little bit of land, but there's the cabin and the spring. Something for Jamie. Land anyway.

'So, you have your quarter acre and your cabin,' this is Tadhg in his cups, 'you can go in the poorhouse, get fed, come back in better times.'

The good stuff's gone. I've told them, this'll rot you from the inside out, but will they listen?

'Aha though, but can you?' he continues, waving the bottle, and answers himself: 'you cannot! Of course not. You know what happened over the way?' He jerks his thumb as if an event twenty miles away were just in the next hollow.

'Soon as you leave the house, they torch it. Tumble the whole blamed thing in! If the poor man once gives up his plot he's ruined. He can *never* come back.' He's slurring his words, waving his arms about. 'The peelers and the soldiers out in all their glory. Oh yes, it's a fine thing for the landlords, this mess, and we all know whose pocket the peelers and the soldiers are in, don't we? Don't we?'

'We do indeed, Tadhg,' Phelim says mildly, waving away the bottle's neck and turning away from the fire, 'we do indeed.'

I'm sitting by quietly, listening and watching Tadhg. He's grown shaggier and rougher, this past year. There's no business at the shebeen any more, and he sold his boat and his nets, for which he curses, but Curly's da helps out. He's a daddy himself now, Tadhg. It was a girl, Sorcha they named her. Hasn't stopped him going about, he gets a bit of wood here and there for the coffins, but there's not enough now, what with the demand from Boolavoe and Kildoran as well. It's been very bad at Kildoran, he says. They're using the same coffin over and over there, they're tipping them out of the coffin into the trench then taking it back to use again. I think that's terrible. I wouldn't allow it if it were one of mine. They're bad enough anyway, the new graves up over Briggan, you can't tell who's who. That's where they took Margarita. It's just lots of big mounds on those bleak cliffs by the sea and they're all put in together. You could be lying in there face to face with anyone, all rotting away into each other, a lively business, one imagines, but it's only matter. She was buried already by the time Darby came back two days later with a bag of meal on his back.

Now here's a surprise. Since her baby died, Sal Quinn hasn't cried once. I thought she'd have screamed the place down but she just went stupid. She let me and Peader take care of everything, and didn't say a word even when we lifted the child out of her arms to take her away. Poor Darby did all the crying. He was still at it when I went up on the Sunday, his big boyish face with a wrung-out look though the skin was very red. But then he's always been a weepy sort of a man. Sal now, she's gone like a doll. She just does what she has to do, empty-faced, and when there's nothing to be done sits useless with her mouth open, clinging onto her one well child, the one who stole her little sister's death moment. That one. Look at her sitting there in the corner of the room looking at me. Smiling.

I had a dream last night, very like the ones I keep having, where I'm always alone and wandering somewhere. Last night I was just walking through some small town like Boolavoe only it wasn't Boolavoe. I was a stranger there, that was the whole point of it. At first I was inside, in a large, light, warm place where there were many other people. There were stalls selling ginger beer and apple cake and a thin lumpy snow-white broth made out of fish; lots of sweet things I can remember. Everything looked lovely, but whenever I tried to choose something from one of the stalls something went wrong. Either there was no money or the woman serving couldn't see me, or else when I looked closely at the thing I wanted I realised it was actually completely unappetising. Nothing had any taste. Well, anyway, somehow I had to leave that place, and this seemed to be an act of bravado. I knew no one well enough to stay there with, and there was no one with whom I could leave. Outside I found myself in the night-time streets of a strange town. Here and there was a light but it was all very quiet, and no one at all was about. It must be very late indeed, and I had nowhere to go, nowhere to be, no one anywhere waiting, so I just kept walking because there was nothing else to do. If I just keep walking, inescapably I'll walk into my future, I thought. It was beginning to rain

252

but it wasn't really cold. Well, yes; a little, but in fact it was quite pleasant.

'Look at her,' Phelim says, 'where in this world has she gone to.'

Oh, I've not gone anywhere. It's all one. I can be in two places at once. Maybe I should go and see Cloverhill again, but what's the use? It's not him that makes the laws, is it? You'd have to go all the way to the Parliament in England, wouldn't you? Even the Queen of England, she can't make the laws on her own, it's the Parliament that does it. How do you go to a Parliament's door and ask for a word?

'Wait and see,' Tadhg says, 'we've seen nothing yet. There'll be such a vicious sweeping of the land, we won't recognise it after. They'll not stop now. Oh Lord, no, they'll not stop now.'

A grand sweeping of the land. I was thinking of his words the next time I was up on the ridge and looking down on Kildarragh, and I imagined a huge besom coming down out of the sky and rattling about in all the lanes and gaps between the cottages, clearing everything out the way you'd sweep all the woodlice from the crannies of a shed. I imagined it was me wielding it, God's charwoman, making all the bugs run for their lives. This idea pleased me, so I was smiling as I descended like the wolf on the fold, the delivering angel, being Legion. I have to pay a visit to the Scanlons. Becky's sick again, wouldn't you know it, but then whenever wasn't she? She'll always be like that, one of those that takes everything going. I'm amazed the fever didn't sniff her out months ago. Still, some of those sicklies can be remarkably tough. I wouldn't be at all surprised if she just floated straight through and out the other side. As for the Sheehans, the whole lot of them are right as rain, hungry of course but then aren't we all? She's good with food, Alma; she'll make a pudding out of anything, God knows what she's giving them. I don't ask and she's very close is Alma.

I look in on the Quinns as I'm passing. The boys are rally-ing. The big boy smiles at me. They remember me being there when they were sick. Sal's still dull, but Darby gets up and greets me gratefully. 'How nice to see you, Eliza,' he says, grinning, his big blue eyes shining brightly, 'you're a breath of fresh air.'

I smile on him graciously, the good lady, the lady who is always clean and fresh and serene, bringing comfort no matter how small. Darby Quinn suits hunger, I have to say it. He looks lovely now he's thinned down, his face is showing its shape. There was something of the lump about him before but that's gone altogether, and a queer quick thrill happens to me when he turns and ushers me to the hearth, where straw is strewn about and the ashes neatly cleared away. He's been home since Margarita died. They're making the meal stretch, and I must say the place is looking the better for his presence. He's the woman here, she's just a drab. The muscles in his back move under his thin shirt. Ragged suits him too.

'How are you, Darby?' I say.

'I'm keeping.' He smiles.

She doesn't deserve him. Hunger doesn't serve her so well, she needs the flesh on her cheeks. She looks awful. 'Hello, Eliza,' she says, not smiling, 'is that a drop of milk? That's kind.'

'I'd give it the girl if I were you.'

Little Eliza. I don't like to look. I can feel something coming off her I've never known before, some new foe in whose presence I'm wary.

'And how are you, Eliza?' I ask her.

She gabbles nonsense.

'Come here, *allanna*,' Sal says, holding out one arm, 'come for a nice drink of milk.'

Nothing at all under that rag, her private parts showing, the girl sits in the corner with her bare knees up about her

254

face. Two perfect curves of deep brown skin, rough and pimpled, have been gouged out under her watchful eyes. I can see the taint under her skin. Something walks across the back of my neck, a louse no doubt. When I scratch, it cracks under my nail. Little Eliza crawls like one much younger to her mother and is hauled up onto the lap. Sal smiles. Very pretty, Madonna and Child; till slowly the child turns its head and smiles its goblin smile at me, and I know for sure what my bones have always sensed: that she is the only one that can bring me down. She is my doom.

She jumps down suddenly from her mother's knee and scampers towards me.

'Look how strong she is!' Darby cries and at the same moment I scream.

'What's the matter, what's the matter?' Sal gets up heavily, eyes wide. The boys are watching.

'Eliza!' Darby has my elbow. 'It's all right now, Eliza, soft now, you're all right.'

The child has stopped still, looking up at me.

'What is it?' says Sal. 'Did you see something?'

I shake my head.

Sal's lips have gone white. 'You scared me!' she says accusingly, 'I thought you'd seen something.'

The child touches my hem and I jerk back in mortal terror.

'What's the matter, Eliza?' says Darby.

'I won't touch her.'

'What?'

I take my arm away from his grip. I have been badly frightened, it's not like me. My heart pounds, making me sick, knock knock knock old thing, bang bang bang on my gullet. 'I won't touch her, Sal,' I say.

They're all looking at me.

'Why not?' she asks.

'I can't touch her. Don't you know what that child is?'

I meant to say: Don't you know what that child has? Don't you see the fever under her skin? But it came out wrong.

Sal began to scream at me. 'She's just a little girl!' she shrieked, 'she's just a little girl, what are you suggesting?'

They wouldn't understand. A little girl with my name and the fever marked for me. When she moves, I flinch.

'How dare you!' Sal screams, flying at me and shaking me by the shoulders. Little Eliza starts to cry. 'How dare you! How dare you, you old witch!'

'Sal!' Darby says, pulling her away from me. 'Sal! Easy, Sal.'

'I will not be easy! How dare she be afraid of my daughter. How dare she!'

'I'm sure she didn't mean –'

'There, Darby,' I say, 'give her the milk.'

Sal's still screaming as I walk on down the hill to see Becky Scanlon. I'm shaking. Well, if she wants it like that she can have it. I've been good to that family. I feel something bitter rise in my throat and my eyes burn, but I will not have it, I will not have it. Becky's not too bad. Coughing up phlegm and scratching herself silly, that's all, but she'll do. I say to John and Cliona, 'What is it about Sal Quinn these days?' I say. 'Do you think she's getting very nervy?'

'She's always been a nervous type,' John says.

'It's the loss of the child,' says Cliona.

'She just flew at me,' I say, 'flew at me like a frighted hen, screaming.'

Cliona looks closely at me. I suppose I'm still shaking from my fright.

'Are you all right, Eliza?' she says.

'I'm a bit upset,' I say, but my heart's still much too fast. 'I don't know why she went for me like that.'

Tears start up in my eyes. I will not have it.

256

'Ah, pay it no mind. She's not herself.'

'I'll not go back,' I say, 'I was trying to help. The other little girl's coming down. I was trying to help, and she just flies at me.'

Their faces are kind. 'Sit a while,' John says, but I can't. I have to keep moving. I rush home. The tears keep coming like silly waves washed in but I won't take any notice of them at all. I will keep on walking and walking ever onwards into the future. Every footfall of mine along this path over the rath is a heartbeat. The sea is pounding in on the stone strand, booming under my feet. Another heartbeat, down in the earth, in the Middle Kingdom.

When I get home, the lights are on. Jamie's asleep, so's my da. Once I'm by my own hearth again the tears flow freely. Phelim is distraught.

'He cried for you,' Phelim says. 'He wanted his ma. We want you here, Eliza. Look at you, look at the state of you. Please don't go any more, don't go, don't go, Eliza. Oh, *please* stop crying.'

'She shouted at me,' I sob, 'she shouted at me and called me a witch, and I was only trying to help.'

He puts his arms around me and crushes me. 'They don't deserve you,' he says stoutly.

I'm staying at home now. I'm no fool. They're putting it about that I spent time with the fairies. Well, that's the Quinns for you. What nonsense these people talk about the fairies. They don't know anything and they have no respect. Well, they'll find out. They'll find out. As for me, *I* never saw a fairy in my life and I never spent time under the earth. I'll have none of that madness. They ought to take a look at themselves. The only thing that was of the Middle Kingdom I ever saw outside of my own head was Eliza Quinn.

Of course no one's taking any notice of them. I heard it

from Alma Sheehan. She says she thinks Sal's lost her mind since the baby died, and I'm not to worry about anything she says. I don't know what they all think. I don't know what Sal's told them. I only meant little Eliza was coming down with some really bad thing, something I have no power over. What do they think I am? Immortal? Anyway I've been so good. I never said a bad word about that child to anyone. They can draw their own conclusions, they can do without me. I've been sitting here by the back door now for ever so long biting my nails. I didn't mean to be so scared of her. I can't help it. I haven't been as nervous as this for years, not since my mother died I don't suppose. I put my hand to the little blue charm bag as I do a hundred times a day, and there's nothing there. Oh my God! It's gone. I feel sick. Where did I lose it? It's gone. I'll not be able to take another step without it. It's always been there, always hanging there between my breasts, always a comfort. It's like my mother's died all over again. How is it possible I didn't feel it go? When did its weight leave me, it's small, sure, secure weight, the difference between the dark and the light?

Then I truly despair. I throw my apron over my head the way I've seen the old ones do, and I weep and howl and groan my despair.

When I put down my apron, Jamie's standing there.

'It's all right, Mamma,' he says. 'If those Quinns come round here I'll chase them off with the loy.'

That makes me laugh, and I grab him and hug him fiercely, and he hugs back.

'I'm staying with you now, my love,' I say, wiping my eyes on his narrow shoulder, 'I won't be running off again. Not any more.'

'Good, Ma!' he says, 'Good!'

It's a black omen. I don't know what I'm going to do. If I was scared before, what is this? I pray with my bones. I don't need to say the words, I put the prayers singing in my bones and they pray all the time like chimes while I do other things. While I smile for Jamie the whole world perishes. But he needs this smiling mother face more than I need to scream out loud. 'I'm sad, Jamie, because I lost my little charm bag your granny gave me,' I say. 'Will you help me to look for it?'

'*I'll* find it,' he says.

My father comes rambling out of the house in his under-wear, scratching his belly. Everything's going to seed. 'Get in!' I order him. 'Get in!' and he does it at once like a stupid dog. Everything's going mad. I can't lose control. I must keep calm and keep upright.

'Come on, Jamie, we'll have a look.'

I take his hand and we go on the hunt, trying to make it a game for him, poor little thing's not got much fun with no other young ones around, and God knows he must get sick of his granda. God knows I do. I don't know where the hell Phelim's got to. He's off at Tadhg's maybe, I don't know what goes on down there. I've not been. I don't know, I wouldn't feel welcome somehow, even though Tadhg himself has always been very thick with me one way or the other. I've not even seen the baby. Do you know – oh my God, I'm stopped in my tracks, what is happening to me? – I cannot even remember whether it's a boy or a girl. Was it a boy? A boy? What name had it?

We look everywhere. All over the house and all over the mounds at the back where I might have gone and sat, and up and down the lane, and up towards Kildarragh and all that way, but there's no point going too far. I had it yesterday cer-tainly so it can only be about here somewhere. What else have I lost? I've lost time, that's what I've lost. I have no idea how much time passes. I think I remember feeling it there this morning, surely I must have done, because surely I always do. But I don't think I know my own mind so well at this minute. I think I remember feeling it there quite recently. But I'm not sure. Phelim stops me as I'm attacking the dung heap and weeping.

He says, 'Hush now, my precious, my lovely little Queen Eliza, it's hard times for us all but we're getting by. We're getting by, love. We're getting by.'

'Did Tadhg have a boy or a girl?' I ask him.

He looks at me strangely. 'A girl,' he says.

'What's her name?'

'Sorcha.'

'Where's Jamie gone? Where is he? When did I last see him? I want Jamie.'

'Oh, he's around somewhere. Don't you worry about him, he's fine.'

'I lost my mother's charm bag,' I say, breaking down.

'Ah! Your nice little charm thing. So *that's* what it is. Of course you're upset. Come in here, come in here, Eliza.'

He takes me in and we go behind the curtain and lie down together on the bed, rocking each other for comfort. I nearly fall asleep. Wouldn't you think there'd be time for a little peace, just a little time at least? If we don't even have time, what *do* we have? But someone's coming. Phelim gets up and goes to the door. It's Tadhg. I'm not getting up, I don't look my best. But I listen, sitting up and wiping my eyes and smoothing down my hair, as Tadhg rumbles on in his ranting, rambling way. He says Lomas has been keeping back some of the meal for the distribution and giving it to his cronies, people north of here by the name of Terence. They're using it to fatten up pigs. Lomas owes these people apparently. It's true you don't see Lomas getting thin, and he's not the only one. They say they're feeding meal and turnips to the cattle inland. That's the way of it, says Tadhg. You don't see many a thin Protestant or a strong farmer, do you?

Swish, swish goes the big besom from out of the sky. Into

the sea they all go, flying out like specks of dust towards the sunset. Blow them all the way to Amerikay. What will they do with the empty land? Tadhg'll not go willing, that's for sure. Tadhg'll get him another gun, he thinks his other's in the sea. He was mad about that, the cost of a gun's not to be sneezed at. It's all wet and rotten and useless by now. I'll get one anyway, he said. You can't save me, Eliza. When did he say that and why is my mind going? What have I done wrong? Where's Jamie?

I jump up and run out past them, looking for him.

'Jamie!' I shout hoarsely in the lane. 'Jamie!'

Phelim comes up behind me and puts his arm round me, saying, 'There he is, see.'

He's coming down from the top. He went searching.

Tadhg walks by, nods at me, serious-faced.

I'm fine now. Fine

'Tadhg,' I say. 'Baby well?'

'Grand.'

'And Curly?'

'Grand, too.'

He's very grave.

'Don't you go getting in any trouble now,' I say as he goes.

In the lane, passing Jamie, he puts out a large square hand and ruffles his hair. I wonder, has he heard anything about me? These fools of men are all soft on Sal, they'd listen maybe to her rubbish. She's never liked me, I know that. Never. I don't know what I ever did to her, why she thought she could always get the laugh on me. Well, I've gone up and she's gone down; she has no bed any more, only a sop of straw. It's all gone, all her nice things; anything she had could raise a penny. The mighty are now fallen and she knows it and she's biting back, that's all, and I'm to take no notice.

'I didn't find anything,' says Jamie, coming in the gate. 'I've been up nearly to the top.'

261

'You're a good boy.' I bend to kiss him and see my feet are bleeding, both of them, between the toes. Now when did that happen?

'Could be anywhere,' Phelim says. 'Leave it and let it come back if it will.'

But I hate thinking of it lying lost somewhere all through the winter.

'It's like the story,' he says as we go in and he blows up the fire. There's broth in the cauldron, and a little steam rising. 'Where the ring turns up in the fish's belly. If it's meant to be, nothing will stop it. And if it isn't –' but here he breaks off, smiling. 'Your poor feet,' he says.

'Are you feeling better, Ma?' asks Jamie.'

'Ma's fine now,' I say.

They were so sweet. They washed my feet by the fire, and we laughed and it was like old times. Even my old da comes and sits with us, he's put his breeches on at least, but his frontage gapes and we have to look at his freckly white chest. Even so, something calm has settled against all the odds, something from Phelim. Jamie creeps up to me. His hand slides into mine. I keep thinking about the gun I put in the tree, and that night when I sleep, Juliander comes along and takes it out and stands looking down at it in her hands in a thoughtful way. Now, what will she do? When I awake it's deep in the night and I sniff winter coming in the air. I put up my hand to curl my fingers on nothing. Omens are no more than tides in the blood. It isn't the occurrence, the losing of the charm, the calling of the bird, the crawling of the snail; it's the turning of the tide in the blood. I've sat out there on the rocks at the moment when the sea tide turns, and it's just the same, the strangest sensation. A moment of perfect poise comes, like the moment between the drawing in and the sending out of God's breath, and for that moment there is the silence of a great change. This is to know some-

262

thing of what it must be like in that moment after the final breath, when the soul realises there's no more to come. I've seen that in others.

Sometimes, everything in the world echoes my great perception. The tide in my blood turned today.

15

There are soldiers bristling with their big guns and bayonets down below Corrabreac. They have swords by their sides, and the swords are freshly sharpened every day. Me and Cliona Scanlon saw them from the heights, the soldiers walking with the peelers, bringing three carts of meal over Corrabreac down into Boolavoe, armed for a war with their carbines at the ready and their pouches full. They must be brave or mad the lads who go for them these days. I wonder, does Tadhg still play that game? He says they're all in England's hand; well, of course. And Lomas is in Cloverhill's and Cloverhill's in Tarlton's and Tarlton's in England's. Tadhg says the landlords want nothing more than to lick John Bull's arse, but John Bull hates the landlords and doesn't care a fig, and now that they're all whingeing and whining and begging for mercy he's left them high and dry.

I couldn't care less about the landlords going under, serve 'em right's what I'd say, if it weren't that we're all going down with them.

We have a curfew now, if you don't mind, on account of someone taking a shot at Cloverhill. That's what they do, they make us all pay. Well, they're not keeping me in. Nobody tells me not to walk about at night in my own country.

No one knows what happened. Someone must have let them in, one of the guards must have been in on it or something, or someone's just turned a blind eye. It was eleven o'clock at night and he was just going up to bed with his candle when someone shot him through the window. They said whoever it was must have got past all the guards to get over the outer wall and across the fence, then past the big dog with the fierce bite. Did someone know the dog? Like one of the guards? Someone familiar, a regular visitor? All kinds of things people are saying. Even Martha Colgan's fallen under suspicion in some quarters, but she wouldn't have the cleverness to do a thing like that and act the way she did that night, running about in her nightgown in the mud screaming for the guards. No. She would never willingly lose her dignity like that, she's a stolid woman. Anyway she's in love with him, the pathetic old sow. But then again, some say – but some always would – that perhaps it was a jealous conflagration. But I doubt it. No, it was one of those wild boys for sure though not Tadhg since he's become a father.

Cloverhill's not dead. His left shoulder took the force. Doctor Carmody tended to him in his own house so it can't have been that bad, but he's not gone out since. His daughter's up there with him, and Martha Colgan of course, so he's not too badly off, but I bet he's scared. I bet they all are. I bet they run. If they run, what happens to his big house and all the things in it? I'd like to go up there and get that picture he's got on his wall of the girl on the sofa. What would I do with it though? It makes me laugh to think of that picture hanging up on the wall in our house. How could you have it there with Phelim and my da and Jamie? You couldn't. So why do people like Cloverhill have things like that in their houses? I wonder what his daughter thinks of it?

So everyone's scared and here we are with a board across the door. It's not fair on us having to be scared like this, having to keep the child in. I used to roam all over when I was his age. We've not done anything wrong. Well, I'm not keeping in. From now on I will not be pulled about by everyone, picked at like bones. I will do exactly as I want. I'll go out if I want. And if I don't want to I won't. I'll stay in bed if I want. I'll not talk to anyone unless I want to. And if anyone wants me and I don't want to go, I just won't.

So when Darby Quinn comes into the yard, I run and put the board across.

Phelim looks up sharply. 'What's the matter?'

I've scared him. He thinks it's the bayonets.

I grin. 'It's Darby Quinn,' I say. 'I don't want to see him.'

He looks relieved. Only Darby. We haven't seen him for so long and he used to be a friend of sorts. Darby raps on the door.

'You don't have to see him if you don't want,' says Phelim, 'but we should ask what he wants at least.'

'Why?'

I know what he wants: another bite of me. These people are sapping my strength. Then it occurs to me that maybe my mother's charm was lost in their house that terrible day when Sal Quinn screamed at me and called me a witch. It gives me a sick feeling, thinking of it being up there in that place with that creature.

Darby raps again and calls, 'Phelim!'

'What is it, Darby?' I lean against the door.

'Eliza,' he says, 'Sal's asking for you.'

I laugh. 'Is she now?'

'Please, Eliza.' The voice pleads through my door. 'Let bygones be bygones. She says things without thinking some-times and then she's sorry. She didn't mean any harm. Our little one's sick and she's out of her mind with worry.'

I look at Phelim and our eyes talk. He's saying, I don't want you to go but God, isn't this awful? I'm saying, watch me now, see how it is to be strong. I raise my voice. 'No, Darby,' I tell him, 'I'm all through with that now.' I don't take my eyes off Phelim, whose face is taking on that distant echo of a plain child with a trembling lip that means he's holding down tears.

266

'At least tell me what to do!' shouts Darby.

I'm silent.

'Eliza! What should we do?'

'I don't know, Darby. What do you want me to do?'

'How am I to know!'

'How am I to know, Darby!' I shout. 'Why am I the one? I don't know any more than I know, and you've had all that already. Go home!'

'She wants *you*, Eliza! She wants *you*!'

'She can't have me.'

'Eliza!'

'Nothing I can do, nothing you can do, nothing anyone can do.'

'Eliza!'

'No!'

Phelim comes.

Darby cries out very loudly: 'You've always held us in contempt, Eliza Vesey! But not anywhere near as much as we hold you!'

'Leave her!' Phelim says darkly.

'Eliza!'

'Go away! I'll not open this door!'

'Leave her, Darby!'

'Our little girl's going,' he sobs. 'She's going! Eliza, Eliza, what can we do?'

'You can't do anything. Nothing at all in this world.'

'You helped the others!' he cries.

'There's what can be done and what can't. I can't help you.'

'Why?'

'I can't.'

'Because you won't!'

I sense him weeping.

'Only because you won't,' he says.

267

I suppose he's right, after all. If it were Jamie, if it were me, I'd do anything, step out of any door. But I'll not for her, not for Sal Quinn and her weird daughter; not for them. I'll put myself out for a complete stranger, but no more for her and hers. Why should I do a thing for that woman? She has not the wrinkles I have. She has not the blood vessels that have burst under the skin and in the whites of the eye; she has not the small hairs growing out of her nostrils, or the furrow between her eyes. She has never had bad breath.

'Your daughter,' I speak it clearly through a crack in the door, 'will go where she is going.'

'What?'

'Home.'

'What?'

'Home.'

'What do you mean?'

'Leave her alone, Darby,' Phelim says firmly, his hands on my shoulders. 'Take yourself away from here now and leave her alone.'

'You could help her,' Darby says, quieter, through the door. 'Eliza, you could help her if you wanted to.'

'But I don't want to,' I shout very loudly, 'I don't want to. Do you understand? I don't want to help her, Darby Quinn! I do not.'

Phelim puts his hand over my mouth gently. 'Queen Eliza,' he whispers against my neck.

'This door is locked and bolted,' I call out, 'you'll never get in,' and fall to my knees with Phelim, a swoon, altogether silly and wrong. Sometime in the swoon, Darby must have given up and gone away, because when I come back to the real world Phelim is caressing me. Such is life. My boy was sleeping an hour ago. Did the shouting wake him? My old dad's in a drunken snore, he found Tadhg's poteen we'd hidden away and so were the mighty vanquished. Ha! So, undisturbed we lay, I don't know how long, on the cold floor. Phelim falls asleep because he always does. Wherever love deposits us, it's me has to rouse him and lead him to bed.

I'm a little laughing rocking lady, rocking all the time. I rock into the future. I have seen the ones who rock, the old ones with their aprons thrown over their heads, the poor ugly children like Eliza Quinn with slimy thumbs in sticky mouths. A whole night I sit and rock before deciding what to do.

In the early morning, a little before light, I set out and walk to Samuel Cloverhill's house. I love this time of day, the beautiful silence full of the wash of waves on the distant shore. No one about. Curfew, ha! So what if I meet a group of soldiery? They have no power over me. As the light comes up and the line of the roofs of Lissadoon appears, purple in the dawn, and the blue falls off the mountains beyond, it's as if the last three years have fallen away and none of it ever happened, and the day will soon begin with all the people getting up and going about their daily tasks, the opening of doors and stirring of pots and coaxing of beasts and emptying of bowels and bladders. Nothing's changed. There was a bad dream in the night, no more of it remembered than the sense it's left me with, the patch of shadow in some closed place, but now the light's up again and life goes on and I'm off on a message. This is the place I've always known, the twists and turns in the lane as familiar to me as the feel of my own breath going in and out of my lungs.

Moisture grows, teeming and drifting in the air. At Cloverhill's gate I pull heartily on the bell and wait. A man with a gun comes out from the trees and asks me what I want.

'A word with someone. Martha Colgan, she'll do.'

269

I'd not get near him now, Samuel Cloverhill, whose lips I remember, full and red.

The man slopes away and leaves me waiting long enough to sing myself all the way through *The Green Linnet* and *Paudeen* and *Carlingford Lough*, till the broad solid figure of Martha Colgan comes bustling down the path with her hands shoved up her sleeves. There's no accounting for tastes. She doesn't speak, just stands there looking at me through the tall locked gate with her mouth like a trap and her eyes nasty.

'The gun's in the tree,' I say, 'at the back of Darby's house in Kildarragh.'

Which is simple and true and makes no claims. I don't wait to watch her face or hear her questions, I just turn and walk away home along the lanes with my back to the sea. I feel so light. I swear I'll leave the earth in a second. During the night when I was a little rocking lady, I believed I was thinking; but now I don't believe I was. Now I think I was just passing away the time in a whirlpool of words that flew and swooped and chased and rose and dropped like nothing more than a few blown leaves. Blown brown leaves are lovely, but they come to nothing. It's like words. They are pushed about like bottles and in the end you do what you do anyway, and after, you feel right or wrong as the case may be. I feel right. I feel sonorous with import. I smile, walking. My lips are dry and I know I'm not very well. It's only later that afternoon when the whole world is stiff with sameness that the voice begins, going, Why? Why? Why?

The voice a high whining in my head, a horrid child that needs a slap.

Why? Why? Why? Why? Why?

By this time I'm back in my bed. Phelim's sitting beside me wiping my face with a cold cloth.

'What's happened?' I ask.

'Nothing,' he says, 'nothing at all has happened.'

'Why? Why, why, why?'

'You've got yourself a little bit upset,' he says, 'now hush, there's nothing wrong, you're right as rain.'

'Where's Jamie?'

'Gone for wood with your da.'

'Did he see me?' I say, rising up, 'did he see me coming back?'

He pushes me back down. 'Not at all.'

'Did you know,' I say, 'that there are things that suck the breath out of living creatures? Not human things.'

'Hush!'

'Yes, there are.'

He'd never understand. A single basilisk can poison an entire nest. There's nothing to be done, you have to burn out the lot. It's a dangerous game. I am a dragon-slayer. Sometimes in the struggle, others are scorched. But someone has to take on the dragon or it delivers the whole land to desolation.

I stayed in bed and waited for news. Jamie and my da came and looked at me.

'Is she ill?' I hear Jamie say.

'Only a little bit,' Phelim says, 'she'll be up and about in no time.'

'Oh, certainly,' Dada says.

'Hello, Dada.' I put up my hand.

'Hello, Eliza allanna,' he says. He smells of smoke.

'Have you a pipe, Dada?'

He smiles. 'I still have my pipe,' he says.

'Will you light it up for me, Da? I could really fancy a little smoke.'

'Of course, lamb.'

I stayed in bed and waited for news. They were all so kind to me. Even my stupid da, he could do nothing but light up his pipe for me and give me a smoke now and then. At night

I was too hot for Phelim to sleep with, I burnt him up, he said. He came to me three or four times every night and wiped my forehead with the cold cloth. The water smelt funny. They had no idea what to do, the only one who could have helped was me; and I, of course, knew exactly what to do, or at least I would have done if only I hadn't been so damnably hard to reach.

Then, after some time, I don't know how long, but I do know Christmas came and went, the news came, but it wasn't what I'd thought, not crisp and clear like a cut. It was Phelim told me. 'Eliza,' he said, with me sitting up against his arm. I'd had a drink and was feeling better and wondering if soon I could get up and walk about again. 'They've arrested Darby Quinn. They've taken him to Clonmel.'

Clonmel. That's on the other side of the country.

'They found a gun on their place.'

'The Quinns had nothing to do with guns,' I say.

'We don't know,' Phelim says.

'I do. I know everything.'

He chuckles. 'I'm sure you do, Queen Eliza,' he says. 'You're pulling yourself through. There is such strength in you,' he says.

Then he tells me they found the gun and took Darby away, soldiers and police in all their glory, and Sal screaming blue murder and the boys trying to kick the shins of the peelers and getting themselves a whack of the head for it. I hadn't thought it would happen like that. I thought they'd just go, swept out by the big broom. I thought they'd be gone from my sight overnight and I wouldn't have to think about them any more. They'd put them out and they'd go and it would all be over. It's happened to hundreds of others, and they were moving that way anyway. All I did was give them a little push. The gun, after all, was an old thing. But that's not what happened; what happened was they took Darby away for trial at the next assizes, but *she* remained, she and those poor boys, and that thing with my name.

I'd thought she'd die, but she didn't die, she was much too crafty for that. She was up again, running about. Everyone was so pleased about that. Let's be thankful anyway, people were saying, at least the little one's thriving again, we'd thought the poor mite was going the way of her little sister. Blessed Jesus, what times we're living in!

And shouldn't she have been grateful she had her children, all three of them safe and sound in these times? But did that stop her with the weeping and wailing? Not at all. I wouldn't be up there listening to her for a pound of gold. He's so far away and she can't get to him.

'What'll happen to him?' I ask Phelim.

Now I think I'm well enough to get up and go out and about again.

Phelim licks his lips and shakes his head. 'It doesn't seem –' he didn't finish.

'Surely not!' I say, 'Surely you're not saying.'

'I don't know, Eliza,' he says, 'it all depends.'

'They wouldn't hang him. Oh God, no, they wouldn't hang Darby Quinn, would they? That's brutal! Oh, not poor Darby!'

'Well, no one knows what'll happen,' he says, 'but they'll not let him off a thing like that, will they?'

I burst into tears with my face in my hands, and my shoulders shake with laughing and crying.

'Now now now,' says Phelim, 'it's a sad thing but it's happened. Let's hope for the best.'

'I'm going back to sleep now.' I lie down again and he leans over to kiss me.

'That's right,' he says, 'you get a little more rest. You're much better than you were.'

I am, I feel it. I could get up tomorrow. But now I'm

going to put the blanket over my head and lie here away from them all and think about this. I want to know exactly what I've done.

I didn't tell any lies. I didn't intend harm to Darby Quinn, he's a nice enough man. The worst thing he ever did was take up with that Sal. Now that was stupid, a woman like that was bound to bring a man down. But he shouldn't die for it. No, no, they won't do that, not for the one old waterlogged gun. Far more likely he'll go to Van Diemens Land. So he'd have his life, and where he's got that there's a brand new story. Now see it thus: that the best thing that ever happens to him, looking at his life as a whole, is getting free of Sal and everything that binds him to this ditch his life's become. Who knows? He's a young man still. He might make something of himself, find himself a wife who won't give birth to creatures of the Middle Kingdom. Who's to say I'm not the kind hand of fate that seems to deliver a blow but really offers a great blessing? It needs a wiser eye than mine, and I know one thing for sure (yes, the more I think of it the more I realise how fortunate this may conclude) that if Darby Quinn stays in this country the best there is for him is turning a capstan mill or breaking stones in the poorhouse, where he'd be separated from her anyway; and the worst that could befall him is death. Perhaps I'm saving him from death. Who knows? Perhaps in twenty years time he'll bless the day he left Ireland.

And then there's her. She'll not suffer. She'll get another man in no time, but not here. She'll have to go in the poorhouse for a time. Well. Think about that. It'll not kill her, she'll get out again, a young strong woman like that; though she's not strong in the mind. Still, that's not my fault. The boys now. The boys. I'll say a prayer for them, a serious one, and I'll send Juliander to their father tonight whatever cell he's lying in. She can sit on his chest and kiss him and bring him dreams of reassurance. Courage, my good boy, she'll say, don't cry – and oh, what a cry-baby that man is – courage, I'll give you a kiss. Hunger's made you sweet. The times have given you a wild gaunt look that was never there before, and I do find it very becoming.

In the night I wake again, refreshed, with a burning urge to get out of my bed and go up and see how things fare with Sal Quinn. Did I say the middle of the night? I don't know, time has become so strange lately. I have no idea what the real time was.

It seems there's a smell almost of spring in the air. But then the weather's so strange, who knows? Then it occurs to me, what if Martha Colgan, that ridiculous plodding woman who gets to share Samuel Cloverhill's bed, what if she told on me? What if she tells it was me who told about the gun? Oh God, what would they think of me? What have I done? I'd have to go away. How could I face a soul after that? How could I say it wasn't me? I never told a lie. I said one small thing, a fact, not an untruth. Others took it up, but that wasn't me. I said a fact. How did I know? Why haven't they come for me with guns? Soldiers with bayonets and guns, asking why. Why, why, why, why did I know there was a gun in the tree? Who told me? Who put it there? Me? No! I had a gun but I threw it over the cliffs near the caves, it's long gone. That's what I told Tadhg but of course it was a lie. It was me who put the gun in the tree and that's all of it. Has it occurred to him? A gun lost and now a gun found. Isn't it funny and terrible? It would seem as if I planned it, but I never planned a thing in my life. What if Tadhg thought I was an informer?

Imagine, Tadhg sent with a big gun to shoot me.

Fear comes at me like a burning in the gut.

But she's said nothing. Martha Colgan's said nothing. Like a cow she goes about her business, as she always did. Bovine,

275

she sways her graceless swathe. A peasant woman, she says – I heard it was said in Boolavoe and Lissadoon: a peasant woman in a shawl, a starved thing, who called through the mist as she passed the gate. That was me. That was what I looked like to her. And now another night falls and I'm still here lying on my back looking up at our ceiling, and Phelim sleeping peacefully quiet next to me.

I've got away with it. A thin cold tear trickles into my ear. It makes you wonder, doesn't it, just what you can get away with in this life?

I rise up from my bed as I have always done, and walk across the floor barefoot, making no sound. I don't dress but I put on my shawl and my cloak and my boots and get out of the house without anyone knowing I even woke up. It's dark, but there's a nice big moon, not quite full. As long as I've been alive I've walked at night. Who can stop me? Those who loved me never tried. Curfew. Ha! Sometimes, I think when I die it won't matter as much to me as to others. I'm only half in this world as it is. I love this time of night, this time when there is no known hour. When I'm alone with the great sounding swell of the night, and cannot doubt that the swell is in my blood as well as out there in the sea and the sky and the earth. Sometimes in the night my joy is bigger than this world alone, this small world of valley and mountain and sea and road shining and misty looming heads of flowers and nodding reeds; than all this, and even than the night sky with all its stars and beckonings. Bigger than my own heart beating in the middle of it. Big enough to kill me with its fierceness.

I walk in delight through the beautiful moony night. Why is it they say a sunny day but never a moony night? This is a moony night. It settles on the wild mountain in soft shawls of silver-grey. On the hillside I am not the only thing alive. I think not of the little running, creeping, hunting, busy

276

things, I think of those living things that have always hung between us, between the worlds, between every comfortable restful place. I think of the things wild beyond my understanding, that have always lived on the mountainside.

But no time to stand. Up across the rath, as bright as, no, not day, as bright as the rath in silver moonlight with the sea presenting small sabres to the sky. This is a brilliant madness, one not to be missed.

I know there are people say I'm mad, since I was small and very easily hurt they have said those things. But I've been given mad moments on raths in timeless parts of the night, wanderings I could never have lived without. I wouldn't have missed them for the world. Tell me this, if we are to be born, are we not born to drink as deep as we can from the cup we're given? This is my given cup. Mad raths in moonlight. And over the crest above the bright sea, and down to a small light in a small window, the small apologetic light of Darby's house.

It will be nothing to me when I am forced to be a ghost.

(I suppose I will be. I suppose I have not been good enough to be released from the earth. No, certainly I have not been good enough.)

When I am a ghost, I'll feel I've already had plenty of practice. I have the gift of it. I can haunt. Yes, I can, and here I come. Why should I be afraid of anything on this mountain when I'm here with them, the same substance, a substance not of the life of broad day? Not of the true midday, the fully awakened real of day. When I'm a ghost I'll float all over this mountain. Shall I wail? Like the banshee? To see the desolation! The empty hearths and the places where the children used to play, grown over with weeds; and the places where the young people went courting, those too. The broad patches beaten flat by the beating of many dancing feet. I could wail so beautifully. Someone surely must wail in the wind for these things, and if not me, who is filled with so much, then who?

Under the window I listen.

'Bring him back to me,' she croons in Irish, the poor sad rocking lady. 'Bring him back to me, blessed Mother of God, he's not a bad man, bring him back to me.'

Being good never saved a man.

She'll make me weep soon, this woman in the night, crooning by her hearth with her hand on the horrible child, the poor little grub there, sick again I see now, sick again – they must draw it to them, these creatures – that thing I can't touch, savouring its every breath upon her broad lap. The sights you see are the sights for you. The things befalling are for you. My life joined to hers.

I open the door and run in and throw my arms about her and let her sob.

'Sal, ssh!' I sigh, 'Sal, don't fret, my pet, I've come.'

Her eyes are slitty red and pouring water, her mouth agape, her upper lip shiny with snot. 'What will they do to him, Eliza?' she pleads, as if I have a say in these matters, 'they won't hurt him, will they?'

'No, no, no,' I comfort.

'He's never had a gun in his life! He wouldn't touch a thing like that. He got a turnip or two once upon a time but they can't take him for that, can they? Cloverhill will speak for him, won't he?'

'I don't know what Cloverhill will do. Darby's not a bad man, he'll do fine.'

'He's not a bad man! No, he's not! Why should they hurt him? They won't hurt him, will they? Please don't let them hurt him!'

As if I'm God.

'I won't let them hurt him,' I say, 'There! How long's she been like this?'

She looks down at her sick child. 'You wouldn't come,' she says, 'I sent for you.'

'Well, I'm here now. How long has she been like this?'

'Since Sunday this bad.'

This is the child's first relapse. Shall I give her her own caul? Her lips are white, and a caul's a powerful thing, particularly hers. Lusmore would help too, I can get that. She smells bad. There's a greyness on her leg, spreading from her toes. This is not the fever I've seen in others, this is not even the fever she had under the skin the time she scared me so. I have lost my luck so I'll take no chances. I won't touch her but I'll bring her lusmore, then no one can say I'm not a good woman.

'Tomorrow,' I say, 'I'll bring her something to help.'

'Will you? Oh, please, Eliza, will you? I don't know what I'm to do.'

'You're to get some sleep,' I say, standing up and looking round. The boys are in a huddle under a blanket, a sleeping heap in the straw. She lies down where she is with the girl, wrapping her shawl about them both. I can't spare her any more turf. What does she think, I'm to give her my own cloak?

'I'll come tomorrow,' I say.

She nods, dull, wriggling for a little comfort. Little Eliza gives a thin sharp cry like some unknown bird you might hear close by in the dark as you're walking.

'Hush, baby,' Sal whispers, suckling her goblin. Away from here, shuddering over the top as the light begins to threaten. I thought I'd get away with it, but he's already there in the yard, watching me down the mountain.

'Where've you been, Eliza?' Phelim says.

'To see Sal Quinn.'

'And why was that?'

'You know why.'

279

He sighs. 'Do I have to lock you in to keep you home?' he says, and we both laugh at the very idea.

'I want to help her because of what's happened to Darby,' I say, 'she's off her head about it.' I walk into my house, where it's warm enough, and safe enough, because we still have a bit of turf for the fire and a morsel in the pot. I sit down, suddenly weary. 'She's very lonely up there,' I say, watching the hot small flames lick around the wiry fibres of the turf. 'If it wasn't for the smell of the sickness, she'd have a man with her in no time.'

He sits opposite me, hugging his knees. 'What am I to do with you?' he asks, forlorn yet amused. 'Is there anything I can say to keep you home? Does it matter that we all want you home?'

'It's all right, Phelim,' I say, smiling. In spite of it all, everything, we've kept our home nice. I feel so tired in the warmth. The idea of taking myself back up there is outrageous. I've been trying too hard for too long and I should give up the ghost. 'I only have to go back up there one more time and that's that. I said I'd take her some lusmore.'

'No,' he says.

I close my eyes and feel the fire gentle on my eyelids. Jamie's waking up. My da, he'll sleep on for a while.

'Enough's enough, Eliza. You've got Jamie to think about.'

I open my eyes and the curtain parts around Jamie's round face, yawning in the early light, his poor damaged cheek. The brown pucker of his skin has grown with him, and is now part of his charm. When he's a man, I think, some woman will fall in love with him because of that. He opens his eyes, sees me and grins. His bare feet pad across the floor and he gets on to my knee, not even knowing I've been gone.

Then, as if to side with Phelim and keep me in, the weather turned. Suddenly we were battered again, and the sea came right up as far as Scarran. It went on bad then, and the four of us went under like small animals in their shelter, for a long time. So there could be no getting about, and secretly I was glad. I kept saying, guilty and in comfort by my own fireside, 'As soon as this clears, I must take some lusmore up for Eliza Quinn.' But it didn't clear enough, so she couldn't have been expecting me really; and soon we were into another time, with trouble abroad on the roads again, so I couldn't go out. I thought, I'll just sit here in my house and let the times move on outside; I'll be just fine and sweet in here. I took out the old caul, Eliza Quinn's caul, and I made a little bag for it out of a bit of blue cloth, as near as I could get in colour to my Ma's old charm bag. Oh, Ma! I thought, I wish you were here. What d'you want to go dying so young for? Leaving me so half made. I always felt like that, Ma. Half made. And you seemed finished somehow, the strongest thing in the world.

So, trouble abroad again. Not here but near enough, Malahies, one of the guards at the manse knocked over and his ears cut off. That's a foul thing, I don't hold with it at all. There's no need for us to be butchers. I'd rather you killed him clean actually than cut his ears off. My God, how cruel we are to one another, how truly vile we are. I went into one of my places, one of my times, when all the others are out there looking in, going about the house smiling and being nice and saying the things to be said and doing it all so well. What are we coming to? Tell me that. No one, no one can make it make sense. Outside the flies are beginning to gather in blurry clusters, like dots before a fevered eye, in clots above the stagnant pools in our yard. The walls drip. Every now and again I go out and throw something on the dung heap. Inside my head are such lonely thoughts. Such fearful thoughts I dare not think. Sometimes everything runs into one and I forget who is my enemy and who is my friend and it all seems silly. Sometimes I feel I'm falling into fragments that are spreading out all over these fields and mounds and bogs and raths and all the houses and cabins and even the low turf-covered hole with the buttercups beginning to spring on top where Peader Fox lives. And all the while I walk about and talk in the world as if everything were normal.

There's a hardening. Cloverhill's shut up in his house with Martha Colgan and sees no one. His girl's gone to Dublin. Soon be the gales. Rent day. I hang Eliza Quinn's caul in the blue bag on a knotted string around Jamie's neck under his nightshirt. No harm will come to him now, I know, it's a thing was passed to me when the time was right and now it's leaving me and going into him. It's the way it moves on. And then the news comes, the news awaited one way or the other, as the news always does come, as things must move on whether you want them to or not. The one thing you can have no power over is time's revelation. And he's who the caul's for, not she. I had not seen her. It wouldn't have made any difference anyway, the lusmore. She was beyond me, that child, she always was. I don't know what she was. I know it was from her I got whatever it was I got, that stopped my reign. But I did not know it then, when the news came in. First, that Darby Quinn was to be transported. Then, within a day or two, that the rents were to be collected in full. Enough's enough, they said, Lomas in his house with the soldiers all around, Cloverhill in his, with his mantraps and ditches and guard dogs and endless circular patrols. I suppose Tarlton clapped his hands. Bring in those rents, boys, he said.

Those who can't pay must go. They've got till the end of the month.

I'm staying in again. I've had enough. I'm not slipping and sliding over to Kildarragh in all this. The potatoes we lifted are stored upstairs where no one can get at them; we'll do nicely, and enough to keep back for the next planting if we're careful. We can't pay all. They'd never put us out, would they?

Tenants-at-will? Surely. But things are happening that haven't before. I asked Phelim, he said we'd be all right because we have the one cow still and she's not a bad little thing even though we've bled her. They'll take her. We managed to keep her all this time. They'll take the cow and they can have all we get from the oats too. Will that do? Surely that'll do.

Evening. As if to remind us that the roads will be hard, it starts to rain. But we're still cosy in our house. Phelim stands at the door looking out at the rain, one leg crossed over the other. I know what he's thinking of: Darby Quinn being taken all the way to Cork City and put on a sailing ship and setting out on that terrible long voyage to the other side of the world. No one ever comes back from there. If it were America or Canada I could imagine that, but where he's going to is very wild, I believe. Still, he's got his life, which is more than can be said for many another. I imagine him riding into Cork City, down to the quay where the prison ship lies. I could envy him. Like Juliander when she walks on and on and on, forever brave, now *he* must guide his steps up the gangplank into a new life.

To sail away forever on that great shining ocean! To a wild place. Well, there's hundreds gone before him so who knows what he'll find?

Phelim turns his head and smiles at me. I married the right man. 'Come here and look at this,' he says quietly.

It's nothing, just our hedge dripping wet, but he's standing smiling at it as if it's a thing he's never seen before.

'What?' I say.

He snorts a laugh. 'Nothing. Only, doesn't it look nice?'

It's wet and covered with cobwebs that have turned golden in the light from the setting sun. Evening sun and rain.

'Yes,' I say, 'it does,' and all of a sudden my teeth begin to chatter.

★

283

I'm coming down with a fever, I know it. It started with that rush of cold as I stood at the back door. I had a fever before, a small one, but not like this. This one speaks to me deep inside, a dark something coiling in the base of my womb. This is something that has come to live in me. I've been aware of it from that moment when my teeth lost all control and rattled madly, when I felt such cold at the heart of me it was a silver dagger of ice that made me yawn and forced water from my eyes.

Then we went in and got warm and drank some of Tadhg's poteen (not the best) and I was very bright and gay and full of laughter because of the chills striking here and there and now and then, because that's the best thing to do when it's that or scream and frighten them all, and the child just gone off to sleep. But I'm not stupid and I understood that something new had got inside me. When I stood up it set my knees to knocking under my petticoat.

I felt very light, almost as if I could have made some game of these knocking bones and flown away dancing out through the window or up the chimney. Phelim put his arm round my waist and rubbed his face against my side, and we were very happy. I suppose the drinking helped. I don't really remember going to bed. But here I am once more awake alone, the dark, the breathing all around me in cadences all over the house. Everything is as it should be. Soft rain on the roof. Soft ticking of the turves, the sweet smoky tang of it, and my eyes wide open in the dark. My mouth is very dry. Slowly, very slowly, my organs begin to heat. They quiver like jelly. There's a hot slick drying on the ice-cold of my brow, and a fat and nauseous worm runs up my gullet. I have to get out of bed, it's the thing to do. But my head is spinning and boiling. I get down and lie on the floor. Everybody sleeps on. This is it. It's the fever, one thing or another, they call it the fever but there's a hundred fevers, they're swarming in the air, invisible, crawling in and out of us like grubs in apples. It's one thing to be brave, it's another to die. I don't know how to do this. I know what my ma did. She just carried on the same as usual, but that was a different thing. That was something big that grew strong inside her. This came from out there. Eliza Quinn put it in me when I was there that night, even though I never touched her. I can't remember how long ago that was now. It seems like only last night, but there have been so many rainy nights, so much rain I've been worrying for the crop again. So it must be some time. She put something in me then, an egg that lay there in the warm, another baby, how disgusting, a baby thing that cracked its shell as I stood at the back door with Phelim looking at the shiny webs in the hedge. And now it unfurls its cold little wings in me.

The sickness passes and I fall asleep on the floor, waking up very cold. It takes me about five minutes to sit up, but by the time I've done it I think I probably will not be sick now. It's still pitch black, I have no idea at all how far away is morning. I know what happens, give or take it's never quite the same. I have time, there'll be ups and downs. I have to get away so Jamie doesn't get it. Thank God I gave him the caul. This is a strong one, it came at me with its teeth bared: that's what Eliza Quinn was for, she's the vessel for my deposer. I'll not be the vessel for his. If I go now, quickly enough, and if I say a prayer in my every waking moment for him, and if the caul does its work, he'll be spared. The caul is of her substance so it will be proof against her, and there's something else in with it too, something very pure and powerful I put there. I won't even look at him, I'll just go. I've done this so many times, you could say I'm practised. I dress warmly, silently. I feel in the dark, slow and careful, thinking myself a ghost and letting my eyes get used to the darkness, which now seems only very slightly less thick than before. I take a cake of bread and a couple of pennies, and walk as far as Tadhg O'Donnell's shebeen at the crossroads.

The moon's come out and is making a reddish ring about itself. I'd say it's maybe four in the morning. I stand outside and the dog barks. I don't want to wake the baby but I knock on the door. After a while I see a light in the house, then the voice of Tadhg comes gruffly through the door: 'Who is it?'

'Eliza Vesey.'

The baby doesn't seem to have woken. Tadhg's quietened the dog, and I can hear him breathing heavily as he shifts the bolts. I walk back as far as the gate and stand just beyond it.

There he is with a lantern, peering about. 'Eliza?'

'Tadhg, I have an illness,' I say clearly, 'so I'm standing over here.'

'Oh God, Eliza, not you!'

There is such despair in it, quiet as it is. I suppose Curly can hear every word. He starts towards me.

'No!' I back off.

He stops a few steps away, and the wall between us. 'Not you, Eliza,' he whispers miserably.

'Listen, Tadhg,' I say, 'I can't have Jamie catching anything so I'm going away. I want you to go and tell Phelim for me.'

'What!'

I laugh. 'Don't look so shocked. I couldn't tell him myself or he'd have stopped me from going. Let him sleep the night out, God knows he needs it.'

'You should have told him, Eliza. Does he know you're not well?'

'I don't think so.'

'What shall I tell him? Where are you going, Eliza? The hospital?'

I laugh again. You'd have to be a fool to go in there, it's full of sick people. I have absolutely no idea where I'm going, it will come to me. I'm just taking the demon as far away from Jamie as I can get it.

'Yes,' I say, 'I'll go into Boolavoe.'

'You go straight to the hospital now, Eliza,' he says, 'straight there, do you hear? They can help you there.'

'Yes, Tadhg.'

Some do come out of that place, now and then, but I'd rather anything else than go in there. I'll seek my fortune.

We stand a while, awkward and stupid.

'If I could, Eliza,' he says, 'I'd step right over that wall and give you a big squeeze.'

I smile and blow him a kiss. 'Tell Phelim,' I say, and away I go, walking briskly and never looking back.

16

'Am I just to be kept worried all the time?'

Jamie had never seen his father so angry, but here he was, breathing hard with it. He said, 'I'll have no more of it. Jamie, keep inside!'

Jamie retreated as far as the door and stood there listening.

'No, no, no,' he heard Tadhg O'Donnell say to his father, 'it's not that way, man, she's ill.'

'Of course she's ill! Going up and down the bloody hillside in all weathers and at all times of night. What does she expect?'

Tadhg O'Donnell looked very serious. He said he was just going to repeat the message she gave him and say no more. She'd said she was not well and did not want to pass on whatever it was she had to the family, so she was going to the fever hospital at Boolavoe.

'I told her!' Phelim burst out. 'I told her not to keep going up there to the Quinns. What did she expect? Anyway, what good did it do? They're all going to be put out now, and poor Darby might as well be dead. Jamie, get in!'

Jamie, who knew a lot about sitting quietly and watching, retreated to the dark corner beyond the hearth and stood completely still. For a while his father's voice went back and forth with Tadhg O'Donnell's, then his father came in bringing the cold, gnawing away at his lips and the skin inside his mouth, the sockets of his eyes brown but the rest of his face long and pale and hunted.

'Patrick!' his father yelled, 'Get you down here!'

His grandfather came on the third shout, his face all screwed up with the indignity of the morning light, his hairy bare legs, knock-kneed, groping down the ladder like those of some peculiarly ungainly wading bird.

'She's gone again,' his father said grimly. 'I've got to go into Boolavoe and get her back. She's taken herself off to the fever hospital, the stupid woman, but if I'm quick enough I can catch her up before she gets there.' He was pulling on his lumpy jacket, throwing his sack over his shoulder as he always did. 'I'm not having her in there,' he said. 'Jamie, you stay with your granda,' and throwing open the door, he set off at a fine pace down the lane towards town.

It was very late when he got back. Jamie was used to being left with his granda but not usually for this long, and by the time he heard his father's footsteps in the yard he was thoroughly scared. His granda, who scarcely spoke a word to anyone else, was a great talker when he was alone with Jamie. He'd given him a smoke of his pipe and let him sit up late while he told him all about the banshee and the weird washing woman over at Corrabreac, and the seal that came out of the sea near Briggan and said to a man fishing from the rocks, 'Seven more years and I'll come for you.' And the man vanished seven years later to the day. Then his grandfather had gone quiet and just sat there stupefied looking into the fire and using too much fuel. Jamie knew his mother would be angry when she saw how much fuel he'd burned away. She'd call him an old rap. Hours passed. Jamie fell half asleep on the floor, but woke up and clearly heard his grandfather say in a tone of great awe, 'I don't think she's coming back, Jamie.'

His mother always told him not to worry. Not to worry, she and he'd be fine. She'd told him so many times it must be true, and it was true. She always came back. He'd fall asleep and when he woke up she'd be there, just as it always happened. But the next time he woke up there was only the firelight still, and his grandfather snoring behind the curtain on his mother and father's bed. Jamie lay on the floor covered with a blanket his granda had thrown over him. He listened to the darkness outside and waited, and fell asleep again. Next time he woke, the door was grating open, and his father coming in.

He sat up. His father strode across and took him up in a great bear hug, smelling of the cold in the yard. 'Not in bed?' his father said.

'Where's Ma?' Jamie asked.

'I can't find her, Jamie.' His father's voice was no longer angry – his anger never lasted very long – just puzzled.

'When's she coming back?'

'Oh, soon, very soon, I'm sure. You know your ma, she always turns up.'

'But she's been gone ages and she never said anything to *me* about it.'

'No, well, I think she was in a big hurry.' His father picked him up and carried him across the room. 'Patrick,' he said, pushing back the curtain, 'get up to your own bed now.'

Granda rose grunting and yawning and groaning. 'Where's Eliza?'

'I don't know.'

'You don't know? You don't know?'

Jamie had not heard a note like that in his grandfather's voice before. But his father hushed everything and put him into the big bed, where he lay awake behind the curtain listening to his father stirring up the fire as quietly as he could and putting some water on for tea. The pillow smelt of his mother. Then he heard his father say, 'The hospital knows nothing about her, she never went there. It's as if she's vanished into thin air. No one's seen her.'

His grandfather's voice then, a horrible low keening like

an old dog they used to have that ululated in the night. 'Oh, Eliza, my daughter,' his grandfather mourned. 'I'll never see you again.'

Jamie curled up tight and screwed his eyes closed. If he only waited long enough his mother would come and pick him up and put him on her knee like she used to, singing some silly old song that made no sense straight out of her head. But he could still hear the high keen of his grandfather, and his father's sober voice going, 'Hush. Hush, Patrick, let him sleep.' And then he did sleep.

When he woke up it was morning, his grandfather was asleep upstairs, and his father was out again looking for his mother. He didn't know what to do. It was so long since he'd been out and about and seen any other children that he'd become a great stander and starer, and for a long time he just walked up and down the lane, every now and then stopping and looking at something or other, a patch of grass or a pattern on the wall or a particularly mesmerising, murmuring cloud of small darting things hovering on the air. Sometimes he cried and rubbed his face, making a dreadful mask of smeared dirt, through which his blue eyes peered fiercely. Then it occurred to him that he might as well go look for her himself, since he was doing no good at all hanging round here, and he set off with a great sense of purpose that gave him sudden energy and sent him right down to the shore, and all over the land between here and the back of Lissadoon. Shyness made him avoid people. He kept thinking he'd see her familiar shape walking ahead of him at every turn in the road, but it was never her; and when finally he returned to his house it was getting dark and his grandfather was lighting the lamp and grumbling about where was his da gone off to now, was the whole world just going to up and vanish on him? The old man flung a handful of meal in the pot, swearing.

They'd eaten by the time his father came back, looking very tired and sad. Granda dished up the stirabout.

'You lazy old devil,' his father said. 'Could you not at least have thrown in a few greens?'

A tear dripped down Granda's face.

'Come on, Jamie,' said his dad, 'come and sit on your old man's knee.'

When he was settled, his father put his sharp chin on the top of his head and his jaws worked. 'I didn't find her,' he said. There didn't seem to be anything to add to that. Jamie sat on his father's knee all night, even while he was eating his supper. Once or twice he thought his father had fallen asleep, but whenever he stirred, his father's hand would cover his forehead and stay there for a few minutes. Much later, Phelim spoke. 'That's what her goodness brought her,' he said wearily. 'If she'd stayed away from the Quinns like I told her these past few weeks –'

Then he stopped and from the sound of wet blinking and tiny catches in the throat, Jamie knew that he was crying.

Later still, his father said, 'What do we do now?'

Over the next two days, Jamie continued looking for his mother, even after his father had given up. His father sat at home all day, staring into the back of the fire and thinking hard. He'd never seen his father lost for what to do and it scared him more than anything else. A knot of unease sat low in his guts. He wandered this way and that way over the foothills of the mountain, as if she may be hiding some-where, behind a bush, in a fox's hole. Sometimes he even called out as if she might be in earshot. In bed on the third night, his fingers touched the pouch she'd put on a bit of string round his neck. She'd made it. He thought of all the other times he'd watched her small hands, no bigger than his own, making and mixing and measuring deftly, and the thought popped into his head that she'd taken lusmore up to that horrible girl. Of course. It seemed obvious now. She'd mentioned it several times over those last few days before she left, when she was so restless and kept walking backwards and forwards in the house. How many times had she muttered to herself, I must take lusmore up to the Quinns? She'd gone over to Kildarragh, that's what she'd done. Surely that's where she was. But then surely his dad would have looked there? And why hadn't she come back by now? Maybe she'd taken ill there?

It was very dark and he had no idea just how much of the night had passed. It didn't matter. A small smoky blur on his wall showed that there was some light outside to see by. He got up, just as he knew that she had done herself so many times, not making a sound; crept across the floor, put on his coat and tied a muffler round his neck, and went out into the night. Before these bad times she used to let him go with her, sometimes at night. He hadn't been this way for a long time now but he knew the way and found just the right track, the one that forked up and off to the right, to the rath. Seeing in the dark was easy once you got used to it and sometimes when the moon showed through a hole in the thick bustling cloud, the sea lit up and shone on the land. He could hear it whush-whushing away in the caves below the rath, which was very wide, so far he could hardly see the other side. Daring anything to come, he set off right across the middle. He wasn't scared. Nothing had ever frightened his mother, nothing but the girl, the bad one, the one she crossed herself against. 'I don't want you playing with her,' she'd said to him once. 'She can't help being the way she is, but you don't want to get too near. She's –' here she had paused and thought. She was very wise. '– not right. She's not right.'

He wasn't scared of a little girl like that. She couldn't do anything to him, he could knock her over if he wanted to. He'd done it once, a long time ago, and his dad had slapped him for it. She was unsteady on her pins and he'd only had to give her a little nudge and over she went. She'd frowned but she didn't cry.

'She's of a different substance,' his mother had said another time. 'She's from the Middle Kingdom.' This was a place under the mountain, with the rath on top like a stopper in a bottle. His mother was scared of it but he wasn't. He whistled softly through his teeth as he went over the ridge and down towards Kildarragh. Near the bottom, he turned silent. There were no dogs any more in Kildarragh, no goose to rise up and hiss his approach. He went round the back of Darby's house, stood on tiptoe and looked in the window. There was a bit of light from a wispy fire in the grate. Sal Quinn was sitting on the floor with her knees apart and one hand resting on the girl, who lay sleeping next to her on a bit of straw. There was no sign of his mother. As he watched he saw movements in the lumpy darkness. It was the boys, Young Darby and Mal, pushing each other about and whispering when they should have been quiet.

'*Is feidir liom thu a chloisteail*,' Sal said, '*Teigh a chodladh.*'
I can hear you. You go to sleep.

He went round to the other window and looked in there too, but there was still no sign of his mother. Perhaps he ought to go in and ask, but now that he was here he felt too shy. His mother and father had both forbidden this place to him. Supposing Sal Quinn told on him? He walked away from the cabin a short distance down the hill in the direction of the other houses, stood irresolute looking at the ragged rows of dark humped cabins, smelling faint smoke, sickly-sweet, rotten dung, and the sea. He felt funny out here all on his own and everyone else in their houses. He picked up a stick and walked up and down between the cabins with an odd feeling of power. After a while, he went back to Darby's house and looked in the windows again. Sal had lain down on the floor and closed her eyes. Everything was still.

Jamie pushed open the door and went in. In the weak light of the smouldering fire he saw at once that his mother was not there, not hiding in any of the corners. Everyone was asleep. He went over and looked at Eliza Quinn. She lay on her side with her knees drawn up, mouth and eyes open, face resting on one hand, which was small and wrinkled as the paws of a monkey he'd once seen on the shoulders of a glee-man on fair day in Boolavoe. The stillness of her was final. Her eyes were glossed over, and the lice were walking boldly on her neck. Then with a shock he saw a braided ribbon against her throat, put down his hand and pulled on it, and found locked in her other paw his mother's lost charm. This made him look round wildly as if his mother might be watching. Then he thought his mother was in the little blue bag and he had to get her back off this girl, but when he tried to prise the tiny fingers from the charm they wouldn't move; he even thought they tightened a jot, and the icy wrinkled feel of them sent a shiver to the roots of his hair. He sat back on his heels and wondered. The firelight, flickering, prepared to die. Why had she got his ma's charm that she'd always had, that she went mad without? She'd killed his ma.

His face crumpled up. He shoved a filthy fist into his mouth and bit down on it hard. Then he picked up Eliza Quinn, stiff and cold in her raggy old dress. It was like picking up a rabbit, the lightness of her bones. She was nothing. He took her out through the door and closed it carefully behind him, making no sound. He stood listening. No one stirred. He couldn't see a thing, the moon had gone in. Black clouds moved swiftly above. Then it cleared a little and he saw the winding black arms of the wicked old tree where the cat bit him, reaching out and throwing into sudden relief a swollen indigo sky. Far away a bird called out on the mountain, sweet and quivering. Then a hole appeared in the sky, lined with silver and red, and the moon looked through and lit up the abomination in his arms.

He dashed nimbly, bare-toed, up the bank. He had to stand on tiptoe to reach the hole in the tree where his mother put the cat. She thought he didn't know, but he knew everything because he followed her sometimes, watching the things she did, and he'd seen the cat go in. Down, down, down, far, far below. He tipped her in. A soft crunching sound followed, like the soft grinding of teeth. The earth from which she'd come took her back where she belonged.

It seemed to take a long time to get back up the hill. He kept stumbling, and his knees scraped against the rocks and bled. He fell in a pool up to his knee. By the time he was nearing the top the light was up: ahead of him the sun's sloppy yellow gaudily rising, behind him the moon going down. He turned and looked back.

From here he could see most of Kildarragh, from the tiny hovels by the edge of the cliffs, to Darby's house on Quilty's doorstep. Morning was bringing the people out, but they were not behaving in the usual way. Some of the men and a few boys were gathering in the fields along the lower path, congregating here and there in clusters and talking very seriously. Father Buckley was there, and Peader Fox standing a little distance apart on his own. He saw Alma Sheehan come out of her door at the same time as Cliona Scanlon, the pair of them meet in the middle between their two houses and put their heads together and talk.

Then two strange things happened simultaneously, as if someone had given a signal. A band of soldiers came marching round the bend of the road from the shebeen; and Sal Quinn came tearing out of her door in a terrible state, with her heavy white breasts hanging out and her hair wild, shouting, 'Eliza! Eliza!' in a sore voice. The boys came running after her, all dishevelled. She was mad, screeching, and Cliona Scanlon put out her arms to catch her. After the soldiers came dragoons, six of them, two abreast, and constables on foot. Some of the men in the fields started shouting. Father Buckley strode out in front of them and faced the soldiers, and a sergeant on a white horse rode out before the bailiff and the men with the big ram and all the tackle. Then the priest and the sergeant spoke together for a few minutes. Jamie could hear Father Buckley's high voice but not the words, because Sal Quinn was making so much noise as she ran from house to house, in and out, round all the walls, searching for her daughter.

'She's gone! She's gone! Someone's taken her. She couldn't have walked on her own, someone's taken her. Where is she? Eliza! Eliza!'

The boys ran here and there with her, but Cliona and Alma had realised something was starting up below, and they set off running down through the cabins. A voice in the crowd reached him where he stood, crying, 'Shame! Shame!' Sal fell down on her knees and covered up her face.

'Eliza!' the boys called helplessly here and there.

More people were emerging from their cabins. Jamie saw the sergeant ride forward into the crowd and address the people directly, but he still couldn't catch the words. The big white horse rode here and there; bit by bit, the edge of the crowd fragmented. A neighbour woman he didn't know ran up and put a shawl round Sal's shoulders, covering her breasts. Sal sat down on a rock, called the boys to her and pulled them in under the shawl.

Jamie counted.

Eight houses down below nearer the sea, just hovels really. Three further up the village, and Darby's house. Twelve then. He didn't really know any of the people except the Quinns. The houses by the sea went down easily: the people came out of them and stood watching while the bailiff's men set up the ram and tumbled them all in. They were just dry sod and went: Poof! Dust. Eight heaps of dust. You wouldn't have known they'd been homes with people living in them.

The whole village was out watching by now, standing here and there on rocks to see better. There was no more shouting. Whatever the man on the white horse had said had quietened things down. Those who had to go were gathered all together where the track to the crossroads began, some with bundles, some with nothing. So many people had come out of those eight cabins, Jamie tried to count, but the children wouldn't keep still. Then the dragoons formed up on guard, at attention, and the bailiff's men went further up the hill and got the people out of another three houses, this time bigger buildings made of stone.

Cliona Scanlon came running back up the hill.

'Have you got everything you're taking now, Sal? They're here.'

Sal looked blankly at her. 'Where's Eliza gone?' she asked.

'Sal, *allanna*,' Cliona said, 'she must be dead.'

'We can't leave her!'

Sixteen people, seven of them children. He had time to count this time. These three houses didn't go down like the others. Instead, the bailiff's men boarded up the windows and drove big metal hasps over the doors, then bashed the thatch in on the roofs while the people stood watching with their hands in their pockets and their bundles on the ground. When they came up to Darby's house, Sal jumped down from her rock and ran desperately towards them.

'My little girl's gone missing,' she cried.

A man with a pale blue waistcoat, who seemed to be in charge, turned a sad, cold face towards her, then talked to Cliona Scanlon. Jamie couldn't make anything out. Sal gave a little scream and ran back to the house, crying her little girl was gone, her little girl was gone, she couldn't just go and leave her. Everyone thought she was mad, even Cliona Scanlon did, you could tell by the way she was looking at her.

'I don't know,' Cliona said to one of the men, 'I didn't see the child this last week at all. She was very ill, I do know that.'

So many had died, they must have lost track.

Sal ran about like a panicked hen, the boys trailing after her, then she flopped down exhausted out on the stony track. She didn't look round to see them banging in the staples, but she screamed when the roof fell in, as if the child was still in there, with the thatch and heavy roof beams falling on her. A man hammered something on the door, a sheet of paper. Another came and spoke to her rapidly, and another, then they got Cliona to sit and comfort her for a while before they took her down the hill to where all the others were gathered. She walked with her head down, flanked by her boys, each holding a hand.

Everyone came out, the women with the children round them, and stood in the fields on either side of the road with the men and Father Buckley, saluting those who passed out of the townland, even those they'd had very little to do with.

17

Don't ever think you can get away with it. Whatever you do goes with you for ever, wherever you go. Remember that, Eliza, I think as I walk on along this road that winds up and down and everywhere and takes me nowhere. I'd call it running mad if it were not me, but I am not running and I'm certainly not mad. I'm seeking my fortune. Everything's coming with me, my home in my head. I've never gone far before. None of us has, except for Darby Quinn and the men who go on the fishing. When all this is over and the fever's gone and the crops back, and when my feet have walked enough steps, then I'll go home.

I took ten pence from the sideboard. I hate to leave them short but it's better than giving them this thing I have. This is for me alone.

I had a piece of bread but I ate it a long time ago. How long? Oh, I don't know. Long, long. Long since I saw anything familiar. These lanes all look the same to me. It's not as pretty here as home. I walked as far as I could after Boolavoe, till I had to sit down. I have to be very careful and preserve my strength. I felt tired as soon as I stopped and could have just lain down right there at the side of the road and had a nap, but I didn't want to make a spectacle of myself. I pulled my cloak about me because it was chilly. It's not rained at least, but there's something in the air says it will. I thought I was getting weaker as I sat there, so I thought I'd better keep on, and now I can't remember how long I've been on the road. There was a night, very long and cold, when I just kept going. Very slow progress I think, because I was getting dizzy. It was the dark making me dizzy. It seemed full of lights that came out of nowhere and pricked my eye, voices shouting loudly from a place in the centre of my skull, blasting outwards. The country is haunted, for sure. Why wouldn't it be? Some of the time I sat under a bridge by a stream. It was nice there. I could hear small night-time things moving in the dark. The stream made a soft singing sound.

This day that's passed since then has been very strange. Long as a lifetime, yet a mere flicker. I went alongside a forest that went on for miles, and there was a farm where they sent out a girl with a dish of thick gruel that lay like a lump of stone in my stomach, but it kept me going.

There was a man followed me and asked me questions once, but I wouldn't speak to him.

And now it's starting to get dark again and I've not got to anywhere. There've been cabins here and there, and the odd cluster of buildings, but nothing like a town, nothing even as big as Lissadoon. If I can get to a town I can buy food. I haven't touched my money yet. I'm not my mother's daughter for nothing; she always knew what to do. You put one foot in front of the other, that's what you do. Even in the dark I can do that. In some ways it's easier, no one to see you in the dark, but it gets colder, and the cold sends quarrelling scurries of wind round my ankles, waking me up and giving me hope. I'm getting on, and if you get on, eventually you reach somewhere. Actually I'm not feeling too bad. I was awfully low yesterday, so bad I had to go off away from myself, get right out and look over my own shoulder. The right one, always the right one I look over, because the left's where I throw salt at the devil, and who wants a faceful of salt? Oh, look, I thought, she's sitting on the bit of rock because she doesn't want to wet and muddy her clothes, and it isn't pleasant to think of all the worms in that loamy earth.

If she lay down on there, they might come up in the night and walk all over her. So she keeps going.

That's what yesterday was like, but now I'm back. I'm all here. The night's a beauty. I have enough air in my lungs and the only things hurting are the soles of my feet. I've never quite known this before, this onward push. I feel like a small sliver of something caught in the swell, borne abreast, landward. I might as well sing, softly in respect of the night. *Sleep, oh babe, for the red bee hums, the silent twilight falls. Aoithal from the grey rock comes to wrap the world in thrall.*

I knock at a house along a winding lane and stand far back. A woman comes out.

'What is it you're wanting?' she asks.

'A lodging in your cart shed till the morning,' I say.

She looks thoughtfully at me.

'It's going to be a wet night.' I look at the sky. At that moment it begins, just a few small drops for now, and a gust of wind.

'Oh, go on then,' she says. 'You can get up on the cart, you should keep dry up there.'

'Thank you,' I say graciously, 'it's very kind of you.'

'Go on with you.' She shoos some children back inside. 'I'll fetch you a sup.'

The cart fills the shed, which smells of damp turf and mould and old dung. But it has a wooden door hanging crooked on its hinges, which you can pull across to keep out the worst of the wind, and the roof appears to be sound. It's dry up on the cart anyway, away from the ground chills nipping my feet. I pull my toes in under my skirt and petticoat. I'm glad of my cloak. I wonder what Phelim, who is here in my head, would say if he could see me now? But I can't think of him, it doesn't work. I can't see him unless I see him just as he is and was and always will be, the long grey man sitting between me and my cloak hanging on the wall. And Jamie.

Jamie. Leave it. Some day you'll see him again and you'll explain.

The woman comes and sets aside the door and leans into the darkness. 'I'm putting you something here on the end of the cart,' she says. 'Now don't knock it off.'

This is good of her. She'll probably want to wash the cart down with something strong when I've gone, certainly before she'll let the children ride in it again. I wonder is there a man about?

'God bless you,' I tell her.

God bless you, God bless you, the voices say, *God bless you, Eliza Vesey*. If I had a penny for every blessing of God called down upon me, I'd not be on this road. But then again –

'Here,' she says, putting the warm bowl to my groping hand, careful not to touch me.

'Thank you.' I wrap my two hands around the bowl and lift it towards my nostrils: a faint savoury aroma makes the juices spurt in my mouth. Look how God has blessed me.

'Come far?' she asks.

'Boolavoe.'

'Boolavoe! You're the first from there.'

'Is there a town if I keep going east?'

'Where are you heading?'

'Cork.'

'I wouldn't go to Cork. Everyone's going to Cork. Got people there?'

I shake my head but I don't think she can see me.

'You keep on this way and you'll reach Closheen. Eight mile away. There's a depot there. After that it's Macroom.'

'Macroom,' I say. Well, now I am going to see the world. I'd rather it were Mallow, I'd like to see Mallow.

'Can I get to Mallow?' I ask.

'That's a fair way north.'

We shall see.

'You watch out for yourself.' She pulls the door across. Her footsteps retreat and I hear her closing up for the night and wonder what it's like for her in there with her four children. She has a light; it's what drew me through the darkness. But I'm snug in the dark, out of the wind and rain, eating my supper, broth with boiled cabbage lying at the bottom of the bowl. I feel well, better than when I left home. I feel very strong in my mind.

Early morning when I left, the rain was over and there were some very bright stars out, low in the sky. I thought I'd get into Closheen before it was mobbed, but by the time I got there it must have been getting on for midday, and for the past couple of hours there'd been more and more people on the road: things I never thought I'd see, horrible sights to look away from, then look back furtively till your eyes get used to it. Then look and look and look because you must see; ghostly women, aged children, ancient madmen, their bellies swelling up and their mouths green. Closheen is a grand place, with a big church and a poorhouse and a dispensary, but it's all over-run with these people. I couldn't get near the depot. I didn't know what to do. I thought, if I buy some food now with some of my money, I can take it with me and eat along the way. Then I'll get to Macroom or Mallow and maybe I can find a place, a lodging somewhere, and I'll keep some money back.

The way I feel, this thing may not after all be such a death's-head and I'll weather it out. So I walk up and down in Closheen, looking for a shop, keeping away from the scurvied lot sprawling round the poorhouse with no chance at all of getting in. I don't know why they do it. I'd rather take my chances in a field alone than sit down with that lot, at least you'd have a chance, 'stead of breathing the air of someone bringing up their guts and coughing all over you. They don't cover their mouths.

304

But after I've spent four pence on bread and found it stale, and walked on out of Closheen into some wild, mist-ridden highland that goes on throwing itself higher, I begin to wonder. The fine mist covers me and turns the bits of my hair I can see pearly. The sides of the road are bare and run with rivulets. Anywhere you sat for a rest you'd get wet, no hedges, no walls, only ditches, deep ones like shallow gullies. Pray God it doesn't go on like this till night. What am I to do? What for the love of God am I to do? Suddenly my head races. Pulses hammer. Here in the mist, coming up from below, falling down from above, thick white clouds, flowing and billowing down the mountainside, this strange mountain, not the old mountain I walked over a million times. This one's much bigger. A real mountain, I suppose. I suppose wherever you go there'll always be a bigger mountain, if you keep on marching forward and forward and ever forward in the world till they shoot you down in your tracks, and that's what they'll have to do with me because I am immortal, the only one; I created Juliander, who has materialised on the very top of nowhere and stands in front of me now in the mist in her plain black shawl, completely unadorned, yet far, far more beautiful than I could ever be.

She trails me all down the other side in the rain, sometimes behind, sometimes before. She doesn't scare me. She's the gentlest thing ever born, she wouldn't hurt a fly let alone me. And she's on my side. Thank God, we're lower down now, and the mist is more kind. This is a beautiful valley. A flat dish with a lake and walls all round, and the sweet small cluster of whitewashed cabins there ahead. Oh God though, but it's very poor past Closheen.

I'm stopped in my tracks by the grey pillar of a gate post. Someone's taken a lot of care with the wall by the house, the stones have been lovingly placed. There's a goat, white-eyed, very high up, watching me, but no one in any of the houses.

305

Not even a skinny cat. I don't know what this place is. I walk on. When I look back I see the eyes of the houses watching me, dark and hollow.

Sing, Queen Eliza, to shorten the road. *Sleep, oh babe, for the red bee hums, the silent twilight falls.* I have a beautiful voice. The road keeps forking and I never know which way to go, and there's no one to ask, so I guess. But then the land evens out and goes this way and that, a pretty, sweet kind of a prospect, with a stream where I see a heron and wonder why no one's killed it. You used to see herons under Briggan. Wonderful to see a heron take flight close by. Wonderful big long-legged bird. I don't know what call a heron has. Reed beds line one side of the road. Where am I coming to now? There are people. Faces along the road. I don't think anyone can see me. I'm walking. I was always a walker. I love to sing as I walk but not too loud. *The pale moon has drained her cup of dew.* I think the whole country must be on the move. *And weeps to hear the sad sweet song I sing, oh love, to you.* That so unnatural a mass of us are on the move makes me afraid more than anything yet. This is death, isn't it? The death of something very big. It's like throwing a log on the fire in the old days and seeing all the woodlice run this way and that, hopeless. Here we are, running this way and that, woodlice. Dying under the hedges, under the stairs, in the drains and in the boreens, lying on our insect backs kicking our frantic insect legs.

I passed a roof of sods over a ditch. A white face peeped out, a child, girl or boy I couldn't tell. I smiled and the face smiled back. I gave a little wave, as you do to a child. I kept on and met a man and a woman from Limerick making for Cork and hoping to get on a boat. She was pregnant and said she didn't want her baby born in this country. America for me, she said cheerfully. This country's finished for me. The man's small and shy. They wonder about me, a woman alone. I say I'm going to meet my husband, he's working in Cork and has a place for me, and we keep each other company as far as Macroom, where we split up at the gate of the union poorhouse. A foul crowd waits in the cold there. Their eyes look blank, as if they've waited for days. The pair say they'll wait and try for a place. He can get eight pence a day in there, he says, but God, the work, it's killing. Still, for a few days, and you're fed; and the money will see them through till they're on their way.

Well, it's no use to me. I'd never be strong enough, and anyway you wouldn't get me inside that place in a million years; so we wish each other luck and part.

Macroom's full of lost raggedy people, wandering here and there trying to find someone to beg from, but everyone's just as hopeless as they are. No one bothers me. I'm just another one of them, lost and raggedy, I suppose. Looking down I see how the hem of my skirt is muddy and decaying, the dirt spreading upwards through the fibre. That's just how the dark shadow spreads through the skin, starting at the feet, at the cold, cold ground; sucking up the badness and pulling it up through the body. I've given up avoiding people though; there are too many about, too many of us, and half of them are far worse than me. What can you do? We'll all wash around in this and some'll sink and some'll swim.

I'd never have gone out looking this dirty before. Look at *her*, Juliander standing looking in a window at things she can't have, her white face sideways against the dark lining of her hood. She's dirty too but dirt becomes her.

'Wait a while,' the man says.
'What?'
I hope he's not going to stick to me.
'Hold back,' he says.
We're in a barn, waiting in line for stirabout. I've been here two or three hours, I'd say, and I'm scared they'll run

out. It's got dark while I've been waiting but they've lit lamps next to the boiler.

'What are you on about?' I ask him.

'Give it another ten minutes,' he says, putting his face, small and deeply seamed, loose-skinned, too close to mine and speaking confidentially. He's being too familiar with his eyes. His breath smells of meat. 'Honestly, Miss,' he says, 'if you can wait another ten minutes, the screb from the bottom of the pot's much, much better. Here.' He takes my arm. 'Stand just here, you'll not lose your place.'

He's short and slight, I hardly have to look up to him at all. I saw he had his eye on me from way back in the queue. This could be good or bad, I think, he may have his uses. He's some rough spalpeen from nowhere, the kind used to dig for us in the old days.

'What's your name, Miss?'

'Juliander.'

'That's a funny name. I've never heard that one before. Julie-what?'

'Juliander. It's a very old name.'

'Is it now?'

'What about you?'

'Me?'

'Your name?'

'Cornelius Dunne.'

There's no harm in him and he's younger than he looks, going by his voice.

'Where you from?' I ask.

'Fermoy.'

'Why d'you leave Fermoy, Cornelius?'

He grins and shrugs, liking my familiarity. 'Now,' he says, 'move forward a little now, Miss. We'll be just in time. I'm famished.'

He's right. By the time we're there with our cans they're

down to the crust, prising it from the bottom and the sides with knives so it comes up in great big chunks, nice and thick and burnt on one side. The old woman at the boiler packs it down in my can.

'That'll put a lining on your belly,' Cornelius Dunne says.

'It will, my dear,' the old woman says kindly.

The burnt bits are lovely. It's like eating bread. We take our cans and I walk away and find a place where I can sit and eat, not too close to anyone else. All around, the ground is filling up with the filth of us. And here comes Cornelius Dunne following Juliander. He says nothing, just sits alongside, companionable but not too close, eating screb from the tin with his fingers.

'You going to Cork?' he asks me.

I nod. Everyone's going there, we're on a tide. You can get a lodging in Cork, and there's work.

'You eat very dainty, don't you?' he says.

'Just because it's hard times doesn't mean we're pigs,' I reply.

He cocks an eyebrow. It's his teeth put me off, they look worm-eaten. They must pain him. Another wave of fear is rising in me. Very like a sickness, the moment rushing on unbearable, the moment before your body forsakes you. Oh, forsake me not, not here, not now. I think I sway. A rushing in my head and my eyes blank out for a second or two, but it passes and I'm back, just.

'It's the food,' he says, 'too quick. Lie down for a bit, you can keep the rest for later.'

God, don't let me, don't let me, not here. I hand him my can, still with a fair amount in it, and down I sink very, very slowly to my stomach, till my cheek is against the cool earth floor. Sweat breaks on my forehead, hot but freezing at once. My teeth give that vile skeleton chatter, that mad clatter, insane. 'Look away!' I say before my teeth clack again.

309

I don't know whether he looks away or not, I don't care any more, I close my eyes and welcome the darkness. If I can just stay still and quiet and not get too hot. Leave me alone. Oh God, this is hell. How long can hell last? Walk a straight line. Give up. Thank God for the cold coming up through the earth.

Then I remember what this is: it's nothing but fear flexing its slow wing over me. Let the earth seep in, purifying, drawing heat down into the underworld, into the Middle Kingdom, which has gone to ground.

So I slept, I suppose. Since I left home it's become so hard to tell the difference between sleeping and waking. But now here I am waking up on the ground. It's dark and very cold. I'm not sick any more. I'm fine, in spite of the rotten smell in this place. Still, it would be wise to do everything very slowly. Sickness is like a hawk, it can drop like that. I sit up and look around. Light comes in through the gaps in the barn walls. Attempting sleep, the shadowy humps reek steadily all around me, as far as the eye can see. If I open my mouth the tainted air will get in, already it's coating the insides of my nasal passages. I must be mad to have come in here, but I needed to eat, and I need to keep something by for Cork. I got a ticket for this, it cost me a ha'penny. I can stay one night and in the morning I get to fill my can again before I go. That's not too bad.

Three or four feet away, Cornelius Dunne is sleeping gracelessly. Where's my can? I'll need it. I start feeling about for it. These people don't sleep easy and quiet. They whisper and groan and mumble, quietly sob into soft things to muffle the sound. A baby's restless, its mother's desperately trying to keep it quiet. Of course it'll cry, poor thing, it's hungry. She's got no milk for it. I can hear it, champing away frantically at her empty teat, every now and again spluttering with frustration.

He sits up. 'How are you, Juliander?'

'I'm better now.'

'Got your stirabout here,' he says, leaning forward to place the can in my hand.

'Good man,' I say.

'Shall I stay with you?' Cornelius Dunne asks.

How should I say? Cornelius Dunne, you are a sweet good man, but I don't want to be saddled with you. How I say it I don't know, but I do say it.

'Juliander,' he says, 'you don't have to explain a thing to me. How if I stick by you while it suits us both?'

We sit close, heads together, and talk quietly through the night. I have a husband and a son. He has a mother and a father and a wife who's dead. It's fallen to me to be his comfort.

We stayed together next day, then there was a lane, darkness, a night of stars. A hedge. His wife was called Mary. Well, I'll be Mary, said I. You'll be Tadhg and Phelim and Jamie.

I lost him somewhere the next day.

My cloak is lost too. I have been dizzy, wandering. I wish I could get a ride on a cart but I haven't even seen one since Closheen. The road to Cork's too crowded. Truth to say, I don't know where I've been, I don't know anything. God's pitched me in with this lot. So many faces here next to me looking at me in the crowd. I'm hungry. I go on. Moment to moment, I have no idea beyond moment to moment. Old man, face of a saint in a window. But people are ugly, all told, and where are *my* people? My people are far far away, gone, back there where they knew my name.

Roads. Lights. Rain.

I hear of food. Shelter.

I learnt a thing or two on the road to Cork. I learnt: Wait if you can before you eat, give it time to thicken up. I learnt:

let yourself go, like falling in a pit, let go, let go, let it happen. I learnt: Wait and see. Wait and see.

I always had a feeling one day I would see Cork City. Beyond it, there is the whole world. Seeing the dove-grey of its spires springing up on the skyline, I say: Stay with me, Lord, I've made many a mistake but I'm still trying. Take me somewhere. Show me the next sight.

A long river approaches the city. I cling to its side as closely as I can, for a river is always a good thing to keep near, and this is a great one, the size of which I've never seen before. At home we just had little streams running down everywhere to the shore, but no real big river like this, with the other bank very far away. I feel strangely joyful. The marshlands are full of poor people, all of us flowing into the city along with the river. Tall-masted boats accompany our progress. Sometimes a carriage goes by with high-stepping horses. The meadows roll on, up and down, and the road is good, graced by tall trees. Here and there on the hills I see beautiful houses with sweeping gardens, willows, lawns sloping down to the water's edge.

Cork is really very beautiful, with its houses so large and clean and sombre. I find myself walking through an area of long streets with terraces and crescents. The wild hurricane could blow all night long and nothing would touch these houses. The streets are paved on either side.

I drift on, further on. The buildings become grander, great stone frontages and doors wider than any doors I've ever seen. I have to stop and just gape. No one takes any notice of me. When I turn the corner there are raggy boys whipping their tops on the pavement, sweet, barefoot babes, dirty, silly and proud. I have to stand and smile at them, but one of them says, 'You're silly in the head, missus,' and another picks

312

up a stone, so I walk on, tears coming into my eyes. I haven't a clue where I'm going. I just wash about here and there, tossed like a bit of wood on the surf. My feet are killing me but I can't stop and sit down, not here. The streets are just too fine in this quarter. A whiskered gentleman in a fine silk waistcoat walks from his front door to a high black carriage waiting at the kerb. I've never seen such lovely horses, they look as if they've been polished.

I watch people very closely, following anyone who looks poor, who might lead me to somewhere more suited to my condition. At last I come to a bridge with a whole road going over the river, with pavements and people teeming upon it, and carriages and carts pulled by great snorting horses, and I see shops on the other side with bright crowded windows, and people with money to spend going in and out of them. Downriver there's another vast stone bridge reflecting in the water, three massive legs and wide shallow arches. A heavily laden boat is passing underneath.

But when I've crossed the river, I can't get over the road to the shops because there are too many horses and so much shouting, and I start to feel weak and peculiar. So I stick near the wall and walk back across the other bridge, letting myself be carried along just anywhere the tide goes. I soon discover that Cork is full of bridges. Wherever I go there's one to cross. The river is everywhere. There must be more than one river, I decide. Tired out at last, I lean on the wall. Looking one way I see wharves and warehouses, factories. The other way there are buildings like palaces, with columns and great flights of steps and stone people carved above the doors. The river is as busy as Weavergate on fair day. Boats line the walls, three deep in places. Men shout to one another, hauling bales and pallets up and down the high walls of the quay.

I close my eyes. It's too big, all of it. Why did I come here?

I don't know what to do. Think. Think. First, am I ill? That's important. Stand still and consider. What is there of pain, sickness, weakness, unease, disease? I know I'm not well, but am I ill? Where's the brooding thing I felt within?

Yes, it's there, like a dragon sleeping in a cave underground. Ssh! Let sleeping dragons lie. Tiptoe.

After I time I swallow the thing in my throat, sickness or fear or both in a clot. I open my eyes and look around. On a corner across the road a coarse-faced woman is begging from passers-by, her apron very dirty, the flounce of her skirt all fouled with muck and dung. She'll know, I think. I wait till some other people are crossing, then run over in their wake and approach her. She sees at once I'm no good for money and looks through me, but I walk right up and ask her where's the food depot.

'Adelaide Street,' she says.

'Is it soup?'

'You can get soup,' she says, 'but you need a ticket.'

'Where can I get one?'

Another beggar woman has appeared from nowhere, this one with a big mole on her face and a couple of dirty little scrubs dancing attendance. 'Go to the Society of Friends,' she says, 'they'll give you a ticket.'

The paving slabs are flat and smooth and even, so my feet don't trip up; I can see them walking on beneath me, flap, flap, flap, with the last bits of the soles of my shoes just about falling off. I'm going round in circles. I listened very hard, but I can't find the Society of Friends and I can't find Adelaide Street and I can't keep going either, so when I see some steps I stop and sit down and lean my head against the wall, my hands keeping hold of the iron railings. That'll keep me fixed to the earth. I close my eyes. I shall wait now. Just wait here quietly and see what happens.

After some time – who knows? – a shadow falls across me.

I look up. An old gentleman with a round pink face, watery eyes and a moustache is leaning down kindly towards me. 'Are you after the depot, Miss?' he asks.

I nod.

'Well now, isn't it just around the corner from here,' he says cheerfully, 'Come on now, I'll show you.'

He puts out his arm to me but I'm afraid to take it because he is so scrubbed and shiny and I'm so dirty.

'Oh, come now!' he says, 'Come, come, come.'

I stand unsteadily, take his arm and walk along with him. I feel so strange. So dizzy.

'I haven't got a ticket,' I say.

'Well now, we can fix that,' he says, and walks me round the corner and through another street, and down a lane that comes out at the side of a building where a great mass of people are queuing on the pavement, some standing, some sitting, some even lying, so it looks as if no one's moved in a long time. 'Now, Miss,' he says, 'you take your place here and if you wait you'll get your soup.'

I sit down on the pavement at the end of the line. He stands, looking this way and that. I suppose he thinks I'm silly in the head. I can't help it. It's just that I'm so tired I have to put my head down on my knees at once. It's so rude, I haven't even thanked him and he's being so kind. How many of them would want to touch you, let alone give you their arm? I can't keep my eyes open, not even for a second, even the burning in my feet won't keep me here.

Next thing I know, I've slept; maybe for a long time, because I'm numb from the pavement and the lamps across the street have been lit.

'Miss! Miss!' Someone shaking my arm.

All around me the people have hemmed me in. I'm packed up tight against the wall.

'Miss!'

315

It's him, my deliverer, his kind eyes pale and wet, his grey moustache sticking to his lip and getting in his mouth. 'I've got your ticket, Miss,' he says, 'you'll be all right now.'

I take it.

'Keep it safe now.' He folds it into my fingers, enfolding my hand with his two big warm ones, squeezing briefly. A quick smile, a firm pat on the shoulder, and he's gone.

I look down at the ticket between my fingers. How small and dirty my hands are, like a child's that's been playing out all day. The ticket has three numbers on it but they swim before my eyes. I try to see down the street, but the kind old gentleman is long gone; tears spring into my eyes, hot and sudden. Taking out my hankie, I blow my nose, hold my bundle close and wait.

There's no movement, just more and more people coming.

Waiting for soup in that endless line I think of all the songs I ever learnt about Cork City.

When I was on horseback wasn't I pretty?

Me. Straight-backed on a horse. I never rode on a horse in my life, and I never was pretty. When I was a child we had a book on the shelf: *The Songs of Sweet Cork*.

> *When I was on horseback, wasn't I gay?*
> *Wasn't I pretty when I entered Cork City,*
> *And met with my downfall on the fourteenth of May.*

Some of the people around me have got spoons tied to their cans. They're all families by the looks of them. Awful, plucked-looking families, their colours all greyed over by the dust of the road. Down the line there's a baby that cries all the time. A little girl, missing her two front teeth, smiles at me. A man down the line has a big boil on the side of his neck and a wide trap of a mouth, loose and dripping like a broken gutter. Thank God, some of these people look worse than me. Ah well, I suppose I fit in nicely. I've fallen down a drain, found my place. I haven't got a spoon. Poor me, all alone. Where can I get a spoon? Will they give one inside? Should I ask?

Some sleep, some sit and stare. Two women chat quietly as if by their own firesides.

So very icy cold it gets in the night, and worse towards morning; I thought I couldn't bear it, kept thinking, shall I die soon? Now?

I wanted to sleep, I tried and tried but couldn't. Then something terrible happened.

I wanted to pee, it got worse and worse, a sharp pain that had me doubling over, but I was scared to move and lose my place, so I stayed and stayed till there was a sweat all over me, and then it just went – a great pain, stabbing – and I peed myself under my skirt and petticoat. I pretended to be asleep. No one said anything. It was such a relief I could have cried, and all the sweat dried up in a second and I felt much better. Then after, as the wet turned cold and clamped against my skin, I shivered and my teeth were set click-clacking again, old chattering skull that I am. It brought back drifting cobwebs of memory of a time when this feeling was familiar. But then someone would come and whip off my sopping drawers and sit me by the fire. That was the first fire of my life, with the straw and turves burning yellow; and the round cauldron steaming on the chain, and my mother and father there. There've been other fires since, fires I coaxed up of a morning, tamped down last thing at night; I've set potatoes roasting in the amber glow of the soft live ashes.

But now I feel as if every fire in the world has gone out and I'll never be warm again.

Morning at last. The cold lifts a little. Sluggish, my blood begins to flow again.

As if at a signal, a lifting comes. A long wave movement all

317

along the line, and we are standing at last and shuffling forward. Standing makes my head spin. Sweat pops out. If the light gets any brighter it'll split my eyes open. Really, I'm only slightly here. A breath could take me. I'm the first-gone, the not-strong, the poor one, the weak one, the giver-up, the one you look away from. People are walking past now on the other pavement, normal people who don't want to see us. The only ones who look are those like us. If Phelim were here searching for me, would he see me, I wonder? Don't look for me among the ordinary people, you'll have to go down for me, down among the doomed things. I see that a dark rivulet of pee has run down across the pavement and into the gutter from where I was sitting.

A man asks me where I'm from but I don't answer.

Someone else is talking behind my back.

'Skibbereen,' a voice says. 'And your people?'

'Dunmanway.'

A woman puts an arm round my waist. 'Come along now, bonny,' she says in my ear, 'keep moving.'

I start. There are pains in my ears.

'Have you got your can?' she asks.

I have my can.

Slowly we troop forward. Dogs bark somewhere in the city. Under my breath to keep me moving I sing *When I Was On Horseback*, a pretty song about a dreadful thing. Funny. That a young man dying of the clap could make such a lovely song. He had a terrific funeral though and a great wake, I dare say. We're not getting our proper funerals these days. Briggan they were putting them in the ground any old how all on top of one another. How would you find your people, all this being over? Then it strikes me that if I die, Phelim and Jamie won't be able to find me, they won't be able to come and see me in the earth. I'll be in a paupers' grave with a lot of strangers. How vile. I must go back, if only for that. I will, as soon as I've eaten. I still have some money kept back for lodgings, I wonder if it's possible to get on a coach from a place like this?

I'm inside, in a dark hallway, and the smell of us all packed in is atrocious. The babies loose their full-throated morning howls. We stay in the hall for a long time, looking at the brown walls. Over the smell of our bodies another settles, something good and thick and heavy, government soup. I feel sick. My knuckles have gone white on my can, which has become to me like Phelim and Jamie and my da and ma all rolled into one. It's mine, my only one, it's been with me ever so long. Since – when did I pick it up? When? – I don't know, I can't remember. A long time ago, and it's gone everywhere with me from far back, very far back, when there was a place to return to. My stomach's all knotted and cramped, I must eat and then I'll be able to think straight again.

It took another hour to get into a big room with a very high ceiling and people sitting all over the place, on the floor and on benches round the walls, drinking their soup. I don't know how long I waited in there. I slept, I think. I lost my place twice and was scared the soup would all be gone before I got there. My God, I thought, I'll never be so stupid again, I'll buy some bread and make it last. I'll make it so there's always just a little bit left in my pocket. The strong smell of the soup was making me feel sick but I wanted it. Oh God, how I slavered for that smell even as taking it in made me retch. I kept my breathing very shallow but it was like drowning. All the lines moved forward at a snail's pace. You were supposed to wait for your number to be called but any system had gone long ago, and as long as you showed your ticket you got something. Every now and then one or other of the lines would slow down completely and stop while they topped up the pot. It happened with mine just before I got to the long

319

table, where grim-faced men and women, too rushed to bother with talk and palaver, ladled green-yellow soup as fast as they could. Sweat greased their foreheads. I'd have preferred the stuff from the bottom, but what can you do?

At last the man fills up my can and I go to the side and blow on it. I drink, burning my lip. Tears fill my eyes. The soup's just water, hot, coloured water. A few bits in it, pooh! Cabbage. I can't do this. I can't do this any more, I need to be home in my bed; oh God, more than anything in the world I need to be home lying in my own bed. I need a spoon. Where can I get a spoon? How stupid, if I'd known I could have brought a spoon with me from home. You live and learn. I get a sudden vivid picture in my mind, the open drawer in our kitchen with the knives and forks and spoons all thrown in any old way. I could almost pick up that apostle spoon we have. And Jamie's old teething ring. But it doesn't really matter. You don't really need a spoon for this watery stuff, there's nothing to it really. It goes straight down, scalding my throat, too quick I know but I can't help it. It's nowhere near enough. I want more, something solid. I've never been so hungry in my life.

All those hours waiting, I thought I was hungry, and now I've eaten it's worse than ever. My tongue bleeds, which seems appropriate. I think I must have bitten it while I was eating. I'll have to go for another ticket. I'm swallowing blood. Will I spend eternity in a line, waiting my turn? Now what? Live on my blood till I get my hands on a loaf, that's what I'll do. Buy a loaf, it's more important than rent money.

First, buy a loaf.

My ticket's gone and I can't stay here, so I'm out with my stomach churning, into bright sunshine and a white sky. What a fool I am, I drank that much too fast, you'd think I'd know better by now, wouldn't you? I walk along for a while, dizzy in the sudden sunshine, nowhere to go, and I wonder what they're doing at home at this exact moment. I have to sit down. Where? All these big buildings and so many people. Get away from the main thoroughfare. An alley. A doorway. The waves of sickness are rising, jostling each other. Something comes up and I swallow it down, an effort that makes my throat sore. I waited so long for that, I'm not letting it go all over this filthy ground, rubbish strewn everywhere. I bet there's rats. I sit on the ground and my head goes down between my knees. I wait, fighting with all my might, trembling, till the spasm has abated; then wipe my forehead with the edge of my shawl and look about me.

I'm not so bad now it's passed, I'll do for a while. This is a narrow mean sort of an alley, with three or four dirty-fronted shops and scruffy people standing about the doorways and staircases. No one seems to think it at all funny that I'm sitting here in the gutter with the rubbish. Maybe there'll be a room here somewhere, where I can go and lie down for a while. That's what I could do with, a place to lie down till I'm feeling stronger. When I feel a bit better I'll ask.

I give myself a few more minutes then slowly get up. Could be steadier but I'll do.

First, get a loaf.

I must have left that place, though I can't remember it. There are holes in time. I'm in a slow dream of a walk. The city's too tall and I can't get across the wide streets – a brewer's horse nearly knocked me down when I tried. Everywhere I go there's people, more people than I've ever seen. I have no idea where I am or where I'm going, I'm just wandering about. Now I see stalls, a few barrows in a side street. A woman's selling soda farls. But when I walk towards her, suddenly I'm so light I might lift off the ground and float away. This becomes a real fear, so that every few steps I have to stop and touch the wall. I know what this is, it's one of those dreams where you know you're dreaming – at least, you're sure you are, but then again you might be wrong. You have to get a hold on these dreams and anchor them, refuse the next soaring step that will carry you higher and ever impossibly higher than anyone could ever go and live. Keep one foot always on the ground. One then the other, one then the other, one foot always on the ground. Keep an eye on them, they're very important.

If I want to look around me I have to stand still because I can't do that and control my feet at the same time.

When I reach the barrow I say, 'How much for one of those?'

'Wait your turn,' says a woman's voice, not the barrow woman's.

The barrow woman is rushed off her feet, you can see. Her mouth moves all the time as if she's talking to herself.

'I'm sorry,' I say. I hang my head and look only at the pavement and hot tears pour from my eyes and splash on the ground.

'Oh for heaven's sakes, let her go,' someone else says.

'What do you want, dear? Buck up now.'

'One of those.' I point.

'A farthing,' she says and hands me the soda farl.

I'm wiser now, I won't rush. I'll wait a while before I even start nibbling it. I put it in my bundle and walk away, feeling better knowing it's there. I can smell the river. That's where I go, to stand on one of the bridges and nibble slowly at one torn off corner of my bread while watching all the activity. A great ship is being loaded up. I'll eat a tiny bit now and save the rest. It occurs to me I could get on a boat like that and sail away. I wonder how much is a passage to America?

The sky is light and I have no idea of the time, and though the sun's bright it's still cold. I turn to walk away and a woman no bigger than me pushes her beak into mine. She looks like a blackbird, bright brown eyes on the sides of her head. 'Hello, my dear,' she says, blotting out everything else. 'Are you not so well then?'

She has a scarf tied under her chin, dark hair on her forehead. 'All on your own, are you?' she asks.

'I'm looking for a lodging,' I say, my voice floating out startlingly from a place on the crown of my skull.

'What is it, dear?' Her voice is crude but steady. 'Looking for a lodging? How are you off for money, love?'

I'm no fool. I'm not telling her how much I've got left.

'How much is a lodging?' I ask.

'Tuppence a week,' she says, 'sharing.'

I can get two weeks with what's left after the soda farl. I can get off the streets, rest, get better.

'I can pay,' I say. 'Is it near?'

She puts a hand on my shoulder to steady me as I rise.

'Come with me.'

I walk beside her, nearly running to keep up with her even strides, like a child walking with its mother, though she's no size. She's wearing a dress cut high above her ankles, all patched and tattered in many different shades of blue, and her mouth is set in a natural upturn that is not a smile. She's carrying a three-legged stool. 'I have to hawk this,' she says, shaking it by one of its legs. 'I'll be a while.'

We stop on the corner of a street wider than any I've yet seen. It takes my breath away.

'Straight up there,' she says, pointing a thin downward-bending finger with a long black nail as thick and ridged as a ram's horn. 'Follow the curve round. Near the top, ask for Harper's Row, just off Paul Street. Number nine, top floor. Just knock and go in and say Margaret Foley sent you. I'll be along within the hour. What's your name, dear?'

'Eliza Vesey.'

She repeats it, nodding once, conclusively. 'Go on now,

Eliza,' she says, blinks her bird's eyes sharply and leaves me there dazzled.

You could fit a score of Weavergates in this street. Smart carriages line the kerb, the horses snorting in their nosebags. The men are dandies and wear top hats. Surely she doesn't mean down here, this can't be right. Look at me. Oh God, just look at me. No one does, but I stare at them. A lady is getting helped from a gig, her foot reaching down from the step to the pavement, pointed and dainty in its tight black boot, the leather old but shined up beautifully. I can smell food, delicious, unbearable. A boy is shouting, selling something, and a carriage rumbles by, the sound of the horses' hooves bright and smart in the road. I look up and see grand bay-fronted houses and shops. The street is a magnificent curving highway of great pillared buildings, with columns, turrets, graceful arched windows and doors, here and there a dome. In my dream, knowing once more that I'm asleep and wandering in that other world where a second changes everything if you let it, I drift up this bright highway.

I have somewhere to go to: Number nine, Harper's Row. First thing I'll do in my lodging is get rid of my stiff clinging drawers and let the air to my skin under my skirt. I'm dry now, but they feel terrible. How can my lodging be near here? I walk past a building with semi-circular steps running up to an arched doorway wider than a barn. A man in uniform stands bent-kneed at the top. A beautiful blue gown flashes at me like a kingfisher from a window high above the street. Heads and plants and figures and bunches of grapes are carved in stone.

'Harper's Row?' I ask a little boy selling papers on a corner.

He points me down to Paul Street, a narrower, flatter and altogether more modest and rambling kind of a lane, down around a corner and off to the side.

I'm back in the alleys, and yet so close to that marvellous thoroughfare. An old woman points me deeper into the warren. It teems. So much for sweet Cork, it stinks to high heaven too. No one sees me. Men in doorways, women walking here and there, the crying of children incessant, sad and unlusty. Blood pounds insistent in my ears, the steady pound of the surf washing in. Well, Eliza, my mother's voice says encouragingly, now you *are* having adventures. We are insects, we are too many, the great besom in the sky is sweeping us all before. These people look like goblins, all of them, an old woman swallowing her nose, a woman with cheeks of scalded red, eyes blackened holes. She laughs in my face. Of course, it's still a dream. They can't all be goblins. Unless, here in the city, at last I have wandered into the Middle Kingdom.

Harper's Row is a narrow high-walled court you have to go under an arch to get into. The front door of number nine stands open onto a dark hall. I can't see anything inside, so I call out, and a young woman opens a door, sticks her head out and says, 'Yes?'

'Margaret Foley sent me.'

She twists brown hair in and out of her fingers. 'Ma!' she calls back over her shoulder, 'which one's Margaret Foley?'

'Top right,' says a deep voice.

'Upstairs,' the girl says.

'Where am I to go to?'

'Top floor.' She turns back into the room, stifling a yawn, 'door on the right for Margaret Foley.'

I stand a while till my eyes are used to the dark. The stairs are narrow and smell like damp rags forgotten for months. On the first floor landing a small window is open to the calls of the yard and the nip of the cold. Four more doors, another staircase, bare, groaning as I walk up it. There are two doors at the top, left and right. The left is not really a door, just a wine-red curtain hanging over an empty door frame; the right has four green panels, on one of which is neatly written the single word: *here*.

I knock.

A small pale man with long straight hair and the look of a noble rodent opens and stares at me: Lord Rat.

'Margaret Foley sent me,' I say.

His lips part on broken teeth. 'For what?'

'For a lodging.'

He sniffs and blinks, throws wide the door. 'Oh yes, yes,' he says, stepping back, 'come in, of course.'

The room's small, with a sloping ceiling and a fire smouldering in the grate. The corners have beds, three straw, the fourth a raised truckle bed where a woman with dark tousled hair lies snoring lightly. On one of the straw beds, a little girl is on her side with her knees drawn up to her chest. Two young boys and a girl with a poor froggy face lurk in other corners.

'Have you money?' asks Lord Rat, and it occurs to me that I've been sent here to be murdered.

'Who am I to see about the rent?' I ask cautiously.

There's no floor space, no room for anything. The rag smell is on everything, and another smell under it, darker and even more dirty.

'Margaret herself,' he says, 'she'll be here soon, I suppose,' then sticks out his hand. 'John Cullinane,' he says, 'from Fermoy.'

I shake his hand.

'Have you money?'

'I'll pay my way.'

'That's good.'

'And where am I to sleep?'

I hoped he might say, over there across the landing, beyond the curtain; and I'd go over and find a tiny room, a garret, with nothing in it at all as long as it's mine and I can take off my drawers at last and get a jug of water and drink half of it and throw the rest over my private parts. But he smiles apologetically and says, 'It's as you see. The boy'll move over and sleep closer to his ma and sister,' and I see that this is it, my lodging, and I'm to sleep on the straw where those dirty little boys slapped their fleas last night.

Pale Lord Rat has a rapid blink. 'Let the lady rest, gossuns,' he says, 'move,' and the young ones rise like flies and reassemble elsewhere. He indicates the corner to the right of the fireplace for me.

'What name do we call you by?' he asks pleasantly enough as I sit down slowly with my back against the wall and my bundle on my knee.

'Eliza.'

'It's better you keep to this side of the room, Eliza. My wife and little girl are not very well.'

I nod. I understand. I am so tired and stiff I can't help but lie down and close my eyes.

I drift. I'm home at last, in the old feather bed we hung onto through all the bad times. I'm wandering along the great curving street, looking sideways down the narrow lanes where rain beats on the awnings of the stalls selling red apples. What I'd like is some of those apples made into red juice. I feel I've done wrong and must be paying for something but I can't think what it is. I think it has something to do with that slimy seal thing I put out under the hedge in the rain. I never should have done that, even though it had me all ashudder. It had a mouth that cried wide for help, straight into my face, poor ugly thing no one wanted. Now it's got into my dreams, and once a thing gets into your dreams you're stuck with it. Not a thing you can do.

A sound wakes me.

Margaret Foley is sitting by me, still wearing her headscarf.

What a peculiar thing she is, eyes bright black droplets with the candlelight in them. 'How are you feeling, honey?' she asks.

I swallow. My throat's bone dry.

'Sissy,' says Margaret Foley, 'get us a drop of water.'

Sissy is the froggy girl. She comes with a baby's cup, which Margaret Foley holds to my mouth. The water is blessedly cold.

'Would you like to sit up now, honey?' Margaret Foley says, then leans close and whispers, 'I've took your old stuff for washing, and your petticoat, but you're fine with what you have on now.'

I'm wearing a strange shift. It's not clean. I rub my spiky hands down it and a shudder follows my fingers, a great icy convulsion.

'Up now, honey,' she says, her hands under my armpits, raising me. My head whirls round and then the room settles, and I'm sitting up.

'Cold,' I manage to stutter, my teeth going mad again.

'Sip,' she says.

One candle lights the darkness.

I look at faces looking back. Two pointed boys' faces, white and ghostly; Lord Rat turning toward me from where he bends over the woman in the truckle bed, who was sleeping before but now is moaning and tossing. 'Oh God!' she cries, her white arm a bone ending in his strong fist. 'Oh Francy!'

Her head is thrown back. Her legs kick, her nightgown reveals her nakedness, and her nakedness is plucked and raw and florid as a game bird hanging by the neck.

I can hear someone else in here, out of my sight, in pain. A child it is, groaning like the devil.

From the handsome white blur of Lord Rat, my eyes pass across Margaret Foley and the Frog Princess. I have sunk into the Middle Kingdom. I am attended by a bird, a frog and a rat. No doubt there is some meaning in this.

'Sip,' says Margaret Foley.

If I was home I could give that child something for the pain. I can't see her, she's in the alcove on the other side of the fireplace. Sissy's gone to her.

'Bread and a quart of soup,' Margaret Foley is saying, 'a pennyworth.'

I nod as if I know what she's talking about.

'Sip.'

Cold soup, watery. The other smell, the dark smell, is our insides, seeping out of us.

'Good,' she says, 'now you've eaten you'll be better.'

My skin is tight on my hands.

Like the tide washing out, I'm gone again.

It's dark. Aha, I think, I still have my bread, and I feel for it in my pocket but my pockets are gone, all my clothes are gone, everything is gone. All I have is someone else's shift. How can I go for a walk along that lovely street? I'd like to get a peek at the shops just once, I didn't see them properly before, didn't take the time to stroll, just dandering along and looking. I'll go when I feel a little bit stronger. But then I'm stronger than I think, I always was stronger than anyone thought, strong enough to get up and float away down those brown stairs made narrow by the thin moaning of the damned behind every closed door. On the street my head is weighed down, so that I can only look at the pavement, the black flagstones my shadow slowly crosses. Till it leaps up bright, the street of promenading people, the lanterns lit, the sky pale above the darkened rooftops, and Juliander walking towards me in a peacock-blue dress, low-cut to reveal her pale shoulders and the plump rise of her breasts. Her black hair hangs in ringlets about her throat. She smiles at me very warmly, then slips her arm through mine, and we walk along together looking in the shop windows. But we don't go far. She wants to take me across the road, but I can't do it, it's too wide, and when I look at the other side I feel weak.

A big wagon flies past and I step back. Her little fingers are very pale and graceful in my rough brown ones.

'Shall we take the stairs?' she says. The stairs are through a featureless door in the wall, between two grand buildings. Up and up and round and round they go, through the wild dance of spiralling dust through which she ascends before me, lit by some unearthly light. At the top there are two rooms and she goes into the one on the left, the one with the wine-red curtain, turning as she lifts it and looking back at me with a smile of such sweet, clear-eyed goodness that she scares me. I follow her into the darkness. Her hand seizes mine, pulling me along with a sense of excitement, as if we are children on a bold adventure.

'Look,' she says.

We're in a room, both of us very small, holding hands and looking down. The slimy seal thing is dying on straw, it has nothing about it of a human but the mouth that wails. It's an eyeless, noseless, sticky thing you'd never want to touch. God! Wouldn't a thing like that contaminate a saint? I draw back from its stink with a gasp. But Juliander croons somewhere above my head. She's grown very tall, a high soaring tree of a woman in a grey dress, unadorned, a sorrowing queen of the olden times, beauty sharpened and purified by grief. From her parted lips comes an ancient sound. As everything she does is fully done, she's weeping fully, from the soul. When I wake I still hear her for a moment, then I realise that what I've woken into is just another part of the dream, that she's gone and that I'm still here in the room behind the curtain, this time alone. I stand for a moment absorbing the darkness and the soft pale moonlight pouring in on this quite glorious mid of night, settling into an ashy wash over things which are becoming distinguishable by discernible stages. Something ripe and foul is on the air.

Someone's in bed under the window. I go closer and see it's an old man and a boy. They remind me of Jamie and my da in our big feather bed at home, the two of them that afternoon when Tadhg ran from the peelers, and the thought makes me smile. Then a cloud moves, and the moon shows me the stillness and the blue skin, telling me they're dead.

A little boy is looking at me, his fresh face sweet and dirty.

'What's your name?' I ask him.

'Tommy Cullinane.'

I turn my head on one side and see Margaret Foley and John Cullinane turning the sick woman over in her bed on the other side of the room.

'Tommy, come away from there,' someone says.

The sick woman's nightdress rides up again and she screams. She's all sores on her back and backside, from the straw. I can feel her pain. It's in the room, in the shadows, in the high parts where I can't see, outside in the air, there on the stairs. She screams, then her daughter, the one I can't see, groans even more deeply than before, a sound you shouldn't hear from a child. It's as if something inhuman has come, the voice of some passing demon that's lodged low in her chest.

'Mamma!' shouts Sissy, 'the little woman's being sick.'

Tommy Cullinane's face goes away and Margaret Foley's pinched and withered one appears, smiling benignly down at me, a kerchief that once was white wrapped round her head. Her bird transformation is almost complete.

'Is she a little girl, Dad?' Tommy Cullinane high up on his father's shoulder asks Lord Rat.

'No,' Lord Rat replies. 'She's a little lady.'

Margaret Foley bends over me, smiling down warmly and stroking my face. I know nothing of time any more. I've been away. In pain. 'Poor little creature!' she says with infinite love, 'you're fading all away from us, aren't you?'

The child in the alcove keeps moaning very softly.

My mother puts her hand on my forehead. 'Let's see,' she says. 'There, close your eyes.'

I close my eyes and see Juliander walking on the quay among the crowds that wash around a great ship bound for America. Her shawl is blue, the hood thrown back. The mass of her hair is soft and clean. She's smiling, even though she's scared. Now she's on the gangway. She turns for a moment and looks straight at me, straight at all she's leaving though she loves it painfully. Her eyes glitter. What she is going to she cannot imagine. She looks her fill then turns and walks on up the gangway, and never looks back again. I watch her till she vanishes into the crowd of people milling about on deck. Sailors cry their wild, rough cries.

I hear the striking of a match. It lights the Frog Princess, whose odd wide-mouthed face is curiously beautiful, as if she was begotten of a frog and a fairy in the reeds at new moon. She looks over her mother's shoulder. The light hurts my eyes.

'Look, Sissy,' Margaret Foley says, 'just like with Jojo and your dada. She's going.'

I have to close my eyes now.

18

1850

When they redivided Kildarragh, Phelim, who was working off his debt clearing drains for Lomas, had put in a bid for the top land, which included Darby's old house. He was going to put sheep there. Tadhg was now working the lower reaches of the townland, putting in fences and planning for cattle, no longer such a foolhardy proposition now that the land was so empty and quiet.

Phelim's last cow had been bled to death one night down by the shore. He'd cried about the cow. 'Poor bloody creature,' he kept saying, 'poor bloody creature.' But when Jamie said something about wanting to kill whoever it was that bled her, he shook his head. He looked very old, Jamie realised, and sad about life.

'They were poor people,' his father said, fingering a tear from the corner of his eye, 'they'll have made a pudding.'

Sometimes Jamie rambled for hours on the mountains with his dogs and his gun. At ten he was already taller than his mother had ever been, a lean but sturdy boy with a broadness of face that was neither hers nor his father's but from his grandfather, who sat by the chimney corner more and more now, hardly ever going out even into the yard. Jamie's wanderings often took him over the top, across the rath, down into Kildarragh. It was very different there from the days when he used to trail over with his ma and go in and out of the cabins and play with the children of the cottiers. All of that was so distant. Walking down towards Kildarragh now with the dogs' white-tipped tails waving before him, he felt only a sense of dislike for its dreariness, the bare and flattened places, the grassy heaps of rubbled stone now hosting a comfortable growth of vetch and thrift, and the open-mouthed, hollow-eyed houses with their tumbled roofs. A few families had hung onto their places here and there. There was smoke from three or four chimneys but there weren't many young people left, and no lads of his own age any more. They'd all gone, drained away by the bad times: first the rains that caused the sheep to have liver-fluke, then the crops unbelievably all rotten and mouldy again, and the familiar smell rising up from the earth so that once more people took to walking about with cloths over their faces.

That was when the Scanlons took ship. The Sheehans and a whole other gang were put out when the Gregory clause came in, but they only moved as far as Carraroe. His father said it was cruel and hard. And the Quinns, they were well and truly gone – Darby to Australia, Sal and the boys to Eskean, according to Tadhg O'Donnell, where she had people who took her in. The only person still here that Jamie really remembered clearly was old Peader Fox, who'd moved into one of the empty cabins and was managing to pay the rent by booleying for Samuel Cloverhill. And of course Tadhg O'Donnell, who sometimes came knocking at the door with a bottle late at night and would sit and talk politics with his father till the early hours. The Terences who'd fattened their pigs on Indian meal were better off now than ever before, Tadhg told his father. He said they'd get a shock one day. Memories were long, and there was all the time in the world.

'No, Tadhg,' his father replied, 'you've lost the fire, and why wouldn't you with a family to raise up?'

Then when Tadhg had gone he'd said to Granda, 'Anyway,

hasn't Tadhg done well enough himself, when all's said and done? He can't look askance at us.'

There were no sounds in Kildarragh.

Jamie sat on the cliff tops, his dogs panting on their bellies in the grass, looking out to sea. He thought about his mother. Great feelings surged inside him, too much to understand. What became of her? He remembered her, he always would. She was a saint gone to heaven, his father said. But one night lying in bed he heard his grandfather say she was in a famine grave somewhere. His grandfather said that was the worst of it, that she was lying somewhere in a famine grave with no one taking her flowers.

'She did it for the boy,' Jamie's father replied.

PART FOUR

LUKE
1970 – late Summer

19

It's not often I get a letter, and now two. Bill Tiernan the history man came up to me outside the post office in Weavergate. 'Here,' he says, 'this came quite some time ago, but I've been bad with the flu,' and he had two letters for me from America, one dated a couple of months ago, one only last week. Sent care of him. What did she want to do that for? God knows what he thinks. I suppose it's all over the place by now. He looked embarrassed. I acted casual-like. I went into Finn's and sat in the far corner with a pint. Her handwriting on the envelopes was not as I would have expected; it was round and looked like a child's. It came back to me how I used to wait till Ma was asleep and then creep out and go over the mountain all those nights, four weeks or so of it, and the quietness and the tap-tap-tap on the door and the drawing back of the bolt, and seeing how much I unsettled her. I was always away again before six, back in time to get Ma's breakfast.

There was nothing particular doing and no one taking any notice, so I opened the oldest letter first, the fat envelope. There was a letter and a photograph of a baby in a red baby suit lying on a striped blanket.

'*I send this by Bill Tiernan,*' she says, '*because I think the other two letters I wrote you didn't make it. Your mother maybe? I have news, which if you did not get those first two, will come as big news. You have a daughter. Her name is Eliza Quinn Conrad, which I think is a very good name. She's extremely beautiful, as you can see. I've thrown everyone out of my apartment except for one or two good* friends, so there is plenty of room now and you are welcome here whenever you want to come. Do whatever you want to do though, not just whatever reason says or what duty demands. No pressure, Luke. No strings. Things are fine. I don't know if I'll come back to Ireland. Sometimes in the wee small hours me and my friends talk about it, going over when Eliza's a bit older, living in Darby's house and planting vegetables. But to be honest I doubt it. I wouldn't stay there too long with a child. Too lonely. Still, I do like the idea of the house being full of children again, to think of them climbing about on the old dead tree, just like your great-grandfather used to do. I imagine the little townlands rising up again. I would never have the tree cut down. I filled it up with earth on my last day and planted forget-me-nots. Go over there, if you would, and take a look for me. Tell me, how are the forget-me-nots? Last week a couple wrote me from Dublin and asked if they could rent the house. Back-to-the-land types, I suppose. Of course, I said yes. It's in pretty good shape now. Dec's fixing up a bunch of men to even up the track.

About the name. The name's important. When she's older I'll tell her where it came from. Eliza from my grandma Lizzie, because that was her real name. That's from the Veseys. Quinn, of course, from you. I'm having her christened at Corpus Christi on the Upper West Side, the whole works. For some reason I've invited my aunts and my brother and his wife and kids, and I'm not normally a family and fuss person. I don't know why I did such a thing. I seem to think she's significant, the way she brings the two sides together, like the ending of the Wars of the Roses or something like that. Anyway. It would be so nice if you could be there. If money's a problem, don't even think about it. I have money, just you let me know.'

The baby in the picture was lying with its head on one side looking straight at me, its hands raised up in the air. It was a nice enough baby, not that I knew anything about them. I looked at the picture for a while waiting for something to happen. I didn't know what to make of it. I felt as if I should do something but didn't know what. The baby had

340

a serious face and looked as if it knew more than I did.

I put the photograph back in the envelope and took a drink. There was a sweat on my forehead. Who does she think she is, I thought. *I have money, it's not a problem, just ask.* As if I'm lower than her. She thought she knew it all, but she didn't. She said to me once, this is just the flare of a match, this thing with me and you, it's like rain, it just happens.

No, it doesn't, though. I planned it, everything. If you wait long enough, things come to you, you don't have to go anywhere. *She* came. I can't say I knew she would, but I knew exactly what to do when she did. She liked it with me. It was good. She couldn't hide that, the last time I saw her, when they buried the bones. She's one of those people who has it all there in the eyes to see, unlike me. It was in the churchyard in Boolavoe, pouring with rain, and everyone was there from miles around, the local press and one or two reporters from the nationals. She was standing with the Veseys. She was looking at me and I was looking at her and I suppose people noticed, people always notice. Father Lynch said when he put down his hand and felt the little skull he experienced a sense of profound grief that the remains of this fledgeling soul should have lain uncared for so long, while the world and all its changes passed on above. And at the same time, he said, there was a sense of humility and wonder. None of us standing here today will ever know the story of this child's life.

There was a silence while we all stood and thought about it.

Nevertheless, he said, God who sees everything saw fit to raise her up at this precise time. Truly, nothing and no one is ever forgotten by God. And he spoke some more about her soul being at peace now and far beyond all suffering, before they lowered down the very small coffin into the earth. The rain was running in on top off the mud.

I met her on the path outside the church. She was going away in a few days.

'Hello, Beatrice,' I said.

She had tears in her eyes. 'Luke,' she said, 'how are you?'

'I'm OK.'

What I liked about her, she was like those women in the old stories, big fierce warrior women with heavy hair. What I liked, she acted big and tough, but under it all she was shaky.

'When do you leave?' I asked.

'Sunday.'

She leaned towards me as if she'd put her arms round me in spite of them all.

'You'll be back,' I said.

She laughed. 'Who knows?'

'Beatrice,' I said, low, 'am I to come up to you one last time? Am I?'

She laughed again. 'OK, sweetheart,' she said, 'one last time.'

The night after she'd gone I went back up there in the middle of the night. It had become a habit. It was very quiet, not a breath. Little moth-things hovered round the tree. I thought about how I used to sometimes watch her when she thought she was alone, she'd be roaming around and around the ruins, and I'd appear without warning right next to her and scare her with my eyes. I thought she was brave to live there alone. I sat on the rock outside her house and lifted my muzzle up to the full moon and howled, and the sound made me think of packs of wolves pacing the tundra, of snow whirling, blinding.

I finished my pint.

Who does she think she is? Why should I go? Let it be her that comes back over here. She will. She will. Nothing's more sure.

Then I opened up the second, the flat envelope dated only last week. There was just one thin sheet. It said: *Eliza Quinn Conrad christened today. Family should be here. You're a grown man. Get yourself a passport and fly.*

You can order other Virago titles through our website: *www.virago.co.uk*
or by using the order form below

☐	Turn Again Home	Carol Birch	£7.99
☐	Little Sister	Carol Birch	£6.99
☐	Life in the Palace	Carol Birch	£6.99
☐	Fair Exchange	Michèle Roberts	£6.99
☐	Stuck up a Tree	Jenny McLeod	£6.99
☐	Like	Ali Smith	£7.99
☐	Alias Grace	Margaret Atwood	£7.99

The prices shown above are correct at time of going to press. However, the publishers reserve the right to increase prices on covers from those previously advertised, without further notice.

Virago

Please allow for postage and packing: **Free UK delivery.**
Europe: add 25% of retail price; Rest of World: 45% of retail price.

To order any of the above or any other Virago titles, please call our credit card orderline or fill in this coupon and send/fax it to:

Virago, PO Box 121, Kettering, Northants NN14 4ZQ
Fax: 01832 733076   Tel: 01832 737526
Email: aspenhouse@FSBDial.co.uk

☐ I enclose a UK bank cheque made payable to Virago for £ . . . .
☐ Please charge £ . . . . . . to my Visa/Access/Mastercard/Eurocard

Expiry Date ☐☐☐☐   Switch Issue No. ☐☐

NAME (BLOCK LETTERS please) . . . .

ADDRESS . . . .

. . . .

. . . .

Postcode . . . . Telephone . . . .

Signature . . . .

Please allow 28 days for delivery within the UK. Offer subject to price and availability.

Please do not send any further mailings from companies carefully selected by Virago ☐